Praise for Tim Hemlin's first mystery,
If Wishes Were Horses ...

" A very promising, quite smart, launch to a new series ... a Southern-fried tale blessed by an unconventional cast of characters."
—*Publishers Weekly*

"Tim Hemlin is a thoroughbred among mystery authors. This debut novel serves up down-home characters and a delicious, fast-paced plot that readers will want to devour in a single sitting."
—DEBORAH ADAMS

"What a debut! ... Gourmet cooking and spirited horseflesh combine to make this premier first at the post!"
—*Meritorious Mysteries*

Tim Hemlin's *If Wishes Were Horses* ... is one of the most entertaining first mysteries I've read in several years, and aspiring writer Neil Marshall is the most engaging amateur sleuth to come along since Jeff Abbott's Jordan Poteet. This novel is so good I'd like it even if it weren't set in Texas."
—BILL CRIDER

By Tim Hemlin
Published by Ballantine Books:

IF WISHES WERE HORSES . . .
A WHISPER OF RAGE

A WHISPER OF RAGE

Tim Hemlin

[signature]

10/20/97

BALLANTINE BOOKS • NEW YORK

Copyright © 1997 by Timothy Hemlin

All rights reserved under International and Pan-American Copyright Conventions. Published in the United States by Ballantine Books, a division of Random House, Inc., New York, and simultaneously in Canada by Random House of Canada Limited, Toronto.

http://www.randomhouse.com

Library of Congress Catalog Card Number: 96-94876

ISBN 0-345-40319-3

Manufactured in the United States of America

First Edition: March 1997

10 9 8 7 6 5 4 3 2

This book is dedicated to the kids:

> Katie (budding teacher and my baseball aficionada)
> Erin (the artist who brings beauty into my world)
> Michael (my first son and someday famous broadcaster)
> Kara (the indomitable, who had the good sense to marry
>   Alex)
> Paul (the steadfast, with a chess master's mind)
> Tony (who knows everything, a born politician)
> Elizabeth (my buddy and a true joy to my life)

and, after great anticipation, a special welcome to David.

Acknowledgments

Special thanks to Joe Blades for his faith and hard work in getting this novel into print. I have come to realize how truly blessed I am to have him as my editor. Appreciation to the Houston Police Department's Citizens' Academy for their training and access to a wealth of knowledge. Also, loving thanks to my wife, Valerie, who pored over this manuscript with me—in fact, she read the earliest of early versions and encouraged me to send it to Joe to begin with. Again my parents' enthusiasm has been contagious. And finally, to Dale Pinkerton, my father-in-law, old warrior, and frighteningly similar to a character I've come to know quite well—C. J. McDaniels.

1

The first time I met C. J. McDaniels was not the first time he had been shot.

It was early on a hot Sunday morning and the air was so thick with humidity it wept. My Willie Nelson T-shirt was drenched. I was finishing my run along Allen Parkway, my battered '73 Bug in sight.

With haze-ridden eyes I scanned Buffalo Bayou. On Memorial Drive, a vacant and run-down Holiday Inn stood out like a decaying tooth. I was wondering if that building would ever be used again, when, through the misty sweat of my glasses, I noticed a red Mustang pull into the parking lot alongside my car. I kept running, lightly stepping, the rhythm with me, my muscles loose, my breathing easy—I felt good. I felt strong. I was in the calm comfort of physical exertion.

A heavyset man climbed out of the Mustang and I watched as he tried to touch his toes, then push against the car in a modest effort to stretch out. I smiled. Here was another executive dinosaur scared of the shape in which he'd awakened one morning, determined now to fight mortality. Most likely, though, he'd start out overly aggressive, attempting to turn the clock back thirty years in thirty minutes, and run square into a heart attack.

Well, I thought, at least he was beginning at the right time of day, before the sun rose too high. I was playing with the idea of jogging up to him when a midsize white sedan came rumbling from the downtown side of the parkway. Traffic was light, almost nonexistent, so every

1

car stood out. But this one was like a shriek in the dead of night.

The heavyset man had edged away from his Mustang, but now quickly sprang back to it. He opened the passenger door and was reaching inside when the sedan jerked to a stop at the entrance of the parking lot.

And then I saw guns.

A fistful of panic punched my heart into my throat. I stopped in my tracks. The shooting came in a couple of quick bursts. Four, maybe five rounds, two of which sprang from the large man's gun. One before he went down, the other as he cringed on the pavement. The last shot chased the car away as someone on the passenger's side fell away from the window. Tires screeching, the wide sedan swerved from left to right, then burned past me.

I stood there like an idiot, not running for cover, not hitting the ground, wide open on the edge of the bayou. They could've taken a shot at me. I was a witness, or was it a spectator, a one-man audience? Exposed and vulnerable, I felt dazed like a deer caught in a poacher's headlight. But now lights were off and a heavy silence filled the violent cracks of gunfire.

There was no traffic. No sirens. There were no planes growling by or police helicopters incessantly searching for criminals. The skyline was before me. Houston, Texas, a city in a coma. I shook my head. I shook it again, then began running, recklessly, half stumbling toward the man lying on the pavement beside the Mustang.

It felt like an uphill run into a stiff, hot wind. My legs were soft and numb, exhausted. As I drew close, I saw the man had a thick neck and almost no hair on his head. He wore a plain white T-shirt covered with yellow sweat stains and threadbare black shorts with pencil holes on the thighs. His sneakers weren't Reeboks as I'd originally thought, but black high-tops, court shoes a basketball player would wear. I placed him in his fifties and, despite the big paunch, he had the look of a football coach or ex-Marine.

"Oh, Christ," I prayed. My breathing was thick. His disgusting T-shirt over his big belly was soaked with blood and his eyes were closed. A huge gun was still clenched in his hand.

Last time I reached out toward a broken body, it was my best friend's. And all I felt was cold. I touched this man's meaty shoulder, not expecting a physical chill as much as a shiver from an empty shell losing its heat. "Oh, God, are you alive?"

His eyes popped open. The hand with the gun started to rise, then paused and fell to the ground. "I ain't sure," he drawled, his eyes widening then squinting as he focused in on me. "I ain't sure at all."

"I'll go call an ambulance," I said quickly.

"No!" he barked, his empty hand reaching up to me. "There ain't no phone around here."

"Don't you have one in your car?"

"No service."

"Great."

"You've got to get me out of here."

"What if they come back?"

"Get me out of here."

"Doesn't look like I have much of a choice."

"You're right, son," he said, slightly nodding his head, "you don't." He grimaced and tried to sit. I grabbed him under his shoulder, pulled, and steadied him. With his empty hand he clutched his stomach, and soon blood was seeping through his fingers. So much for Willie Nelson, I thought as I took off my T-shirt, wadded it up, and slipped it under his hand and onto his wound.

"Goddamn," he snapped. The man was gulping air and he tipped his head back and looked straight up at the milky sky. He sat with one knee bent, the other leg stretched out. I noticed scar tissue by his eyes. "Son," he said, again trying to bring my face into focus, "you got to get me the hell out of here."

"I am."

He glanced at the gun in his hand. "I think I nailed him, too."

"Some consolation," I muttered.

"Huh?"

"Want me to take that from you?" I asked, nodding at the huge gun.

"No." He paused. "I don't know where my keys are."

I reached over and pushed the car door closed. It hadn't offered much protection, I thought as I noticed a deep, dark bullet hole. The keys weren't in the lock.

"It's all right," I told him. "We'll take my car."

"You ready?" he demanded, as if I were the one holding us back.

"On three," I said. And as we counted, a low, guttural grunt of pain escaped him as he forced himself to stand. It took every ounce of strength I had to help him. I was a good four or five inches taller than this man and fairly strong, but his iron bulk made him difficult to maneuver. It felt as if I had an anvil on my shoulder as I staggered the few yards toward my Bug.

"What's your name, son?" he managed to ask.

"Neil Marshall. What's yours?"

"C. J. McDaniels."

"From a distance you looked like some kind of corporate executive."

"That's a hell of a thing to tell a dying man."

His words set the hair on the back of my neck on end. Keep it light, I thought. "Don't worry," I told him. "Up close you don't look like one at all. Unless you're slumming." I tried to smile, laugh, anything—but my face felt frozen in deadpan horror. "You a cop?"

"Private investigator," he wheezed.

The fear in me was rising strong.

"For some idiotic reason I came here," he added, "to run, trying to lose—" He stopped talking when we reached my car, and I fumbled in my pocket for the keys. There were two of them, flat and worn like old pennies, fastened together on a weak and narrow metal band. I knew they were in there, but my hand was like a mechanical claw unable to grip the prize.

"You mean you're the kind of guy they make movies out of?" I asked, mostly in order to hear my own voice.

"What?"

"Private investigators. They really exist."

"This one still does," he replied. His breathing was shallow, growing in its quickness, and his voice was turning from gravel to thin glass, threatening to shatter into shrieks of pain at any moment. Or so it seemed to me.

Finally I felt the coarse curves of the keys, and my hand shook as I unlocked the car door. I avoided looking at his right side.

"Seat's awfully far down," he said. "Why couldn't you drive something real? Say something, son. You're supposed to be taking my mind off this shit."

"I've been trying."

"Trying don't get you nowhere," he yelped, and dropped himself down into the car. He was still holding the gun. "Damn me for listening to Bedford. Never have before, client or not. The old bastard's out to take everyone he can with him."

I helped him swing his legs in.

"Gardner said I'd gone soft, too, said I was too fat and old for this business," he grumbled, the words riding the high crest of his frail breathing. "Damn cop."

"Lieutenant Gardner?" I blurted.

"But I don't need help," the man continued, apparently not hearing me. "I don't need him. The hell with him!"

Rambling. That's good, I thought. Still coherent, still alive. I slammed the door. As I ran around the front of the car I half tripped and almost fell. My heart was still lodged in my throat, and for a split second I saw the black spots of darkness close in on the white of day. No, no, no, I screamed inside my head, fighting it off. I unlocked my door and threw myself into the seat.

"Don't go passing out on me, son." He wheezed moisture like an old man who'd been smoking all his life.

"I won't."

"Speak up! Are you okay?"

"I can't help it. I mumble. It's a bad habit."

"I don't care if you mumble. Just don't pass out."

"Trust me."

"Kind of looks like I have to." His head bobbed back against the seat and he closed his eyes.

The keys rattled like wind chimes as I stuck one—and after that, the correct one—into the ignition. When the car started, I ground the gears into reverse, then first, and we whipped out of the parking lot and flew down Allen Parkway. C. J. McDaniels was quiet.

"You there?" I asked. What I meant was, *Are you still alive?*

He didn't respond. I glanced at him. His chest rose in short breaths. The gun gently slipped from his hand to the floorboard. I gulped a breath and shakily released it.

This was unbelievable. Something my ex-wife said would happen. I couldn't take care of myself, Susan claimed. I was a dreamer. But the dreamlike feeling that closed in on me now was more thorns than rose. I was fighting for air, surrounded by something like water, and I was in danger of drowning. I could see the light above me, cracks of distorted yellow grins; I needed to breathe, but I couldn't trust what was water and what was air. Then I realized I was holding my breath, afraid, and I let it go. It all came bursting out in a great rush.

Wake up! This was actually happening. I glanced at the man beside me. He could die. He was bleeding. I was taking him to the hospital. Shut up, Susan. I could do it. But what hospital?

Jefferson Davis, half a mile down the road, had closed its doors. LBJ, the new charity hospital, was miles and miles away. The med center was too far. The man drew in a sharp, gurgling breath. Held it. Think! Goddamn it, Neil, come up for air and think! I ran a red light at South

Shepherd, as I blocked out his irregular breathing. Or lack of it.

Wait, there was a medi-clinic on West Grey. It was around the fourth ward, or in the fourth ward. A tough part of town. Traffic was picking up. I didn't care. I knew where I was going. And that was good. I was going where they treated gunshot wounds. They could stop the bleeding. They'd seen a lot of it. Probably bored them by now. Second nature.

And they'd be calm, in control.

Yes, that would work.

That was good.

Thank God.

2

Three days later, I caught my breath. Once again, I'd stumbled upon crime firsthand. Front page. It seemed I'd had the good fortune to salvage one of Houston's best-known private investigators. Media coverage centered around the shooting, the lack of suspects—or overabundance of suspects, as it was hinted that almost any felon in the surrounding area could've been involved. McDaniels had more enemies than the bayou city had roaches.

Some of the news reports proclaimed me a hero. Hell, I was no hero. I was a twenty-eight-year-old divorced man hiding out in grad school at the University of Houston. I was a poet, a living poet, and I intended to keep it that way. I didn't want any vendetta against me because of coincidence, because I'd performed a humane act. Christ, all I did was drive a dying man to the emergency room without fainting. And that was what I told the reporters, which only made more of a hero out of me. I was *real*.

Then out came the fact that I'd been acquitted of murder for gunning down a man in self-defense. The man that I was supposed to have killed had, in fact, killed my best friend, Jason Keys. If I'd allowed myself, I could've relived the whole episode through the morning newspaper. I chose not to.

Media shy anyway, I withdrew from further interviews.

I hadn't seen C. J. McDaniels since he'd been whisked away by the medical crew, and I hadn't spoken to anyone

8

outside of the police and, foolishly, a reporter or three—except my landlord, Jerry Jacoma. For the most part I'd been keeping to my garage apartment in the Heights, sleeping on the couch with the doors double-locked, and checking the small windows each night to be sure they were secured.

As the 30-30 was stored at the stables under Candace Littlefield's care, my little .25 was always within reach. Actually, I had brought the small gun for Susan, my ex-wife, but she'd wanted nothing to do with it. According to her, it was another example of my paranoia. Turned out, the .25 was one of the few material possessions I wangled out of that marriage.

As for my bootleg album of the Beatles' 1965 Houston concert—I never did rope that away from Susan. Wasn't fair, as JFK said of life. So you move on.

I hadn't fully realized the impact of the stress—of driving the wounded investigator to the hospital—until after C. J.'d been safely tucked away and the burn of adrenaline turned stone cold in my system. Despite all the effort I'd exerted to get back in shape, I had the shakes so bad I wasn't jogging. I wasn't writing. I hadn't gone to my literature class at the university. At Perry Stevens Catering, where I worked as an assistant chef, I phoned in sick. I was doing nothing.

Possibly worst of all, Susan was repeatedly trying to contact me. When she phoned, I wouldn't talk to her; I was screening my messages. Susan had read the news accounts and was concerned. She had a boyfriend who was living with her, but for some reason she wouldn't leave me alone—or let me go.

Perhaps she still thought I was incapable of taking care of myself. Ever since she passed the bar exam and hooked up with one of the big firms downtown, she was the great provider, the moneymaker. Most of my married life was spent putting that little green-eyed blonde barracuda through school. And I was all for it. But when it was supposed to be my turn, college was no longer necessary. I didn't need it, Susan said. I could stay home and write. Wasn't that what I always wanted to do? Besides, we had accumulated enough debts with her student loans. We didn't need any more.

That was the straw.

When I left, I was suddenly the scattered, addled artist unable to cope with the real world. Couldn't hold a serious job, she told my mother. Had grand, literary ideas, she told my lawyer. Would never make it on my own without her paycheck or guidance, she told me. She was furious, bedded down with her current accountant-boyfriend before our signatures scarred the divorce decree. Was I jealous? Yes, some. My heart had been strip-mined. I kept thinking this raw hole would eventually fill with soft memories until it was a pool of sore love. Lost love. And maybe it would, given more time. But after these last few months, and the Jason Keys incident, my relationship with Susan remained fuzzy, heavy, like trying to see and breathe underwater.

For now, though, there was someone I'd been lucky enough to help who wanted to see me, and I couldn't stay away from that person any more than a tree could stop reaching upward for sunlight. C. J. McDaniels had telephoned and asked if I'd come "pay my respects." I gasped, thinking he was on his deathbed after all. Sensing his words had chilled me, however, he quickly laughed his deep, hearty laugh and changed it to "drop by and shoot the shit."

C. J. had been transferred to Memorial Southwest Hospital. He was going to live. The bullet had torn his side but not plunged into him. The police had told me what size the bullet was, what kind of gun it had been fired from, and what would have happened if the shot had struck him a little higher and a touch to the right. I remembered none of the details, however, only that they were putting him up at Memorial Southwest and that, for his own protection, arrangements had been made for a guard to be stationed at his door.

I entered the mass of concrete, steel, and disinfectant that was Memorial Southwest. A nurse was wheeling a new mother and her tiny baby out to a waiting car. Senior-citizen volunteers governed the front desk. I walked hesitantly past them, found the elevator bank, and rode up to the fifth floor. As soon as I stepped off the elevator, I came face-to-face with a uniformed policeman.

"I'm here to see C. J. McDaniels," I told him.

He was slight of build, had dark hair and a thin mustache, and wasn't much older than me.

"So ask at the desk," he replied, expressionless as he stepped onto the elevator. The doors closed. Okay, I thought, I will.

The receptionist's desk was really a counter, almost a full circle that took up the middle of the fifth-floor lobby. Three long hallways jutted off at angles. It was quiet. There were a few people milling about, but for the most part they were nurses gliding around in their soft-soled way. At the desk were two female nurses: a heavyset black woman on the phone and a short blonde woman doing paperwork. The blonde looked up as I approached.

"Can I help you?"

"I'm here to see C. J. McDaniels."

"I beg your pardon?"

I was mumbling again. I repeated myself.

"Do you know what room she's in?"

"What?"

"Do you know what room she's in?"

"No—I mean, she's a he. C. J. McDaniels, the private investigator. I know he's here."

"Young man, this is the maternity ward."

"The what?"

"The place where women recover after having babies," she said sternly.

As tall as I was, looking at this woman shrank me. Like the policeman before, there was no sign of a smile and only a hostile sign of life. It was like encountering the disgruntled ticket taker at the local movie house. Only her eyes held a little spark.

"I swear this is where he told me he was."

"Who told you?"

"C. J. McDaniels," I said, wanting to add, *you stupid woman.* "You don't understand," I continued. "My name's Neil Marshall. I'm the one who drove him to the emergency room when he was shot, gunned down in a parking lot on Allen Parkway. I haven't seen him since, and now he phoned me. Surely you've heard of C. J. McDaniels. He was in all the papers. Me too, front page."

This wonderful specimen of the medical profession raised her eyebrows. "It must have been a slow day for news," she said, straight-faced.

"Listen, lady—"

"Young man, I shall call security."

"Can you tell me who to see so I can find out where he is? Maybe I wrote it down wrong."

A tall man about my height came up to the desk. He was thin-faced with a long, sharp nose and dark hair with wisps of gray in the sideburns.

"I don't believe it," I muttered.

"This case caught my interest," Lieutenant Paul Gardner replied.

"My luck."

"Thank you, ma'am," Gardner told the nurse, "but everything's, ah, okay. I'll take care of it."

"It's just that the young police officer had left and—"

"Yes, thank you, ma'am."

The nurse gave a short nod and went back to her paperwork.

"Come with me, Mr. Marshall."

I followed the lanky man down to room 512. The door was slightly open. Before going in, Gardner stretched out a hand. "I find it damn coincidental to discover you're involved in another shooting," he said.

"I'm sure you do."

"And I don't believe in coincidences."

"I didn't shoot the old geezer," I said firmly. "I came to his rescue."

"I don't believe you've ever shot any old geezer."

"What?" I asked, and ran my hand across my forehead and over my hair. A cold thin film of sweat covered my fingers.

"Though I suppose we're talking history now."

I touched my chin and realized I had a heavy stubble of beard on my face. "My wife and I divorced at the beginning of the year."

"Yes?"

"Nothing." I guessed I was trying to fill him in on what had happened since Jason's murder, which he had investigated. Also, I wanted to divert his questioning. But it came out awkward. My timing was off. Or his appearance had thrown me off.

"I understand. Another shock in your young life. Don't be embarrassed."

More like humiliated, I thought. You son of a bitch.

"Goddamn it, Paul!" came a shout from inside the room. "What are you talking about out there? Let the boy in!"

Lieutenant Gardner flashed his soft, easy smile but added, hand across the door frame blocking my way, "You still don't remember what they looked like?"

"I was too far away," I told him as I had the officer on the scene. "And my glasses were sweat-stained. I couldn't see very well."

"Paul, they were Mexicans or something like Mexicans. Colombians or El Salvadorians. Goddamn cops, what do you have to do to make them believe you?" C. J. McDaniels sounded hale and hearty.

Gardner, wearing the same type of blue suit, white shirt, and snug tie as when I'd first met him, relaxed his grip on the door, raised his palms, and let me enter. The room was a double, but only one bed was occupied. McDaniels was by the window. His broad frame took up the width of the bed, and he was propped in a sitting position with his thick arms crossed.

When Lieutenant Gardner entered behind me, a scowl streaked across McDaniels's face. However, I paid little attention to that. I was more interested in the young woman with the lustrous black hair. She was seated at McDaniels's side. Her presence helped pull my mind to the now.

"Well, Neil Marshall," said C. J., "it's mighty kind of you to answer my call and pay me a visit. My dear," he added to the woman beside him, "this is the brave, mumbling poet who saved me. This beautiful lady, Mr. Marshall, is Linda Garcia, my secretary."

She surprised me by standing and reaching out her hand. I took it hesitantly, but then firmly met her strong grasp.

"I thank you, Mr. Marshall," she said, with a trace of an accent.

As she sat down again, I smiled and stepped to the end of the bed. Linda was a light-complexioned Hispanic. Her face was long and thin, her mouth small but with full, pouty lips. There was a strange familiarity in her appearance. Perhaps it was her trim figure or her luminous eyes, but Linda reminded me of Keely Cohen, a poet, a professor at the University of Houston, and a close friend.

"A man of many words," McDaniels drawled. "Poets are known to be frugal in that regard."

"I'm glad you're okay," I told him, though the words scraped dryly across the roof of my mouth.

"Are you?"

"Well, yes!"

McDaniels grunted.

"This is the first day he's shown any life," Linda Garcia announced.

"Don't bitch, McDaniels," Lieutenant Gardner said quietly. "You're alive." His soft smile was a fixture on his face.

"Because of him." McDaniels pointed a thumb at me.

"I suppose he did save a friend this time instead of avenging one."

"Goddamn it, Gardner, what the hell are you talking about?"

"Past history," I muttered.

"You two know each other!" He caught my eyes, then stared at Gardner.

"What I can't quite figure is how whoever did this knew you would be there," Gardner stated. "It's not like you go jogging every day. And you usually don't miss a shadow."

"Guess I did this time. I was damn mad enough to, people saying I'm soft, fat, and washed up—"

"McDaniels, I never said anything of the sort."

"Yeah, you and—" He stopped himself.

"And who?"

"You got anything to tell me, Gardner, or is this a social call?" C. J. twisted, then grimaced, as he took a pillow from behind his back, pounded it with one of his big fists, and held it against his belly. He folded his arms across it.

"I let the guard go, as you requested."

Linda sat straight and stared at C. J. She was wearing black slacks, a long-sleeved purple blouse that looked to be made of silk, and a little gold cross around her neck.

"You requested what?" she asked.

"Good," C. J. said to Gardner, ignoring Linda.

"But you're getting sloppy," the lieutenant told him. "You need someone to watch your back. Linda can't do it all."

"I can watch my own back," he bellowed.

Linda slapped C. J.'s arm. "You requested what?"

"I can watch my own back," he repeated, in a softer voice.

"The guard was to keep you in."

"I'm fine."

"We are going to wait for the doctor before you go anywhere," Linda said firmly.

C. J. sighed. Apparently, then, it was settled. This petite woman, I thought, obviously wielded considerable power over the burly private investigator. Not that size had anything to do with power, of course. Only size of intellect, and the varying needs of the parties involved. *Need*, the key word . . .

I realized I was drifting off into my own world when I heard McDaniels tell Gardner: "Anything else?"

"We found the white sedan," Gardner said casually. He walked from the door and leaned against the sink by the mirrored wall.

"Burned out?"

"Surprisingly, no. There were bloodstains on the seat, so they must've ditched it in a hurry. Guess you hit one real good."

"Prints?"

"Not a chance. It was a stolen car, of course."

"You'd think they could've stolen a quieter car," I commented. I backed up so I wasn't blocking McDaniels's view of Gardner and I bumped into the empty bed.

C. J. grinned. "Ain't that the truth, son. Have a seat." And I did, on the end of the vacant bed.

"We've been checking the hospital and clinic reports but haven't come across anyone with one of your slugs in him," Gardner said. "A couple of leads, but they didn't pan out. Guess he's got some private help somewhere. Private help and money." He paused, tapped his fingers together as if he were forming a cage or spider's web. "So now, McDaniels, you want to tell me what case you're working on?"

"Paul, you know I can't do that." He glanced at me.

Gardner cleared his throat. "Perhaps Mr. Marshall should step outside for a moment."

C. J. shook his head. "I asked Neil here to thank him. Be damn rude of me to send him off on his own."

I stood and started to say it was okay, I'd wait in the hall, but C. J. raised his hand.

"No, son, you sit down. Don't let the lieutenant's rudeness spoil our afternoon."

"Cut the crap, McDaniels."

"I'm on the up-and-up."

"Up-and-up, my ass."

"You said it, not me."

"You son of a bitch, McDaniels. There's something you're not telling, and that's enough for me to start a little fire under *your* ass," Gardner said. He never raised his voice, but it took on a sharp, steely edge.

I sat there, thinking that scenes like this had gone on a hundred times before. These two men knew each other like ocean knows landfall, and the cadence of the conversation determined how hard the waves hit the shore—the shoreline being their common bond. It was a case of old acquaintances wary of each other as they were, in friendly rivalry. They may often not like each other, but something endured, a kind of reluctant trust.

Then again, in the terse silence that engulfed us, I could've been wrong. I knew Gardner, too, and no matter how he felt about a particular person, he had a job to do. And he liked it. Damn my tendency to romanticize things.

Finally Linda Garcia spoke up. "Come on, Paul, you don't need to shoot C. J.'s blood pressure through the ceiling. Give him a day or two more before you do that."

Lieutenant Gardner remained quiet a moment longer before nodding his head and gently stating, "Okay. For you." He stepped away from the sink. "You don't deserve this child, McDaniels."

C. J. grinned, then put up a hand and wriggled his fingers at Gardner. "Later, Paul."

"Count on it." He turned to me. "Goodbye, Mr. Marshall. I'm sure I'll also need another word or two with you in the near future."

I shook his hand. I didn't know what else I could tell him, but I nodded in agreement.

"By the way," he said, before closing the door, "I never learned who your favorite poet is."

"Keely Cohen," I replied without missing a beat.

"Really? I don't know him."

"Her."

"Mine's Shakespeare." And he was gone.

"Ain't that goddamn fine and dandy," C. J. called after him. "Shakespeare, hell."

"Actually, Shakespeare's very good—" I started to say, but C. J. cut me off.

"Yeah, well, that's great, son, but I need to hear what you saw the other morning in the park." He spoke quickly.

I glanced at Linda, who simply shrugged her shoulders.

"I didn't see them," I said.

"At all? I was going to ask you to describe the car, but since they've found it that don't matter much anymore."

"I told the police—"

"Sometimes things come back to a person after events have settled a bit."

"I know."

C. J. glanced at Linda.

"I was too busy looking at you and trying not to be scared," I added.

C. J. sighed. "I appreciate your honesty, Neil, but if anything comes back to you, all I ask is that you tell me first."

"I'll do that. But is that why I'm here, so you can pump me for information?"

C. J. shifted his weight in the bed. "Oh, no, son, not at all. I called to express my heartfelt appreciation for what you've done for me."

I smiled, reckoning he could get rich in used cars or real estate.

C. J. turned to Linda, who stood.

"Mr. Marshall," she said, "Mr. McDaniels has asked me to take you to lunch. And I would be delighted if you joined me."

I found that a curious proposal and, though I thought Linda was attractive, a little voice in the back of my mind asked *why—why her and not C. J. when he felt better?*

But I ignored the unspoken question. Lunch with Linda might be interesting.

I responded with a reasonable amount of verve. "That sounds fine."

I assumed they thought Linda Garcia could unearth something that neither Lieutenant Gardner nor C. J. had. Hell, I reinforced, it could be interesting.

It really could be.

3

Shortly after Lieutenant Gardner left, in walked a man wearing a white golf shirt and tan slacks. He was as old as C. J. and about the same height but much heavier, like an offensive lineman who'd seen his best days thirty years earlier. Beneath a sandy-colored hairpiece, he was doubtless as bald as C. J. His face was ruddy and his nose flat, as if it had been broken a time or two. And he had a hell of a black eye, the right one. I hadn't seen a shiner like that since the fourth grade—when Johnny Morris and I tangled, and he'd tagged me with a sharp right.

"C. J. McDaniels," he bellowed, "what the hell are you doing in bed?! You never have done a day's worth of honest work."

Without missing a beat, C. J. replied, "Coming from someone who should know."

"I see you're still alive and kicking."

"How'd you find me, Ray?"

"Aw, C. J., I always knew how to locate you. Times haven't changed none."

"Times have changed plenty, Ray. And it's been a lot of years. What do I owe the pleasure of this sudden visit?"

Ignoring C. J.'s question, he turned to Linda and said, "My dear, you have grown up into a fine young woman. I haven't seen you since your mother died, but you don't remember me, do you?"

Linda's smile was polite but tight. "I'm sorry, but I don't," she said. Though from the sharp light that emanated from her eyes as she studied him, I suspected she knew full well who the fat man was.

"I'm C. J.'s old buddy, Ray Westview," he said.

"Oh, yes, of course," Linda said, nodding her head as she stood. She extended her hand.

Westview hesitated, then awkwardly took her hand in his. "Strong girl."

"Thank you."

"Linda's my secretary," C. J. told him.

Westview held on to her hand for a moment and eyed her carefully before releasing it. Linda's expression never changed from its piercing politeness as she sat back down. Then, as if what C. J. had said just registered, Westview turned to the detective, eyebrows knitted tightly together, and barked, "What the hell you doing bringing your daughter into a business like this? You want *her* to end up in a hospital bed? Or worse?"

My mouth dropped. "Your daughter?" I asked.

C. J. frowned. "You always did have a goddamn big mouth, Ray."

"You mean it's not common knowledge?" he asked.

His daughter? I thought. His daughter?

"I go by my mother's maiden name," Linda told me. "It puts a stretch of distance between C. J. and me. He believes my life is safer if people think I'm simply his secretary."

"And not his own flesh and blood," Westview added. "Probably not a bad idea, but if someone ever wanted to find out exactly who Linda Garcia was, he would."

"Still an effort someone would have to make," I said. Looking at father and daughter, I began to see the resemblance. Of course, I thought, of course. The cheekbones, the eyes, the round mouths.

Linda nodded her head. Her smile toward me was warmer than her smile toward Westview.

Then Westview looked in my direction as if he was seeing me for the first time. "Ray Westview."

I took his hand. "Neil Marshall."

"You're the hero?"

"The poet hero," C. J. interjected, and winked at me.

"The what?" Westview asked. "He looks like a skinny college kid."

"He is."

"I wouldn't exactly say skinny," I told him.

"Anyone under two hundred and fifty pounds is skinny," Westview replied, and released my hand.

I didn't like the way he stared at me. It was as if he was stealing a part of my soul with the camera in his mind. I didn't like this man. I couldn't quite figure out why, but I knew I didn't want him to hold on to any part of me.

"That's some shiner you've got," I said.

"Husband abuse." He laughed heartily and slapped me on the back.

No wonder he had a black eye, I thought, feeling the sting from his hand between my shoulder blades. I didn't figure he was capable of talking softly or walking softly. And God knew what kind of stick he carried. He turned to C. J.

"Del always had a mean right hook, didn't she, buddy?"

"I wouldn't know, Ray. She never had reason to use it on me." C. J. edged himself up an inch or two.

"Your loss, buddy." He laughed again. "Always has been."

"Yeah, Del was a fine woman."

"Still is."

"I bet. She still painting?"

"Sure, sure. Why, she just—"

"She did that portrait of me," C. J. told Linda, cutting off Westview. "You know, the one hanging in my bedroom."

I saw a flash of recognition spark in Linda's eyes. Later she would tell me that the painting he was referring to was of a young C. J., shirtless and leaning against the doorway of a small apartment with a cigarette burning hot down by his hip.

Westview forced a smile. "Well, you should see her stuff now. It's not childish anymore."

"I'm sure she's matured, Ray."

"Not like us, huh?"

"Speak for yourself, pal."

"Hey, buddy, I knew you when—"

"Shit, let me tell you, I sure do like that painting. Brings the memories stampeding back."

Westview's upper lip began to twitch and he let out a short laugh. "I'd almost forgotten about that picture," he said. "I don't think about those days too much. You know, she painted one of me, too."

"Can't imagine."

"Oh, yeah, during her little fantasy time. Hell, we never looked that good."

"I did," C. J. said casually as he patted his belly. "That might've been a world ago, but it wasn't a fantasy. In fact, Del told me that painting was so real it scared her. I think that's why she didn't marry me. She saw me too well through that painting."

"That sounds like *your* little fantasy, McDaniels." Westview's smile was falling.

Tension spliced the room. Hell if I knew why C. J. was trying to push Westview's button, and from the look on Linda's face neither did she. The bantering turned to badgering. And C. J. continued.

"Del needed a man she could control," he said. "Or her father could."

"You goddamn arrogant son of a bitch! If she'd listened to you she'd be as dead as Karla."

Linda stiffened. "Mr. Westview, if you have something to say about my mother—"

"It's okay, Linda," C. J. interrupted.

"No it's not."

"Let me handle this."

"Like you've been—"

"Linda!" C. J. snapped, but said no more. His daughter fell into a smoldering silence.

"Okay, Ray, let's cut the crap. What's on your mind?"

Westview paced to the door and back, glancing at me. I wondered if I should give them some privacy, or if it even mattered anymore, but before I could make a decision Westview started to speak.

"I'm onto you, old buddy," he said. "I know the old man's hired you to poke around in my business."

"Now, Ray—"

Westview leaned against the end of the bed. He was between me and Linda, and he faced C. J. "Don't start shoveling shit on me. You've been rattling doors." He gave the bed a shake. "What's the matter, does the old man think I'm ripping off the company?"

"Are you?"

"Fuck you, McDaniels."

"Then what are you worried about?"

"I don't like anyone sticking his nose into my business."

"I'm doing some work for the old man."

"Some bullshit work, McDaniels!" he snapped, and pushed himself away from the bed. His breathing was heavy and he was beginning to talk through a tight jaw. "The old man and Mark Hill were trying to dig up dirt on me, but they couldn't find any. You know why, McDaniels? Because there isn't any. Then Hill had the bad luck of dying, and the old man blames me for that, too."

"Come on, Ray. Why would dear old Mr. Bedford do that?"

"Dear old Mr. Bedford, hell. He's a rotten son of a bitch who's too mean to die."

"Never could please him, could you, Ray?"

Westview leaned slightly forward, hands on hips, and glared at C. J. "But sooner or later he will die," he added, his voice low but rolling with a coarse, throaty rage.

"Company's still his."

"Only in name."

"Good enough for me."

"Back off, McDaniels."

C. J. interlocked his fingers and casually stretched and

put his hands behind his head. The sleeves of his hospital gown fell back to his shoulders, exposing his thick, muscular arms.

"What if I call on you when I'm feeling better and we can discuss this further?" C. J. asked.

"There ain't nothing to discuss, McDaniels."

Westview was so angry I could almost feel him shake.

"I'll look you up, Ray."

For a long minute no one said a word. It was an icy-eyed staring contest, and I wondered what I was going to do if Westview suddenly decided to take a swing at C. J. I supposed if he lunged I could clip him at the knees and with any luck tear a ligament or two. It would be a cheap shot, and the thought of his massive weight coming down on my back didn't thrill me. But, even as big as I was, I doubted if I could stop his forward motion by going for his upper body. Maybe C. J. figured he could slug him with one of his meaty arms and bring Westview down easily. I couldn't see it, though, not without him ripping out all his stitches. Of course, now, he could have a gun stashed behind his pillow. . . .

Then Linda cleared her throat, stood, and picked up her purse. The gesture was enough to break Westview's concentration, and he glanced at McDaniels's daughter.

"Fine!" Westview suddenly said, and threw his arms up. "Just fine!" He took a step toward the door, then turned back around and jabbed the air with his forefinger in short, jerky motions. "If that's what you want to do, then look me up. You want to play your dick games, go ahead. I'll be waiting."

"Be seeing you, Ray," C. J. said.

"Yeah." Westview hesitated, then added, "Just be sure to watch your back, McDaniels. Looks to me like someone's trying to hurt you."

"Count on it," C. J. replied.

The aura around Westview sent shock waves I was sure even the EKG machines picked up. He let out a short breath as if he were snorting.

As he reached the door, McDaniels called out, "And give Del my best. Been thinking a lot about her recently."

Westview paused a second, his back to the room, then left without another word.

Linda set her purse back down on the floor and looked at her father. "What was the big idea?" she asked.

"I wanted to see how easily he'd rile."

"Why?"

"Find out how badly whatever's eating at him is eating at him."

"You think you touched a nerve?"

"Jesus Christ, hit the goddamn mother lode," C. J. said, "and you know it, smartass. He's always been a hothead, but he never loses that smug, arrogant smile in public unless something's really bugging the shit out of him. People don't change, do they?"

Linda shrugged her shoulders.

"But get this," C. J. continued, "I haven't found a speck of dirt on him, or at least I didn't think I had." He paused and now glanced at me. "We'll talk about it later," he told his daughter.

"What now?" Linda asked.

"I don't know. I need to think. You two go to lunch and give me some time alone."

"C. J.—"

"Go on, girl, like we planned. I need to think. We'll talk later."

Linda sighed and picked up her purse. "Let's go, Neil," she said.

"You sure?" I asked. I didn't want my company to be a chore for her. Besides, I thought, I really should run cross town and see Candace Littlefield, my *adopted* baby sister. After her grandfather's death, I'd taken Candace under my wing and treated her like family. The gesture had been reciprocated. If she wasn't working her summer job at Dairy Queen, then she'd probably be at the stables tending her horses. With all this activity in my life, I knew the young girl would be worried about me. I needed to reassure her I was fine.

Instead, Linda replied, "Of course I want to have lunch with you. It's just that . . ." She caught her father's eye.

"Have a good time, kids. I'll be around."

"Around where?"

"Right here."

"You better be."

"Say, girl," he said to his daughter as we were leaving, "I thought that purse was too small to hide a piece."

Linda grinned. It was a beautiful, broad smile.

"Absolutely not," she told him.

"You're coming along fine."

"Yeah, I'll do," she said.

No kidding, I thought. And we were gone.

4

Outside the hospital Linda said, "Let's take my car, okay?"

"I'd prefer to. Mine's a VW Bug, *sans* air."

"How classic."

"That's how I look at the little car, at least in the winter. During the summer, classic gives way to just plain hot."

Linda grinned and ran a hand through her long, black hair. The sun burned in the hazy sky like the end of a cigarette. I was already sweating. Even Linda's faint purple eye shadow was close to melting.

I told myself C. J. wasn't forcing her to lunch with me. Linda was treating me because she wanted to. Any other notion took the edge off a potentially beautiful friendship.

Linda eyed me curiously. "Do you have something else you need to do?" she asked. "Or someone else you need to be with?"

"Not at all," I responded, though I wasn't quite sure why. Did I want to be with this woman that badly? After all, I had missed my literature class—taught by Keely. And besides, I was eager to see Candace, then check in at work.

"You seemed lost in your own world."

I felt my cheeks flush. "Creative trance," I replied.

"Are you one of those weird poets?"

"Weird poets?"

"You know, the kind who writes about his own penis."

The hotness on my cheeks spread wider until I was afraid I would combust. "Actually, I'm a breast man."

28

"Very good."

"And you're just as meek and mild as your father."

The corners of her mouth turned up in amusement. "So I've heard. Come on. I know just the place for lunch."

Linda drove a half-ton Ford pickup, blue. I'd expected something sporty like a Mazda or a Porsche or maybe even a Corvette. Instead it was another Texas Cadillac. Linda cranked up the air conditioner as we headed on our way.

The city of Houston was undergoing triple bypass surgery. Great mounds of dirt banked the widening arteries. Steel mesh and huge blocks of concrete rose half-completed and without purpose. It was a city as modern art, I thought, as Linda drove quietly, lost for a moment in her own thoughts. We twisted along the fringe of organized chaos. Yellow lights flashed warnings of congestion—lanes closed, exits inaccessible, streets blocked off for sewer repair. Hard-hatted workmen moved about like an occupation army. The city had that war-torn Beirut look. Or was it an old soldier gasping for breath, under the knife? Perhaps it wasn't that deep. Perhaps it was only cosmetic surgery to make us all feel better, a placebo—

"What did you say?" Linda asked.

"What?"

"You said something, I thought to me. C. J. told me that you mumbled."

"Yeah," I said, trying not to sound sheepish. I'd found that as my thoughts grew in intensity I started to talk aloud. It was especially acute when I was writing poetry. My ex-wife pointed that one out to me. "I was wondering where we're going," I added, enunciating clearly.

"We're here," Linda replied, pulling into a busy parking lot off Westheimer. "It's called Grotto," she said. "Great Italian food."

"You're preaching to the already converted," I said. "I know this place well."

"Listen," she said, "I'm sorry for not talking, especially after teasing you about your creative trance. My mind took off somewhere else."

"I understand. Private thoughts are another world."

She took a double look at me and grinned. "A quote from?"

"Some fool poet. You read poetry?" I asked as we got out of the truck and made for the restaurant. "I mean, besides the writers who pay homage to their own manhood."

"Not really. And touché. I haven't read the penis pushers since high school."

"Some people think poetry is that stuff on greeting cards," I said.

"Oh, I don't," Linda said. "And I didn't say I haven't read it. I just find modern poetry difficult to understand. It's like looking at a room of black canvases and being told they're paintings. I don't get the message. And those poems I do understand are like photographs where you have to imagine the rest of the picture, which is okay, I guess. I just like stories, whole stories."

"I'll buy that," I replied. "But in your line of work, you see snapshots of people and situations and then have to construct the rest of the picture."

We were at the front door. As I pulled it open Linda said, "Clever."

"What?" I followed her in.

"Are you calling our work poetry?"

We approached the hostess, told her two for non-smoking.

"Yes, actually." The correlation hadn't been intentional but, given the opening, I took it.

"Can you imagine what C. J. would say to that?" she asked. We followed the hostess through a maze of wooden tables to a small two-top by the far wall.

" 'Poetry, hell,' " she mimicked C. J., her voice low. " 'If anything, it's a goddamn dirty limerick.' " Linda smiled slyly.

There once was a dick from Houston
who didn't know just how to shoot'em.

All the cheaters of wives
he was hired to eye—

Linda paused, then shrugged her shoulders. "You finish it," she said.

"Me?"

"You're the poet."

"Okay." My mind rattled like an old steam engine as I repeated,

All the cheaters of wives
he was hired to eye . . .

Then I shot out,

So he'd cut off their balls and salute them.

"Best I could do under pressure," I told her.

"That's great!" she cried as the waiter arrived and took our drink orders. Linda asked for a glass of chardonnay, so I decided to have a beer. Moretti. It was a good Italian brew, rich but not too heavy. I didn't usually drink in the middle of the day, but this encounter somehow called for one. I had to admit that, in spite of my hesitancy, I was enjoying myself more than I had anticipated.

I hadn't been to Grotto in a while, but the place hadn't changed. It was a large, open rustic space. The walls were one big colorful mural, with Bacchic caricatures that were festive and amusing. Toward the front was a stone, wood-burning pizza oven. On one side was a counter with bowls of *tapas*—an array of condiments, Colavita olives, corni-chons, hot peppers, and marinated salads. Deftly managing the pizza oven was a man dressed completely in white—trousers, jacket, and chef's hat. The wall opposite us was mostly windows, and behind those windows was a small outside courtyard with tables. As the tables inside began to fill, a few people braved the summer heat and sat in the courtyard.

When the waiter returned with our drinks, we placed our orders—linguini *pescatore* for Linda, and angel-hair pasta with a seafood Alfredo sauce for me. We both chose to start with a Caesar salad.

"I was offered a job here when they opened," I said.

"Really? As a waiter?"

"Oh, no. Chef. But I had my mind set on getting back to school and didn't want to commit the hours I'd have to put in. And now I have too good a position at Perry Stevens Catering. Decent money, flexible schedule, and some close friends."

"Interesting," Linda said as she broke off a piece of *focaccia* and dipped it into a mix of olive oil, red pepper flakes, and spices.

"It can be. Perry's kind of highfalutin. Once we did a private dinner party for Henry Kissinger. It was at an antebellum in River Oaks. The floors were wood and the decor very arty and old South. With Kissinger in attendance, the atmosphere was that of power and back-room politics. About sixteen people were there, and after the last course I was standing in the hall, all decked out in my chef's coat and hat and such. Well, Kissinger walks over to me, stretches out a hand, and says, 'That was delightful,' in that deep voice of his. It was great. Pissed Claudia off, though."

"Who's Claudia?"

"She actually runs the food prep at The Kitchen, and I work under her. She felt she deserved the kudos, but she was in the other room checking on the coffee. Hell, I even got Kissinger to sign a menu card. Perry has the card framed and hung in his office."

"So tell me more about yourself."

"There's not much else to say," I told her, and drank. "I'm twenty-eight. I'm divorced. I go to the University of Houston. I'm trying to finally earn a master's degree. As you know, I write poetry. I've published in little magazines. After I get my degree I don't know what I'll do."

"You've been married? I wouldn't have guessed."

"Why?" I had a piece of the *focaccia*, too. It was a rosemary-and-onion flat bread and pretty good.

"I don't know," she said. "You seem kind of shy with me. I guess I thought you were like that around all women."

"Finishing your limerick was shy?" My face rivaled the crimson tide.

The waiter brought our salads, grated on flakes of parmesan cheese, then ground some coarse black pepper from a silver pepper mill. I ordered another Moretti. Linda was doing fine with her wine.

"How long have you been divorced?" she asked after sampling her salad.

"A few months. You ever been married?"

"No, and I'm getting to be an old woman."

"Not by my calculation."

"That's because you're a breast man."

I almost coughed out a mouthful of beer. "You do like the shock effect."

"And for your information, I'll be thirty this fall. Who wanted the divorce?"

"I guess I initiated it."

"You guess?"

I shrugged. Usually I didn't like talking about my failed marriage, but for some reason the words flowed.

"She liked the idea of being married," I said. "Even if the marriage was bad, which it was. Or became. I don't know. The relationship felt lousy after she finished law school. Instead of life becoming easier, it grew more difficult."

"Law school? She's no dummy."

"She's a whiz with words. To the point where conversation is confusing." I laughed. "Like I'm being now."

"We don't have to talk about it." She smiled.

"I don't mind," I said, and paused. "Actually, it's been a while since someone would listen." I took a drink of beer. "I know she didn't want to end the marriage. Just control the relationship."

"Control, huh? What's her name?"

"Susan."

"Rather common," she said.

I smiled.

"But then, I've always liked my name," Linda added, "and wouldn't trade it for any other. Any kids?"

"Thank God, no. I could imagine a custody fight. Dividing property was difficult enough. Susan's idea of splitting the blanket was that she got the blanket and I split. Finally, I ended up in the Heights in a garage apartment, while she kept the house, the furniture, and my Beatles albums."

"Hey, bud, it's a community-property state," Linda said. "Unless you were doing something you shouldn't have been—like screwing around—that would've swayed a judge in her favor, you were entitled to your share. We deal with enough messy divorces. I know how it goes." She took a bite of her salad before continuing. "Maybe that's why I've never been married—seeing all the rotten things people who are supposed to be in love do to each other when it comes to divorce."

"I wasn't screwing around," I told her, thinking of Keely Cohen, my literature professor. There was that night I'd innocently stayed with her. Nothing had happened, but Susan caught wind of it and charged me with adultery. In the end, Susan backed down and my blundering hadn't damaged Keely's marriage. And I was careful to keep it that way. "My partnership with Susan simply hit the point where I wanted out."

"Cut your losses and ran? Why? The control thing?"

"Some. I don't know. I just wanted out."

"You have rights, too."

"You need money to fight. Our legal system goes to the highest dollar."

"Is that cynicism or guilt?"

"Disagree with me."

"What do you think went wrong?" she asked instead.

"The problem," I said, finishing my salad, "was that we were too preoccupied with ourselves to be interested in each other. We thought we'd grow together without working at it. Wrong."

"Sounds clinical. Do you still love her?"

I hesitated. "I love being back in school," I replied.

"You think I'm being too nosy, don't you?" Linda sipped her wine.

"Isn't that your job?" I asked, glad she didn't push it. "Asking questions must be second nature for you. It comes automatically, this thirst for information."

"I believe you are a romantic."

"That's a mean thing to say."

"You are," Linda stated. She set her salad fork down on her empty plate. Seconds later the waiter came by and scooped them up. He topped off our water glasses as another waiter presented our entrées.

"I thought if you were going to pump me, it'd be about that incident the other day on Allen Parkway. Although I can't imagine what more I could tell you."

"I know, Neil. You're straightforward. If there's a fact or face or anything else to remember, I'm sure you'll let me know."

"I didn't see them." I tasted the angel hair, redolent of garlic and fresh basil.

"Good, huh?" She was tucking into her platter, over-flowing with shrimp, calamari, crab, and several steamed mussels.

"Delicious," I replied.

Linda seemed pleased. "Mine's good, too," she said. "So you cook stuff like this?"

"Yes."

"It's a wonder you're so lean," Linda said.

"Months of hard work. After the separation I woke up one time too many with smoky lungs and beer on my breath. And I'd developed a Buddha belly."

"So you took to jogging around Houston in the mornings."

"And now I'm beginning to feel soft again. Lately I haven't done a hell of a lot of jogging."

"It's too bad you didn't see the gunmen."

"I was scared," I confessed. "But I remember everything that happened."

"It scared C. J., too," she said. "And me."

We went over the whole scene again, but came up with nothing new.

"Whoever's behind the attack will probably try again," Linda concluded. "Especially if one of them was hurt as bad as Lieutenant Gardner indicated."

I was quiet a minute, then asked, "Do you think it has anything to do with Ray Westview?"

Linda stiffened the way she had when Westview had upset her earlier. "It's best not to jump to conclusions."

I set down my fork. "I don't mean to pry."

"Yeah, you do. Like me."

"Okay, maybe I do. But the deduction's not difficult. For God's sake, I've already heard that C. J. is investigating Westview for Westview's father-in-law—and that Westview doesn't like it one bit, to say the least. I know that he and C. J. hadn't seen each other in a number of years, but Westview took the time and effort to locate C. J. And it's obvious that they both were, or are still, in love with the same woman."

"You know too much. We'll have to ice you."

"And who was Mark Hill?"

"CEO for Bedford Oil. He died a couple of weeks ago."

"How?"

"Heart attack."

"Do you believe it?"

She shrugged. "Didn't have any reason not to, until now."

"Are you carrying a gun?" I picked up my fork and shoveled in another bite of seafood Alfredo. "Would you have pulled the piece at the hospital?"

"Yes, and yes." Linda pushed her plate away. "I'm stuffed." The plate was half-full.

"I thought they were going to fight."

"Me, too. It was weird. Ray showing up. C. J. acting so aggressive. You know, I think C. J. was looking into this in order to see Del again. I don't think he expected to find anything. He felt Old Man Bedford, Del's father, was frustrated because Ray's at the helm and the old man never liked Ray. Now with this shooting—and Ray's belligerent behavior—we'd be fools not to suspect something's going on."

The waiter cleared our plates. We both passed on dessert, but I had an espresso and Linda a cappuccino. Then she paid the bill and we were out of the cool, cavernous restaurant and back into the sweltering heat.

All too quickly we returned to the hospital, and I realized we were about to go our separate ways. Christ, Texas was still a republic when I last asked for a date and, even then, smooth had not exactly been my style. What the hell, I gave it a shot as we strolled into the reception area.

"Say, Linda, what if you let me buy you dinner sometime? Or lunch? Or something?"

"Why, Neil Marshall, are you asking me for a date?"

I was going to have to work on this blood-to-cheek thing. "Yes," I replied, "I most certainly am."

"I wondered why you were following me. You don't need to go back up to C. J.'s room, you know." We were standing in front of the elevators.

"I wanted to thank him again. For suggesting lunch, I mean."

"Of course. And I'd be delighted to have dinner with you."

"How about tomorrow night?"

The elevator door opened and we took it up to the fifth floor.

"Anxious, aren't we?" She gave me a sideways glance.

"I wanted to say tonight."

"You should have, then." She raised her eyebrows and grinned. "But I guess I'm busy."

How obnoxious, I thought, but laughed it off.

The elevator door opened and we walked down the hall to C. J.'s room. As soon as we hit the doorway, though, Linda came to a dead stop.

I glanced over her shoulder. Nothing was as we had left it. The room was straightened. The furniture was rearranged. The bed was made.

And C. J. McDaniels was gone.

5

Linda sighed.

The blinds were open, so the room glared with afternoon sun. The smell of disinfectant lingered in the air.

"All set for the next victim," Linda said.

"Undoubtedly some new mother who, at this very moment, is downstairs in delivery having the time of her life."

"Right."

I cleared my throat. "Do you think the police moved C. J. again?"

"My guess is he wandered off on his own free will."

"They'd let him go, just like that?"

"I wonder if he paid the bill."

"Don't orderlies and nurses generally discourage people from simply walking away, especially people with bullet holes in them?"

"Not C. J. Besides, it was only a .38, not very professional."

"Only a .38? Foolish me."

"And it brushed him."

"Brushed him? Well, I'd say there was a lot of blood for a brush stroke." I walked to the window and looked out at the Southwest Freeway. Traffic was heavy, but not remotely the stop-and-go thickness it would be in a few hours. When I turned back, I glimpsed Linda's sleek figure leaving the room.

"Hey, wait a minute." I followed her to the front desk. "People don't just walk out of here," I repeated.

"I'm sure C. J. was bored."

The blonde nurse was gone, but the heavyset black woman was still around. "Can I help you?" she asked as we approached the counter.

"Has Mr. McDaniels checked out?" Linda inquired as if we were at the front desk of the Waldorf-Astoria. "I work for him. I'm Linda Garcia."

"Miss Garcia, we are not happy with Mr. McDaniels. The doctor did not release him."

"Then he is gone?"

"We can't find him anywhere."

"Then he's gone." Linda opened her purse and drew out her wallet.

"What, are you paying cash?" I joked.

"I didn't even know he had clothes," the nurse said. "Someone must have brought him some."

"I did," Linda replied.

"Then you knew he intended to leave," I said.

"The doctor was scheduled to come by this afternoon and C. J. was hoping to be released, so he conned me into bringing him clothes when I came in this morning."

"Someone needs to do something about the bill, too," the nurse demanded. "Lord, Dr. Stone's not going to be happy about this."

Linda handed the nurse a card. "This is our office address and telephone number," she told her. "Tell them to send a bill. C. J.'s sly and ornery, but he's not a cheat. He'll pay."

"I called the police," said the nurse. "That Lieutenant Gardner gave me a card and I called him direct. He told me don't worry none—they'd find him." The nurse turned the card over in her hands. "Don't you have an insurance company you want to run this through?" she asked.

"It would cost a fortune to insure C. J. Besides, he doesn't believe in it." Linda started walking away. "Thank you and have a good day."

"They're not going to like this," the nurse mumbled.

We took the elevator to the first floor, walked by the little gift shop, past the chapel, and through the bustling lobby.

"I'm sure he took a cab," she said more to herself than to me. Then she caught my eye and held out one of her long, slender hands. So formal. Well, back to business, I thought.

"Tomorrow night?" she asked.

"Great."

"Here's my card with my mobile- and home-phone numbers. The office number's on there, too. Give me a call tomorrow."

"Thanks again for lunch," I said, and stuffed the card in my top pocket. We were at her truck.

"Where are you parked?" she asked.

"Other side, by Toys 'R' Us."

"Climb in. I'll drop you off."

Linda zipped around the back of the hospital and over to my little VW. As she did, she punched in a number on her phone, but she waited until I got out to send it.

I unlocked my car door and rolled down the window, my eyes the whole time on Linda. I was surprised at my growing attraction toward her. Why? I asked myself. The woman was pretty, intelligent, and fun to be with. Simple enough.

I saw Linda pick up the phone. She braked the truck and hesitated a minute while talking to whoever was on the other end. Or perhaps she left or retrieved a message. Whatever it was didn't take long, and I watched her hang up before continuing on her way. I cranked the small engine of my air-conditionless car.

The day was moist and hot, and I couldn't get the image of Linda Garcia out of my head. I hung behind her for a couple of miles. My general direction was Loop 610, but I took a turn or two I really didn't need to in order to keep with her. It was odd that I was attracted strongly to someone I barely knew. I didn't believe in love at first sight, and I rolled over this conundrum in my mind. As I followed, I stayed back a few cars, close to a faded brown Buick. It would be embarrassing if she spotted me and, from then on, thought of me as some lovesick schoolboy.

When I began to feel silly, I decided it was time to head for home. After the third straight turn I made behind Linda, however, the Buick followed. Earlier, this rambling vehicle had half caught my attention. Now the brown car received my full attention. I could make out two men in the front seat. When Linda slowed and I slowed, the third car slowed, and when we picked up speed so did the Buick. My palms were slick on the steering wheel.

At Chimney Rock and West Bellfort Linda turned right. The thought struck me that, wherever she was going, her driving was odd, because now we were headed away from Loop 610. Her path was some big circle, and my problem was how to warn her that she was being followed.

If I had a car phone, then she and I could talk strategy. The thought of having a phone in the Bug caused me to laugh aloud nervously. The damn phone would be worth more than the car. I shook my head. My best bet was to catch up to her and lay on the horn to get her attention.

Problem was, Linda was too far away from me. And she had a lead foot. At any open length of road, she hit the gas and I couldn't catch up. When traffic thickened I had a hard time maneuvering close. Finally, at West Bellfort and Gessner, Linda went through a yellow light. I stayed in front of the Buick so it wouldn't run the red. We waited. The Buick was penned in. By the time the light turned green, Linda was long gone. I continued in her direction to keep an eye on the Buick. But the brown bomb never made an effort to pass me.

When I hit the Southwest Freeway, I hooked a right and headed north. Rush-hour traffic was beginning, but for the most part I was going against the flow. At an easy cruising speed, I fell into the rhythm of the freeway with the Buick as my company.

I didn't know what to do. The men behind me made no bones about being there.

Shit, Neil, I told myself, those bastards are more pissed off than a pair of Brahma bulls that've been shot in the balls. At another time, the thought would've put a smile on my face as it brought to mind my old buddy, the late Jason Keys. When he was a boy he used to air-rifle bulls in their big old sacks. Told me once how he'd been treed by one particularly mean Brahma that had escaped. Little Jason had clung to the upper limbs of a big old oak the better part of an afternoon. Jason's father finally came looking for him and chased the bull back to the field. The old man paddled the boy's behind with the butt of the rifle.

Hell, I'd take a paddling now if someone would rescue me from those two muscleheads.

Someone like C. J. McDaniels. I debated about driving to C. J.'s office. But what if he wasn't there? Or what if that was where Linda went? I'd lead them right back to her. No good.

I wondered what these goons wanted. Better yet, I wondered how I was going to get away. At least they hadn't tried a drive-by. So far. In this stupid car I couldn't spin *Rockford* one-eighties or practice any clever, evasive *Magnum* moves. "Like you know how, anyway, Neil," I said, and realized I was talking aloud.

"This is the last straw. I'm selling this damn VW! And I'm not jogging on Allen Parkway anymore!"

Allen Parkway.

Finally the notion sank into my thick head that these idiots weren't following Linda. They were following me. Odds were they were the thugs who shot C. J. and believed I could identify them. Great.

I was awash in sweat and the blood pumped through my veins like a flash flood through a narrow canyon. If I was going to lose them, I had to get off the freeway.

I tried to make it look as if I was continuing north on 59, but at the last minute I shot over to the left and took the spur for downtown. I exited on Richmond, ran a red light, and took a left to Montrose. The Buick stayed right with me. At the corner of Richmond and Montrose I turned right. Panic began throwing little black spots in front of my eyes when suddenly I remembered there was an HPD substation just off Montrose at Westheimer. I made for the cops.

The police storefront was only a few blocks, but it was one of the longest stretches of road I'd ever driven. Short long rides were becoming a habit, I thought. At the substation I was pleased to see not one but two baby blue cars parked right out front. As I pulled into the parking lot, I heard the thugs in the Buick go screaming away down Westheimer. Of course, it didn't occur to me to get a license-plate number.

After turning off the ignition, I sat quietly for a minute. With a shaky hand I brushed my hair back from my sweaty forehead. I told myself I should go inside and make a formal statement, but I couldn't move. What could the cops do, anyway? I had nothing to give them but a story, and the thugs were gone. What I wanted to do was talk to C. J.

I fumbled in my top pocket and pulled out the card Linda had given me. To my surprise I saw that their office had a Westheimer address only blocks away. The hairs on the back of my neck prickled, adding to the discordant way I felt.

I drove up to C. J. McDaniels's office, which was above a new-and-used record store in an old renovated house. There were no cars out front. My VW idled in the driveway, and my eyes kept darting to the rearview mirror, but there was no sign of the Buick. There was also no sign of the father-daughter detective duo. I didn't feel like talking to anyone else, so I didn't go inside the record store to ask the old guy working behind the register if he'd seen them. I was about to pull into traffic when the door that led up to the office opened and out hobbled C. J. McDaniels.

"Son, you just intend to sit there and take in the view?" he asked.

"You're supposed to be in the hospital."

"Linda point you on my trail?"

I shook my head. Suddenly, my adrenaline fell. I realized my hands were trembling, and I couldn't stop the sensation. Damn it, I thought, I'd been through worse than being chased by a couple of goons. Yeah, and I wanted to avoid a repeat. Only recently had my ribs finally mended.

C. J. rested one of his big hands on the hood of my car to steady himself.

"Don't lie to me."

"Linda and I were followed," I told him. I began to relate the events since our return to the hospital. Slowly at first, then picking up speed, the words dropped like grains of sand through a broken hourglass. Finally, order gave way to chaotic phrases.

". . . like I said, a brown Buick—I know it wasn't the same car as on Allen Parkway because the police found that one, but, I mean, it stayed right with me until I drove into the parking lot of the police station down the street and then the thugs left in a hurry—"

"Slow down, son."

"I feel like throwing up."

"Are you sure they were following Linda, too, or just you?"

"I don't know. Maybe just me. But Linda was driving funny—like she knew someone was behind her."

"Someone was. You!"

"I was trying to warn her, but I couldn't catch up."

C. J. straightened himself, then reached into his pocket for a pack of cigarettes, tapped one out, and lit it. Christ, I couldn't escape smokers. And after nearly six months without a puff, I was still tempted. I gritted my teeth and drew on my incredible willpower. The fact that I still felt like blowing chunks didn't hurt my resistance.

"Wait here," he ordered.

"Why? You want me to be thug bait?"

"I want you to take me to get my car," he said. "I thought those idiots towed it back here, but come to find out it's in a police lot near the Heights. Before we go I'll call Linda in case what you said about those guys following you is true."

"I'm not so neurotic that I'd make a story like that up."

A hand on his side, cigarette dangling from his mouth, McDaniels grunted, then ambled back to the office door. I guessed I'd wait.

I gave the idling VW a pump on the accelerator and listened to the little engine gurgle. My shirt was soaked through with sweat. I fidgeted to the left, then right, glancing every other second in the rearview mirror. If those two knuckleheads returned, I was determined to make a break for C. J.'s office. Let them tree me in there, I thought.

I'd lead those bonecrushers to one of the toughest old bulls still roaming the field.

6

As we drove to the police holding lot, C. J. McDaniels told me he waited a good ten minutes after Linda and I left before starting to dress. Linda knew he was up to something and C. J. wanted us long gone before he made his escape. He was prepared to find us lying in wait for him down in the lobby or out in the parking lot, so he'd planned to slip out the back, walk over to Toys "R" Us, and call for a cab there. It'd worked.

"Linda wasn't the least bit fazed to return to an empty room," I said.

"Not a whole hell of a lot raises that girl's eyebrows."

No kidding, I thought.

The big detective's breathing was heavy. Slouched back in the seat, he twisted and turned uncomfortably. I wasn't sure if his anxiety was a result of his wound or the reminder of the last time he was sitting in that seat.

"Did you get her on the phone?" I asked.

"No. Left a message on her machine. Did you get a license number?"

"No."

"Worthless."

"What?"

"The—" He stopped. "Your information is worthless. All I know is that someone followed you. But that was almost to be expected. You were on Allen Parkway. You helped me and saw them—or they believe you just might've. Why do you think I called you?"

"You wanted to pump me for information."

47

"No, I was scared you'd end up dead. I didn't want your bullet-riddled corpse on my goddamn conscience."

I waded through a moment of stinging quiet before asking, "You don't figure Linda's in trouble, do you?"

"No."

C. J. wore jeans, a short-sleeved white cotton shirt, and a pair of old black leather boots with rounded toes. I'd learn later that he couldn't stand the pointy-toed boots, afraid that after a heavy rain they'd curl up like elf booties.

"You don't look so good," I said after a few minutes.

"I feel a mite puny," he replied. "How about you pull into the first fast-food place you come across. I think I'll be better after I eat something."

"There's a Mickey D's up the road."

"It ain't exactly The Ale House, but it'll do."

"Oh, I know The Ale House. My writers' group meets there a couple of times a month." It was also where you could get a cool pint of Newcastle Brown Ale—on tap—to chase down the best burger you'd ever eat.

"That so," he grunted. Then nothing.

I swung into the drive-through and we picked up some food, though C. J. ended up only picking at his value meal.

"Want some fries?" he asked me. He finished about half his burger before stuffing it back into the bag. "I've had about all I can stomach."

"No, thanks."

"Exit here."

"Where?"

"Right there!" he snapped, pointing at a signless street. "It's faster. We can cut up Washington."

Yes, sir, I thought, and followed his directions. We bypassed most of the area's construction and, as we pulled into the lot and C. J. lit up another cigarette, he spoke civilly again.

"To think I toyed with the idea of dropping smoking and picking up jogging," he said. "Hell, I don't know which of the two is more hazardous to my health."

"Been wondering that myself recently. I quit smoking for jogging after—" I cut myself off.

"After you killed that man," C. J. finished, and pushed open the door.

He noted the surprise on my face and added, "It's my business to know what goes down in this city. Your name sounded familiar, but it wasn't until I watched you and Gardner together that I remembered from where."

"That's a long story."

"Usually is, and at the moment I'm not strong enough to listen." He stepped out of the car, grabbed the door to steady himself, then straightened tall. Or as tall as he could.

"You okay?" I asked.

He ignored me, and I walked with him to the little hut which was like a ticket booth and waited as he asked for his car. A shriveled old man methodically picked through an untidy stack of papers. After checking C. J.'s identification, he handed him the bill. McDaniels cursed for not having Linda pick up his car two days ago and save him a hundred bucks.

"Goddamn it, a man shouldn't be victimized twice," he muttered, receiving the keys through a hole in the window.

"This ain't public parking, buddy," the old man in the booth said. "Ain't got enough room to hold them forever. So we charge 'em a lot and they get 'em out, or we keep 'em." He flashed an array of yellow, crooked teeth. The place looked like a junkyard. There was a hurricane fence with barbed wire on top. The parking lot was a dusty, rocky, treeless patch of land, and there were pit bulls chained close to the booth.

"Cops know who I am," C. J. complained. I helped him locate his Mustang. It needed a washing. "Some young son of a bitch must've had it towed off," he added.

"You going to be all right?" I asked. He was sweating, but pale as the big man was, it appeared to be a cold sweat.

"I swear if you ask me that again I'm going to knock

you on your ass." He dropped himself into the Mustang, sighed, then rolled down the window.

"I'm fine," he said, softening his tone. "Thanks for the ride. Now, go home, but keep your eyes open. You see those two morons again, call me. I'll be in touch."

"I feel like an armadillo staring into the headlights of an oncoming eighteen-wheeler."

"Son, that's why I want you to stay out of the road."

"Yes, sir."

He started the car and began to roll up the window.

"I'm taking a summer class, so I'll be at the university tomorrow morning," I called.

C. J. nodded, then threw the car in gear. Rocks spewed as he tore off down the street. I climbed back into my hot little VW and drove in the same direction.

To my surprise, I caught up to C. J. a few blocks later. He was driving excruciatingly slowly, something I hadn't picked for his style. Fearing that in his condition he might pass out, I stayed with him. In the back of my mind, a little voice whispered that this was how I invited trouble earlier, but I couldn't justify blowing past him, then reading about some bizarre accident concerning C. J. in tomorrow's paper. Besides, he was probably heading for home and a soft bed.

He made for River Oaks. As I wound behind him into Houston's den of riches, I was beginning to doubt I was tailing C. J. to his humble abode. Or, contrary to every PI movie or book I knew, the gumshoe business had paid off handsomely. When C. J. finally turned into a drive-way, I was satisfied. If he occupied this bayou pearl, then he didn't have the largest domicile; it was a mere eight or ten thousand square feet. I supposed, however, everything was relative. The modest mansion was certainly livable.

C. J. pulled into the circular drive and parked directly in front of the main door. It was an old antebellum-style house, white with slender columns—and marble steps leading up to the front door. I wasn't going to play amateur shamus peeking into rear windows, so I rolled the VW in behind C. J.'s Mustang and hopped out. From the look on his face you'd have thought I'd ripped out the man's stitches.

"What the hell are you doing here?" he asked.

"You were having trouble driving, so I thought I'd best follow you home. Nice place."

"This isn't my house, you blanket-head. It's Ray Westview's."

"Your compassionate chum from the hospital?"

"Hit the road, Neil." His hand clutched his side. I half expected to see blood shade his hand. It didn't.

"You're about to fall over," I said. "What if Westview really comes at you this time?"

"I can take care of myself."

"Pain medication's wearing off, isn't it? Listen, I'll hang in the background, take notes for you. Since you missed me shadowing you, I'd say you're still not quite up to snuff. A second opinion on what's said wouldn't hurt."

"You cocky bastard."

There was a heavy knocker, but I chose to lean on the bell instead. I don't know why I made such a brash move, except that the big detective was making me nervous and I needed to redirect his energies. Christ, I felt like Barney Fife bungling his way into a Sam Spade case. C. J. stared daggers at me before taking a final drag on his cigarette. Then he tossed it down and toed it out. Whereupon a short Hispanic man of about fifty answered the door.

"Is Mrs. Westview in?" C. J. asked.

Mrs. Westview? I thought.

"May I please have your name, sir?"

"C. J. McDaniels."

"C. J. McDaniels?" a voice trilled from inside. "I don't believe it. It's okay, Raul, let him in."

The Hispanic man bowed his head, then closed the door after we entered the foyer. It was an open space that went up the height of the house. The floor was marble and a spiral staircase rose to the left, leading to an open balcony on the second floor. A woman stood on this balcony, leaned against the rail, and stared down at McDaniels.

"Hello, Del," C. J. said.

"I don't believe it," she repeated. Her voice echoed throughout the house.

McDaniels stood, hands on hips, and grinned up at her. This could've been Tara, I thought, but Del Westview was as different from Scarlett O'Hara as C. J. was from Rhett Butler. She was a tall, slender woman, sleek as a model but almost boyishly flat chested. Her black hair was graying and she'd made no attempts to hide it. She also wore no makeup, though her hazel eyes, high cheekbones, and pouty lips reflected a girlish passion. And from the way C. J. was coolly eyeing her, I reckoned he'd been involved in some of that passion many, many years ago.

"My God, C. J.," she said, "you've gotten fat."

"Widened the road some, that's all, " he replied.

"I'd just finished working," Del told him. She was wearing jeans, brown sandals, a black tank top, and she was holding an old white shirt that was streaked and smudged with dark-colored paint.

"Is Ray here?"

"Is that who you came to see?"

"No."

"No, he's not. He's at work."

"Can we talk?"

Del started down the stairs. "Yes," she said, "but I have to be somewhere shortly. I wish you'd called."

"Didn't have the chance."

"Who's your friend?" she asked, glancing at me and smiling broadly.

Suddenly C. J. recalled I was with him, and his whole attitude ballooned into a big, black-bellied cloud.

"Mr. Neil Marshall," he announced.

I wanted to bolt out the door. "Pleased to meet you," I said.

"Del Westview," she replied. "Likewise."

Del was not as tall as C. J., but she had no trouble kissing him on the cheek. Her eyes betrayed her immense pleasure in seeing her old friend, but there was also a sense of wonder as well as a spark of something else at play, something like mischief. I wondered why the hell I invited myself along.

As I was sure C. J. did, too.

"Would you like a drink?" she asked him. "I mean the both of you," she quickly added.

"Ice water."

"What?"

"I'm finding that I have to restrain myself more and more these days, especially after being shot."

"Yes, I heard about that unfortunate incident," Del said as she turned to Raul.

I waited for C. J. to explain how I'd come to his assistance.

He didn't. Del turned to me.

"Ice water's fine," I said.

"Would you bring two glasses of ice water for Mr. McDaniels and his associate, and iced tea for me?"

Raul nodded and left.

"Raul's very good," she added, taking McDaniels by the arm and leading him into the study. "He and his wife both work for me as live-ins. It's much nicer than having only one maid. But you didn't come here to hear me talk about my domestic help, did you? Perhaps you want to see my latest work. Oh, but there isn't time today. I have someplace I need to be. So you'll have to come back. You will come back, won't you?"

"I haven't left yet."

I tagged behind them like the younger brother sent in the living room by Mom to make sure no hanky-panky was going on. The den was a small room with a big oak desk, a couch and a matching chair, bookshelves filled with mostly art books, and trophy heads on all four walls.

A ram, an elk, a six-point buck, and a black bear. C. J. and Del sat on the couch. I stood by the door.

"Ray bought the bear, you know," Del told C. J.

"I'm not surprised." He lit a cigarette.

Del smiled. "Same old C. J.," she said, and reached for an ashtray. "I quit."

Raul appeared with our drinks on a silver tray. I accepted my refreshing glass of water, then he set the platter down on the coffee table. He left quietly, not giving me a second look, and closed the door behind him.

Del reached out and touched the nape of C. J.'s neck. "What happened to all that beautiful hair?" she asked. Her voice was fluttery.

"Been butting too many heads, Del. Speaking of which, did Ray tell you he came by to see me this morning?"

"He said he might."

"Did he say why?"

"For old times' sake. Why—did you two have another rivals' spat? I told him that was what would happen, but you know Ray. 'That's water under the bridge,' he says."

"Was that all he said?"

"That's all he said. He was never too bright."

"Then why'd you marry him?" He snuffed out the cigarette before he was finished.

"Feel free to smoke if you want," she said. "You don't have to stop on my account."

"I'm trying to be polite."

She laughed. "I know it's hard for you."

"So why did you marry him?" he repeated.

Del was still playing with the hair along the back of his neck. C. J. shifted uncomfortably. I wasn't supposed to be here.

"Because he let me paint," she said casually.

"I'd have let you paint, too."

"And he was a stay-at-home guy. I never had to worry about his running off in the middle of the night or where he was going next. Or if he was going to get shot. If I

wanted him to stay home, he would. Now he runs
Daddy's company, something you'd never have done."

"You're right."

"I've always felt bad about Karla," she said quietly. Del
was staring at the dull light coming into the room through
the partially closed, floor-to-ceiling curtains. "Did you ever
find out what happened?" she asked.

"Officially, no. But the man I suspected was gunned
down outside one of his clubs about nine years ago."

Del looked at C. J. wide-eyed.

"No," he said, "it wasn't me. I wanted to kill the son of
a bitch, but it wasn't me. I was trying to do it the right
way, digging up evidence against him."

"How's your daughter? I know she took Karla's death
hard."

"Linda's as headstrong as her mother, God help her."

"And you," Del added, and smiled.

"God help me. Or are you calling me headstrong?"

"Both." Del paused, started to reach for the tea, then
pulled her hand back. "I often think about Karla," she
said. "I liked her. And I think of Linda, what she's grown
to be like."

McDaniels sipped some water.

"I guess I did play it safe," she mused. "And for years I
thought it could've been me instead of Karla, and I hated
myself for feeling glad I'd married Ray. Do you understand? For a long time that was the only reason I was
glad it was Ray and not you." She gave him a sideways
glance.

I've got to get out of here, I thought, and set the glass
down on the tray.

"My dear Mr. Marshall, you don't need to leave," Del
said.

"Yes, I do." I had expected to help C. J. deal with the
bullish Ray Westview, not an old love.

McDaniels cleared his throat.

"I'll be in the foyer," I informed him.

C. J. gave a short nod, then asked Del, "How's Ray doing with the company?"

"He's stressed out. It's a burden coming in on the heels of a man as successful as Mark Hill, God rest his soul. And you know Daddy doesn't think much of Ray. Still swears he's a gold digger."

"Ray wouldn't have any reason to have me shot, would he?" McDaniels eyed her carefully. I hesitated, hand on doorknob.

Del tugged hard on his hair. Her smile fell, but then slowly came back. "That's silly," she said. "He's not that jealous of you." And then her face was close to his, her eyes watery.

"I always wanted your baby," she whispered. "If it wasn't for Ray—"

"What?!"

And she kissed him. I opened the door.

"Oh, I've really got to go, C. J.," I heard Del say quickly. "But promise you'll come back." The earlier poise she had worn had been ruffled.

I stood in the open foyer and took a deep breath. I felt I'd invaded an intimate moment from thirty years ago. I could picture a young Del straightening her plaid skirt, afraid her father was about to walk in.

"Promise?" I heard Del say.

"I promise," C. J. replied.

Del burst into the foyer. C. J. followed, pale and sweaty.

As they walked across the marble floor toward me, something else drew our attention. Out on the front porch Raul was talking to someone whose voice was getting louder and louder until finally it reached a pitch of anger that stopped Del in her tracks. I couldn't make out precisely what they were saying.

A moment later I watched as Raul came sailing backward into the house, landing flat on his ass.

Forcing his way in after the servant was a large, muscular, red-haired man. His fists were positioned as a boxer's coming to meet his opponent at center ring, until he saw

Del. He dropped his left hand to his side but pointed at her with the index finger of his right.

"My name's Willie Burns," he said, his voice exploding like cannon fire in the foyer, "and I've come for my sister! Where is my sister?"

7

Del froze. Raul jumped to his feet, but waited for a signal as to what to do next. I watched as C. J. calmly lit a cigarette. The movement caught Willie Burns's attention.

"McDaniels?"

"You're out of the pen, Willie."

"Last week."

"Don't you know forcible entry is illegal?" He stepped up. Willie Burns was six feet four and a solid two hundred and twenty or so pounds. I appeared small next to the man. I wished C. J. had his gun.

"I'm looking for my sister," he said. The decibel level of his voice had dropped considerably.

"You two know each other?" Del finally managed to say.

"He busted me," Willie said.

"I never busted you," McDaniels shot back. "He tried to rip off Linda's truck," he told Del. "She busted him."

"She never—"

"Shut up! She had your ass and you tried to take a swing at me."

"What a pleasant reunion," Del quipped. She headed for the stairs. "C. J., I have someplace I absolutely have to be in half an hour. Would you please deal with this . . . this person?"

"Yes, ma'am."

"Don't be an asshole."

"I want to know where my sister is," Willie repeated.

C. J. thrust out a hand as if he were going to push the breath from Willie's chest.

Del paused halfway up the stairs. "Mr. Burns," she called out, her voice strong and deep, "as I told you on the phone, Pauline left my employment about six months ago and I have neither seen nor heard from her since."

"What did she do for you?" C. J. asked, exhaling smoke and not taking his eyes off Willie. McDaniels flicked the ashes on the floor.

"Raul," she said, "get him an ashtray." Raul nodded and left the room.

"Del?" C. J. said.

"Pauline was my maid and cook before Raul and his wife. I liked that girl and begged her not to quit. But she had her reasons, which she wouldn't explain, so I gave her a very good recommendation and released her. And, like I said, I haven't heard from her *or* a prospective employer since. Now, I must go. Please, C. J., deal with Mr. Burns."

"Yes, ma'am."

"Oh, shut up." She turned abruptly and disappeared upstairs.

Raul appeared with an ashtray, but C. J. was ushering Willie Burns outside. I thought he was doing an amazing job of not limping, or doubling over.

"Let's go," he said. "She's not here." Willie hesitated. "You want me to call you on parole violations." It was a statement, not a question.

"That kid never busted me."

"Goddamn it, Linda did. And if you hadn't been such an asshole she'd have let you off. I used to take her to your fights." He shoved Willie out the door.

I saw the pain flare from C. J.'s side as it etched across his face like cracks on a rock-damaged window. Burns didn't notice the touch of weakness, though, as he half stumbled, then spun a three-sixty from the push.

"I'm trying to go straight." Willie bounced like he was ready for round two. I didn't particularly relish dancing the canvas with the ex-boxer, but I didn't see much of an alternative with C. J. in pain and his only weapon being his demeanor. So I hung close. But neither noticed my presence. All this neglect was beginning to hurt my feelings.

"Hell of a start," C. J. stated.

"My sister's missing!" Willie stood still.

"Well, she's not here, so cool your heels and think where she might have gone." C. J. tossed the remnants of his cigarette on the marble steps. "And if you take another swing at me, I'll have Lieutenant Gardner personally haul your ass off to the state pen in Huntsville. Got it? Well?"

"Yeah, yeah, I got it. All I want is to find my sister."

"When's the last time you heard from her?"

"About seven months ago. She wrote me."

"So you didn't know she'd quit this job."

"It don't make sense, McDaniels. Pauline wrote she had a job with good people and was making decent money. She was going to help me when I got out, said she'd have some money saved up. Pauline's a swell kid, McDaniels. She's steady, you know? It's not like her to just run off, not without telling me. It don't make sense."

McDaniels walked down to his car. I shadowed him like a Secret Service agent on the president. Willie followed. It was late afternoon, but there were two or three hours of daylight left. Irritating the hot air was the high-pitched whine of cicadas.

Then Willie stopped. "Who's the dickhead?" he asked, glaring at me.

I tried not to let my knees knock.

"My associate," C. J. replied without hesitation. "And don't fuck with him. He's saved my ass with guns blazing."

I paused, angled myself tall, still as death.

Willie grunted. I met his eyes, hoping he wouldn't rip off one of my limbs like I was a smoked turkey.

He turned back to C. J. "Pauline's the only family I got."

McDaniels eyed him. There was sweat on Willie's pock-marked face. His red hair was curly, grown long, and it stuck out wildly. Willie's nose was flat and crooked, as if it had been broken repeatedly. I figured the man had always led with his head. In his eyes, between the flashes of anger, was a pleading. Willie was a proud man who, for better or worse, had done things his way. He'd never had to ask for help.

"How'd you get here?" McDaniels asked him.

Willie nodded toward an old beat-up white Cadillac.

"Where'd you get that?" Suspicion rose from his voice.

"I'm borrowing it from a friend. I didn't steal it. It's on the up-and-up, you can check it out."

"You're awfully jumpy, Willie." McDaniels opened his car door. "Where were you about three days ago, early in the morning?"

"What?"

"You know, the morning I was shot."

"Hey, now buddy—"

"Where were you?"

"In bed."

"Got a witness?"

"Yeah."

"Know her name?"

Willie set his jaw tight and narrowed his eyes.

"Yeah."

"Is that her car?" C. J. demanded.

"Yeah."

"How'd you hook up with someone so quick, Willie?"

"I been locked up two years, McDaniels. First thing I did was find an old friend."

"And just moved right back in. Lucky you."

"Lucky me."

"Then you started looking for your poor little sister. What a guy. Has it crossed your mind Pauline doesn't want to see you, Willie? Maybe that's why she skipped out quickly, afraid you'd be back any minute? Maybe that's why she left without telling anyone where she's going?"

Willie's hands balled into fists. He shook. McDaniels took out a cigarette, lit it up, and waited.

At long last Willie spoke. "I treat my sister good."

McDaniels blew out a large cloud of smoke and nodded his head. But his shoulders dipped into a slouch. I didn't believe he could keep up the tough-guy act much longer.

"I want your girlfriend's name," C. J. barked.

"Lucy Hayes."

"Have you checked with the cops?"

"After two years in the slammer you think I want to march down to the police station?"

C. J. smiled and his posture gained back some of its stiffness. "Suck it up and do it," he said. "I'll put in a word, too, but that's all I can do right now."

Willie stared at him hard. "The cops ain't going to do nothing."

"I'm on a case, Willie."

"I got some money," he told him.

"Check her old hangouts. Look up her old friends, but don't go pushing your way into any more houses. Got it?"

Cicadas droned. I prayed. C. J. smoked.

"Yeah," Willie finally responded, and spat on the ground by McDaniels's car, then walked off. "I'll call," he said over his shoulder.

"I can hardly wait," McDaniels replied.

We both watched Willie hike down the driveway, muscles bunched in catlike fashion. Large cat.

"Willie once went four rounds with Big George," C. J. muttered under his breath.

"Thanks for the information. Now."

A soft laugh escaped McDaniels. "Would you just go home?"

"Yes."

He eased into his car. "You stood up good," he added, then closed the door. I remained like a lawn ornament as he sped around the circular drive and down the road.

The world's gone nuts, I thought. Again.

As I was about to proceed to my little limo, I spied Del Westview open the front door. She was shouting instructions at Raul. Until she saw me. The front door closed abruptly.

I felt like box-office poison—no one wanted me.

I reentered the comfort of my Bug and gurgled out of the drive. A hot breeze slapped at the sweat on my face as I cruised by the houses of River Oaks, some Spanish style, some Southern plantation takeoffs, some European gingerbread houses. Here and there were palm trees and banana trees, all transplants that may or may not survive the next annual freeze.

There wasn't a Buick—brown, red, lime green, or polka dot—behind me, though I kept a nighthawk's watch. The desire for a cigarette haunted me. In a similar situation not so long ago I'd have relented and bought a pack. If I was a narrow-minded religious man, I'd have thought this was God's temptation. Fortunately, I was strong. Or at least not narrow-mindedly religious.

So what the hell was going on? There was a bullet hole in C. J. McDaniels's side. A pain in his ass in the neurotic Ray Westview, who I gathered hadn't shown his fat head since McDaniels's wife, Karla, had died. A paranoid, bitter old man gunning for his son-in-law and spoiling his dear little daughter, Del, who was making passes at C. J. Which confused him. Or he liked.

Damn you, McDaniels. You know better.

At the freeway, I hooked a left. Once I worked my way free of rush-hour traffic, it was a fast shot to my apartment.

Let us not forget the dead CEO, Mark Hill, I thought, or the hotheaded ex-boxer/ex-con and his runaway sister.

But over the whole scenario, my mind couldn't shake Del Westview. After all these years there was still something between C. J. and her. What a tragedy. That iron confidence she must have exuded thirty years ago had rusted. *Promise you'll come back?* she'd said. *Promise?* She'd said it twice, about begged. No wonder C. J. McDaniels was worn.

I always wanted your baby, she'd also said.

I should never have been privy to that.

Your baby.

What would Linda say?

8

Not long after I'd returned to my apartment the phone rang. I grabbed it, assuming it might be C. J. I thought he might confirm that Linda had realized we were being followed. I sensed C. J. didn't know whether or not to believe me.

Damn, was I wrong.

"C. J.?"

"Neil?"

"Susan?" My ex.

"Are you okay?" Her voice was soft, concerned, cautious. Though I received these calls periodically, this was not her style. It made me nervous.

"What do you want?"

"I'm asking you if you're okay?"

"I'm fine, Susan."

"Why haven't you returned my messages? I've been worried about you. I saw the article in the paper."

"Then you read that I'm all right," I calmly told her.

"What, Neil? I can't hear you."

"The other guy was shot," I said, louder but controlled. My mumbling bugged the hell out of Susan.

"Well, fine then," she snapped.

Ah, curtness. Much more like it. I said nothing. Silence pissed her off, too.

"Neil, talk to me."

"I have nothing to say. I'm fine. That's what you asked. That's what I'm telling you. I'm fine."

"I don't believe you. I'm coming over."

"What?"

"You shouldn't be alone."

"What's gotten into you, Susan?" This was weird. Ms. Big-Time Lawyer was living with someone. Why, after all these months, did she want to see me?

"What?" She adopted her Poor Wounded Wife tone.

"Susan, I don't want you to come over. I'm about to kick back with a strong drink. You don't like it when I drink."

"You're not taking care of yourself, Neil. I knew you wouldn't."

"Susan, I'm fine," I repeated, anger creeping into my voice.

"Oh, my God, you have someone with you, don't you? Is it that cute little married poet?"

"And if I do?"

"You *do*!"

"Not yet."

"Go to hell!" she shouted, and hung up.

Jesus Christ, I thought as I placed the receiver back on the phone. And she's the one shacking up with somebody else.

I paused. *That cute little married poet. Marriage—* what a cruel word.

Beneath the kitchen sink I kept a large bottle of tequila. For medicinal emergencies only. Like literally running across a gunned-down man. Or being followed by a couple of heat-packing gorillas. Or stumbling into a thirty-year-old love affair. And to top it off, a strange call from an angry ex-wife. I grabbed a bottle of mix from the refrigerator, gave it a shake, then fixed a short margarita. I had to rough it without lime or salt.

I picked up the drink and pressed the icy glass against my forehead. If I hadn't had to move out in order to go back to school, I might still be with Susan. The fact that another man had soon insinuated himself into her life (and her home) simply showed how dissatisfied she was with me. We weren't meant for each other. The bottom line. Simplicity—that was the ticket. Tell yourself to let it all go, Neil. Stop writing about the break. Tell yourself you're glad she's with someone else. Makes the letting go easier, right?

Right.

And now? "And now I'm goddamn hungry," I said aloud, then tossed back my drink and slammed the glass against the table.

It was after seven. I still had a brief paper to write for my short-fiction class the day after tomorrow. Keely Cohen taught the course. I planned to compare and contrast stories by Raymond Carver and Hemingway. Perhaps there was nothing new to discuss, but I was banking the paper would be relatively easy, given the little time I had left.

There was nothing in my refrigerator. Usually I kept at least a pound of chili meat in the freezer, along with a couple of sliced chicken breasts marinated in fajita seasoning. Yes, fajitas, I thought. I could almost hear them sizzling, smell the spicy aroma as they came off the grill. Strips of smoky chicken, covered in a mix of peppers, served with sautéed bell pepper and onion, fresh *pico de gallo*, tomatillo sauce, and warm flour tortillas. Toss in a side of *guacamole*, some cilantro rice, and refried beans, and I could almost taste it. But *almost* wouldn't put food in my belly, so I made myself another drink. As I sipped the margarita, a heavy knock rippled the door.

My little .25 was tucked on the bookshelf behind Tolstoy. I reached around *War and Peace,* then slipped the small gun into my pocket. I didn't know why I was nervous. After all, a couple of muscleheads weren't about to come calling like the Avon lady. Most likely.

The bottom corner of the door stuck and reverberated as I yanked it open, only to come face-to-face with my landlord, Jerry Jacoma.

"You're a pretty sight," I told him. Jerry was about

forty. Short and stocky, he wore a Fu Manchu mustache and a constant smile. Tonight there were beads of sweat along his forehead and dotting his mustache.

"Hey, thanks." He walked into the room. "I biked ten miles. Man, I'm getting to the age where it's healthier to stay fat. I thought I was going to have a fucking heart attack."

"Good for you." I hung on the door, then decided to close it.

"Good for me, huh?" He laughed. He fingered the bottle of tequila. "You eaten? Or you drinking dinner tonight?"

"Now you sound like my ex-wife."

He picked up the bottle. "Mind?"

"So much for health."

"The hero-runner talking."

"Go ahead."

"Listen," he said, "I ordered a pizza from Leo's. You pick it up, I'll pay."

It wasn't fajitas, but Leo's had great pizza, real stuff, not cardboard with fake cheese and a few shavings of pepperoni. The only disadvantage was they didn't deliver. Even so, I said, "Jerry, I've got work to do tonight."

"So do I. Got a client flying in from Tulsa in the morning." He poured himself a stiff drink. Jerry made good money as a technical writer for Exxon and often ragged me about being a poet. Poetry didn't make money. And seeing Jerry drive a nice truck and buy all the toys he wanted wasn't always easy. Of course, the fact that he inherited this house and a tidy sum from his mother hadn't hurt.

"I need to hang around," I told him, thinking perhaps that C. J. might call.

"Aren't you hungry?"

"Yes."

"You aren't too drunk, are you?"

"No," I said defensively, before I realized that could've been my out. But I was starving. I hesitated, for only a second. I shouldn't go anywhere after a couple of drinks, but the cosmic forces were against me. Or with me. I didn't know—maybe I was drunk. At any rate, I gave up. I took a sip. "I'll pick up the pizza," I told him.

Jerry handed the money to me, right on cue. "Knew you couldn't resist, man," he said.

"If a guy named C. J. McDaniels calls before I'm back, get a number where I can reach him."

"Sure, man."

I closed the door behind me.

Carefully, I stepped down the stairs, not wanting to fall and break my neck. I pushed open the hall door and walked to my car. The air was muggy and held a mossy smell. I felt dumb as a dog that chases parked cars for not jotting down the license-plate number of the Buick, or getting a good description of the driver and passenger. My sloppiness had not only irritated C. J. but also damaged the credibility of my story.

I had the wrong key in the door lock. For a minute it jammed, and I began to feel thoroughly humiliated. Finally I managed to yank it out. After taking a deep breath, I found the right key and unlocked the door. As I fell into the car, I felt the pressure of the gun in my pocket. God, I didn't want to get caught with this. Opening my glove compartment caused an avalanche of papers. That was no place to stash a gun, anyway. If I was ever pulled over and asked to show my insurance card, sure as hell the gun would tumble out in front of the friendly traffic cop. A roll of electrical tape had fallen out. I ripped off a few pieces, strapped them across the gun, and stuck it under the passenger's seat. Now my little pistol wasn't going anywhere.

I took Twentieth to Heights Boulevard. About three miles down was the pizza place. The food wasn't ready, so I ordered a beer, sank into a red-vinyl booth, and waited. This pizza parlor was like those back east. White floor, open counter where the white-uniformed cooks flipped the dough and slid pizzas into the big ovens, and a jukebox in one corner. Someone dropped in a few coins and on came the throaty sound of Tom Waits. The place wasn't actually in the Heights. If it had been, Leo wouldn't have been able to serve beer. The Heights was dry.

One song ended and another began. I was getting antsy. I was certain C. J. would phone, and I wanted to be home when he did. It could've been a two-beer wait, especially since I drank the first quickly, but I stuck to the one. When the pizza finally hit the box, I was out of Leo's and up the road before I even began to smell the basil and pepperoni.

In five minutes I was coasting into my driveway, parking behind the house near the garage. There was music blaring from my apartment above. Through the muffled, droning sound I could make out the deep voice of Springsteen. Jerry loved Springsteen. Other than that, all was quiet. I was pleased.

I was stepping out of the car, holding the pizza carton high above my head like any respectable waiter, when the famous Buick screeched to a stop in front of me. My heart burrowed into my throat for cover. I dropped the pizza. Two guys jumped out of the car. Before I knew what was happening, I was facedown on the concrete.

A thick hand grabbed my long hair and pulled me up. Then the one whose left arm was in a sling hit me a hard right in the stomach. I couldn't breathe. The pain hurt worse than any dry heaves I'd ever had.

"You're going for a ride, kid," the larger man said with a Hispanic accent. He had a round face, long black hair, and a bushy mustache.

I tried to jerk away, but he hit me flush in the face with a big fist, knocking off my glasses. Then he grabbed my arms and wrenched them behind my back. I was not small, but I was wrapped like a longhorn about to be branded. My vision was blurred. I started to call out to Jerry when the other thug, short and with one healthy arm, drilled me in the stomach again. Then he flashed a knife and brought the blade in close. There was no mistake as to what the man held.

"You should've stayed out of it, kid," he said. I could smell garlic. His unbuttoned shirt revealed a chest full of black hair, and I noticed that he had a gap between his top front teeth.

"I never saw you," was all I managed to say.

"You lie!" He put the tip of the knife just below my eye.

"Let's go!" the big one snapped.

"No witness, no proof," the one-armed thug said.

I was thinking that I would kick him in the balls as soon as he moved that knife away from my face. I'd then jerk around so the big thug would take the blade in his back when the one-armed thug retaliated in anger. My plan never took hold. Sensing I was up to something, the big one tightened his grip on me, sending bolts of pain through my arms. He rattled something in Spanish, to which the other musclehead rattled something equally harsh back.

"We're going to slice you up, señor," the one-armed thug hissed. "Slowly."

The short, gap-toothed bastard cut me. The blade inched from the corner of my eye down the side of my face to the corner of my mouth. At first I didn't realize I'd been hurt, the pain in my arms subsuming anything else. Then he held the knife in front of my eyes. Blood dripped from the blade. He gently wiped the sharp edge on my blue Izod and laughed.

The one-armed son of a bitch snarled, stepped back, and waved the knife in my face. Then there was a shout, a growl. I felt myself pulled back a couple of steps. Pain was like a tiny wire digging through my veins. Gunfire—and I went down. Thrown down. Two, three, four shots. I wasn't sure. There was a scuffling, a heavy thud, and running. For a minute I felt pale. A shroud of cold sweat left me light-headed. When I came to, I was on my ass by the hall door that led up to my apartment. My arms were free, but there was a numb ache to them. When I looked up, C. J. McDaniels was standing over me.

"Am I shot?" I asked.

"No, son," he said. "Damn him."

"What? You wanted me shot?"

"What are you talking about?" He knelt beside me and drew out a handkerchief for my face. It was soon saturated with blood. He also handed me my glasses.

"The little gun did me a rat's-ass bit of good," I muttered.

"What? I killed the son of a bitch with his arm in a sling," he continued. "I had to shoot fast. He was about to run that blade through you. But the tall bastard got away."

"How?" I asked. McDaniels was coming into focus—his round face, bald head, flat nose.

"I missed."

"Missed?"

"He used you as a shield, then threw you at me."

"Threw me?"

"Kind of spun you like a poorly tossed top. But his plan worked. You were in my way. He slipped off behind the garage, and I'm in no shape to run after him."

"In your way?" I shook my head. I was talking like an idiot.

"You fainted, didn't you? So he was carrying deadweight."

"Deadweight? I don't like the sound of that."

"I bet you don't. Damn!" He stared at the one-armed man sprawled on the driveway. "The bastard can't answer questions now." The back of the dead man's shirt was soaked in blood.

"But I can describe him to you," I said.

"Funny. Did you get a good look at the second guy?"

"Yes."

"Good."

The hall door burst open and a wide-eyed Jerry Jacoma came running out. "Oh man oh man oh man. Is he dead?"

"Of course he's dead," snapped C. J. "Did you call the cops?"

"No, man, I heard the shots and—"

"Go call the fucking cops and tell them we need an ambulance. Now!"

I heard Jerry stumble back up the stairs. The night air was still. My arms ached. The evening was hot. There was a dead man next to me. I could smell my own blood. The one-armed bastard's eyes were open as wide as Jerry's had been. I watched McDaniels look at the gun in his hand, then tuck it into the holster at the small of his back.

"Don't stare at him, son."

"He's the one you shot down on Allen Parkway, isn't he?"

"Bet on it. But he's hired trash. I need to find the old boy behind it all."

It was the eyes—shocked, white, glazed—I'd seen first. Next, the growing pool of blood and the crimson smeared against the side of the white garage door.

I noticed the handkerchief was bright red. My legs were once again softening like butter left out in a hot room. C. J. McDaniels bent down. "You're going to need stitches," he told me.

I nodded slowly. In the distance I heard sirens. They grew louder. Jerry came racing back downstairs. I watched as he took it all in, spun around, caught himself on the banister, and choked back the heaves.

I was in a daze. I'd almost forgotten I was half drunk. I couldn't believe this blood on my fingertips was from my face. "I'm going to have a scar," I said, then realized I'd spoken aloud.

The police slammed into the driveway.

C. J. McDaniels grinned. "We'll talk later. Meanwhile, you ever thought about growing a beard? You know, Hank Williams Jr. fell off the side of that mountain, scarred up his face. Now he wears a beard. At least that's the story I heard. It can do wonders, a beard. Gives a man a rougher edge. Lord knows, you need one."

9

The police sealed off the area. I was taken, with Jerry, into Jerry's house, which served, for a few hours, as a sort of headquarters. There was a medical examiner, an ambulance, and tons of flashing lights. They sat me at the kitchen table. Activity swirled. I felt like a piece of meat inside a pot of boiling soup. Somewhere amid all the commotion a hand gripped my shoulder and a voice said, "Neil, they're going to take you to the hospital and stitch you up."

I looked at C. J. "What the hell are you doing here?"

"Some gratitude."

"Mighty coincidental."

"Not quite," he replied. "Thought they might show their ugly faces."

"So I was thug bait."

"Kind of a harsh assessment, Neil."

"I'm going to have a scar," I said.

"I heard." McDaniels stubbed out his cigarette, lit another. I put my fingers against the roughness of my face and wondered if Susan would be shocked or if this is what she figured would become of me once we split.

"They thought I could identify them," I said. "But I really couldn't. Now I'm going to have a scar."

"Son, you could be dead."

"I guess that's one way of looking at it."

"The only way. And we've got something to go on."

"Good."

"They'll want to keep you overnight for observation," C. J. added, pointing at me with an unlit cigarette.

"What?"

"At the hospital."

"I'm not staying overnight," I told him firmly.

A paramedic examined my face, swabbed it, and put a temporary bandage on it. "Any higher and you'd have lost an eye," he said. "You're lucky."

I shuddered. "Some luck."

"Listen, Scarface—" C. J. began.

"Scarface?"

"What's the big deal about staying overnight at the hospital?" he asked me.

"You're a fine one to talk about staying in hospitals."

"We're talking about you, Scarface, not—"

"Don't call me Scarface."

"Forgive me."

I narrowed my eyes. "Sew me here," I stated.

"You're in a little shock," the paramedic spoke up. "You need to be examined. Also, to fix you right is going to take time, care, and a bunch of stitches. You don't want a bad scar."

"As opposed to a good scar?" I asked.

"There is a difference," he told me. "You *could* be Scarface. Some lacerations are more difficult to sew than others."

"Well, I'll go, but I'm not staying overnight." I looked directly at C. J.

"You'd be safer there," C. J. said.

"He won't be back and you know it," I snapped.

"No, I don't."

"I'm not staying overnight."

"Son, you grow belligerent when you drink."

"I'm not staying overnight."

"Suit yourself, kid." C. J. McDaniels started to turn when Lieutenant Gardner walked up.

"Jesus, another delightful story for the press," he

snapped. "Don't let up, Marshall. Pretty soon you'll have a regular front-page serial running."

"I'm leaving," C. J. barked as he tucked the loose cigarette in his mouth and stomped outside.

"What's his problem?"

I shrugged innocently.

"I'll send someone around for an official statement later," he told me. "Go get patched up."

"Yes, sir."

The medic helped me to my feet. I heard Jerry Jacoma on the other side of the room babbling to the police. He told them about the Allen Parkway incident, as if they didn't know, and then every detail concerning this evening, including his biking feats, until the cops had enough and escorted him to another room. We went outside. There was quite a crowd standing in the shadows of the trees that surrounded the house.

"You're not going to strap me in, are you?" I asked as we approached the ambulance.

"Procedure."

"You serious?"

"You need to remain still until you're thoroughly examined."

I was tired of arguing. This fracas was worse than the time Chip Gunn's men beat the crap out of me. And now the indignity of forced restraint. If I had had to lay a bet, I'd have said that McDaniels set this up so I couldn't leave.

They mummified me on the stretcher and slid me into the ambulance and away we went.

C. J. had said nothing about Linda. I wasn't convinced they were only after me. What if they'd been following Linda and I had screwed up their plans? A bolt of panic shot through me.

Of course, they thought I could identify them. They wanted me. I was sure. Yes. No. I didn't know. My mind wasn't working straight. Disoriented. Not calm. I didn't have a handle on life. I wanted to see Linda.

This time I entered the hospital on wheels. I much preferred my feet. C. J. might be accustomed to such procedure, but I wasn't. I didn't think I ever would be. Bright lights, sterilized floors, and concrete walls were much more intimidating when you viewed them from flat on your back. It was no longer simply an uncomfortable atmosphere. You were out of control, and in someone else's hands. It was damn frightening.

The young doctor on duty was no conversationalist. He had short brown hair and a baby face with bags under his eyes. I told him I didn't want to be knocked out and he looked at me like that was not even a consideration. He examined my face, gave me a couple of shots, and did his work. The nurse assisting him made a comment here and there, but I didn't dare respond. I didn't move a centimeter and I barely breathed. The only time I was nervous was when he worked close to my eye. Despite his graceful bedside manner, however, he was patient. His hands were soft and he was careful, so, when he hit a sensitive spot or two the local hadn't quite deadened, I didn't scream.

It could have been eight hundred stitches over eight hours for all I knew before I was able to sit up. I was sipping on a glass of water when the nurse came back and said I had a visitor. I expected Lieutenant Gardner or C. J. McDaniels, or both, to push through the curtains. As luck would have it, however, I drew Linda Garcia.

I smiled on the side of my face that wasn't numb.

"You're getting quite a reputation," she said. She was wearing jeans tucked into black boots with fringe on the top and a black dress shirt.

"What do you mean?" Words were hard to form.

"You want things to happen, send Neil Marshall into the world. Trouble's magnet."

"Did you have to come in black?"

She smiled. "You still have your sense of humor."

"Is C. J. with you?"

"No. He's exhausted. It's not every day he runs around with a bullet hole in his side and winds up killing someone."

The last part of her statement chilled me.

"They identified the dead man," she added. "His name was Roberto Españada. He was a petty criminal, did time for theft and assault. And it looks like he was the one C. J. hit the day he was shot. They're still trying to identify the man at large. The cops will need your help."

"My pleasure."

Linda smiled.

The curtains were pushed aside and in walked a uniformed Houston police officer. He was young, about my age, tall, thin, and had a blond mustache. He asked for a statement, and I proceeded to describe the events from being followed after leaving the hospital to when C. J. arrived at my apartment. Linda listened carefully. I was sure to point out that the bastards said they were going to kill me and would have had it not been for C. J. The cop scribbled it all down. He asked me to read the document. I did. Signed it. He left.

The doctor wrote out a prescription for codeine, then released me. I gave the hospital my insurance information and once again I was in Linda's truck.

"We don't think you ought to stay at your apartment tonight," she said.

"Why not?" Surely she didn't mean I should stay with her, did she? The night, which seemed so dark only moments ago, now appeared beautifully multicolored.

"It might not be safe. You're the only one who can identify him," she said. "C. J. didn't get a good look. Who's to say the killer won't come back to finish the job?"

"The killer?"

"He wasn't at your apartment to share your pizza."

"Okay, okay," I said, and touched the side of my face. It was beginning to hurt. But I could live with it in anticipation of the answer to my next question. "So now what?"

Linda pulled into a parking lot. "First we're going to

get you drugs." She grabbed the prescription slip out of my hand and jumped out of the truck. I waited, wondering why she was being so attentive.

A few minutes later she returned. She handed me a white bag with a small plastic container of pills. Again we hit the road.

"Wait," I said, "I didn't give you any money."

"I know. You owe me."

"How much?"

"We'll figure it out later, okay?"

"Okay," I said, almost cheerfully. "So *now* what?"

"We're going to swing by your place so you can pack a bag."

Okay, I thought.

"And I'm going to drop you off at a friend's house."

"A friend's house?"

"She's the dearest woman you'll ever meet." She paused. "Oh, I see."

"I'll take my chances at home," I said.

"But you already agreed and, besides, you should have someone keeping an eye on you for the first twenty-four hours or so. Those pain pills will send you for a loop."

I didn't respond. Perhaps I could bunk again with Robbie. Or Keely or Perry, for that matter. As fast as the idea came to me, though, I realized I'd be putting them in danger. Damn.

Linda released a long breath. "Listen, Neil, I'm fond of you, but it isn't right for you to stay with me. I'm not ready for that. I'm sorry—"

"All right," I cut in. "I misunderstood."

"I didn't mean to give you any false impressions."

"I read too much into what . . ." I let the explanation fall.

"Neil, I care for you," Linda said. "I owe you for my father's life."

"That's not why I want you to care for me," I responded. "And C. J. evened up any IOUs earlier."

"Tonight wouldn't have happened to you if you hadn't

been there on Allen Parkway for C. J.," she told me. "And that's not why I care for you. I like you."

In the dimness of the truck, against the varying light from outside, her profile was stunning. She glanced at me once, then turned her attention back to the road. I took a deep breath and silently released it.

"Fair enough," I told her.

"Good. Thank you, Neil."

"For what?"

"For understanding, or trying to."

"Of course." I paused. "Listen," I added, "I'll go to your friend's house on one condition: I follow you over there in my car."

"Why?"

"I want the freedom to be able to leave."

"You're going to get along with Mama just fine."

"Mama?"

"She's a close family friend. She won't ask impertinent questions, but she will be there to keep an eye on you."

"I'm sure I'll get along with her fine. But I'm thinking I might get out of town for a while, head to Austin to see Terry, a friend of mine."

"Oh," Linda responded flatly.

"I spent time there while I was going through my divorce," I explained. "A getaway, to ease the stress."

"That means our date for tomorrow night's off?"

"No," I said, surprised.

"I thought you said you were going to Austin to see Terry."

"I am. I mean, I might."

"You can't be in two places at once."

"We can go out first."

"How nice. How old is Terry?"

"About my age."

"You've her for a long time?"

"Her?"

"Terry."

"Terry is a guy, a great guy," I told her. "He has this place on the lake and we do a lot of fishing. Do you like to fish?"

"Uh, yeah, I like to fish."

"Fly-fish?" I asked.

"Never tried it."

"It's the poetry of fishing. Everyone should experience the joy of a perfect cast at least once. Maybe you'd like to come. Sometime."

"Maybe."

I thought I saw her smile.

"You're okay to drive?" she asked.

"Fine."

"Don't take any codeine until we get there," she said.

"Why?"

"It'll put you to the canvas, as C. J. would say."

When we pulled into the driveway at my apartment, I felt a chill knife up my spine and cut at the hairs on the back of my neck. Everything was quiet. The only sign there had been trouble was the police outline of the dead man on the concrete and the remains of the infamous pizza piled in a heap that strongly resembled roadkill.

"Relax," Linda said, putting a hand on my arm.

I nodded my head. "I'm all right."

"Want to wait in the truck?"

"No," I said quickly. "Let's grab my stuff and get out."

We walked in silence up the staircase. My door was unlocked and ajar, and with two fingers I pushed it open. I still carried the codeine. The apartment was as I had left it, in its generally messy, clothes-strewn condition. The tequila bottle was the first thing I picked up. It was three-quarters full, and I'd be damned if I was going to leave it.

"That stuff will stunt your growth," Linda told me.

"I'm six four."

"I'm not talking height," she replied dryly.

"Want a drink?"

Linda eyed me carefully. "One."

I dumped out the watery mixture that remained in my

glass, then poured about a jigger's worth in, found Linda a clean glass, and gave her the same. "Want some mix?" I asked.

"Straight and neat."

I handed it to her. She tipped her glass toward me, then tossed the shot back. No grimace, nothing. I looked at mine. Straight. No salt. No lime. Shit, I thought as I gulped it down. The hardness of the liquor twisted my smile. "Ah." I sighed and released it in a shiver.

"Pack what you need and let's go."

"Yeah, let's go," I agreed, my voice hoarse. Then I stuffed my Nike gym bag with underwear, a pair of jeans, sweats, a couple of T-shirts, and a couple of polo shirts. Then I filled my overnight kit with soap, toothbrush and paste, shaving cream, and razor—though it crossed my mind that I didn't really need those last two items anymore. I was ready.

"Mama doesn't like drinking," she said, eyeing the tequila.

"I'll keep it hidden." On my way through the living room I grabbed a slim volume of poetry by Keely Cohen and tucked the book in the bag.

We stepped out, and I locked my door. As we eased down the hall and outside, the dogs next door barked and I half expected Jerry Jacoma to come barging out of his house, shooting at the two shadowy figures in his driveway. Luckily, there was no sign of him. Hell, he was probably triple-locked inside, still babbling to himself.

Linda gave me directions to where we were going. I nodded halfheartedly, and finally she said, "Just follow me."

I climbed into my car, set the bottle on the floor on the passenger's side, and put my Nike bag over it.

The night's humid air rolled in through the open windows. On the radio was Gershwin's "Rhapsody in Blue." A couple of times I caught sight of my face in the rearview mirror, and I wondered what I had done to invite this violence. Taking the rap for fatally shooting a man might've had something to do with my misfortune. Made me wonder if I was destined for a life of debauchery. A stone erroneously cast had rippled my karma and was now washing to shore. I could blame the ill fortune on divorcing Susan. Even though leaving that situation was like breaking out of a viper's cage, splitting the blanket had brought on more pain than I realized. I now had to stand on my own.

Gershwin lofted into beauty. But I didn't feel beautiful. The sound was enough to make a man change the music to a country-and-western station.

Linda headed down North Main to Loop 610. We went east until we exited at North Wayside Drive. From there we turned north and drove for what seemed forever. Here and there were long stretches of forested areas. It was as if we were no longer in Houston. These, however, were balanced by densely active intersections. At one of these intersections—I didn't catch the name of the street, as the green signs were either gone or bent so they faced the ground—we turned right. Five minutes later we were in a seemingly quiet little neighborhood pulling up in front of a small ranch house.

Linda parked behind a brown Toyota pickup. I coasted in next to her behind a silver Cadillac. Before getting out of the car, I stashed the tequila bottle in the Nike bag, hoping it wouldn't leak.

"She was going to play bingo tonight," Linda told me as I pulled myself out of the car, "until C. J. called her."

The front door opened. Light poured onto us. "Well, Linda, my baby girl," a woman said, "you get more beautiful every day. Is your daddy all right?"

"You know C. J.," Linda replied as we walked up to the large, shaded figure standing on the border of the house's light. "He's indestructible."

"No, he ain't," she said. "He only thinks he is. That boy's been worrying me more than fifty years."

"And he'll never change."

"Hmm," she muttered, turned her back, and stepped into the house. We followed.

"Mama," Linda said, "this is Neil Marshall, the young man who saved C. J.'s life."

She looked at me. "Mr. Marshall, it's very nice to meet you." She held her hand out and I shifted my Nike bag to my left hand and took it. Mama was in her seventies, at least. Her gray hair was the color of the Cadillac. She had a round face and a broad, openmouthed smile that flashed a number of gold-capped teeth. Heavy, dark bags were tucked under her eyes, which somehow radiated a tremendous amount of melancholy. Her eyes ran the length of my scar.

"That boy means the world to me," she said, and released my hand. "Thank you very much for what you did. He told me what happened to you when he asked if you could come stay awhile."

"C. J. and I are even."

"He needs help but he don't know it," she continued. "Baby here does a wonderful job, but she can't do it all and she got her own life. He needs help."

Not knowing what else to do, and feeling awkward, I simply said, "Yes, ma'am."

Linda stepped up and took Mama by the arm. "Neil," she said, "your room's around to the left. That's where you're going to put him, right, Mama? Yeah, Neil, to the left. Now, come on, Mama. Let's go in the kitchen and make some coffee. Okay, tea, then."

I walked into the living room.

Mama's house was a scavenger's dream. It was a permanent garage sale where nothing was ever sold, only collected. I began poking around. Bottles, jars, tin boxes, and clocks were scattered throughout. A warehouse of furniture, some usable, some not, brought the walls in tight. In the living room was an old hundred-gallon aquarium, dry, filled with a rainbow array of yarn. There were mannequins in various stages of dress, forms with wigs and partially finished straw hats. In one bedroom were needlepoint stands and bundles of quilting material piled against a wall. In the room where I was to sleep there were bolts of fabric stacked in one corner and a sewing machine in another. Mama was into crafts.

I unzipped my Nike bag, left the bottle in it, and set the bag within reach of the bed, on the side opposite the door. Then I noticed that this was a hospital bed, the kind where the top half cranked up and down. For some reason, I wasn't surprised.

I didn't want to disturb them, so I lay on the bed with my hands behind my head and waited for Linda to come to me. The bed was soft and I felt as though it sucked me in. Any farther down and I'd have needed rope to get out. I hoped this was going to work.

My face was beginning to throb, as the local was wearing off. My head also had a dull ache to it. I decided to take my pain pill, and a nightcap. After all I'd been through, I deserved it. The nightcap. I popped the pill, grabbed the tequila, and chased it down.

All I needed now was a glass of ice water. And I needed to sort through this all.

This strange life. I took another slug of tequila, then set it down. Maybe going back to work would help bring life back to a routine. Normality. Tomorrow I'd call Robbie at The Kitchen. Routine. Work. Where was that tequila? I swiped for it, but my hand felt like a wrecking ball that missed its target.

I propped myself up by my elbows and looked for the bottle. But as soon as I was up, I was down again. Slippery sheets. Should I give rising another try? I closed my eyes. Linda in the other room. God, do I want her . . . I think I'm in . . . Susan? Not Susan. Why should I call Susan? I'm not going to embarrass myself. Ask for her. Humiliating. So what? A scar. Big deal. Grow a beard, C. J. McDaniels said. I can take care of myself. Susan's no longer my wife. Ms. Lawyer. I tried. Now a master's degree, then . . . Susan, I'm going to call Robbie. Or Perry Stevens, my boss. They're both freaking. I know it. And call Keely. Yes, my poet, my friend. In the other room, very beautiful . . .

Later, Linda Garcia would tell me that when she popped her head in to say goodbye she found me fast asleep.

10

Mama was good to me. Unable to sleep, I arose before the sun, surprised to find Mama fixing biscuits and gravy, sausage links, and scrambled eggs doctored with red pepper, green onions, and cheddar cheese. And some strong coffee was percolating. My cholesterol level rose just by smelling the rich, homestyle food. And though it was delicious, I had difficulty eating. There was a long line of pain on my face, and when I chewed this image of my scar ripping apart like a bad seam on a pair of old jeans kept flashing across my mind. So I picked at the eggs and sausage and a large fluffy biscuit and drank gallons of coffee.

I didn't say much. I read the newspaper, but it was a collection of words without meaning. There was some article about someone like me, the *acquitted killer*, referencing my well-publicized justified homicide in the Keys case. The only twinge of pain I felt was when I came across Jason's name. He'd been a good friend and an irascible source of cantankerous strength. I about said something to Mama, but I didn't want to dig up the body that was supposedly credited to my account. Of course, my story might not faze her a bit, or she'd think I was nuts. Perhaps I was. Or heading that way. At any rate, I kept quiet.

Mama didn't talk much, either. While I ate and drank coffee, she sat on the couch in her little work area, wearing the same blue housedress she'd had on the night before, and watched TV while making hats out of blood-red straw.

Once the hour turned semi-respectable—eight o'clock—I put in a call to Linda and left a message on her machine. This was not the best night to go out, but there was no way I'd miss seeing her. What I had was a little discomfort. If C. J. were in my position he'd go. Don't be a wimp, Neil.

After yapping at Linda's machine, I called Robbie Persons, beverage manager and my best friend at work.

"Oh, God, what's happening?"

"Robbie, it's déjà vu."

"Are you okay?"

"I feel like a lamb that's wriggled out of a wolf's mouth," I told him.

"Can I do anything for you? Want to sack out on my couch for a few days?"

"Thanks, but I've got a roof over my head. What I could really use is some work to reorient myself."

"You know how scarce jobs are in the summer," Robbie replied. "Half our clientele leaves Houston."

"There's usually something to do."

"Nothing that Claudia can't handle herself. But I have a check cut for you."

"Money helps."

"I'll be around The Kitchen until ten-thirty, and back after two. Perry's out of town visiting his father."

"I'll catch you in a little while," I told him. "I can't sit still."

"You need to relax."

"No shit, Robbie. It's like I've walked into someone else's story, or someone else's nightmare."

"Yes, child, déjà vu."

After hanging up, I telephoned my apartment to check the messages on my answering machine. There were only a couple. One was from Candace Littlefield, and though she was a tough kid, I detected the worry in her voice. I immediately phoned the Andersons', where Candace was staying, but received no answer. Odd their machine wasn't on, I thought, and made a mental note to call back tonight, after Candace got off from Dairy Queen. The girl was working hard—too hard, I often thought, much like her mentor, my late friend, Jason Keys. But she was ambitious, wanted to be a veterinarian.

The second message was long and rambling and from Susan. For the most part she expressed her *concern* over my *condition*. What condition was that, Susan? My face or my stupidity? I know, I can't take care of myself. Again she wanted to see me. Why? She losing interest in Stud, Super Accountant? Bizarre.

I thought about trying to write. After all, I still had a short paper to do. And usually I wrote something every day. Not everything was worth reading, but at the least it organized my thoughts. When I picked up a pen and my small notebook, though, my mind blanked. I couldn't relax. Forcing it only brought words that were deaf and flat. I gave up.

The pain was strong. I took another pill, then, with Keely Cohen's book of poems on my chest, dozed for most of the morning. When I awoke I realized I'd have to catch Robbie this afternoon. I wandered into the living room.

"I was going to fix pork chops, mashed potatoes, and green beans for dinner," Mama said at my appearance.

But wait a minute, I thought.

"That was before Linda called and said you two were going out. I didn't know that."

"I wasn't sure our date was still on."

"She said to meet at her house at—now, was it seven or eight? Well, you just meet her at her house. She told me to give you the address. That girl's taken a shine to you, and I don't think it's 'cause you saved her—C. J.'s life."

"Her father," I said. I supposed by her hesitancy that Mama had forgotten she'd already referred to the relationship in front of me—to Linda when we'd first arrived.

"You know that? Not everyone does. She must like you, boy." She rose from the couch and walked into the kitchen.

I hope, I thought. "How long have you known them?" I sat down at the kitchen table.

"Would you like some iced tea, Mr. Marshall?" Mama came around with two glasses.

"Thank you, ma'am. Please call me Neil."

"Thank you, Neil. Most everyone just calls me Mama. You can, too. Now, how long have I known them? Well, I worked for C. J.'s parents for thirty-five years. I raised C. J."

"Thirty-five years?"

"Had a house in River Oaks, they did," she said proudly. "Little house, but still in River Oaks. His daddy took good care of Mr. Bedford and he took good care of him, too. And his mama was so pretty, had a piano that she played with those long white fingers. Oh, they're dead now. Happened right after C. J. got back from the war. A plane accident outside Odessa. Too bad. They was good people."

"Plane accident?"

"One of them small ones."

"C. J. went to war? Which war?"

"Vietnam. Early, too. There and back before anyone cared to complain about it. About broke his mama's heart. Daddy's too. C. J. volunteered. His daddy wanted his son by his side, but C. J., his ideas and theirs weren't the same. C. J. always was a restless child. Wanted to be a policeman from the minute he could speak. His daddy felt he'd outgrow it. Never did. I tried talking to his daddy, but Mr. McDaniels wouldn't hear it. Figured I was just filling C. J. full of boyish nonsense."

"That's sad," I said, more to myself than anything.

"No, boy, that's life," Mama told me.

I glanced up at her.

"I may forget things, but I still hear fine," she said.

"I guess so. And I always thought I mumbled."

"You do."

I smiled, took a sip of tea. I was about to stand and excuse myself to get ready to meet Linda when Mama slipped in one more observation.

"That girl's his pride and joy."

"I know," I told her.

"Treat her good."

"She'd beat the crap out of me if I didn't," I joked.

"She ain't as tough as she thinks. And C. J., he needs help, now he's getting up in the years."

"C. J.?"

"He thinks he ain't ever going to die."

Why are you telling me this? I wondered.

Mama looked at me and smiled. "Oh, I'm just talking," she said. "You best get yourself ready so you don't keep that girl waiting."

I had hours before meeting Linda, so I took that as the end to our conversation.

"Will you be coming back tonight?" she asked.

"I don't know," I replied. A nice idea was to stay with Linda and give the relationship a shot, but I doubted she'd changed her mind in just one day. And I wasn't going to push it. "I've been thinking about going to Austin. Maybe I'll head out after I drop off Linda. I like driving at night."

Mama nodded. "You're welcome here should you change your mind."

"Thank you."

I went into my bedroom and picked out clean clothes, then took a bath and washed my hair, being careful not to get the stitches wet. I was half serious about going to Austin. I didn't want to stay at my place until the police corralled this guy. Mama was nice, but I felt useless out here. What I needed were familiar surroundings, like Terry's place in Austin.

At one point I caught a glimpse of myself in the mirror. There it was, long and black like a water moccasin marking the surface of a pale lake. A rough five-o'clock shadow was beginning to cover much of my face. I touched the stubble with the tips of my fingers. Even a beard wouldn't hide it completely, but maybe C. J. was right. It might help. I didn't shave and I told myself it wasn't so bad, if I could accept the gangster look.

I wrapped my dirty clothes around the tequila bottle, then stuffed it and my book back into my Nike bag.

Before leaving, I asked Mama if she'd heard from C. J. today and she said she hadn't.

"But if I do, I'll be sure to tell him you and Linda are together," she added.

"Later on," I said. "Before I meet Linda, I'm going in to work."

"Well, I'll let him know."

I wondered what C. J. would think of my date with Linda.

Mama waved from the doorway as I got into my car. I tapped the horn gently before backing out, then I chugged on down the road. My face was hurting again, but I didn't dare take a pain pill. I concentrated on seeing Linda and tried to ignore it. Every once in a while I caught the image of my scar in the rearview mirror. It wasn't so bad. I smiled deviously. I could just imagine Susan's reaction— her shock, her feigned concern, and her smug I-told-you-so attitude.

As I entered 610, I had a funny feeling I was being followed. The sun was angling down, but it was still strong enough to make things hot. My windows were down and the warm wind blew my hair wildly. I wore my mirrored shades with my scar. I felt tough. I was driving a low-powered imitation of a car, possessed a toy that resembled a firearm, and was acting paranoid. Yeah, tough.

A long half hour later I coasted to a stop in front of the converted ranch house that we, at Perry Stevens Catering, lovingly referred to as The Kitchen. Robbie's car, as well as the van, were parked in the driveway. Instinctively, I scoured the area as I pulled myself out of the VW. But there was no sign of anyone following me. In fact, there was no sign of anyone. Even the hookers that hung out at the corner were taking the afternoon off. Or maybe they were busy.

Robbie was sitting at his desk by the front window when I entered the building.

"Child, you look bad enough to scare the makeup off a drag queen."

"Funny, I was just noticing our ladies weren't around."

Robbie smiled softly, gray eyes landing sympathetically on mine. I closed the door. The Kitchen was quiet
except for the buzz of refrigerators and freezers. The back
half of the building was dark.

"Claudia gone?" Apparently even my immediate super-
visor wasn't on the premises.

"You just missed her."

"My loss, I'm sure."

"Candace called for you," he informed me.

"From work?"

"I don't know. She just called."

"She's been trying to track me down. I tried getting
back to her, but the message machine was off."

"The girl's scared," he stated. "She considers you the
only family she has left. And even though she's staying
with Sondra Anderson and her husband, they don't rank
in that category." Robbie stood, handed me an envelope
with a check in it.

"Thanks," I told him. "Don't worry; I'll comfort
Candace."

"Looks like a couple of small functions came up for
next week," Robbie said. "I can get you on those, plus
the kitchen hours."

"That'll help." I paused.

"You want to talk about it?" he asked, and leaned
against a stainless-steel work table. He was still dressed in
his black and whites from the lunch he'd waited earlier.
Despite the proper attire, he appeared hard and rugged.

"I met someone," I found myself saying.

"Yeah, a big private investigator with holes in him."

"No, I mean, I met someone. A woman."

Robbie's eyes narrowed. "When in hell did you have
time between all this blasting and slashing to fall in
love?"

"I have no idea. And Susan must have on her radar, because she's called me more in the last few days than in all
the months combined since the divorce."

"Who is she?"

"The PI's daughter."

Robbie folded his arms across his chest. "You can't find enough trouble on your own without marrying into a situation that invites incidents?"

"Who said anything about marriage?"

"I know you. Figuratively or literally, you'll be married to this girl for a while."

"For a while? You act like it's a tumble in the hay."

"Yeah?"

"Go to hell, Robbie."

"All I know is that when a person's in love he's supposed to be happy."

"I am happy, goddamn it."

"I'm convinced."

"I kind of like the idea of having some companionship," I told him.

"Don't get your nose all bent out of shape."

"Oh, shut up." I reached for the door.

"That's more like it," he said, and straightened himself. "Come on, why don't you stay with me a few days?"

"And suffer more abuse?"

"Then head to the stables for a break."

"I think someone's still out for me, and I don't want to lead anyone close to Candace. She tends the horses at the stables every day."

"Smart."

"I'm going to roll, get this money in my account."

"If there's anything I can do."

"Believe me, I'll be in touch." I opened the door, felt the blast of heat.

"Listen, child, go with the happiness," Robbie said.

"Sounds familiar."

"But watch your back," he added.

I glanced back, touched the scar on my face, and left.

My first stop was the bank not too far away, close to my apartment. It was then that I noticed a black pickup a few car lengths behind me. Staying with me. Okay, I wasn't going to panic. I drove the speed limit; so did the truck. I sped up. It sped up. I slowed. It slowed. Now I could panic. It was happening again.

The first thing I did was to keep a good pace. If I got pulled over for speeding, so much the better. But I didn't go on a tear, either. I wasn't going to lose control. Next was to decide where to go. That truck kept right with me, not gaining, not slowing. At least he wasn't shooting at me.

The police station worked well last time, so I headed for it. This time I would go in and talk to them, mention Lieutenant Gardner's name as well as C. J.'s. And this time I managed to get the license number. The thug had probably stolen the truck, but it was worth a shot.

By the time I hit Westheimer I was almost out of gas. But there were no cop cars in front of the substation. Could be someone was in there. Could be they were out on patrol or could be they were plain closed. These substations were hard to figure. I wasn't stopping without a sure bet.

The truck was two cars back. Now what? I was trying not to shake and not to be a bundle of sweat. C. J., I told myself. I hustled down the next couple of blocks and tore into his gravel lot, stopping next to his Mustang. It didn't occur to me that he wouldn't be here, that this wasn't a sure bet, either.

I hit the door, which this time was unlocked, and tore up the stairs, which were strangely like those that led up to my apartment. I found a door marked C. J. MCDANIELS, PRIVATE INVESTIGATOR. When I burst into the office I found a desk immediately in front of me, and sitting at the desk was Mr. C. J. McDaniels. He had his feet up and grinned as I entered.

"So you have a date with my daughter tonight, huh?" he bellowed.

"I'm being followed," I shot back. I moved to his side and faced the door I'd just entered.

"Mama likes you," he added. "But I thought you were

supposed to go to Linda's house. What are you doing here?"

"I'm being followed," I repeated.

"Stick around," he continued, not hearing a damn thing I was saying. "Linda's going to stop by on her way home. Might as well meet her here as anywhere."

I looked at him. *I'm being followed!* I wanted to scream. Remember? One of the killers got away. Instead I kept quiet and stared at this big man in blue jeans, a large, white Mexican-style shirt, and a deep blue Astros cap. His eyes were on the open door. Then I noticed the huge handgun that rested in his lap. A cigarette smoldered in an ashtray to his left.

A killer was stalking me. I started to say something about C. J.'s casual attitude, but the words lodged in my throat when I heard the hall door open—then close. The sound of footsteps galvanized us. They were the heavy footsteps of a man who didn't care if we knew he was coming.

Only then was I aware of a small desktop radio tuned softly to country music. The song that played was about some redneck shooting a jukebox. A gunned-down jukebox wasn't what I was worried about.

C. J. was calm. I stood at his side, trusting he knew what he was doing—trusting the big gun in his lap and resisting the urge to run into the back office.

In strutted a heavyset Hispanic man of about forty. His hair and thick mustache were salt-and-pepper. He wore a beige suit, a blue shirt, a red paisley tie, and he smiled broadly at McDaniels.

C. J. stood and tossed his gun on the desk. "Mr. Marshall," he said, "this is Sergeant Victor Hernandez, HPD."

Hernandez held out his hand and I took it. He laughed. "So this is the boy wonder, eh?" he said.

"The one and only." C. J. sucked down the remainder of his cigarette, then stubbed it out. "Hernandez is assigned to my case," he added through a cloud of smoke and sat back down.

Hernandez laughed. "We're old buddies. I'll tell you, McDaniels, you picked up a live one, man. The kid made me almost as soon as I was on him. I was sloppy about it, but he did good."

"Huh," C. J. grunted, and half smiled. "Prior experience, I guess."

"Sure, man," Hernandez agreed, as in, whatever.

"Why were you following me?" I asked.

"I was out to pay you a visit. You see, I have something to show you." Hernandez pulled a photograph from an inside pocket and flapped it at me. "But then I saw you leave, so I wondered to myself just what you were up to. I wonder if you two have something you're not telling me."

I shook my head. "I thought I was being stalked. You scared the shit out of me."

"So you came here instead of the police station. Not smart, kid."

"No one was home down the road," I shot back.

C. J. laughed. "You done fine, son. Show him the picture, Vic."

I thought it might be hard identifying someone I'd seen briefly from some black-and-white mug shot taken who knew when. It wasn't.

"That's him," I said strongly. The little hairs on the back of my neck tingled as if the shadow of the grim reaper had stepped from my heart to face me.

"Name's José Ramirez," Hernandez stated. "Some punk caught in a drug raid a few years ago. Been put away on assault charges, possession of illegal weapons, possession of drugs—the usual. Out on parole again. Was checking in with his officer, until recently. I don't think he's left town. I put the word out and received a tip he frequents a little dive near the Heights called Los Coyotes."

"That's not far from my place," I said.

Hernandez's eyes lit up. "Let's take a look," he said.

C. J. nodded, stood, and slipped his gun under his big shirt in a holster against the small of his back. He grabbed his pack of cigarettes and lit one.

I started to follow. Hernandez jerked his head at me while looking at C. J.

"What are you doing, son?" C. J. asked.

"Going with you."

"No you're not."

"I'm in this, too."

"This ain't no game, son, and I don't have time to play wet nurse to a greenhorn."

"Okay, John Wayne."

"It wasn't John Wayne. But it should've been."

"Yes, it was John Wayne."

"Which movie?" he asked.

"Who gives a damn!" I snapped. "You weren't talking like this the other day when I was dragging you into my car."

"I was when I shot that son of a bitch who was knifing you."

"Listen, you two," Sergeant Hernandez piped in, "I've got to get going."

"Don't you need me to identify him?" I asked.

"You just did," C. J. told me.

I hesitated, long enough for him to add, "Son, you've got a date tonight, remember?"

"A date?" Hernandez asked. "What are we talking about here?"

"Linda will want to go, too," I said.

"He's got a date with Linda!" Hernandez exclaimed.

"Yeah." C. J. puffed out a billow of smoke.

"I've got to go, man," the sergeant said, and then proceeded down the stairs.

"I'm in this, too," I repeated. "And so is Linda."

"Linda works for me." C. J. sighed. "Okay, son. There's a .38 in the bottom drawer of my desk, on the right. Go get it."

All right, I thought. I stepped quickly into the back office and sure enough, the gun was right where he told me it would be. But as I slid the drawer closed I heard the front door click shut and then the sound of a lock snapping in place. I raced into the other room, gun in hand,

and tried the door. Locked, all right. And there was no manual dead bolt on my side, only a keyhole. An empty keyhole.

"Damn it, C. J.!" I yelled. "This isn't funny. Let me out of here!"

The only response I received was the sound of the lower door closing and the echo of another lock slamming into place.

I had half a mind to shoot the lock on the door. It always worked in the movies. But when I checked the chamber I saw it was empty. Not only that, the firing pin was broken. Now, why was this hunk of junk in his drawer, anyway?

I tossed the gun on the desk as C. J. had tossed his earlier. It thudded, bounced a couple of times, then rested, barrel pointing at the radio. What was that about shooting a damn jukebox? Damn him. Damn his redneck ways. And damn his music.

A steel guitar twanged. I leaned back against the desk in his office, his locked office, collecting my thoughts. What to do next? The presence of C. J. McDaniels lingered around me like a cloud of cigarette smoke.

But I was very much alone.

Wonderful.

11

I rummaged around for a key, determined not to phone for help. After all, who was I going to call? Linda would think I was an idiot for falling for C. J.'s con. Robbie would laugh, then dial 911, and have half of Houston's emergency units here for yet another news story. Susan would let me sit and think about how badly I'd screwed up for divorcing her. Then I heard someone unlock the door downstairs. Back already? Decided I'd learned my lesson and now I'd listen to him respectfully, as the professional. The authority. Was I prepared to do as he said? Well, goddamn it, I had a thing or two to tell him.

I picked up the useless gun and tossed it from one hand to another. If worse came to worst and the visitor wasn't C. J., I supposed I could swat someone on the side of the head with the revolver. I paused. If C. J. was approaching, maybe I'd swat him anyway. And leave the country.

I sat behind the desk, as C. J. had, looking as calm as I could. The country music was now killing time, and I waited anxiously as the front door opened and in stepped Linda Garcia.

"Neil?"

I forced a smile. "Your father locked me in."

"What?"

"Oh, he sent me in the other room for this old useless gun, and while I was digging for the piece he locked me in."

"How embarrassing." She laughed. "He must've gotten a lead and didn't want you tagging along."

"Exactly."

Linda set a short stack of folders on her desk. "I'm sorry," she said, grabbing my arm. "A typical C. J. move. You'll learn if you stick around."

Stick around? I thought. Why wouldn't I stick around? And it's not that funny.

"Do you know where he went?" Linda asked.

"Sure do. And Sergeant Hernandez is with him."

"Vic is with him? Good. Vic's the kind of cop you want backing you up. Not much gets past him."

"Vic?"

Linda grabbed the open door. "Come on," she said. "You can't let C. J. get away with these things or he'll get spoiled."

I hopped up, Linda closed and locked the doors, and we were back on the street.

The air was spongy and the leaden sun hung heavily over the horizon. There was a good hour and a half of daylight left, before the wash of pink sky darkened to crimson, then violet, then blue black. The pain beat strong on my face. The scar itched and I wanted to claw it. But, sitting next to Linda, I kept still and said nothing.

"What's the quickest way?" she asked.

"Allen Parkway to 45 north, exit Cavalcade."

"Easy enough. How you feeling?"

"Better."

"Good. Well, I have some interesting news," she said. "While you've lazed around I've looked into the life of Mark Hill. Remember him? The CEO who died, allowing Ray Westview to gain control of Bedford Oil?"

"We were discussing him at lunch."

"Exactly."

"You're going to tell me he didn't die of a heart attack," I offered.

"No, that's not it, though C. J. needs to call for the autopsy report. What I discovered was that Mark Hill and Del Westview were involved in a little liaison."

"Really? Most interesting. How'd you find that out?"

"That's my job, Neil." Linda glanced at me. Her furrowed eyebrows smoothed, and she smiled softly. "Don't let C. J. get to you—"

"He didn't."

"Good, because if he knows that he can, you're sunk."

"I'll keep that in mind."

"Listen," Linda said, changing the subject, "most of the time all you have to do to find out about someone is to ask questions. People love to gossip. Hill had a maid, a part-time cook. I talked to a neighbor or two. After a while information begins to surface."

"You have any idea how long the affair was going on?"

"Years, off and on. The cook, Edna, had been working for Hill about five years and she remembered seeing Del from the day she started. She said Del would be around for a while and then weeks or even months would pass before Edna saw her again. Edna knew Del was married. I guess Hill had a lot of woman friends, some married, some not. At any rate, Del wasn't the only one. One of the neighbors, a man named John Webster, confirmed this. He said Hill was often with a different lady. Though he remembered seeing Del the most. In that respect, I guess she was an exception to Hill's habit."

"Think Del knew about the other women?"

"I don't know. Probably. Being married, she wouldn't have much to say about it. I think they got together every once in a while for a little fun."

"You think Ray Westview knew?"

"I'd wager he did. If Hill was the womanizer he appeared to be, news like that travels." She paused, then added, "Hill was married for a while, too, but that broke up ten years ago. Her name was Melissa Allen, twelve years his junior and a former rodeo beauty queen. I haven't been able to track her down."

We edged up the on ramp to I-45. Linda had the windows up and the cool air on. The discordant sounds of the freeway were away from us and her truck rode high. I didn't feel like I was going to be flattened any moment as I often felt in my car. In fact, this whole experience was much better than in that squat ex-hippie-feeling Bug I drove. I needed to get rid of that vehicle.

"I know what you're thinking," she told me.

I laughed. "I don't think so."

"You're thinking that Ray Westview heard about the affair and somehow murdered Mark Hill. Maybe Westview found out about the affair only recently, went to threaten Hill, and Hill suffered a heart attack. But that's weak. More likely Westview knew about the relationship early on, put up with it for a while, then demanded Del end the affair. Perhaps she did. Time passed. She went back to Hill. Westview again found out, demanded she stop, and the cycle continued for years until, finally, Westview decided to do something about it.

"I'll bet Ray was getting some on the side, too."

"I'm sure you're right," Linda agreed.

"Perhaps they had an arrangement."

"Possible. Unspoken, though. Wives of rich executives don't get permission to take on lovers."

"Whereas husbands can do any damn thing they want."

"Absolutely. But let's get back to what we know."

"Okay," I said. "Westview wouldn't divorce her because it's her money and her father's company, right?"

"Right. And he wouldn't go to Bedford because the old man's so loyal to Del that he wouldn't believe Ray. Period. Then Ray's chances for running the company would be nil for bringing these false accusations against Del."

"But if Ray took Hill out of the picture, not only would he put an end to this insipid affair but also have a shot at gaining control of the company."

"Very good, Neil. You're catching on. The only problem is the heart attack."

"Couldn't some kind of drug induce that reaction, some kind of poison?" I asked.

"Possibly," she replied. "Usually, though, something to that effect would show in the autopsy report."

"Unless they weren't looking for that effect."

"Long shot."

We exited on Cavalcade, swung left, back under the freeway. At Airline, not too far from The Kitchen, we took a right and in a couple of blocks we were at the bar where José Ramirez was said to hang out. This fine blue-collar establishment was diagonally across the street from the Farmers' Market. I spotted C. J. and Hernandez sitting in Hernandez's truck by the bus stop that was in front of the busy market. I didn't think they had seen us. Linda turned right before we passed in front of them and then left into the parking lot of the market. We were a good football field's length away. Staying behind them, we crept up until Linda found a spot that put both the bar and C. J. to our left. She parked. We waited.

Linda talked aloud. "What do we have? We have C. J. investigating Westview. C. J. shot. You were almost a statistic in homicide for fear the would-be killers could be identified, which, ironically, leads to their being identified. We also have the Westview-Hill affair. For years. Then Mark Hill dies. Heart attack? I don't know, you call it. But Ray Westview ends up with Hill's job."

"Also his wife back," I added.

"So it seems."

"The scenario ties together rather neatly."

"Or too neatly," Linda replied. "If you can't prove Mark Hill didn't die of a heart attack, then all you have is an on-again, off-again affair. Big deal."

"Do you believe in coincidence?" I asked.

Linda smiled. "No." The smile then dipped and Linda fell into silence. I knew she was mulling over events in her mind. I kept to myself, figuring she'd talk again when she was ready.

The Farmers' Market bustled with business. People pulled in next to us and left without so much as a second glance. Shopping carts rattled across the broken pavement. Car doors slammed and shouts in Spanish as well as in the slow drawl of the Texas twang filled the sunlit air like particles of dust. Bursts of car stereos intermittently stirred the atmosphere with their rap and Tejano music, then as abruptly as they disrupted, they faded.

The main portion of the market was a large, one-story warehouse. In front were stands of strawberries, walnuts, pecans, and a big wooden bin full of watermelons. Inside were aisles upon aisles of fresh vegetables and fruits, eggs, and shelves with a few dry goods like honey and spices. Behind the building was the open market where local farmers came in with their seasonal produce and set up from the back of their trucks or at little booths.

My attention drifted to the bar across the street. Los Coyotes was a small bar with a white-stucco facade and a purple neon sign spelling out its name in script across a darkened bay window. There were black burglar bars across that window as well as across the small window on the front door, which was propped open. The inside was dimly lit with the red, yellow, and blue sheen of more neon.

The pub was beginning to fill, mostly with jean-clad Hispanic men. Many were from road crews, caked with dust and dirt. Some were from the produce companies around the Farmers' Market. There was a legion of dirty off-white straw hats and few clean ones. A handful of patrons were dressed in silver-studded Western shirts, black-leather pants, and black boots. For the most part, though, there were men stopping by on their way home from work.

Linda cleared her throat. "I think the bottom line is that Ray Westview had something to do with Mark Hill's death. But murder is going to be very hard to prove. The only way we'll get Westview is to keep badgering him and wear him down into a confession."

"You think that'll be C. J.'s reaction, too?" I asked, looking over at them sitting quietly in Hernandez's truck.

"I don't know. Probably."

"Is there more?"

"Maybe. Or maybe it's the angle. That's the only other thing that bothers me."

"What?"

"Maybe someone else murdered Mark Hill."

"*If* he was murdered."

"Say he was murdered, for argument's sake."

"Okay, Hill was murdered and he was murdered by"—I paused—"by someone Ray would protect." I surprised myself. "But who would that be? Del?"

Linda shrugged her shoulders.

"Seems to me she had a good thing going—"

"We don't know that."

I leaned back in my seat. She's right, I thought. We don't know that.

"You have to look at everything," she told me.

"And dig."

"And dig."

I glanced over at Hernandez's truck and realized that Hernandez was no longer in the driver's seat, but crossing the road. C. J. was out of the passenger's side, leaning against the closed door and watching.

I edged forward and put my hand on the dashboard. "Linda, Hernandez is going in."

"I see. Did you spot Ramirez?"

"No."

"They might've. Or they're going to stir things up."

"What do we do?" I asked.

Linda smiled. "Wait," she replied simply.

Hernandez slipped between sunlight and shadows and into the bar.

I gathered all my willpower to remain cool and calm and to restrain the barrage of questions that popped into my head. What was C. J. going to do? How were they going to get Ramirez? Was Ramirez in there? What if he wasn't? Wouldn't Ramirez be tipped off later that a cop was asking about him? What if shooting erupted? Did Linda have her gun? The only gun I found was dysfunctional and sitting on her desk back at the office. And C. J., why was he hanging back? He wasn't exactly in shape with that wound to go quickly running in if all hell broke loose. Is that what Linda would do? Do I ask too many questions?

Suddenly a big guy in a black T-shirt with long black hair and a bushy mustache burst from the darkness of Los Coyotes and into the long-legged yellow light of the fading day. On his heels was Sergeant Hernandez, gun drawn.

"Holy shit!" Linda snapped. She jumped out of the car. I followed, noticing C. J. try to take the angle to cut Ramirez off. He couldn't pick up speed. I saw the pain on his face.

Ramirez raced across the street without looking, causing a car to screech and slide toward the bar in order to avoid him. The car didn't hit Ramirez, but it slowed down Hernandez, who had to stop and jump back to keep from being a hood ornament. He pushed at the car hood as if to shove it out of his way and was off again. Linda pulled her gun from her purse and took off full stride. She wasn't going to catch him, either. I could see that. Short of shooting Ramirez, he was going to get away. Hernandez had the best chance, before the car cut him off. Now he'd have to make the hundred-yard dash in less than ten seconds. He wasn't going to.

I did the only thing I could think of: I ran after him myself. Questions came to me. Why weren't there any uniformed cops here as backup? Did those two old men leaden with fat and iron think the capture was going to be this easy?

I knew the area and took off down Service Street, hooked a right at the cash-and-carry place. Linda had taken the direct path, but for a big guy Ramirez was fast, too fast for her to come close.

I expected to hear gunshots. There were none. All of them were out of sight. I was running parallel to Airline Drive, thinking that old José would duck into one of the neighborhoods, when I asked myself what I was going to do if I did catch up to him. I was fast, had great stamina, and was totally unarmed. Great, I thought, and slowed. I pictured the headlines: IDIOT JOGGER SLAIN WHILE CHASING EX-CON—OUTRAN COPS AND INVESTIGATORS TO BE THERE FIRST—NEVER SUSPECTED PROTECTION WAS AN ISSUE. The son of a bitch tried to kill me once. What better to do than give him a second chance?

I began to sprint and decided to take my next right back to Airline and try to locate Linda, C. J., and Hernandez. It was possible I could get a glimpse of which way Ramirez was heading. That was as far as I'd go. But when I turned the corner and hoofed it onto Link Road I ran square into José Ramirez.

José was big. I was larger. When we collided, I landed on top of him. On the way down I somehow managed, quite accidentally, to knee him in the groin. He'd been looking over his shoulder and never knew what hit him until, curled in the fetal position and moaning, he glanced up and caught my eye. He reached into his pocket. I was on my knees, scared to death he was going to pull out a gun and blow me away. I was unable to move or think or do anything but stare at his round, unshaven face and wide, dark eyes when I heard the others come chugging up behind me.

"Damn, the boy wonder strikes again!" Hernandez cried. He wasn't quite gasping for air, but he was panting. The sergeant grabbed José by the hair and turned him on his face. "Spread-eagle, Ramirez."

Ramirez snapped something in Spanish.

"Yeah, same to you. Now, try." Hernandez frisked him and lifted out a snub-nosed .38. "Kid, you're lucky. Vicious but lucky."

Linda had me by the arm and helped me to my feet.

C. J. was beside her, breathing heavily.

"I figured you'd have to shoot him to catch him," I said, and smiled weakly. "Funny thing is, I was on my way back to find you when we banged heads."

Linda patted me on the shoulder. "Always did like hardheaded men."

"You're one of the luckiest sons of bitches I've ever seen," C. J. muttered.

"Ain't he, though," replied Linda. She winked at me.

"It's the scar, man," Hernandez added. He handcuffed Ramirez, who was still groaning. "You scared the hell out of him," the sergeant said. "You don't see too many gringos with scars, only the bad ones." He laughed; his breathing was slowing to normal.

I leaned toward Linda, who squeezed my shoulder again. C. J.'s eyes narrowed and focused intently on the big, injured man.

Hernandez, standing behind Ramirez, had him on his feet. He held him with one hand on the man's arm and one hand with a fist full of dark hair. C. J. stepped close.

"Mr. Ramirez," he finally said, his voice low and soft, his eyes burning into the man's face. "Let me introduce myself. My name is C. J. McDaniels. And we're going to have us a little talk."

12

Slowly, José Ramirez's moans eased into a barrage of expletives. An understanding of Spanish wasn't necessary to realize this, and I gathered that much of what he had to say was directed against me. I did well to stand with an expressionless face, arms crossed, and stare at him with unflinching eyes. Of course, C. J. was between us, Sergeant Hernandez had a good hold of him, and Linda was beside me, gun in hand. For a long time no one but Ramirez said a word. We stood beside a scrubby mimosa tree, behind the general rush of things on Airline, casting long shadows from the thick yellow light of the day's end.

Finally C. J. snapped, "Shut up!" His bark didn't work. McDaniels shook his head, sighed, and in one swift motion went with the bite. He drove his right fist into Ramirez's gut. From the gasp that escaped the captive man, I could tell the punch had hurt and would have doubled him over had Hernandez not been holding him up.

"Oh, man, you know I can't let you do that shit," the sergeant stated.

"Who hired you, José?" C. J. asked. He grabbed Ramirez by the cheeks with his forefinger and thumb and squeezed. Ramirez spat on the big detective.

C. J. didn't flinch. Instead, he again hit the man in the stomach.

"McDaniels, I told you I can't let you do that."

"You mean you can't watch me," C. J. replied.

"He's got a point, man," Hernandez whispered to Ramirez.

I glanced at Linda. She stood calmly, gun still drawn, her attention on Ramirez. I kept my mouth shut, but I didn't know what to do. I had no stomach for watching C. J. beat this guy senseless. I'd follow Linda's lead. She was a hard woman, harder than I'd thought. But my gut reaction was that she wouldn't let C. J. get carried away. She could help Hernandez stop him.

"Who hired you, José?" C. J. again asked.

Ramirez's breathing was hard and pained. He was leaning forward, and Hernandez had to tug and wrench the man hard to keep him relatively upright. Ramirez said nothing.

"Neil, is this the man who said he was going to kill you?" C. J. asked.

"Yes. He's also one of the men who tried to kill you." I didn't say I'd seen him on Allen Parkway. I was simply going by what the thugs told me when they'd cut my face.

C. J.'s breathing bordered on the heavy side. His shirt was plastered to him, and he looked ready to take a bite out of his gun and spit bullets.

"He drove," I added.

Ramirez snarled. "Espanada should have killed you quick instead of fucking around."

"Who hired you, José?" C. J. again asked.

"Hey, cop, I want a lawyer and I want to press charges against this bastard."

Hernandez jerked Ramirez's head back and said, "You resisted arrest and were duly subdued. You need a lawyer, all right. You need a lawyer to defend you for two counts of attempted murder, for resisting arrest, for carrying a concealed weapon, for breaking parole, and for anything else I can think of. Now, *amigo*, answer the man's question."

Ramirez's eyes darted from C. J. to me to Linda

and back. "I don't know," he blurted. "Espanada was the contact."

In a flash C. J. drove another right into the man's stomach.

Hernandez sighed. "C. J., man, there you go again."

"Vic, I'm out of patience."

"C. J., let's just haul his ass in and lock him up for a long time."

"He's going to get that anyway."

"Unless maybe he wants to talk," Hernandez said. "Answer the man's questions, then we say how cooperative he was. We'll put in for a plea bargain, so he won't rot the rest of his life in jail."

"Who hired you?" C. J. persisted.

A cyclone of Spanish began again and we all remained silent until it ended in English: "I been in fucking jail before. It don't scare me."

I expected C. J. to hit him again, but he didn't. He only looked at Ramirez blankly.

Suddenly Sergeant Hernandez tossed Ramirez to the ground. "Come on, kids," he said, and waved an arm over his head dramatically, "let's take a little walk around the block. I think José busted loose again. But he won't get far with those cuffs on. Come on, help me track this tough *hombre* down."

Linda started after Hernandez. I followed Linda.

"You can't do this, cop! I can make trouble!"

Ramirez's threat was lost behind the fear in his voice. He was beginning to rise and we weren't ten feet away when C. J. hit him with a right cross. It sounded like a yardstick slamming against a table. Flesh on flesh exploded into a thousand splinters of pain. It sent the big man sprawling.

Linda didn't look back. I flinched, thinking that had to have torn C. J.'s stitches. Even Hernandez hesitated.

"I don't think the gringo's in a good mood, *amigo*," Hernandez called back. "Long hours in a hot car make a man ornery."

"I don't know nothing," Ramirez said hoarsely.

"C. J., we'll be back."

"No, man," pleaded Ramirez.

"Take your time," C. J. told us.

Linda stopped, turned back. "C. J., you don't think he'll plea-bargain?" she asked.

"He doesn't appear too interested."

She was still carrying the gun, but when she crossed her arms and seemingly glanced at her nails it was like she was holding a looking glass instead. "You haven't exactly been approaching this delicate situation properly."

"Take your walk."

"He's pretty tough, C. J."

"Either he talks or he doesn't," C. J. growled. He was on the verge of kicking Ramirez.

"What can we offer him, Vic?" Linda asked.

"I've been thinking about that, too," Hernandez said. "Maybe we can talk aggravated assault instead of attempted homicide, third-degree felony instead of first. That's up to the DA. I can only make recommendations. But I can control resisting arrest and flat-out breaking parole by carrying a concealed weapon." He repeated what he had just said in Spanish to Ramirez. *"Comprende?"*

"Comprendo," muttered Ramirez.

For a moment no one uttered a word. Long shadows were blending into the graying light. Hernandez struck me as a very honest cop, and if he and C. J. had been playing good-cop, bad-cop then it was a rough version of the game. Ramirez was on his knees, disheveled, the left side of his face beginning to swell. How were they going to explain that welt? Or did they need to?

Then there was Linda, gun in hand and looking on critically as if she were the director of a play and it was rehearsals. I wanted a drink.

Ramirez stirred. "Sam Contella," he said.

"Who's he?" McDaniels snapped.

"No sé."

"Good enough," Hernandez said, and walked over to Ramirez.

"We made a deal," Ramirez shot out as the sergeant grabbed his arm and pulled him to his feet.

"I'll do what I said."

C. J. stepped close to Ramirez. The handcuffed man's eyes widened. "*No más.* I answered your question."

"Come near me or anyone in my office again and I'll kill you," C. J. stated slowly, his voice deep and his tone cold. "*Comprende?*"

"I'm not afraid of you."

"Yes, you are."

Ramirez tried to meet McDaniels's stare, but instead his eyes darted to Hernandez, to me, to Linda, to the ground. Hernandez jerked him away from C. J.

"I'm going to take him to the market and call for a blue to take him in," the sergeant said. "You all get lost."

"You going to run a check on this Contella?" C. J. asked.

"I'll call."

C. J. nodded and started slowly down the road.

Then Hernandez grinned. "Hey, Linda, some date you and this guy have, huh?"

"Night's still young," she retorted.

"Bet he behaves himself. When McDaniels gets a hair across his ass you never know who's next."

"I run fast," I told him.

"That's right, you do. He does, doesn't he, José?"

Ramirez said nothing, and after both Linda and I looked at his swollen, bitter face the conversation died. We all filed to the market, parting ways as we came back in contact with civilization. Hernandez, in control, escorted Ramirez into the building. People backed well away from them like they were a couple of stray pit bulls. Hernandez talked to one of the clerks, who pointed toward the manager's booth, and they were gone.

"Where are you?" C. J. asked sharply.

Linda pointed to her truck. She had the palm of her hand around the gun and kept it down close to her side so it wasn't very noticeable.

"What's to keep Ramirez from pressing charges?" I asked.

"He'd hang his own goddamn neck," C. J. snapped.

I glanced at Linda like, *What's his problem?*

"We've presumably got the information we wanted out of him," Linda explained. "For him to start screaming brutality will only bury his chances of being brought up on lesser charges."

We reached the truck. The windows were down and it was unlocked.

"You ride in the back," C. J. ordered me.

"There's room for all of us in the cab," Linda said.

"I thought I told you to stay put." C. J. poked me in the chest with one of his thick fingers.

"You tricked me after saying I could join you." I didn't move.

"He could've blown your head off."

"And you'd never have caught him."

"You were goddamn lucky."

"Will you boys stop arguing and get in," Linda said.

"I'm talking!"

"Damn it, C. J., you're stubborn."

"Stubborn? Me, stubborn?"

"Yeah, you."

"And who came charging over here like John Wayne? After being told not to."

"Look who's calling who John Wayne," Linda told him. "You can't cover everything yourself."

"I swear I'll kill the next person who says that."

"A little sensitive, aren't we?"

"I went to great lengths to keep Neil out of this," he said.

"What great lengths?" I asked. "You pulled a fast one. Besides, who used me as bait, and also carted me over to the Westviews'—"

"Hardheaded—"

"I come by it honestly," Linda cut him off.

"I wasn't talking to you, or about you."

"Yes, you were. Don't lay it all on Neil. Get in."

C. J. sighed. "I'm too tired to tangle with either of you," he grumbled, gingerly climbed in first, and edged over to the middle. I closed the door and locked it, rested my arm on the open window.

Linda slipped her gun back into her purse and started the truck. "You ripped your stitches, didn't you?" she asked her father.

"No."

"Damn you if you did. I hope you bleed to death."

"Fine. You have your mother's tongue."

"You were never treated so good."

We hit Loop 610 and headed west. C. J. closed his eyes and leaned his head back. The hot evening air blew harshly in at us. I looked at C. J.'s side, but didn't see any blood coming through. At one point Linda bumped up the window. I moved my arm and she closed both windows, shutting out the night, and turned on the air-conditioning.

"I'm taking you to my house," Linda finally told C. J.

"No, you're not."

"If you bleed to death, you can do it in the spare bed-room, where I can keep an eye on you."

C. J. grunted. "Masochist."

"Come by that honestly, too."

"You're driving. Not much I can do about it."

I was thinking that, with José Ramirez heading down-town, my apartment was probably safe. I said nothing. Linda said nothing, and we drove uneventfully to Linda's small house on the southwest side of town.

"C. J.?"

"I'm awake."

"We're here."

She clicked open the garage door automatically, drove

in, and parked. "There's something I've been wanting to tell you," she said as we all got out of the car.

"Yeah?"

"Concerning Mark Hill."

"Spit it out, girl."

"He and Delores Westview were having an affair."

C. J. froze. "What? Are you sure?"

"Positive."

"Jesus Christ," he muttered.

Linda hit the button to close the garage door as we stepped into the house. It was a one-story bungalow with wooden floors, a small living room, a dining room, a couple of bedrooms, and a small kitchen. A stereo was on low, playing jazz. At a quick glance I noticed that much of the art on the walls and objects scattered around were Native American, including a shield hanging above the couch and a rain stick resting in the corner by the front bay window. The walls were white. The house had a crisp, clean, intelligent feel. C. J. went to the bar and fixed himself a drink.

"Tell me about it," he said.

"Make yourself a drink, Neil, if you want one," Linda told me. "There's a bottle of chardonnay in the fridge under the bar. I'd love a glass."

As I poured her wine and made myself a strong whiskey and water, Linda filled C. J. in as she had me earlier, sticking to the facts, leaving out her theories. When she finished, I handed her the glass of wine. C. J. ran a hand across his face, walked over to the couch, and sank down in its whiteness.

"What do you think?" he asked her, pulling out a cigarette. He lit it and took a long drag.

Linda set an ashtray on the glass table in front of him, then sat in the matching chair perpendicular to the couch. "I think Ray's behind it all," she said. "I think Ray Westview had something to do with Mark Hill's death. I think when you began poking around in his business he panicked and had those two idiots come after you and then Neil."

"But what about this Contella guy?" he asked.

"Go-between?"

"Or more. We need to find out about him."

"What are you afraid of?" Linda asked.

"Maybe this is the person Westview's protecting," I spoke up.

"What?" C. J. grumbled.

"We were talking about it earlier," I explained. "Perhaps Westview is protecting someone." I shrugged.

"Or the opposite," he said. "He's under someone's control."

I was sipping my drink when I realized it was almost gone. I slowed.

"Did you rip your stitches, Dad?" Linda asked.

C. J. looked her in the eyes. "I don't think so."

"If you did, will you tell me?"

"Yes." He stood. "Tomorrow I'm going to see Del Westview and find out what the hell was going on between her and Mark Hill. Linda, I want you to find out what you can about Sam Contella. Talk to Hernandez, too. But don't do anything until you talk to me first, hear?"

"Yes, I hear."

"I mean it. Don't go jumping into anything. I thought I raised you better than that."

"Of course you did."

"I'm going to my room," C. J. grumbled. Then paused. Smoke rose from the cigarette in his hand. In his other hand was his half-full drink. He looked at me like a grizzly sizing up an intruder. There was a silence.

"If the gun had worked, I'd have shot the lock," I told him.

"You noticed the firing pin, huh?"

"Yeah. And I was on a mission."

"We'd have had to call the blues in if you hadn't run over Ramirez," C. J. said. He turned and left the room.

"That's as close to a thank-you as he ever gets," Linda told me. "He likes you."

"He feels obligated," I said, and sat on the end of the couch closest to Linda.

"C. J. doesn't feel obligated to anyone very long."

"Except maybe Del?"

"No, that's not obligation."

I finished my drink.

"Want another?" Linda asked, and took the glass from me without waiting for a response. I told her it was a whiskey and water. After she fixed it she topped off her wine.

"Thanks," I said as she handed me the drink, then sat back down on the chair.

"Why don't you stay here tonight, Neil?"

"My apartment's okay by now."

"I don't feel like going back out."

"Couch looks good to me." I remembered the night spent on Keely Cohen's couch, though this situation was mighty different. Then was reaching for the unattainable. And at best temporary. Now was scarily within reach. Did I really want another relationship? Of course I did, I immediately thought. Of course. But I was determined to play it cool. I didn't need to move too quickly.

Linda smiled warmly, sipped her wine. "You're a good man, Neil Marshall."

"I don't know about that, but I'm a patient one."

"You're worried about C. J. being right in the other room."

"Don't push it," I told her. "I'm not that patient."

A sparkle danced across her eyes like starlight over ocean water as she peered at me over her wineglass. If I hadn't had the self-control I prided myself on, I'd have squirmed. As it was, I thought she'd better keep her bedroom door locked, and I pictured a gun resting on the top of her nightstand as more incentive to stay away. Drink your drink, Neil, I told myself, then have another, then after Linda goes to bed, another if you need to and with luck you'll fall asleep quickly.

Instead, Linda rose and, without a word, took my hand in hers. I didn't question the change of mind in little more than a day; I simply allowed her to lead me down the hall.

I didn't land back on the couch until daybreak.

13

I awoke at first light. Linda's back was to me. I had a arm draped around her narrow waist, and the back of he head was tucked under my chin, against my chest. He skin was smooth and warm and smelled of moonlight i Vermont. The cool spring air, the scent of pines, firs, an dew on rolling fields of thick grass. It was a scent tha threatened to pull the blackness from within me an replace it with a bud of hope.

I pressed against her slender body and felt the new da begin as the old had ended. A soft moan. A gentle turn Lips caressing, then tracking down the hot curve of th neck. Hands upon shoulders, small of back, cupping hips A cleansing of the soul. A thrusting out the hardness the city. The sounds and smell of hot rusty steel givin way to sweet breathing, sweet breathing that slowe from quickened gasps. And, for a poet's moment, w melted like shadows into a bright dawn.

After Linda fell back asleep, I dressed and floppe down on the living-room couch. I wondered if C. J. reall cared whether or not I was sleeping with Linda. Probabl Of course, she and I were big people. But C. J. was big ger. And meaner. I wasn't sure I was ready to find out he cared.

Then I smelled the coffee and dashed into the kitcher

"Morning," C. J. grumbled.

I smiled weakly. "Morning."

"Coffee?"

"Black."

He slopped the steaming liquid into a mug, thumped it on the counter in front of me, and lit a cigarette.

I spun my mind like a crazed Rolodex, searching for the right cue card. The awkward silence twisted on as C. J.'s cigarette burned. Finally, I figured there was only one way to approach the subject.

"It's Linda's business. Hers and mine," I stated.

"Never said otherwise."

"Maybe not in words."

"A man's urges can get him into a shitload of trouble."

I touched my face. "I'm along for the ride."

"Ride, hell," he said. "You're thinking with your balls, not your brains."

"That's a hell of a statement after watching you and Del Westview yesterday."

The mug stopped halfway to his lips. C. J. looked like a papa bear who'd just been told someone had eaten his porridge.

I sipped coffee. I could take a cab to my car. The old man could order me to hit the road. I would explain to Linda. She'd understand. Wouldn't she?

"Go ahead," I spoke up in the silence, my voice hoarse, "tell me to go to hell."

"Maybe I was wrong about you." He drank his coffee.

"You mean I don't need a beard?"

"Yeah, you do. To keep mirrors from cracking."

I laughed, pulled out a wooden stool by the counter leading into the kitchen, and sat down. God, I wanted a cigarette.

"Linda's been alone for a long time," he added, stubbing out the remains of his cigarette.

"I care." I thought of Keely Cohen. If there was anyone I'd have been dedicated to, it was her. Out of reach. Safe. But now there was this chance, and I'd taken it. Still, why did I feel so apprehensive?

C. J. responded by lighting another cigarette.

"Chekhov said something like don't run from your

happiness when it offers itself. Later you'll chase after it, but you won't be able to overtake it."

"Who the hell's Chekhov? Some commie president?"

"Far from it."

He grabbed a stool and sat on the opposite side of the counter from me.

"Never mind," I added, uncertain if his ignorance about the Russian playwright and short-story writer was actual or feigned.

"Son, I'd never begrudge Linda her shot at happiness."

"But?"

"Nothing." C. J. stubbed out his cigarette.

I knew that the focus of his silence was Del Westview. Not the Del we had seen the other day, but the Del of twenty-five or thirty years ago. I waited.

"Galveston," he muttered.

"What?"

C. J. hesitated, stared me in the eyes. "A lifetime ago," he began slowly, "after Del had broken her relationship off with me for Ray Westview, she ran away. It was before they were married, and she was still living at home. Old Man Bedford—and he was an old man even then—found her note that said she needed to find herself. To the old man, this was balderdash. Ray was sure Del had made for New York City. So he hiked up there, an arrogant, LBJ-like Texan searching the coffeehouses and beatnik hangouts of Greenwich Village for the misbegotten artist. What a fool. I encouraged his trip.

"Del was my first missing-person case, and one of the easiest. I had a gut feeling where she might have disappered to. I started slow, close to home. And it paid off."

C. J. lit another cigarette and splashed more coffee into our mugs. I said nothing, not wanting to break his train of thought. He was talking to himself more than he was talking to me.

"Mickey," he continued, blowing out smoke, "a mechanic friend, had replaced a belt in Del's car. She'd also had him check all the other belts, the hoses, the oil, and anything else she could think of. He asked if she was fixing to take a trip. Del replied that maybe some fresh salt air and a little painting would clear her mind. Bingo. Gut reaction confirmed."

I sipped the piping hot coffee and bit back the desire to ask questions.

"I only had to try one hotel," he said. "Even then I knew that a runaway never totally lets go of her past. There are old habits or attitudes or expectations so ingrained that they fingerprint a person, and they are as much a part of second nature as are breathing or walking. Del, not through stupidity, but through a desire for safety in her rebellion, went to the hotel her father had taken her to as a little girl, to the hotel she and I once escaped to, and to the hotel that surely she and Ray Westview had now visited many times."

C. J. ground the cigarette into the ashtray. "The Hotel Galvez was stepping in high cotton in those days. Presidents, movie stars, and sports figures all hobnobbed there. And so did Del Bedford.

"I took one day and shadowed her. All she did was leave the hotel early in the morning, sketch down by the ocean all day, then lock herself back in her room and not come out. The second day began the same way, and I waited until she was by the water before I approached her.

"Del was spread out on a blanket. At the sound of my voice, she clutched her sketch pad to her chest and scuttled back a couple of feet. I assured her I was the only one who knew where she was. She asked if her father paid me to find her."

C. J. shook his head. "Old Man Bedford hadn't, but I bet he would've. Del indicated she'd only go back when she was damn good and ready.

"I sat on the hot sand, my back against a large, half-buried rock, and I smoked. I'll never forget that day. There was a breeze, a salty smell in the air, and high humidity. At one point Del snapped that she could sell her car. I listened quietly, and she then charged that I was going to force her to come home. She stared at her sketch pad, striking and marking it like she was branding a calf, not creating art.

"I proposed we get an apartment in Galveston, but Del pointed out that Galveston wouldn't be any different than Houston. She wanted me to marry her." C. J. glanced down at his coffee and forced a smile.

"Part of the problem was Del wouldn't commit to the kind of life she wanted. She liked to think Bohemian, but she didn't want to lose hold of her aristocratic affluence. Of course, she accused me of not committing to anything. Called me a cross between James Dean and a Texas Ranger who wouldn't slow down for anybody. She was probably right.

"Her voice betrayed the bitterness," C. J. added. "Del was scared, too. Kept harping on commitment, couldn't see why I didn't understand.

"But I did. I'd have married her, son. Just wasn't about to change the direction of my life.

"And I wasn't one to rehash old arguments. So Del shifted her back to me. I remember the sounds of the surf, the gulls, the cars on the boulevard above, and the steady, hissing burn of each cigarette I smoked."

C. J. McDaniels poked at the ashtray of butts, finished his coffee, and pressed his hands flat against the counter as if to push himself up. Then he paused.

"Son, I understand exactly what your Mr. Chekhov meant," C. J. told me. "On that late-summer day in Galveston, I took Del home."

14

I wondered why C. J. had opened up to me. Not that the experience was unique. I've had people from associate professors to gay waiters to a mob boss confide in me—confessions I was certain they wouldn't tell their own mothers. On occasion, even Susan opened up to me. I didn't know what it was in my personality that invited such trust, and if I ever discovered the trait, I was half convinced I'd endeavor to change it.

C. J. picked up the phone. "I need a cab," he muttered. "My car's at the office."

"I can drop you off. I have a late-morning class at the university."

C. J. hung up. "Obliged for the offer, but your VW is next to my Mustang at the office."

"True." My cheeks reddened. "Then I'll split cab fare with you."

"I have a better idea," he announced, and picked Linda's keys off the rack. "We'll take her truck."

"How will both of us get our cars then?"

"You drop me off, then skedaddle back here. Hell, she'll still be sleeping."

I slipped my running shoes on, having grave doubts about this plan. Some not-so-little voice in the back of my mind cried that it was Linda's truck and she was rather protective of the vehicle. When C. J. stepped back to his room, I ducked into the bedroom to consult Linda. But she was sound asleep. I left a note explaining that I was going to help her father retrieve his car and that I'd be back soon.

C. J. was waiting for me, holding open the door that led to the garage. He said nothing about my coming out of the bedroom. From the way he gripped his side, the pain had to be significant. Then I noticed a pint of bourbon in his hand.

"I can feel it in my guts, son," he said. "It's going to be a bourbon day."

"Not unlike the last two," I replied.

"You drive," he ordered as he eased into the passenger's seat.

"Me?"

"You think I want to take a chance and scratch Linda's truck?"

What was this? I thought. One minute I saw the man's heart spilled before me, the next he was determined to prove he no longer had one. I clicked the garage door open, started the truck, and eased back, making sure we were all the way down the drive before I signaled for the door to close.

As I blended with traffic, C. J. spoke.

"If you're not in too much of a hurry, I want to make one quick stop," he said.

"I really want to get back as quickly—"

"Fine attitude, son," he broke in. "Head for the Westviews' *hacienda*."

"Why am I not surprised?"

It was only a matter of minutes before we were again in front of the Westviews' River Oaks mansion. The bustle of Houston was far removed from the stillness of this neighborhood. Gingerly, C. J. climbed out of the truck and quietly closed his door. Spanish moss should have shrouded the trees above him. Cicadas droned. I felt as though I was walking into a mausoleum.

Ray Westview answered the door. He was unshaven and wearing a maroon bathrobe.

"What do you want?"

"I've come to see Del."

"She's not here."

C. J. hesitated. Westview was half leaning against the open door.

"You been drinking?"

Westview didn't reply.

"Can we come in?"

"Who's we?"

C. J. nodded in my direction.

"I don't know you," he slurred at me.

"Del was having an affair with Mark Hill," C. J. stated. Westview continued to lean lazily as if he hadn't heard, then suddenly he pushed the door wide and walked into the dim shadows of the house. We followed.

The house was as quiet as brush strokes on canvas. The marble hall echoed C. J's boot steps. Westview was already shoving open the door to his den, which showcased elk heads mounted on the walls and a zebra rug on the floor. C. J. signaled for me to close the door to the den behind us.

Ray Westview was at the bar, pouring himself a drink.

"Want one?"

"I figured it was going to be that kind of day, but I didn't know it was going to start so early."

"You're a bourbon drinker, ain't you?"

"Neat."

Westview slopped some bourbon at an empty glass and handed it to him. Then he glanced at me and repeated the procedure without asking. The outside of the crystal glass was moist with liquor, though there was plenty on the inside.

"To what's going on," C. J. said, tipped the glass toward Westview, then tossed back a hefty shot. I consumed a respectable amount, though I hadn't felt an early-morning burn like this in a long time. But damn if I was going to let these good old boys show me up. If they even cared.

In one corner the pawlike pendulum of a grandfather

clock was slapping time's face. C. J.'s first tactic appeared to be to wait for Westview to speak. However, after Westview dropped himself into a large leather-backed chair by the fireplace, sloshing a good portion of his drink on himself as he did, and let his head loll so he was staring at the floor, I recognized it was going to be C. J.'s task to elicit conversation.

"Had any sleep?" C. J. sat in the matching chair on the other side of the fireplace. I stood by the couch.

"No."

"Del's not here?" C. J. asked.

"Told you that already. Don't you believe me?" His words were a mix of bumbling consonants and droning vowels.

"I'm not sure. She leave you?"

"No!" Westview's head snapped from his chest. "Don't get anything into your head."

"Just wondering why you're sitting here alone on the tail end of a night's binge. Were you afraid she was with me?"

"Don't flatter yourself, McDaniels. I knew she wasn't with you. She's, she's, she's—"

"She's out again, like she used to be with Mark Hill?"

"It's not like that—I mean, it wasn't like that!" Westview wove back and forth as he stood. After one particular stagger, he steadied himself by grabbing hold of the mantelpiece.

As upset as Westview was, I believed that Del wasn't in the house. Not only that. Judging from Westview's appearance, she hadn't been around for most of the night. She was up to something. And I wondered if, with a little pressure and fast talk, C. J. could crack Westview's silence. Or at least tell him what had gone on between Del and Mark Hill. Pressing a drunken, distraught man could almost make a person feel guilty. Almost.

C. J. stood, put a hand on Westview's shoulder, and guided him back down to his chair.

"Guess you're not going into the office today, huh, Ray?"

"I work every day. I'm never not working."

"Company going okay?"

"It's going great. You take that back to the old man."

"It's a lot of responsibility, isn't it, without the help of someone like a Mark Hill?"

"Mark Hill didn't do nothing but undermine me. I'm glad he's—" Westview cut himself off, grumbled, and stood to get more liquor.

"You didn't kill him, did you?"

"Goddamn you, McDaniels, you son of a whore. Hill died of a heart attack. I know. It was in all the papers."

I watched as C. J. tapped out a cigarette from a box and lit it as he sat down again. "But there's something that wasn't in all the papers, isn't there, Ray?"

Westview took a messy sip, then waved his glass at the cigarette. "That shit's going to kill you, McDaniels. I take pleasure in knowing that."

"Or you will."

"I didn't do no—"

"The papers didn't say anything about Hill's association with Del."

"They weren't supposed to."

"I guess the old man pulled that juicy info from their slimy hands."

"He doesn't know shit about it, and he never will. It was me who kept that out of the press! Me!" He jiggled the rest of his drink onto himself, then weaved his way back to the bar.

C. J. finished his bourbon. I was tempted to offer him mine. It was too early for me, even on a bourbon day.

"You have clout, Ray. Always knew it."

"I have fucking clout."

"So what was it with Hill and Del? Ego? You afraid the cops would accuse you and you'd never get control of the company? Yes, that's it. You'd never get control if there was such a scandal—or wasn't. Maybe Del was going to leave you for Hill. That's it, isn't it? She was—"

"Shut the fuck up!" Westview wobbled over and

pointed a finger at McDaniels. "She'd never leave me.
She only fucked him! She'd never leave me. She just
fucked him one too many times and he—" His arm
dropped to his side.

"He what?"

For a moment Westview seemed like a rampant bear,
albeit drunken. Then suddenly his whole demeanor
sagged as if he'd remembered he was only a circus
animal, caged and beaten.

"He had a heart attack, McDaniels," he said softly, and
sank back in his chair. "A fucking heart attack and Del
was there. Naked, in bed. She got scared and called me.
She called *me*, McDaniels!" His voice was on the rise
again. "Now, tell me how you think I feel, coming to
save my wife—who's fucking freaking out—after her
lover's keeled over?"

"And the old man never knew?"

"No."

Chalk one up for Westview, I thought. He'd taken the
brunt of abuse to protect her from public disgrace and her
own father's wrath. There was more, though.

"Is that why you tried to kill me?" C. J. asked.

"I didn't have anything to do—"

"Strange how you showed up at the hospital."

"Well, I—"

"After all these years, too."

"McDaniels—"

"And strange, as I was working for the old man and
coming close to Del and Hill's little relationship."

"Now, listen to me! I wanted you to keep the fuck out
of it," Westview spat, sat up straight. "But I didn't do no
shooting."

"No, you hired—"

"I didn't goddamn hire anybody!"

"Then you're stupid coming to the hospital like that."

"I ain't stupid. Just drunk. Was drunk. Been drunk . . ."
His voice trailed off.

"What's going on, Ray?"

"Nothing. He's dead."

C. J. leaned forward, cigarette smoldering between his fingers. "So, let me get this straight. You came to see me, to chase me off the case, because you were afraid I'd find out Del and Hill were having an affair, that Del was with him when he died, and that I'd tell the old man?"

Westview grunted.

"You've told me what you were trying to keep me from finding out. I don't get it."

"You were onto the affair. Sooner or later you'd have found out they were together when he died. And she left the scene. Couldn't she be in some sort of trouble for that?"

I had to listen carefully and noted that C. J. scooted up even more. Westview was beginning to mumble and his words were becoming more and more slushy.

"You helped her, Ray," he said.

"I don't worry about me."

"You don't worry about you, how chivalrous. There's something missing, Ray."

"I do love her, McDaniels."

"Where is she?"

"I told you she's not out fucking around."

"Where is she?" he repeated.

"Del's still Del, goes flying half-assed down the road whenever she wants. Still needs her *space*." The word slithered off his tongue.

"Still think of her as a little girl, don't you?"

"Huh?"

C. J. snubbed out his cigarette. "What's Sam Contella got to do with this?"

"Who?" Westview slowly lifted the glass to his lips. He was staring at the floor.

"Contella, Sam."

"Don't know the man." Westview gulped the liquor, then banged the glass down on the end table. He rested his head back against the chair and closed his eyes. "Only care about my wife," he muttered, "not a damn thing about—

Not fucking around, McDaniels. She's not. But you're
back. Why are you back, huh? Why . . . are . . . you . . . ?"

We watched Westview fade. From C. J.'s scowl,
could tell he despised self-pity.

The old bastard snored, his chins folded against his
high-cholesterol chest, hands hanging at his sides. No
even nine o'clock in the morning and he's three torn
sheets to a blue-norther of a wind. And alone. Yes, alone

Where was Del?

C. J. ran a thick finger around the rim of his bourbon
glass. I held mine out to him. He stood, grimaced, and
accepted the drink. In one smooth motion, he poured the
liquor into his glass, then down his throat. He placed the
crystal on the bar, and I opened the door for him.

We left the house to the harsh snoring of Ray Westview

15

I punched the truck through River Oaks and toward the office. Big, powerful—I was growing fond of the smooth-riding vehicle. "Ray Westview is a wreck," I commented.

"Your professional assessment?"

"And I've only met him twice. Where do you think Del is?"

"How the hell do I know?"

At first I thought he was kidding, but my smile dropped when I caught his eye. No hunch this time. Or one he wouldn't share.

I glanced at my watch. "I'm running into a problem," I told C. J.

"What?"

"That little jag to Westview's cost me time. I have to be in class in half an hour."

"And you can't get the truck back."

"Not for another couple of hours."

"Don't worry. I'll call Linda."

"I'll trade her truck out for my VW."

"Don't bother. You'll have to pick up Linda later, anyway. I have miles to go."

We bumped into the gravel driveway. My car, bunched on its haunches, eyes closed, rested in front of the office like a fat, lazy, old cat. Fierce. Protective. Half-dead. And not alone. C. J.'s car stood guard as brightly as a police line around a dull background.

"So you'll get in touch with Linda," I said more than asked.

"You always this nervous?" he replied, and shoved the door open.

"Only when—" I started to say, but was unable to complete the sentence over the sound of the door banging closed. I watched the roll of the old man's shoulders as he plodded into the worn building. He never looked back, and I believed, until recently, that was how he'd lived his life. Deal with the situation at hand and forge ahead. Now C. J. found himself forced to face a past that never quite went away. And I also believed it awakened him to just how many years he'd packed on this mortal coil. Perhaps realizing those years, the physical slowdown, was another reason he included me, however reluctantly, in the investigation and personal history. Perhaps he was considering me part of the audience to which he was going to impart his knowledge.

Then again, perhaps I was riding shotgun because of coincidence as well as the fact I was a nag who wouldn't quit. So much for poetic sentimentality. Pour it out in class, Neil. I whipped the big truck into traffic.

As soon as I hit campus, I realized my literature book and notes were in my Bug. Also, my face began to throb again. And I felt like a fox carrying a hen through the barnyard for having Linda's truck. I hoped the dear girl didn't own a double-barrel.

Keely Cohen was in her office.

"How is one of America's premier young poets?" I quoted from the *Times* and rapped my knuckles softly on the open door.

Keely frowned. "Writing's the only business that considers a person closing in on her mid-thirties young."

I stepped into the small, book-filled room. Her eyes widened.

"I look like an alley cat that's been tangling with a pit bull, don't I?"

"I've been reading about you," she said.

I pulled a chair up to her desk and sat opposite her. She

slipped her reading glasses off and rested them on a stack of papers.

"Weird, isn't it?" I said. "A few months ago Jason's death, and now this."

"A life fraught with high drama."

"Aptly put."

"Can I do anything?" she asked.

"Maybe. I know I wasn't here Monday or Wednesday, but I need to miss class today, too," I said.

"No problem. Read the Chekhov story."

"Already have. As a matter of fact, I had a conversation about Chekhov earlier this morning."

Keely reached out to still my own hands as they fumbled with a pencil holder.

"Are you okay?" she asked, soft brown eyes boring into me.

I'm scared, Keely, I wanted to say. Instead, out came the pat response. "I'm fine."

"You losing your voice?"

"It's scratchy, like a pen running out of ink."

She patted my hands. "Okay. Now, go on. Do what you have to do. Call me if I can help, and don't worry about class. Worse that happens is I give you an incomplete. You can make it up later."

"Thanks, hon."

She smiled softly and stood with me. "Oh, you do need to call Candace Littlefield. She hasn't been able to reach you and she's so worried that she had Sondra Anderson call me."

"I heard my adopted baby sister's been trying to reach me."

"Even though I hadn't seen you, I assured them you were all right."

"Again, thanks. I'll phone them."

"Watch yourself," she called as I left.

"Count on it." And my sneakers squeaked down the hallowed halls.

Funny, I thought my budding relationship with Linda

would subdue the feelings I had for Keely. Not. In fact, I couldn't even introduce the subject of Linda in front of Keely. Perhaps, with a little time and a little more Linda, my obsession for Keely would subside. Perhaps.

Linda was in the kitchen working on a second pot of coffee when I returned. She wore a powder blue bathrobe and her long hair was brushed back over her shoulders. Fingers were drumming the mug.

"Have a nice drive?" she asked.

"Did C. J. call?"

"No."

"He said he'd explain, though I'm back sooner than I'd told him I would be. I mean, I felt uncomfortable borrowing your truck, but C. J. needed a ride and—"

"I know, Neil," she broke in. "This is C. J.'s doing. He understands I don't loan out my truck. In the past he's always taken a cab when he wants to leave before I'm ready."

"You mean he set me up?"

"Yes. But I'm surprised you so readily went along with C. J."

"I didn't know I was going along with anything."

She sighed. "Well, look at the picture carefully when dealing with C. J. You should've learned that when he locked you in the office."

"My mind doesn't work on those manipulative terms."

"And that's why I like you," she replied, smiled, and kissed me on the cheek. "C. J. has a mean streak that tends to rear its ugly head when he's frustrated, but his heart's—"

"On vacation."

"Oh, fix us something wonderful to eat, Mr. Chef," Linda said, this time giving me a full-fledged kiss before she disappeared into the other room.

I found a loaf of thickly sliced white bread in the freezer—the kind you make Texas toast out of. I figured this was in storage for C. J. However, it would make perfect *pain perdu*. Why was the bread *lost*? I wondered.

This glorified French toast was usually made with French bread and soaked in a sweet cream and egg mixture with a touch of sherry or brandy until it almost fell apart. It was then pan-fried in hot butter so the outside browned and the inside, though cooked, remained moist. And I thought Mama was into cholesterol poisoning.

Linda lacked cream, so I settled for two percent milk, and all I could find to add was imitation vanilla or whiskey. I opted for both and, along with a half-pound of bacon, I guessed it would do. The *pain perdu* was holding in a warm oven, and I was frying the bacon when Linda returned carrying a phone book.

She poured herself another cup of coffee. "Smells good. I think I'll keep you around for a while. C. J.'s a pretty fair cook, too."

"Think he was upset about where I slept last night?" I turned over the pieces of bacon.

"So what?" Linda asked, and kissed the nape of my neck.

Yeah, I thought, so what?

"Guess he had his suspicions before he even went to bed," she added.

"You think?"

"Yes, dummy. Why? Does C. J. worry you?"

"Naw," I droned.

"You still haven't learned." She picked up the phone book and thumbed the white residence pages. There were three Contellas listed in the Houston area. One with a middle initial *S*.

"Is it that easy?"

Linda shrugged. "Start with the obvious. You'd be surprised."

She placed a call to someone named Marge at the main library downtown. While I finished the bacon, I eavesdropped.

"Come on, Marge," Linda said into the phone. "Don't make me come all the way downtown. I just need a quick check in the city directory. I know you're busy. I know, I

know, ever since the new directory came out, but, Marge,
you owe me. Remember who tracked down your worthless ex-husband? You're getting child support now,
aren't you? Yeah. So I'm not asking too much, am I? Just
this one favor, save me a trip. Okay, who's counting? It
wasn't a cakewalk finding old Joe, either. Harry, whatever. Yes. All kidding aside, it is important. C. J.'s fine.
Can't say. Thanks. The name's Sam Contella. Thanks.
No, I'll hold."

Linda looked up and smiled. "Unlisted in the phone
book will often show up in the city directory. We're
lucky. Word has it this is the last time they're going to
update it." She paused, still holding.

"Marge is actually a nice lady," she continued. "She's
gotten her spunk back since she kicked her ex-husband's
ass in court. Yes," she said back into the phone. "Four Contellas, no Sam. Anything close? What are the initials? I've
got that one. Okay, what about the other two?" Linda wrote
down the addresses. "Missouri City? Thanks, Marge. Yes.
Soon. Bye." She hung up.

I took the *pain perdu* out of the oven, plated up the
food, and served first Linda, then myself.

"A lead?" I sat on a stool opposite Linda.

"Three." Linda broke off a piece of bacon and chewed
slowly as she picked up the phone and made one more call.

Quietly I scarfed down my breakfast. I hadn't realized
how hungry I was.

"Sergeant Victor Hernandez," Linda said, and waited.
"When will he be in?" she asked. "Yes. Linda Garcia. No
message. He knows the number." She hung up.

For a moment, Linda was quiet. She ate her lost bread
and picked at her bacon without comment. Made me
wonder if she liked it. I pushed that out of my mind.

"Now what?" I asked.

"Trying to figure out which direction we should go,"
she replied. "No more bathrobe investigation. We're
going to have to hit the road."

We? I thought.

"You want to take a shower here? We'll stop by your apartment later for a clean change of clothes."

"Fine with me." I set my plate in the sink. So she'd made up her mind I was going with her. No asking. Almost ordering. A familiar feeling crept over me. A Susan feeling. It wasn't good.

I shook off the anxiety, bent down, and gave Linda a kiss, but I could tell her mind was off on tracking down Sam Contella. I walked into the other room, thinking that was okay, she was working. Then I heard her pick up the phone one more time.

The shower was quick, and again I was careful not to wet the scar. My beard was coming in thicker than the last time I grew one, a few years ago, during my first tour of college duty. Right now I had the five-o'clock wino look. It was the appearance I attributed to the man we were trying to track down. Of course, for all I knew, Contella could be a three-piece-business-suit corporate shark like Ray Westview.

The phone rang. "Vic," Linda said. "Thanks for calling back. No, I haven't come up with much. Damn DPS wouldn't even run an auto check. No, the clerk over there's always like that to me. I know, Vic, no one's as nice as you. So you have anything on Contella? *Uh-huh.* What? Goddamn it, Vic! Oh, come on—okay, I'll tell C. J." She hung up.

"What?" I asked.

"No info from them on Contella until C. J. talks to Gardner about the case he's working on. Simple as that."

"But I thought—"

"Gardner's throwing his weight around."

"Seems to be an epidemic."

"So we work our way down the list. Let's hit the road." Linda bounced up. While she got ready, I stuck the dishes in the dishwasher. Once or twice my mind wandered to Keely, inflicting a pang of sadness. I missed class. I missed my friends. But when Linda returned, I shrugged off my melancholy. And we were gone.

* * *

Our first stop was in the Heights. I was getting tired of the Heights. It was a small house, not far from the Farmers' Market, not far from Los Coyotes, not far from where José Ramirez went down. It seemed to fit too nicely into the overall scheme. That's why I was apprehensive.

So, apparently, was Linda. I saw her check the gun in her purse.

A dog barked as we approached. It was behind a screen door. There was an old oak shading a small porch. Peeling white paint on the outside of the house. Peeling green paint on the shutters.

"What do you want?" an old woman called from the darkness behind the screen.

"Is S. V. Contella here?" Linda asked.

"What do you want?"

"I need to talk to him."

The old woman pushed open the screen door. "I'm Sarah Vasquez Contella." The dog's yelping grew louder as she stepped onto the porch. "Oh, hush, Caesar," she snapped at the dog. It didn't do any good. "Are you from Social Security? It's about time you got out here."

The woman was thin and pale and wore small, round dark glasses. She gripped the sagging porch railing.

Linda's hand came out of her purse, empty.

"Maybe it's Mr. Contella we want," I said.

"What!" she cried. "He's dead. Been dead two years now, and I ain't got one payment. My husband might've been a Mexican, but he was a veteran. Fought against the Japs in World War II. I come by that money rightly."

"We'll look into it, ma'am," Linda said, backing away. I followed.

"Ain't there a form or something I need to sign?" she asked. "I need that money, young lady."

"Yes, ma'am. We'll get right on it."

"You do that. I want the check by Monday or I'll call the president himself. Oh, shut up, Caesar." The screen door slammed. The dog's barking was relentless.

"Strike one," said Linda as we got back into her truck.

The second Contella was out by the Astrodome—in an apartment complex. There was no dog.

A huge man answered the bell. He wore only a pair of boxers. There was more hair on him than any three bears I'd ever seen. Though he had a gut, he was as solid as the Transco Tower. And as tall.

At the sight of Linda, he broke into a wide watermelon grin.

"Carlos S. Contella?" Linda asked.

I prayed he'd say no.

"Yeah." His voice was deeper than the bayous around Allen Parkway.

"Can we ask you some questions?"

"Who are you?" he asked.

"Just a couple of questions," Linda stated firmly.

"She said she was twenty-two," he said quickly. "I didn't know." His face went pale. He brought a great limb of an arm across his forehead, wiping away sweat.

"No, Carlos," Linda told him. "We're not with the police."

"What?"

"What's your middle name?" I asked.

Linda shot me a look that said she'd as soon feed me to this guy as anything.

"Slasher," he growled.

"Slasher?" Linda asked.

"Ain't that why you're here?" he asked. "If you ain't with the cops, then you got to be with *Wrestling* magazine."

"Wrestling what?" Linda said. Again she pulled her hand from her purse.

"Ain't you here to interview Carlos 'The Slasher' Contella? I got a shot at the title. If only I didn't have to go through Bubba the Buzzsaw. He's bigger than me." He almost seemed sad, like a big, black-haired Saint Bernard.

"Good luck," I said, exhaling.

"Yes," said Linda. "Good luck."

We were gone.

The next house was a small bungalow out in a section of Missouri City that was maybe five or six years old. We were progressing from inner city to outer. There was nothing special about it or the nondescript subdivision it was in. One story, brown trim, brown-and-white brick. The small front yard needed mowing. It wasn't too bad, but give it another week or two and it would be a minor jungle. In the middle of the yard, half falling down, was a FOR SALE sign.

"I'd say no one's home."

"I'd say you're right," Linda replied.

"How close is this guy's name?"

"Esteban Contella. No middle initial. Come on. Might as well have a look around."

Linda tilted the sign up and wrote down the realtor's name and number while I looked for a window that wasn't fully curtained. Around back, I found one. It was a sliding glass door, and I could see just enough of the inside to tell it was empty. Linda came up behind me.

"Like I said, no one's home."

"But someone was not too long ago. House seems clean. Carpets vacuumed. It doesn't have that locked-up, dusty look. The lawn needs mowing, true, but that may be because it's not on a yard crew's route yet. Let's go see the realtor."

Down by the police station in Sugar Land, we parked beneath an oak and walked by a line of offices with charcoal-tinted glass fronts until we came to the realtor.

"Yes, can I help you?" asked a small woman.

"Lavon Dillon, please," said Linda.

"That's me. How may I help you?" Her head was cocked to one side and the smile on her wrinkled face was strained. Maybe she didn't use those facial muscles often.

"We'd like some information on a house on Eagle Rock."

"Oh, yes. Three bedroom, two bath. Going quite reasonably, I believe." She turned to a large book on the front desk and began paging through it. In the back part of the partitioned office a radio softly played oldies. Occasionally, a phone rang. Each time I heard the deep voice of a man answer.

"Oh, yes, that's right. It's a corporate sale. Not much room for negotiating, but for $54,000 you really can't beat it. Eighteen hundred square feet, two-car garage—"

Linda caught my eye. "Corporate sale?" she asked.

"Yes, and they don't like to hold on to these houses long. Only been on the market for a month. New roof. New carpeting. Pretty little yard. Nice subdivision."

"We've seen it," I said.

Lavon smiled her weak smile. Her eyes ran the length of my scar. "Of course. Now, if you'd like to look at the inside we can go over there."

"What's the name of the company selling it?" Linda asked.

"Ameriwest Pipe and Equipment."

"You have an address for them?"

"Young lady, you cannot negotiate with them directly. I assure you, they will not bring down their price."

"I'm not asking to negotiate with them directly."

"They have requested that any potential buyer go strictly through our office."

"Yes, ma'am. Are they a local company?"

"Why?"

"That's easy enough to find out," I said to Linda.

"They will not talk to you unless you go through me."

"Is Esteban Contella your contact?" Linda asked, ignoring the scarlet that was rising in the old lady's face.

"I don't know anybody by that name."

"Sam Contella?" I asked.

Lavon looked confused as she glanced from Linda to me and back.

"Nobody's trying to go behind your back," Linda told her.

"If you young people would like to see the house, I will show it to you. Otherwise, you may have a nice day."

Linda's lips were pressed tightly together and spread thin. Her eyes narrowed, then relaxed. It was the same look she gave Ray Westview at the hospital. "Thank you, ma'am," she said, then turned to me. "Honey, let's think about it."

My eyes dove into hers. "All right."

"Wonderful," the old lady muttered.

We left.

As soon as we got into the car, Linda got on the phone. "Ethel Taylor, please." She pulled out of the parking lot and down Main to 59. I was patient. Linda was onto something.

"Ethel? Linda Garcia. Fine, thank you. Oh, he never changes. All right, I'll tell him. Listen, can you give me any information on a company named Ameriwest Pipe and Equipment? I understand, Ethel, if you're busy. I'm about to get on 59 out here in Sugar Land and head toward you. No, car phone. Ameriwest Pipe and Equipment. I'll call you back—what? Thanks." Linda put the phone against her chest. "I think they built the Fort Bend County Clerk's office around Ethel. She is a sweet old dear, if she likes you, and she can still move fast when she wants." She lifted the phone back to her ear. "What? Stafford. Okay. Highway 90. What was the street address again?" Linda scribbled the information down on a pad of paper she had mounted on the dashboard. "Great. Is there any—it's a DBA? Contella, Esteban. Any middle name, by chance. No? Okay. You're a sweetheart, Ethel. I'll tell C. J. to stop by and give you a big kiss. Thanks." Linda ended the call and glanced at me.

"Our man?" I asked.

"We'll find out. The business address is only ten minutes from here." Instead of getting on 59, Linda stayed on the feeder until it hit Main, also known as Highway 90, and turned right. In the back of my mind were C. J.'s words about not going headstrong into anything. But that was where I kept them, in the back of my mind.

"Ameriwest Pipe and Equipment," I said. "Oil industry, right?"

"Definitely."

"Don't you think it's odd they'd operate out here and not down around the ship channel? I mean, I don't know much about the oil business, but—"

"You've got a point. There could be good reason for it, though."

"Money."

"Like money. Cheap rent. Who knows? We'll get a better idea after we see what it looks like."

We crossed FM 1092, and Linda moved over to the right and slowed. The address took us to a set of dirty white barracklike buildings. Linda pulled into a patchwork-slab concrete parking lot. Right in front were two auto-repair places. In the middle isle of buildings, near the opposite end from us, some men were loading large pallets of something stored in large blue cylinders. Except for them and the auto shops, the area was quiet.

"This is small," Linda said, more to herself than to me. "Let's walk in."

We drew some attention from the mechanics, and they weren't questioning why we were here. Some of them were whistling at Linda.

"This way," she said. "We want 17-B."

It was boarded up. A huge sheet of plywood riddled with graffiti covered the receiving window in front. Next to it, on the grungy concrete wall, was a large white spot where a sign had been. The front door still had its glass, but there were two boards covering it in a cross shape on the inside.

"Well, dear, we're not having much luck today," I said. "Nobody's where they're supposed to be."

Linda shaded her eyes with her hand and looked through the small openings the boards afforded. "Empty."

"Moved with no forwarding address."

"People do that. Companies don't." Linda started walking toward one of the auto shops.

"Now what?"

"Keep asking questions."

"Do we have to do it there?" I asked. I was half kidding.

"What?"

"Aren't you hungry? It's about lunchtime. Let's grab a bite and regroup."

"Jesus, Neil, later."

The mechanic's shop we chose to enter was small, greasy, and full of harsh light.

A short, balding man approached us. He was wiping his stained hands on a filthy rag. "Yeah?"

"You know who was using that warehouse?" Linda asked, pointing down the drive.

"I ain't the manager, lady."

"You have a phone book? Yellow pages."

"You want some work done on your truck?"

"No."

He tossed the rag aside, stepped into a small office, then came out and handed Linda the phone book. It looked a hundred years old, but it was the current one.

"I need the second half," she told him.

"Lady, you're more trouble than my customers." He lit an already half-smoked cigar, grabbed the book from her, and replaced it with the volume she wanted. "I ain't got no public phone," he added.

Linda ignored him and opened the book.

"Let's see," I said. "Mechanic. M-e-c—"

The stocky guy turned and walked over to where a stoop-shouldered man was digging at the underside of a jacked-up Dodge.

"Ameriwest Pipe and Equipment," Linda said. "No listing."

"Out of business?"

"Or never existed," she said. She tossed the book into the office next to the other one. "Thanks," she called over her shoulder.

"Yeah, lady, come back anytime."

Across the drive, at the other auto shop, a friendlier mechanic offered no more illuminating explanation for the vacant warehouse. Linda took down the number for rental information and we left.

"I'll feed you now," she said. "Let's pick up something and eat at the office. I'll call the renter on that property and maybe we'll run into C. J. Sound okay?"

"Great," I replied. Then again, maybe everything with Linda could be that. Great.

16

We'd stopped at a local deli on the way, and we spread our lunch across Linda's desk. She picked at her salad and sipped a sparkling water, while I bulled my way into an Italian-sausage hero and sucked down the first of two beers.

"Don't you think this one's a dead end, too?" I asked, in between mouthfuls.

"Not like the first two. That sandwich looks scrumptious. Let me have a bite."

I let her have a bite. "I think the man lost his business and moved."

She dabbed her lips with a napkin. "Anyone would lose their business if they didn't list it in the phone book."

"So you think the whole thing was a front for something else?" Linda was eyeing my sandwich again. I took a quick bite.

"We're walking on a shadow right now. We at least have to follow it until we find out where that shadow's coming from." She smiled. I handed her my sandwich.

"Where do we go from here?" I asked as she returned the unused portion of my lunch. For a small woman she had a large bite.

"First, I'll call the number for leasing information on those warehouses. Then I want to talk to the neighbors around that little house and maybe even get back in touch with that charming realtor and take a look inside."

"What do you hope to find?"

"I don't know. People leave things behind. A receipt in a drawer. A note in a cabinet. A small photograph face-down on the mantel. Even cleaning companies don't get everything."

"You think it's worth it?"

"Yes, if only to get a feel for the house, a feel for whoever lived there. I want some sort of picture of this guy. I don't think he's invisible, only his company is. I want to know why. And I need to follow a lead until I'm sure of it one way or another. Right now I'm not."

Before we left the office, Linda put a call in on the empty warehouse. She played like a debt collector and drew some sympathy from the person on the other end. It appeared that Mr. Contella had six months left on the lease before slipping off. No forwarding address. No other name on the lease. And no, the landlord had not seen the company in operation. Contella always paid rent on time, with a company check. Texas Commerce Bank account. With the last check, though, came the keys with a note that said he was moving. When the renter went to check on the building, it had been empty. Phone disconnected. Yes, there had been a business phone number. He gave it to Linda. He also "confirmed" Contella's driver's license number, Social Security number, and home address in Missouri City.

Linda scribbled down a note for C. J. telling him we were still trying to track down the right Contella, and we hit the road.

"I've changed my mind," Linda said in the truck. "I want to check the deed on that house first to find out who the guarantee is."

"Ameriwest Pipe and Equipment, don't you think?" I asked.

"Mortgage companies don't just give loans because you have a company name. There has to be some equity."

So we ended up at the county recorder's office. There was little activity and we spent about an hour going through the index book listings. There was nothing under Ameriwest Pipe and Equipment. There was, however, under Contella, S. E., President of Ameriwest Pipe and Equipment. The purchase was made barely a year ago. Cash.

"We've got to get hold of this guy's bank records," Linda concluded.

"There's decent money floating around somewhere."

"Exactly."

While at the county courthouse we ran a check at the civil office and at the criminal office. No lien on the property. No criminal record on Contella. Clean as a soap bubble that had popped and suddenly disappeared.

"Okay," Linda said as we drove back toward Houston. "Let's stop off and see Lavon, Miss Congeniality of realtors. It seems she's the only one who can get in touch with Contella."

"And how do you expect to get anything out of her?" I asked.

"Lie, cheat, bribe. The usual things a private investigator does, and a realtor accepts."

Lavon Dillon was sitting at her desk doing a crossword puzzle. To her credit, she tried to smile when we walked in.

"We would like to see the house," Linda announced.

"Now, are you sure you can afford it?"

"I beg your pardon!" I snapped.

"I am perfectly within my rights to ask that."

"Should we make an offer, Ms. Dillon, you will receive a complete financial statement," Linda said calmly.

"Very well."

"We'll meet you there," I added.

In twenty minutes we were back in front of the cute, nondescript house. Next door a man was bagging up freshly mown grass. He nodded at us.

As we were getting out of the truck, I asked Linda, "How are you going to get Contella's number?"

Lavon Dillon hadn't kept up with us. We'd hit a

couple of yellow lights. She hadn't made the first. It'd be a few minutes before she arrived.

"Promise her sexual favors with you."

"Funny. I'd rather chew glass."

"If she's really obstinate—"

"You don't think?"

"Then I'll come clean, admit I'm a private investigator, and tell her if she doesn't release that number she'll be obstructing justice."

"Doesn't obstruction of justice have only to do with the police?"

"Depends on how you look at it." Linda winked at me. "And she may not know that."

"Won't it tip off Contella?"

"Because of who we're dealing with, about anything we do will tip him off." She leaned against the truck. "Follow my lead."

"Plan to."

The man next door was a small, potbellied Indian. Shirtless. He approached us.

"You looking to buy this house?"

"Maybe," I replied.

"How nice, how nice. I don't like an empty house beside me. It was almost like that when the last couple lived there."

"Couple?" Linda asked.

"Young woman and an older man. Very strange. Never talked."

"We like to talk," Linda said. "It's good to communicate with your neighbors."

"Yes, it is very good to be friendly. This other couple, they were not friendly."

"Older man and younger woman?" I asked. "Father-daughter?"

He laughed. "I do not think so. And he was not an old, old man. Maybe my age or a few years more."

I judged him to be around forty-five.

"He had this," he continued, and patted his belly.

"Only more. But he did not have this," and he pulled at his thick hair.

"Bet he was a businessman on his second marriage," I said.

"He dressed like a businessman. Or a doctor. I am a doctor—"

"I bet you can tell a lot about a person once you see him. You must've gotten a good look at this gentleman."

"Many little looks. The windows on his car were tinted and he entered through the garage most of the time."

"What kind of car did he have?" I asked.

"Mercedes. I prefer BMW."

"I bet you're right. I bet he is a doctor. And his wife was probably pretty, huh?"

"Yes, but not as pretty as this lovely lady."

Linda smiled warmly and thanked him.

"The other lady was a blonde. And she was very thin. White, white skin. Stayed inside, so I did not see very much of her."

If you didn't get a look at her, I thought, then nobody did. I couldn't imagine living next to him.

"When's the last time you saw them?" I asked. "I'm wondering how long the house has been vacant."

"Oh, do not worry. Maybe one month. One day, while I was at work, my wife said the movers came and they were gone. It is not a bad little house—"

Lavon Dillon rumbled up. "You young people certainly drive fast," she shouted as she got out of the car. "Though I did have to stop for gas." She walked quickly to the door, fumbled with the lockbox, and pulled out the key.

"I understand they're out, right?" Linda asked.

"Yes, he is. I had cleaners come in and scrub the walls and carpets. And an exterminator bombed for fleas just two weeks ago. He had a dog, you know." She hurriedly unlocked the door. "You're the first people I've shown this house to, so if the company is in a big hurry to sell then maybe there is room to—"

She pushed open the door, and it hit us.

"Oh, my God," Lavon Dillon said. "What is that smell?"

Linda touched my arm. The house, sealed and not air-conditioned, was stuffy. The walls and floors were bare and clean. But the hot air was filled with a rotten-meat odor, as if someone had cleaned out the refrigerator and forgotten a couple of pounds of hamburger on the counter.

The odor grew stronger as we edged through the living room toward the back of the house. Neither Linda nor I was listening to Lavon as she rambled on about the wretched smell and cursed the cleaners for having left some sort of trash behind.

Lavon went right to the kitchen and began opening and closing cabinets and drawers, still talking to herself. Linda stepped down a small hall. I followed. We walked slowly. There was nothing in the first bedroom, nor the second.

The source of the smell was in the master bedroom.

I gagged, put a hand over my nose and mouth, but stood my ground.

The body was bloated. Its skin held a greenish-red tint and was covered with blisters. Around it, the tan carpet was stained a deep rust. One wall was spotted in amber. The body lay sprawled on its back in the middle of the barren room, barely recognizable as what it had once been.

A woman. A woman with one side of her head shot off.

17

I couldn't shake the putrefaction from my nostrils, and the taste of bile clung to the back of my throat. Most upsetting of all was that I couldn't imagine what this pulpy shape had been as a living person. When I'd discovered Jason's body, I encountered the mortal coil of a friend. And it hurt. This woman's body appeared to me as flesh-wrapped violence and horror. Her corpse was as fascinating as it was repulsive.

"You all right, kid?" Sergeant Hernandez asked me.

"What? Yeah, fine."

"Maybe you'd better sit down," Linda said.

"I'm fine," I repeated, but I sat down in a chair next to Linda.

C. J. McDaniels was on her other side. We were all in Lieutenant Gardner's office. Gardner wasn't in. Yet.

Hernandez half leaned against a black filing cabinet. I realized he talked cheerfully as if we were all at a party waiting for the guest of honor to arrive. Linda smiled. C. J. said nothing.

"The old lady will never find anyone to buy the house," Hernandez said. "Houses where there's been a murder don't sell. That's a fact."

"What do you mean?" I piped in. "She'll never set foot in there again. As white as she turned, I thought she was going to have a heart attack." Poor old Lavon had staggered outside, trembling like a cowed dog. Linda and I had rushed next door to call the police.

The door burst open and in strode Lieutenant Gardner. His demeanor was curt.

"That's two stiffs in almost as many days," he snapped, glaring at C. J. "Make it two and a half. What's going on, McDaniels? You're surpassing yourself. Or is it the Marshall luck? Box-office poison."

"You got a make on the woman?" C. J. replied.

"Yeah, I do. And more."

"Well?"

"Well!"

C. J. pulled out a cigarette and lit it.

"Put that thing out, McDaniels," Gardner said. "All fucking public buildings are nonsmoking. You know that."

Gardner's gruffness pulled me back to reality. I knew C. J wouldn't stub out the cigarette.

In fact, C. J. emitted a cloud of smoke and said, "Paul, I'm not sure what the hell's going on. Caulfield Bedford asked me to look into company affairs involving Ray Westview. I didn't take it very seriously because Bedford has never liked Westview."

"He's in control of the company, isn't he?" Gardner stated.

"After Mark Hill died, Westview grabbed the reins. Bedford's too old to keep track of his personal business, much less his real business. Only his hate of Westview keeps him going. Why the old man didn't kick his ass out long ago, I'll never know. Except that he always spoiled that kid of his. I figure she's the one who's kept Westview afloat all these years."

"That kid, huh?" Gardner said.

God, he still loves her, I thought. Why else the sarcasm, the taste of bitterness?

Linda wore her poker face.

"So you're investigating Westview and someone shoots at you," Gardner continued. "What'd you find?"

"That's the shit of it, Paul. Nothing. I found nothing."

"Now, come on, McDaniels," he softened. "I don't want to fight over every little point."

"I found nothing. You figure it. After I was shot, I wouldn't have suspected Westview if he hadn't shown his face at the hospital. Then two guys follow Neil, jump him. I kill one. Hernandez nabs the other. We try to track down Contella and find another body. You tell me what's going on. Who was she?"

Gardner sat behind his desk. The silence in his office allowed the murmuring bustle of voices, of printers grinding out more overtime information, and of ringing phones to filter into the room. C. J. finished his cigarette, rubbed it against the inside edge of a small trash can, and dropped it in.

Gardner finally found his voice. "You'd better not be bullshitting me, McDaniels."

"Who was she?"

"Pauline Burns," Gardner replied. "Name mean anything to you?"

C. J. nodded his head. "Willie Burns's sister. He came to me the other day wanting me to find her."

"And you did."

Ice-cold truth, I thought.

C. J. said nothing.

"Now we'd like to locate Willie," Gardner said. "Seems he hasn't been checking in with his parole officer."

"I know Willie. He's a mean son of a bitch, but he wouldn't hurt his sister."

"You know better than that."

"Lieutenant Gardner," I said, "I was there when Willie—"

"And you shouldn't be here now."

"But the kid is," C. J. snapped.

Gardner caught his breath, then relaxed. "Okay, McDaniels, say you're right about Willie. Who would he hurt?"

"His sister's former employers, Ray and Del Westview."

I noticed a tightness in C. J.'s voice, though he hadn't moved a muscle.

"Exactly. Want to know something else? The coroner's examination showed she hadn't been sexually assaulted. But it did show she had a baby not so long ago."

"A what?" Linda asked.

"Kind of interesting, huh?" Gardner asked, then ran a hand over his head and down to the nape of his neck. "Kind of makes you wonder where that baby is, doesn't it?"

"I'd say with Contella," Linda said.

"Who is Contella?" Gardner asked. "We're still trying to get him in focus. The only person who has apparently seen him is that flaky realtor, and she was in no shape to give us a decent description. The Social Security number Contella used to rent that bogus warehouse was that of a kid who'd died two years ago at Herman Hospital. Driver's license number? The kid's father's. Seems they both died as a result of a car accident."

"What about the neighbor?" Linda asked. "He sure seems to know what's happening."

"His description could match anyone in this room," the lieutenant grumbled.

"So the only link we have is Westview," McDaniels said.

"Let's just say the whole bag of crap all comes back to Ray Westview," Gardner told him. "And if we don't find Willie Burns, we won't even have Westview to kick around."

"Talk to Westview yet?" C. J. asked.

"No, but we will. Both Westviews. And I want to compare notes after you've talked to them. As I'm certain you will. Got it?"

"Yes, *sir*," quipped C. J., and stood.

"And when you hear from Willie Burns I want to hear from that nut, too."

C. J. left. Linda and I followed.

Linda waited to say anything more until we were in the open air. "Contella's the key, isn't he?" she asked.

"I don't know," C. J. admitted with a sigh.

"Want us to keep after him?"

"No. Let the cops dig. We need to go back to Westview. I want to know why Del didn't tell me Pauline Burns was pregnant. You need to tail the Westviews. And I need to talk to Caulfield Bedford."

"What about Willie Burns?" she asked.

"He'll be in touch, I'm sure."

Linda simply nodded. "So you want us to follow the Westviews?"

We'd reached Linda's truck. The parking lot was a sea of baby blue squad cars. The day was growing long. Still hot, though. And surrounding us was the cicadalike whine of thick traffic. C. J. stopped.

"You," C. J. told his daughter. "I want you to tail Ray Westview. Tomorrow. I doubt he's gone much of anywhere today, as tanked up as he was this morning." He gave me a slap on the back. "Neil, you've been a great help, but this damn thing's getting strange, and I think you should lay low."

"What do you mean lay low?"

"I mean go home."

"No." I stepped away from him.

"What?" C. J. asked, then drew a sharp breath.

"I can't follow both Del and Ray," Linda spoke up.

"And I'm in this," I said. "I've got the scars to prove it."

"You want more?"

"Now, C. J.," Linda said. "Give the guy a chance. He's been helpful, and I like the backup."

"Backup? You'll be covering your ass and his. You're letting your carnal desires get in the way of sense."

"I thought I was the one thinking with his balls, not his brains," I shot in.

"So that's the problem!" Linda snapped. "You're bothered that Neil and I slept together."

I wiped the sweat off my brow. "Hey, y'all, we're in the middle of a police parking lot."

"I don't give a king-size crap what you two do—" C. J. blurted.

"Like hell you don't."

"As long as it doesn't interfere with the case," he finished.

"My relationship with Neil's interfering with the case?" Linda said.

"You're not thinking straight."

"I most certainly am. And we need the help."

"Hey, guys," I tried to interject.

"He doesn't have a PI license," C. J. snapped.

Linda laughed. "What?"

"I'm worried about you."

"Well, don't. I can take care of myself. So can Neil. And you weren't licensed for a long time, until—"

"Okay, okay. But I've got a bad feeling about all this."

"You think I should go at it alone," Linda said. "Dad?"

C. J. growled. "Someday, girl, I'm going to knock the shit out of you. Should've done it a long time ago." He glared at me, then stormed off.

"I'll phone later," Linda called after him.

No response.

Linda turned to me. "He didn't get his way. Don't worry about it."

"I worry."

Linda half smiled. "We have work to do," she said, "and he's too damn proud to admit he can't do it all anymore. There are stories about that man. Someday I'll tell you. But now we have business at hand. Are you coming?"

18

C. J. McDaniels left the police station, and we followed. I didn't ask Linda why she decided on this course of action, but kept my mouth shut and watched. We headed directly to the Westviews' River Oaks mansion. My gut feeling was that C. J. believed Del was in trouble, similar to the time he knew she was in Galveston. Something was wrong. Gnawing at the back of my mind, though, was why Del hadn't told him that Pauline Burns was pregnant. That's not a minor detail you forget. Or ignore. And a housekeeper that far along wouldn't look for another position, recommendation from Del or not. Unless forced to.

Or Pauline could've found herself a sugar daddy in Contella. Then why ask for a recommendation? It didn't make sense.

There was danger. C. J. in his irascible way had been trying to convey that to his daughter. When a person really hadn't loved in years, you forgot what a fool the feeling could make you. I knew. And from the way C. J. talked, he was only partly afraid of Linda getting hurt physically. His fear stemmed as much from the sense that some idiot with puppy-dog eyes and a chivalrous attitude would throw his body in the path of a bullet and get himself killed, sending Linda into another tailspin of grief. Which could happen.

Not that I had a strong desire to die. At least, not now. Unless . . .

The Westview house was dark. We watched as C. J.

rang, then pounded on the door. Even Raul, the butler, didn't respond.

"I thought C. J. was going to pay a visit on Caulfield Bedford," I said, trying to draw Linda out.

"He is. But C. J. doesn't always explain his actions in chronological order."

What is gnawing at you? I wondered. "For all I know, Ray could still be passed out in the chair in the den. He'd never hear the bell."

"The house looks lifeless," Linda replied absently.

"Nothing to do with whether or not someone's home."

We hovered in her truck across the street, far enough away not to draw C. J.'s attention. Finally, she cut the engine.

McDaniels gave up on the door and walked the well-manicured grounds. He shook a locked wrought-iron gate leading to the backyard, then dug some kind of set of picks from his pocket. The gate proved no problem. He could've used a skeleton key and been successful.

"Hope it's not wired," Linda said. "Half the River Oaks cops will be on our asses."

"Why are we following C. J.?" I asked.

"Got that bad-times feeling."

"Well, don't worry about the gate. Complicated systems are usually saved for the house itself. Outside alarms are easy to trigger."

"How do you know?"

"As a caterer, I come here all the time."

"So what's around back?"

"If the yard's close to other places I've been, there's a kidney-shaped pool with large brown magnolia leaves floating in it like dead lily pads. Maybe a small fountain resembling an oil derrick that's either huffing and puffing or standing dormant with a ring of green mold in its basin. French doors undoubtedly face the pool. Locked. And I'll bet C. J. at this very moment is rapping on the glass with the back of his knuckles. Receiving no answer, he stares at shadows that stretch across the house like black claws."

"You *are* a writer," Linda said.

"And I'll bet you a night's worth of sex I'm right."

"Oh? And what do I get if I win?"

"A night's worth of sex."

"I think you're in a no-lose situation."

She caught the gleam in my eye, just as I caught sight of the large figure moving across the lawn toward the open gate.

"Linda," I said, and pointed.

"Come on."

We both bolted. No doubt the man wasn't the grounds-keeper or a cop, and I hit high gear to catch up to Linda. I reached the entrance first and held up a hand. Linda paused.

McDaniels sat on a lawn chair next to a round table. He was smoking a cigarette.

"Ain't been no one here all afternoon," Willie Burns told him.

McDaniels nodded, narrowed his eyes.

"Plan on breaking in?"

"That's illegal, Willie."

Willie spat. "Yeah."

"It'd send half of River Oaks down on us," McDaniels continued. "Actually, I thought you might've been one of them."

"I ain't. And I still ain't found my sister, if you're wondering why I'm here. I don't know where else to go. None of her old friends has seen her in months, and this was the last place she was. I think that old lady ain't telling us everything."

"I hear you and your parole officer have been strangers recently," C. J. said, releasing a cloud of smoke.

"Where'd you hear that?"

"Cops."

"Why they care?"

"Why haven't you been checking in, Willie? You told me you were going straight."

"I ain't had the time."

"Make it. Or you'll be doing time again."

Willie stiffened. "Just 'cause you sent me up once don't mean you can do it again."

"No one's seen your sister?" McDaniels asked, and cocked his head slightly back to the right.

Willie folded his arms. His forearms were like cinder blocks covering the massive brick wall that was his chest. I started to move in. But Linda caught my arm. She shook her head. I questioned her wisdom, but bowed to it.

"Not in almost a year," Willie finally told C. J.

"Believe them?"

"Yeah."

C. J. stood and toed out his cigarette. "Sit down, Willie," he said, jerking his thumb at the chair.

"Why?"

"Do it. You're already in enough trouble."

"I'll stand."

"I found your sister," McDaniels told him.

At those words, a twisting and all too familiar feeling knifed my insides.

"Where is she?"

"She's dead, Willie."

The large man's arms fell to his sides. "No, she ain't."

"Someone shot her."

"What?" He stepped up to C. J., put a forefinger against his chest. "You're a lying bastard."

"There's more. Not long before she died she had a baby. We don't know where it is."

Willie took a step back as if the burly private investigator had landed a hard right jab.

"I'm sorry," C. J. told him.

Willie ran a hand through his curly red hair. "No! It's a lie! It's a lie!"

"Willie, she's dead."

"I don't believe it. I got to see."

No you don't, I thought.

C. J. said, "Her body's at the morgue."

"Someone's going to pay for this, McDaniels," Willie swore, his voice low and hard. He made a fist at the house. It appeared strong enough to turn the mansion to rubble. "They're going to pay for this!" he screamed.

"Shut up, Willie," McDaniels snapped. Now it was his turn to get into Willie's face. "And you listen. She was found in an empty house miles from here. You know a guy named Contella?"

"No, but I will."

"You're going to go to your parole officer. You're going to tell him how worried you were, how full of grief you now are, and you are going to ask his forgiveness. Then you're going to talk to Sergeant Hernandez at HPD and tell him everything you know about your sister. And you're going to tell him that I sent you."

"I ain't talking to no cop."

"Then they're going to think you're guilty."

"I didn't kill my sister!" he bellowed.

McDaniels held his ground.

"I know that. Now convince Hernandez."

"I'll find that baby."

"You do what I say or I'll haul your sorry ass in myself." He shoved Willie back a step.

Willie's eyes bore hate. His hand was still balled in a fist. C. J. waited.

I noticed C. J. absently touch his side. I was sure he'd taken punches before, but not from someone who could stagger George Foreman. In spite of Big George dropping Willie after four rounds, I heard it'd been a scrappy fight.

"You want my help—" McDaniels began to say.

"A little late for your help," Willie broke in.

"We would've been days too late even if I'd jumped onto the case the minute you asked me."

"What?"

"We were too late, Willie. Both of us. Now, if you want to find who did this, and if you want to find the baby, you do what I say."

Willie hesitated.

"Go," McDaniels ordered.

Willie slammed his fist into the palm of his other hand. It was like a whip popping the air. He turned briskly and, without a word, shoulders tensed and close to his neck, stormed out of the backyard, toward us. Linda and I both scrambled behind a couple of pecan trees.

"You know I'll check up on you," C. J. called.

The only response was the rattling gate.

A second later I smelled C. J.'s cigarette. "You two can come out now," he said. "Hell of a lot of good you did me."

"Didn't want to cramp your style," Linda responded.

"Willie's big enough to cramp the Grand Canyon— and you're worried about my ego. Why're you here?"

For once, Linda turned to me.

"You think Willie's going to follow your directions?" I asked.

"Yes. And the police will probably hold Willie for a while. You didn't answer my question."

A group of cicadas began scratching the air. I wondered why we hadn't noticed them before.

C. J. walked to the gate and quietly closed and locked it.

"I have a hunch we should follow Del Westview," I told him.

He jerked his head toward me, took a hard puff on the cigarette, then tossed the butt down. "So have I," he said. "You two take care of the surveillance."

Linda's mouth fell open as she gazed at me, then back to C. J. "And what are you going to do?" she asked her father.

"Something I should've done decades ago. Parley with Caulfield Bedford."

19

Linda took C. J.'s directions to heart.

"We'll need to pick up your car," she informed me. "In case we have to follow them separately," Linda added at my quizzical look. She gunned her big truck and we left the quiet Westview abode.

A couple of blocks away, we caught sight of C. J. turning down River Oaks Boulevard, toward the shacks where they hung jewelry for wind chimes.

"You ever met the old man C. J. is going to see?" I asked.

"Once. When my mother died."

"Sorry."

"Don't be." She flashed a smile in my direction. "I remember Bedford's face was wrinkled, his skin pale, and he had a thin patch of hair like a scrub of cotton left unpicked. Even then he wore a black suit as if he was already dressed for his wake. His house reminded me of a maximum-security hospital, and it smelled of disinfectant like he was trying to asphyxiate death. To top it off, Caulfield Bedford has more money than God, and therefore thinks he is the Almighty."

"Didn't your grandfather work for him?"

"Now, where'd you hear that?"

"Mama told me," I replied.

"Granddad was one of Bedford Oil's best CEOs. So legend goes. I never knew the man."

"Mama also said that Bedford helped raise C. J. after his folks died."

"Well, not really. C. J. was grown by then and Caulfield tried to help my dad choose a career. 'Course, C. J. didn't want anything to do with corporate horse hockey, and went off on his own. Especially after Del married Ray Westview," she added quietly.

"What's C. J. hoping to gain from talking to Bedford now?" I asked, trying not to let the conversation fall.

"I honestly don't know. Crazy as that old man is, though, he could be behind the whole conspiracy in order to set Ray up."

A sobering thought. "You think he'd go so far as to have C. J. shot? Think C. J.'s in danger?"

A sharp breath caught in her throat as Linda cut a hard right turn. In a moment, though, she said, "No, no. Bedford was too close to Granddaddy."

Silently we drove the remainder of the way back to the office. We picked up my car, and I followed Linda back to River Oaks. She advised me to park by a house that was undergoing construction. My battered VW fit in perfectly with the cars of the workers, and the VW was only half a block away. I casually got out and walked to Linda.

Together we sat in Linda's truck near a narrow, wooded road diagonal to the Westviews' house. Actually, it was more of an entrance that rose up to a small cul-de-sac that gave access to five or six minimansions. At one point, a pale, saggy-faced man slowly drove his Acura toward the houses. Linda took out the key map and played as though we were lost. The man didn't give us a second look, though I wondered how often that trick would work.

The sun was fading into wisps of light. Across from us the humble Westview homestead was dark, inactive. I wasn't worried about my car at the moment, but as the workers slowly left I knew the Bug was going to stick out like a wart on a beauty queen. I expressed my fears to Linda.

"A wart on a beauty queen?" she said.

"Yeah, you got a problem with that?"

"I think this PI stuff has gone to your head. You've just joined the Mickey Spillane school of metaphors."

"Funny," I said. "But what about my car? You know the River Oaks cops keep a tight watch on this neighborhood."

"Yes, I'm aware of that." Linda tied her long hair into a ponytail. "So I put a call in to the cops saying I was with the construction company and that one of the workers' cars had broken down and would be left there overnight."

"It worked?"

"We'll find out."

"Oh." I fell silent and found my thoughts were getting distracted by Linda's thin face and long, tan neck. And the profile of her fine body.

"We could have quite a wait," Linda said casually.

"What if they went out of town? What if they don't come back tonight?"

"Then you get to spend another night with me."

"This isn't exactly what I had in mind," I told her.

She smiled. "Such is the exciting life of a private investigator," she said.

"And what's going to happen when a patrol car cruises by later and sees us sitting here? They're not going to be very understanding. We're doing the stuff that makes up gossip columns, tabloid headlines, and trashy books."

"Neil, you worry too much."

"You have a friend on the inside of the River Oaks cops?"

"No."

"No?"

"Well, kind of. C. J. knows most of them, but you've got to understand they get paid by the fine wealthy citizens of this neighborhood. They have certain loyalties."

"In other words, your contacts are of no use," I said.

"In this situation, you're right."

"Are we trespassing?"

"That's what they try to say. But I'm licensed." Linda hunched down in the seat and put her feet on the dash. "Listen, Neil," she told me, "we might get hassled, but the worst thing that could happen is we get made. The cops contact the Westviews and let them know we're on their tail."

"Is that the worst thing?"

"The worst thing I want to think about," she replied, and closed her eyes.

The sky was slowly turning the color of an open wound surrounded by the deep purple of dried blood. The heavy air pulsed with the sound of cicadas. This time of day now put me on edge. I touched the scar on my cheek, the beard filling in. The urge to scratch was almost unbearable. There were times when I felt that, with a little faith, I could rip the scar off my face as if it were a thick spider's web I'd walked through. Threads of Susan. No, this would never have happened if I hadn't left her, remember, Neil? The hell with it. Call it post-Susan fallout.

My mind, when left on its own, would go back to the dead woman. The missing baby. The mysterious Contella. The dead boy and man's identity he tapped. There was something very moblike about it that gave me chills. If I hadn't known any better, I'd believe Chip Gunn was behind this matter also. The man who positioned me to take the fall for killing Jason's murderer was capable of doing anything. But this didn't have Gunn's sign. And he wouldn't have been shy about making his presence known. Not to me. So if the circumstances were not born from the mob, his mob, it was a relative of the same calculating cold power that fueled this attitude.

I heard a car slowly wind its way up the road and leaned forward.

Linda didn't move. "Is it them?" she asked.

A red Mustang eased by.

"It was C. J.," I told her.

"Checking up on us."

"He didn't even look this way. His eyes were on the house," I said.

"He knows we're here," Linda responded.

"What do you think he's up to?" I asked.

Linda opened her eyes and smirked. "Probably a six-pack of beer, a grilled steak, and a good night's sleep," she said.

"It's tough at the top," I mumbled.

"So I hear."

Streetlights began to pop on. We were in the shadows of one near the entrance of the drive. There was still no activity at the house.

After a while Linda said, "You've gotten quiet. You bored?"

"No. Unsettled."

"I'll give you credit for honesty," she told me. "Why are you unsettled?" She sat straight.

"Contella's a ghost."

"No, he's not a ghost. There's a man out there with that identity. We just haven't hit the right combination to get to him. We will."

"Using that boy's Social Security number and the man's driver's license number bothers me."

"He's no lightweight," Linda said.

"Exactly. How would he get that information?"

"Death certificates are public."

"What did he do?" I asked. "Rummage through them until he came to these two?"

"Are you trying to make a connection between Contella and the boy and man? That's stretching it."

"Maybe he knew about the deaths and, when he needed to shade his identity, conveniently remembered them," I said.

"It's a long shot."

"I don't know. Maybe they didn't exactly know each other but knew of each other. Maybe they went to the same church, had business dealings, once worked at the same place. What did the man do for work?"

Linda's eyes widened. "Not a bad question. I'll lay money the police have dug into that."

"How deep?"

"We'll find out."

I ran a hand through my hair to the back of my neck and began to rub. Tense. It was my turn to lean back. I closed my eyes. My hand touched my face and again I resisted the urge to scratch the hell out of it.

"You've got a good mind for this," Linda told me.

"Thanks."

"Almost as good as mine."

I opened one eye, caught her smile brightening the shadows. "Almost," I agreed. All images of bodies, knives, and guns stuck to the wings of my mind. At center was Linda as I took in her sweet scent, thought of the night before, and, for the first time all day, I began to relax.

A little before eleven Linda nudged me. "Company," she said.

I pulled myself from a groggy sleep as I sat up, fully expecting the company to be the River Oaks cops. It wasn't. Across the street, Ray Westview, driven by Raul, arrived home. Raul parked in front, helped a stumbling Westview out of the backseat and into the house through the front door. A few minutes later Raul reappeared to move the car around and out the circular drive—his headlights swiping the ground just below the hood of Linda's truck—then down to the garages on the lower side of the house.

"Well, there's the goose," I said, then added, "a little marinated, as usual. The man never lets up."

"Apparently not," Linda said, watching carefully. "Okay, where's the gander?" she asked.

"Think she's already found a replacement for Mark Hill?"

"I think she has her eyes set on one," Linda replied.

"C. J.?"

Linda said nothing. I dropped it.

I had that stranded-in-the-airport-after-having-traveled-all-day feeling. My hair was disheveled and greasy and a thin film of sweat clung to me. Again we waited. Nothing.

Then a patrol car turned the corner and slowly came toward us. This time it was flashing the wooded side of the road with a floodlight that was mounted to the driver's door.

"Shit," Linda snapped, quickly turned on the truck, and backed straight up the small hill. She pulled in behind a BMW that was parked in the cul-de-sac. There were only two other cars parked out in the open, and one was a big Cherokee, but it was enough that we didn't stand out too badly.

"Duck down," Linda said. She cut the engine and pulled the keys from the ignition. "If we get caught we're a couple of college kids making out, got it?"

"Absolutely. Making out." I gave her a kiss.

"Not now, dummy."

The patrol car inched up into the cul-de-sac and did a casual swipe with the light as it turned around. It didn't stop and it didn't speed up. There seemed to be an accustomed speed to its rounds and that was simply what it was doing, winding, twisting, rolling like a slow-moving toy. After a long minute, it was gone.

We sat up.

"That was a sign," Linda said.

"That was smooth," I told her.

"I'd been looking for the floodlight. This was the first patrol car to use it."

"What kind of a sign was it?" I asked.

"Big Ray's passed out by now, and who knows if Del will be back. I say we go get some rest, then pick them up first thing in the morning. If need be, one of us will follow Ray and the other will wait for Del."

"Fine with me. I could use a shower."

"Take it at my place?" Linda asked.

"You're going to get tired of me," I said.

"I'll let you know when I do. But, after the passionate kiss you just forced on me, how could I refuse you?"

"Yes, how could you?" I asked calmly.

She batted her eyelids and we went to her house, quietly and together.

20

In the dim recesses of Linda's bedroom—blinds closed and curtains drawn, air conditioner humming, cool, damp sheets resting against long flanks of flesh—I had no sense of time. Or cared. Linda lay across my right arm, her head against my chest, a leg strewn across my midsection, a hand on my shoulder. Her breathing was slow and steady. Sweet beauty. Soft hair brushed my cheek. I drifted in and out of sleep, feeling sated, happily drugged on the aftermath of hours upon hours of lovemaking. And then I caught sight of the digital clock. It glared at me in big, bold red numbers. 2:32.

"Oh, crap," I said. Dull as it was, there was enough glow on the windows to tell me it was afternoon, not morning.

"What?" Linda asked, sleepily lifting her head from my chest.

"We've slept the day away."

Linda squinted at the clock. She kissed me. "After last night and this morning, I'm not surprised," she said, and nuzzled back against my chest.

"Isn't C. J. going to be pissed?"

"If he finds out."

"You don't seem too worried."

"And you worry too much," she told me. "There's nothing we can do about it now. Besides, you deserve a break. Enjoy it."

"But what if they've flown the country and we missed them?"

"Then C. J. will be royally pissed."

"How comforting," I said.

Linda sighed. "We'll rise and shine in a while and run over there. If we come across them, we'll see what they do. If not, we'll give it a couple of hours, then leave, start fresh in the morning."

"What day's today?" I asked.

"Day of rest," she purred.

"Sunday?"

"Close enough." Linda yawned. "It's Saturday."

"What a week," I commented.

"No shit."

A week's worth of missed classes, I thought. I began to feel guilty about neglecting my studies—and my friends—until Linda suddenly wriggled against me. I stirred, pulling her warm body tighter against mine.

"Day of rest?" I asked.

"Hardly."

It was almost five before we returned to River Oaks. The house remained dark. No activity. Around nine, Linda put in a call to C. J. She left a vague message concerning Ray, his arriving home late last night, drunk. And she let C. J. know we had yet to catch up to Del. However, contrary to what Linda said earlier about staying a couple of hours, we toughed it out until nearly midnight when, same as the night before, Ray Westview staggered home.

"We'll need an early start tomorrow," Linda stated seriously.

"Want me to stay at my place tonight?"

"Alone?"

"Well—"

"Do you want to?" she asked.

"No."

"Then that's a stupid question."

"What about my car?" I asked.

"Ah, leave it." Linda started the truck and we cruised

out of River Oaks. "We can run by your place and pick up some clean clothes if you want."

"Could use them."

Only, when we went by my apartment, Linda came up with me. We made it as far as my small bedroom—and my twin-size futon next to the wall-unit air conditioner that blew the sweat off our sore, tired bodies all night long.

In the morning, we both had the exhausted-but-refreshed feeling, ready to face the sun and watch another humid Houston day sweat off the calendar.

Only today it was raining. Intermittently, it went from normal pelting to thick torrents. The thunder-boomers had slammed into the city earlier in the morning, and it was a good bet they'd be back. Fortunately, we were rolling on a day without rush-hour traffic.

Because of the rain, and the fact that it was Sunday, there were only a couple of workers at the construction site near the Westviews' house. As we cruised by I noticed that my car was right where I'd left it.

"What'd I tell you," Linda said. "No one gave your Bug a second look."

"Story of its life."

"But not of its owner," she replied, and winked.

Come on, I thought, let's call the game on account of inclement weather. Let's go home.

But sitting in the circular drive was a little black Mercedes.

"Del's car," Linda said. She drove past the entrance to the cul-de-sac, past the house, then turned around and pulled to the side of the street where the Westviews' lot connected with a small wooded area. The house was on our right, though the view wasn't as ideal as last night's and we were much more visible. But what we had going for us was the sheer cloak of rain.

"I don't figure we'll be here long," Linda told me.

"How are we going to handle this?"

"I'll take whoever comes out first, drop you at your

:ar. You swing back over and tail the second one."
Linda paused, looked hard at me. "Don't do anything
foolish. Observe, don't act. You see trouble, call C. J. or
Hernandez."

"Okay, no problem."

"I mean it, Neil. Especially if you get Ray. Beginner's
luck is just that. It doesn't last forever."

"Please, Linda."

"I had to say it."

"And I heard it. I understand. I'm ready. Got my
notepad and pen and minibinoculars."

"No gun, right?" Linda asked. "You're not licensed."

"No gun," I lied. Actually, my little .25 was still taped
on the bottom side of the passenger's seat in the VW. Not
that I planned to use it, but the piece was a security
blanket. I touched my face. Of course, the baby gun
hadn't stopped me from getting cut. And I figured that if
someone got close enough to me to find it, I'd already be
in deep shit. The fact that I was carrying an unlicensed
gun would be the least of my problems.

"Good," Linda replied. "Oh, I talked to C. J. while you
were in the shower. Passed on your hunch about the dead
man's private life and work and any connection there
might be to Contella. He was going to double-check."

"Maybe something will pan out."

"Sooner or later it has to."

About a half hour later, as the rain softened, Ray Westview emerged from the house. Raul brought the car
around, but this time Westview drove himself. Linda
started the truck.

"Leaving his chauffeur at home today," I said.

"He's walking straight. Maybe he doesn't need him."

"He won't end the day that way."

Westview sped down the road.

"Jump out quick so I don't lose him," Linda told me.

I did.

"And remember," she called as I closed the door.
"Observe."

I gave her a *yes, ma'am* salute and she hit the gas.

The rain picked up and I hurried to my car. I cracked the window on my side, then rolled the passenger's halfway down to let out the mustiness. I cranked on the motor and in a minute I was back where Linda and I had been. The Mercedes gleamed in the beading rain in front of the columned house. A picture out of *Architectural Digest*.

Heavy drops beat against the shell of my car, and I wondered if this was the way a turtle felt curled up in its house in such weather. Eventually, I had to roll both windows all the way up to keep my glasses from being splatted with june-bug-size water beads. Next, I dug around for a napkin to wipe the condensation from the windshield so I could keep the house in view. Nothing.

Then the cops showed. Not the River Oaks cops that got my palms sweaty, but the HPD that sent me visions of dark cells and roommates named Iron Dick. A blue with Sergeant Hernandez riding shotgun jerked to a stop. No rest for the weary, I thought. My Bug's shell was getting too stuffy, so I cracked the passenger window again, then slouched in the seat. I jotted down the time Hernandez entered the house. Then the time, about an hour later, when he left.

The right half of my car grew pretty wet on the inside. Finally, Del Westview appeared. Raul held an umbrella for her as she climbed into her Mercedes. I started the Bug and when she pulled out of the driveway I gave her a few yards, then eased into gear and down the road. Out of the corner of my eye I noticed Raul folding the umbrella as he stepped back into the house. Not spotted by him. Good start.

With the rain slowing traffic, it wasn't too difficult to stay with her. Out of River Oaks, she turned right on Kirby. At the light on Alabama I had to zip through a yellow turning pink, but I remained about three cars behind her.

Del Westview kept on Kirby until University Boule-

vard. She turned right. Now it was getting tricky. We'd
left the main stream of traffic, so I hung farther back as
we wound our way into West University. At a quick left I
almost lost her. She'd gone immediately back to the
right, and I was passing the street when I caught the red
glow of her taillights a block away.

I turned the lights off on my car, backed up quickly,
and was on task again. A slight case of paranoia was
catching up to me as I kept glancing into the rearview
mirror to be sure that I wasn't being followed. I wasn't. I
didn't think.

I wished I wasn't sweating so much.

After another right, Del drove into the driveway of
a powder blue ranch house. The garage door rose slowly
and the Mercedes disappeared inside it. The door closed.

I drove by the house to the end of the block, scribbled
down the street's name, then turned around and parked
behind a brown Volvo station wagon. I was across the
street, three lots away. With help from the binoculars, I
could just make out the house number and wrote it down.
Then, again, I waited.

This waiting wasn't much fun to begin with, but it was
even less fun alone. And in the rain. And hungry. Stop
whining, Neil, I could hear Linda say. I wondered how
she was doing. Fine, I was sure. Why, she was only following a man whose blood was ninety proof and whose
brain was a cell or two short of a full load. God knows
what she was following him into.

I fidgeted in my seat, slouched down. Linda knows
herself and her business, I thought. Worry about your
own self. Like what you're going to do about needing
to go to the bathroom. I could picture myself explaining to C. J. that I'd lost Del when I'd made a quick run
to the local gas station. I hoped she wouldn't be in there
all day.

I missed lunch. And this was a dead street. Very few
cars went by. The only excitement came midafternoon
when a West U cop cruised the neighborhood. But even

that was minor. The rain was coming in torrents again, with thunder and lightning rattling and flaming Houston like artillery fire, so visibility wasn't very good. As far down as I was slumped, I don't think he saw me. At any rate, he let me be.

Around five a battered pickup pulled into the driveway. I picked up the binoculars. The driver was a thin, hard-looking Mexican dressed in a denim shirt and wearing a straw hat. I wrote down the license-plate number. He banged a fist against the horn and quickly, through the front door, came a stout Hispanic woman. She wagged her finger at the man, who responded by placing the palms of his hands in front of his chest as if he was afraid of getting hit. The woman waddled into the truck and the man endured more finger-wagging and some verbiage that I was sure wasn't "How was your day, honey?" He nodded his head, backed up the truck, and they left.

The rain continued into the darkness of evening. Lights came on in the house. I was getting unbearably antsy until finally I had to step out of the car and stretch. My Notre Dame cap was on the backseat. I slipped it on and casually walked across the street. There was no one to be seen on this miserable night, so I eased on up to the house to try to get a look through one of the windows.

God, was I hungry. I tried not to think of the first thing I was going to eat when I was free of Del Westview. Chicken fajitas from The Flower came to mind. Or crawfish from Papadeaux. Or even a Big Mac. I wasn't feeling particular.

Oh, pay attention to what you're doing, Neil. There was a porch light on in front and a floodlight in back. The side windows I faced were curtained, but I figured they were still my best chance for a peek inside since the garage butted the other side of the house.

I slipped against the side of the house. There was no light coming from the first, and largest, window. I couldn't see a thing. The second window was lit up, but pretty well covered. About all I could see, through a slight crack in the curtains, was another window against the back wall. Straining my ears, I could hear music and, I thought, a woman's voice singing along with it.

A short Cyclone fence blocked off the backyard. The gate was padlocked. What the hell, I thought. I grabbed the fence with both hands, jumped, and swung myself over. No noise at all. I paused in the shadows, then slipped a look around the corner of the house. The yard was pretty bright back here. A huge live oak tree hung over most of the lawn. The floodlight was in the tree, and I could see the individual drops of rain pass through its beam.

The window wasn't ten feet away. I'd gone this far. Crouching, I forged on, though my heart was pumping so furiously I was light-headed.

This curtain wasn't drawn as tight and the blinds behind them were partially open. I caught glimpses of Del Westview. She was painting. Painting. I'd been sitting out in the rain all day, hungry and wet, and she'd been in this small, dry house painting. I couldn't make out what was on the canvas, but I noticed the colors were pastels, soft blues and pinks.

"Great," I muttered to myself, pulled away from the window, and stood. Then I saw the dog.

It was a big dog of Doberman persuasion, and the mass of muscle and teeth shot at me. I was quick, but had there not been a chain attached to the dog's collar I'd have been dinner. The chain went taut. The barking exploded. Instinctively, my hands were back on the fence and I heaved myself over. I ducked beneath the lighted window and paused. Del's voice snapped something, and the dog fell silent.

I took a deep breath, gained control, and was about to walk away when I heard someone on the front porch. There was the jangling of keys. The door opened and then closed. I stuck my head around the corner and saw Ray Westview's car in the front driveway.

I leaned back against the house and concentrated all

my energies on trying to hear their conversation. But I couldn't make out a word. Only tones. Sharp tones.

Figuring I'd pressed my luck as best I could, I stepped from the house and slowly headed toward my car. About halfway there I heard a truck pull up beside me. The passenger's door opened and I climbed into Linda's cab.

"What were you doing over there?" Linda asked.

"Observing."

"You could've been observed." She pulled to the side of the street a house or two down from my car, cut the lights and engine. "Since you weren't," she continued, "what did you see?"

I let out a short laugh. "Del Westview painting."

"What?"

"Yeah, painting." I related to her the basic elements of the day. The visit by Hernandez. Tailing Del directly over here. The Mexican woman leaving. The apparent art studio in the back room. The aggressive tones I heard when Ray entered the house. My hunger.

Linda was pensive. "Here, have a Coke," she said, and handed me hers, half gone and warm.

"Thanks."

"No problem." She wasn't paying attention to me.

"You want to know what I think?" I asked her, then continued before she could respond. "I think Del is leaving Ray. I think she's setting herself up in this house to get away."

"Could be. How'd Ray get in?"

"I heard keys."

"You think he'd have a key to her house?"

"Maybe they've owned this house for a while. Rental property. Company buyout."

"Maybe." Linda kept her eyes in the rearview mirror.

"What did Westview do today?" I asked.

"Nothing but the usual corporate crap. Went to the office from home."

"On Sunday?"

"He wasn't the only one. He went to lunch with a young woman."

"Oh?"

"He's fantasizing. She won't have anything to do with him. I could tell." She gave me a sideways glance, then turned back to the mirror. Both of her hands were on the steering wheel.

He wasn't the only one who was fantasizing, but I kept it to myself.

"About two in the afternoon," she said, "the police paid him a visit, but they didn't stay long. Westview then hung at the office until he came here."

"No meetings with someone who could be Contella?"

"From what I saw, no."

"Now what?" I asked, pulling off my cap. I ran a hand through my sweaty hair.

"Here comes Ray," she said. We scooted down. "After he passes by, hop out. Hang around until it looks like Del is settled for the night, or leaves."

"All right, but you owe me dinner." I put my hat back on.

"Why don't you go to your place tonight? I don't know where I'll be. I'll call you."

"Good enough," I said. But it wasn't.

"And if tomorrow's the day for garbage pickup, steal Del Westview's trash."

"What?"

Ray Westview raced by, tires slapping water from the pavement.

"Bye," she said.

I quickly got out and, without a word, closed the door. Linda's lights didn't come on until she was rounding the block.

Trash?

The rain kept coming. My clothes were damp. I hadn't realized I'd cut my hand on the fence until now, when I felt the sting. Hunger was my middle name. I'd taken to urinating under the shadows of a pecan tree. And Linda told me to collect garbage. Ah, the glamour of detective work.

I couldn't wait to see what glory tomorrow would bring.

21

I awoke to the sound of tapping against my windshield. It wasn't rain. The clouds had broken, sky clearing. My eyes focused in on a West University cop.

I rolled down my window and, without a word, handed him my driver's license.

"What are you doing here?" he demanded.

"My car flooded last night," I replied. "I was waiting for it to dry out. Guess I fell asleep."

"You know anyone around here?"

"No. I was attempting to find my way home on dry streets."

He stared at me. "Flooding wasn't that bad," he said.

"I don't care what people say," I explained. "VWs don't float."

He stared at my cheek. I touched the scar.

"That's quite a cut. Where'd you get it?"

"Kitchen accident," I told the man. "I'm a chef. I slipped a couple of days ago. It was a freak incident."

The officer was around forty, in good shape, though not too tall. His black hair was graying. "Kitchen accident?"

"Weird, huh?"

"Unbelievable."

I forced a smile. The rest was best left unsaid. I had no desire to delve into the McDaniels investigation and further incite this cop's curiosity.

He walked over to his car and used the radio.

I glanced over at Del Westview's little ranch house. If she caught any of this activity, I was dead.

The cop returned and handed me the license.

"Try starting it," he ordered.

I tucked the wallet in my back pocket, then turned the key. The Bug whined and sputtered before kicking on.

"Mr. Marshall, go home," the cop said. "Get some rest, take a shower. You look like shit."

"Thank you, Officer."

He waited. I ground the Bug in gear and drove around him. The little house was quiet. At the end of the street I turned left, then left again, and stopped with a large live oak at my rear. In case the cop ran across me, I used Linda's trick and took out my key map. I could play the dizzy, confused artist, and most likely he'd buy it. But I figured that he wouldn't do a short block, and he didn't. He drove right by me.

I circled back. This time I parked beneath a china-berry tree, keeping the house in my rearview mirror. I wasn't planning to stay long. That cop wouldn't be as understanding the second time around. But I was hoping for some sign that Del Westview was in there. And a few minutes before seven, on this Monday morning, I received that sign.

The battered pickup from yesterday chugged into the driveway and out bounced the Mexican woman. The man waited until she was in the house, then rambled off. Not fifteen minutes later the garage door opened and Del Westview backed out her Mercedes. I cranked up my car after she passed me and gave her half a block before I followed.

As she wound her way back to Kirby, I noticed that people had their trash out. Shit, ace detective, part-time garbageman had forgotten half his job. Well, Del hadn't had trash out anyway. I didn't think.

I decided the more important mission was to keep an eye on Del Westview, though her direction seemed apparent. Then she surprised me.

At Westheimer she hooked east and made for the Avalon

Drug Store. I had given her plenty of room, so she was out of her car and inside before I reached the parking lot.

I cut the engine in the middle of the lot, next to a large blue van, and got out. The place had started at the Avalon Center as a hash-slinging diner and drugstore. For years it was an early-morning hangout for many of the high and mighty River Oaks power brokers. Probably remained so, though the Fifties atmosphere had given way to a more art-deco scene. The windows in front were glass and lighting was colorful and abundant, but from where I was, even with the binoculars, I couldn't see anything. I pulled my hat low, dipped my shoulders, and put my hands in my pockets. In a wide arch, I circled to the front of the building.

Ray and Del Westview were both in the full diner. There was a third person with them. I felt the excitement dampen my palms until I realized the third person was the big ex-boxer, Willie Burns. And it didn't look as if he'd been invited to breakfast.

Del held a hand to her mouth, her eyes wide. Ray was trying to wave Willie away, but the big man had sat at the booth on Ray's side and had him pinned in. Willie was alternately jabbing his forefinger at them both, his voice seemingly loud. I didn't need to hear the words to know what he was saying. Finally, Del jumped up and started to run off. Willie stood and grabbed her. Ray, moving surprisingly fast, yanked Willie off his wife. A big right cross sent Ray sprawling to the floor. A chill shook me; I felt that blow from here. I turned my back as the door burst open and Del raced to her car. Sirens were growing louder.

I walked back to the street. Two cop cars, one HPD, one River Oaks, screeched into the parking lot. Only in this part of town are people blessed with a two-second reaction time, I thought. The cops caught Willie at the door. He held his hands up, didn't resist. Del Westview nailed her car into the flow of traffic. I didn't bother to follow.

As I was leaving an ambulance arrived. Willie was cuffed and sitting in the backseat of the HPD car. I wondered if Ray had another shiner or a broken jaw. Del sure didn't seem to care all that much.

If Del Westview was back at her ranch house, she might be on the lookout for company. I was tired enough, though, not to give a damn. I parked two houses down on her side of the street and popped the trunk. There was something to be said for the front-end trunks on these Bugs, big enough for a couple of kitchen bags full of trash with room left over.

If anyone saw me walk up to the brown trash can, lift its tan lid, and take out the two white bags they didn't say anything. The front curtains were tightly closed at the Westviews' house. I saw no movement.

The sun was beginning to blaze, as if it had to make up for lost time. I didn't run or panic but placed the bags in the trunk, quietly closed it, dropped myself into the car, and drove off.

On the way, I stopped at McDonald's and bought eight dollars' worth of food and coffee. To go. When I reached my apartment, Jerry Jacoma was coming out of his house. His smile was weak, and he flashed a second-thought *high* sign before climbing into his truck and leaving.

The message machine blinked madly with red flashes. A couple of calls were from Susan. Another was from Candace. And one I skipped ahead to was Linda's. Her voice sounded concerned that I hadn't called her back. She told me to meet them at C. J.'s office as soon as I could.

First, I returned Linda's call and conversed with her machine. I left word that I was fine and I had a couple of presents for her. Then I called C. J.'s office. The answering service took the same message.

Finally, I telephoned Candace. Sondra Anderson answered.

"Oh, Neil, I'm so glad to hear from you."

"Thanks, Sondra. Yes, I'm fine—"

"Honey, not from the picture Keely painted."

"You know how dramatic poets are."

"Words of experience," she replied.

"Bet class isn't the same without me," I said.

"I'll say. You've become quite the topic of conversation. In fact, dear, you're beginning to scare the youngsters in our group. However, it takes more than a murder or two to shake up a crusty old broad like me."

I laughed. Sondra was old South with more style than the state of Virginia. She and I had met at a poetry fest and become fast friends from the start.

"Let me talk to 'baby' sister," I said. "She behaving herself for you and John?"

"She's a headstrong girl. Once a bee invades her bonnet, no one can squeeze a word in edgewise. Candace had her mind set on going into the city looking for you."

"Why on earth would she want to do a thing like that?"

"The girl's been worried. Neil, you haven't returned any of her calls."

"I'm glad she stayed put," I said. At the silence I added, "She did stay put, didn't she?"

"For the time being. John and I raised a couple of mavericks of our own. We hid her truck keys."

"God, that's all I'd have needed."

"I also make John go with Candace when she tends the horses. I'm afraid she might saddle Granger and ride after you."

"Christ, is she there?"

"Just a second, dear," Sondra said. "She's upstairs getting ready for work." I heard her call for Candace, and then the girl ripped into the phone.

"Where have you been, mister?" she demanded.

"Candace, I've been meaning to call—"

"Good intentions don't even count in horseshoes," she snapped.

"You're right."

"I was so worried that if I was a horse I'd have come down with cholic and died by now."

"I'm sorry, 'baby' sister—"

"Don't you 'baby' sister me. If this is how you treat your family, then—"

"Jesus, Candace, calm down."

"I've been scared."

"I've been hurt," I retorted.

"Are you all right?"

"Yes."

"Then come riding with me at the stables one day I'm not working."

"When aren't you working?"

"Thursday."

"Fine."

"And do one more thing," she said.

"What?"

"Tell Sondra to give me my keys back."

"No." And I hung up.

I took a minute to catch my breath.

Half an hour later, clean and feeling as if I'd made up for a week's worth of not running, I headed out for C. J. McDaniels's office, bearing the gift of refuse.

22

"The stupid son of a bitch did what?!" C. J. bellowed as he threw his cigarette down.

"Don't burn the office down," Linda said.

He stepped on the offending butt.

"Laid Westview out on the floor," I repeated. "Right there in front of God, power, and money. I tell you, if he'd have thrown more shots like that at Big George, Willie might've walked away with the title, after all."

"The cops grabbed him?" Linda asked. She was sitting behind her desk. The radio with its incessant country music buzzed softly in the background like a mosquito.

"They were on him so fast there was no chance for round two," I said, and sat in the wooden chair that was in front of the desk.

She nodded. "I'll check with Vic, see what the deal is."

"And Del took off?" C. J. asked.

"Never looked back," I told him.

"Why were you still there this morning?" Linda asked as she picked up the phone and punched in a number. "I told you to knock off at midnight."

"I had a gut feeling," I replied.

"You fell asleep. Didn't you?"

I sighed. I wasn't going to tell them about the cop awakening me.

Linda spoke into the phone, asked for Sergeant Hernandez. Their conversation was brief. Yes, he'd heard about the altercation. Yes, Willie Burns was being held.

193

Any decision on bail had yet to be made. Ray Westview was filing assault and harassment charges.

"Westview's scared of him," I said.

"That's his nature," added Linda.

C. J. lit a cigarette and walked over to the window. "Can't say as I blame him. Willie Burns is a nut," he muttered.

"You'd be a nut, too," Linda said, "if your sister turned up dead and her baby missing."

"Missing baby, all right," C. J. told her. "We can't even track down where she had it. No birth record. No matching blood types. No name. Nothing."

"Could've gone out of town," Linda offered.

"We're looking."

"Or had it at home," I added.

C. J. flicked the ashes on the floor, turned around. "That'd be my bet."

The window-unit air conditioner hummed and ruffled the white plastic of the two trash bags that rested beneath it. They were still unopened.

Linda smiled. "He's pleased with your hunches," she told me. "Your question about the dead man's work, the one Contella lifted the driver's license number from, played out. C. J. dug. The man was an engineer for Bedford Oil."

"Bedford Oil!" I said. "I don't believe it." What I meant was that we deserved a break.

"So we've linked Contella directly to the company," Linda said.

"The company's being used," C. J. spoke up, "and Caulfield Bedford knows it. He's locked himself inside a library with no books, only art objects he says have stories of their own. The halls reek of bleach and ammonia, and he regrets never having shot his son-in-law, Ray Westview."

"That good, huh?" Linda asked.

"Skin pale as his white hair. Liver spots on cheeks and hands. The old man's waiting to die."

"I'm sorry, C. J."

"Hell, it's taken that son of a bitch a long time to die, and he's scared. Not for himself, but—"

"So Bedford's out," Linda interrupted, "and we've tied Contella to Ray Westview." She sat stiffly.

"Watch your attitude, girl. If anything, Westview lied to me about not knowing Contella," C. J. added.

"I swear, Contella's a shadow," I tossed in.

"A very clever one, Neil," C. J. said, and paused. "Linda filled me in about the West U house. I want you to tell me about it. Slowly. Don't leave anything out."

I repeated what I'd told Linda.

"There's nothing else?" he asked.

I shook my head.

"So you think Del's moving out?"

"Seems obvious to me," I stated. "I think something that Ray's sunk his pudgy paws in has frightened her."

"More speculation," C. J. grumbled. "Don't get carried away."

My cheeks reddened.

"Hey, you wanted his hunches," Linda spoke out.

C. J. said nothing.

"Someone has frightened her," Linda continued. "At the least it's Willie Burns. And now that she's scared, who do you think she's going to call?" She looked at her father.

"Never has before," he responded.

"She's wanted to."

"Is that female intuition?" he asked.

"Yes."

"Keep it to yourself."

"She'll call, invite you over to her little den."

"Linda Marie," he growled. C. J. stubbed his cigarette out in the ashtray.

"She's been dying to call you, been looking for a reason. Now it's perfect, especially with her breaking away from her marriage. She's going to need someone else to take care of her."

"Why don't you can it?" he told his daughter.

"And you think *I'm* being stupid."

C. J. McDaniels narrowed his eyes. "Watch it, girl."

"No, you watch it. I don't think she's the victim everyone says she is."

"More goddamn female intuition?"

"I know you're in danger, but you're too pigheaded to see it."

For a moment there was only the low muttering of the radio and the sound of the air conditioner vibrating against the tension in the air.

I cleared my throat and stood. "What about these nifty little prizes I brought home," I said, and toed one of the white bags. There was the sound of Styrofoam crinkling, cans bumping each other, and bottles rattling.

"Admit it, C. J., you love her," Linda said, and jumped up, knocking the chair back against the wall.

"What's your goddamn problem?"

"Same old shit. Do as I say, not as I do."

"You been drinking?" C. J. barked. His eyes were wide and he leaned toward Linda, hands in fists at each side.

"No, have you?" Linda asked, not backing down an inch, pointing at him with a forefinger. "You're acting with as much common sense as a drunkard."

"All I've done is given my word."

"Who to?"

"To Caulfield Bedford, if it's any of your goddamn business. I promised to help Del—"

"You've always loved her."

"I don't need this bullshit. I don't need to rehash your mother's death again."

"This doesn't have anything to do with Mom."

"Like hell it doesn't. I'm so sick of you feeling sorry for yourself—"

"Go to hell!" Linda cried. "Go to Del Westview!"

C. J. began to speak, then caught himself and turned. Before he could leave, however, I picked up one of the trash bags and dropped it on the desk. It clattered and clanked. The broken glass and metallic rattling caught their attention. They both glared at me. The looks said they'd forgotten I was here and were angry they'd been made to remember.

"Enough of this shit," I said, feigning irritation. Actually, I was afraid they were going to expend their frustrations by beating the crap out of me. "We finally get a break with the Contella link and you two are acting like—" I cut myself off, hoping I hadn't gone too far.

"Neil," C. J. warned.

Linda folded her arms across her chest. The fire coming from her eyes was hot enough to vaporize a man's soul.

"Argue later," I commanded. "There's work to do." I ripped open the bag and poured the contents onto the desk.

C. J. tucked another cigarette in his mouth. "Fuck wor—"

We all stopped.

The three of us stood around the bag of trash and stared at can upon empty can of baby formula.

23

C. J. McDaniels clicked open his brass lighter and lit his cigarette. I wondered if I wore the same shocked look that he and Linda did.

"Oh, God," Linda softly said. She picked up one of the pink cans with white lettering. There was a sprinkling of coffee grounds on it.

"It's worse than I thought," McDaniels said more to himself than anyone else.

I caught his daughter's eye. There was none of the I-told-you-so in her expression toward C. J. It was almost apologetic. A minute ago he was ready to slap the shit out of her.

"Now what?" I asked.

"I wait for Del to call me," McDaniels said. "Linda's right. Del will call." Cigarette smoke slid into the air with each word he said.

Linda went to the filing cabinet and took out a box of clear plastic gloves, the kind food servers use. She handed a pair to me and said, "Watch out for glass and sharp objects like can tops. Go slow."

"Y'all do lead a romantic life," I mumbled, slipping on the gloves.

"You know it," she replied.

C. J. watched carefully. We worked deliberately with no one saying much of anything. Besides the usual kitchen trash and the cans of empty baby formula, there was an empty fifth of Scotch, six beer bottles, and five Diet Coke cans. There were envelopes from the light company, the gas company, and AT&T, but no statements or receipts. Two notes were handwritten, one a grocery list and one a partially legible set of instructions to Esmerelda, presumably the maid.

"No diapers," Linda commented.

C. J. kicked the other bag. "Bet you."

"You open it, Neil," Linda said.

C. J. forced a smile. A leaden feeling pulled at me. I sensed the weight of the years, like burned-out stars, fall cold and hard. I obeyed, and the odor confirmed suspicions before we looked.

"Well, dig in," he told us.

I started first, then Linda grudgingly followed. Disposable diapers, baby powder, baby wipes, a bottle of laundry detergent, an empty can of Diet Coke, and an empty bottle of beer.

We peeled off our gloves, tossed them out, and I quickly tied the bag then set it outside the office in the hall.

"Pauline Burns's baby is in that house," I said, and shut the door behind myself. "Del Westview has it."

"Pointing that way," C. J. answered. He crushed out his cigarette.

"Pointing that way, hell," Linda said. "Goddamn lightning's struck."

I want your baby. I recalled Del's whisper to C. J.

"Why else be so secretive about a kid?" Linda asked. "They could've claimed to have adopted it."

"Unless someone's causing them problems," C. J. said.

Linda brightened. "Like Sam Contella?"

"Or Willie Burns."

"But why wouldn't Contella take Willie out?" I asked. "He seems to be good at it."

"You're getting way ahead of yourself," McDaniels said. "You're assuming that Contella was in on some kind of conspiracy with the Westviews, that he killed Pauline Burns, and that he's still around or on friendly terms with them. All we know for sure is that Contella has circumstantial ties to Ray Westview, the Burns woman was found dead in a house Contella owned, she had a baby we can't account for—"

"And Del Westview's trash at a hideaway house is full of baby formula cans," I cut in.

C. J. drew a deep breath. "I know."

Your baby, I remembered she said. When was that? *I've always wanted your baby.* Galveston?

Which one of the Westviews couldn't have kids and which one of them resented it? I wondered.

"You're thinking blackmail, aren't you?" Linda offered.

C. J. focused on Linda. "There's a shitload of money involved and that dummy company reeks of something," he responded.

I scratched at my scruffy beard. It wasn't nearly thick enough to hide the scar. Yet.

C. J. continued, his voice deep, controlled. "Neil, it'd be taking a hell of a chance to kill both Pauline and her brother and get away with it. Cops don't believe in coincidences."

"Then, since Willie's so volatile, you wait for him to do something stupid you can send him back to jail for," I said.

"Yep," McDaniels grumbled. "People always do stupid things, make stupid promises."

He was getting out another cigarette when the phone rang.

Linda answered, no expression on her face. Without a word she handed the receiver to McDaniels.

"Yeah?"

McDaniels listened.

"What do you want me to do, Del?" The cigarette bobbed between his lips. He thumbed the lighter, squinted through the thin lines of smoke that began to rise.

"Slow down," he snapped, "slow down. Okay, what? Where? Then I'll name it. The Ale House on Alabama. Fine. Half an hour." He hung up.

"Any questions?" C. J. asked.

"You want me to call Hernandez?" Linda replied. She

sat in the chair behind the desk, her legs crossed at the knees, and faced the window on the Montrose side.

"No."

"C. J.?"

"I'm going to get Del's story first."

"Which one?"

"I'll know if she's telling the truth," McDaniels told his daughter. "Then we go from there."

"You might be playing this hand one round too many," Linda said, and swiveled the chair around to him.

McDaniels stood, jerked open the top desk drawer, and took out his gun. It was in a brown leather holster, and he tucked it against the small of his back, under his short-sleeved shirt. There was a mist of sweat on his balding head.

"You two hold down the fort," he said. "I'll call. Give me about an hour."

"An hour before what?" I asked.

C. J. smirked. "Before you think I'm too old to take care of myself."

He left the room.

As he went down the stairs, Linda called after him, "Christ, a public place won't protect you from getting burned by an old flame."

I heard the bottom door slam. Linda stared at me.

We would follow.

24

As soon as C. J. left the office, Linda checked her gun, then slid it into her purse.

"You don't think we're going to do what he says, do you?" she asked. Her sunglasses were pushed up on her head like a hairband.

"Be rather foolish at this point," I replied, and followed her out the door.

"We'll both go in my truck."

"Let me get my shades."

"Hurry up."

I had no shades. Instead, I unlocked the passenger's side of my car, slipped my hand under the seat, and ripped free the .25 that had been taped to its bottom. Palming the small gun, I shoved it into the front pocket of my jeans. Linda was putting off some strong vibes, and I was determined not to go into another confrontation butt-naked unarmed. As I jogged over to the truck, I shook my head, then explained I must've left my sunglasses at my apartment.

We found C. J.'s Mustang parked on the east side of The Ale House. Linda set up watch down the street a little ways in the parking lot of an empty building. Not many people used the front door of the pub, and our view into the back lot where most customers parked was obstructed, but C. J.'s car was directly in sight.

Linda had moved her sunglasses down to the bridge of her nose, and she sat silently, staring at the pub.

"What are you afraid of?" I asked.

"Besides the obvious?"

"Yes," I said, though I wasn't sure what the obvious was.

"Bad judgment."

"I don't think—"

"You don't know!" she snapped.

"Fine." I put my hands up, palms to her.

Linda released a deep breath. "Neil, I'm sorry. I haven't been this wound up since I quit smoking."

"You smoked?"

"Five heavy years," Linda said. She let out a short laugh. "No, make that all my life if you consider second-hand smoke."

"You're so health-conscious, I wouldn't have guessed."

"It's been almost five since I quit. And I still want a cigarette."

I knew she glanced at me by the way she moved her head, but I couldn't see her dark eyes behind her dark glasses.

"Believe me, I understand," I told her. "Just over six months since I've quit."

"You're a hell of a lot calmer than I am."

Then talking to Candace must have taken the edge off me, I thought. And we waited. The sun might as well have been made of sand, each grain falling as a lazy minute. Not ten grains later, Linda said, "Why don't you slip inside and peek at what's going on?"

Her impatience caught me off guard. Not to mention that she wanted me, and not her, to go into the pub.

"Think that's wise?" I asked.

"I'm not sure sitting here is wise, either," Linda replied. "What if they duck out the back and take her car?"

"I can't imagine—"

"Just do it, Neil."

"Okay," I said, and hopped out. "Don't leave me here."

What did I bring out in women, I wondered, to make them all snap at me at the same time? A short time ago Candace. Now Linda. Of course, they received a reaction.

Yeah, I thought as I crossed the street. Desired reactions. So whose damn fault was that?

I completely circled the pub and entered through the back door where I was less likely to be noticed. Despite the midday sun the inside was dark, and I edged toward the rest rooms while waiting for my eyes to adjust. When they did, I focused in on the large, exposed beams that hung above me, then the weathered wood floor I stood on. On the walls were pictures of royalty, noblemen, references to English history, and portraits of men on horseback. McDaniels was at a small table near the dartboards. No one was playing darts at this time of day. Mostly the lunch crowd was young executives, both male and female.

Standing next to McDaniels's table was Del Westview. She appeared animated. C. J., on the other hand, simply shook his head a couple of times and sipped on a beer. There were plenty of tables around them that were empty, but I could only occupy one, a high-backed booth by a front window, without being seen and still have half a chance of hearing what was going on. When Del sat down, I eased to the bar, ordered a beer, then casually sauntered over to the booth.

"Who's following you?" I heard C. J. ask.

"That crazy man. You know, the fighter you chased out of my house. He insists I knew where his sister is or some such thing."

"Stop lying to me, Del."

"How dare you?" she replied. "That man is out to get me."

"He knows where his sister is," C. J. informed her.

A waitress approached and asked if I wanted a lunch menu. I took it for show. C. J.'s voice was soft, but Del's was loud and bordering on hysterical.

"He does?" Del yipped.

"She's in the morgue. Someone took a gun and blew half her head off."

"Oh, my God. That's awful."

"But you knew that she was dead," C. J. continued. "Willie Burns told you this morning."

"What the hell are you talking about?"

"You know, when Willie knocked Ray silly at the Avalon Drug Store."

"Did what to Ray?"

"Stop playing games with me, Del."

"Don't yell at me! I don't know what you're talking about. I didn't know what that crazy man was saying, either. He was raving about this and that and how he was going to get even and kill both of us. I was terrified. And he grabbed me. When he let go, I ran."

The waitress returned. "Made up your mind?"

"Not quite," I answered softly. She smiled and left.

I sipped my beer and leaned back. I had to strain to hear C. J. say, "The doctor's office, probably. Willie hit him damn hard."

"I had no idea," Del cried. "I mean, I ran. I just drove around and around until finally I went home to look for him. That's when the crazy man began following me."

"Are you still telling me you're being followed?" C. J. demanded, voice loud for once.

"Yes, yes!"

"It can't be Willie Burns. He's sitting down in the holding tank as we speak."

"Then who?" Her voice shrilled, and I noticed that I wasn't the only person privy to their conversation. My only regret was that I couldn't see their faces.

"How about Sam Contella?" C. J. asked.

"Who?"

"You tell me."

"I've never heard of him."

"You didn't tell me that Pauline Burns was pregnant."

With my menu down, the waitress reappeared. Before she could speak, however, I waved her away. I'd leave her a generous tip, but damn it, I didn't want to miss anything.

"You didn't know?" I heard C. J. say.

"I didn't know it was of any importance," she snapped. "If you remember correctly, that crazy man first pounded on my door the day you were there. It scared me. I didn't know where his sister went. And the last thing I was going to tell him was that wherever she'd gone she'd most likely had a baby. That bit of information would've sent him into a rage.

"I mean," Del continued, "I told the girl she could stay with us until she got on her feet. She chose not to. Never explained, dear C. J. One day she just up and left. Please believe me."

"I don't."

"Why are you treating me like a criminal! I haven't done anything. All I've ever wanted to do was paint."

"And have my baby."

I heard a glass break against their table. Del said something, but for once her voice was low, and the coldness chilled even a Houston summer.

A chair scraped against the floor. "Come on," C. J. said. "Let's get out of here."

"I don't know if I want to go anywhere with you."

"We're going to find out who's following you," he said softly.

There was a stretch of silence. Then Del said, "Yes, maybe that's a good idea. Yes."

I caught sight of them leaving, tossed down a five for a tip, and followed once they exited through the back.

A familiar Mercedes appeared from the narrow street on the west side of the pub and turned west. I dashed around the pub. Linda spotted me and gunned the truck to pick me up. First thing I grabbed the binoculars and read the license plate, caught the River Oaks logo beneath the letters.

"That's Del Westview's car," I said.

"Are you sure?"

It moved north on Kirby, out of sight.

"Positive. They left together. Is C. J.'s truck still on the other side?"

"Yes."

"How many people in the car?" Linda asked, starting the truck.

"The back window's too dark, but I think only the two of them." The question caught me off guard. It hadn't occurred to me that someone might've been waiting for them. Or him.

"It looks like they're heading to the River Oaks house," she said, forcing her way into traffic on Kirby.

"What happened in the pub?" she asked. "How much beer did he have?"

"One lager, that I noticed," I replied. "And C. J. pushed Del's buttons, asking about Willie hitting Ray, Pauline's pregnancy and disappearance, and Sam Contella." I purposefully left out the bit about Del wanting to have C. J.'s baby.

"And the response?"

"Evasive. Semihysterical. Weird."

"And you're sure they went off together, and he didn't just walk Del to her car?"

"Yes," I replied, though she was placing the seed of doubt in my mind.

"And up yonder is Del's car?"

"It's the same one I've been following around," I responded. But she'd smacked my confidence enough that I put the binoculars back to my eyes.

"Where'd it go?" I asked.

Linda was just as confused. "Shit."

She punched her truck through a caution light at Westheimer and sped through traffic, hitting a green light at San Jacinto. There was nothing shy about her pace.

A quarter mile up she said, "They didn't come this way. We'd have caught them by now."

"The way you're driving, I agree."

As soon as she could, Linda pulled a hard U-turn. The tires whined about the treatment. I hoped no cops were around.

"Back to the pub?" I tried to joke.

"No way."

"What do your instincts say?"

"Semihysterical?" she said, her mind on the conversation. "What does that mean?"

"Going over the edge."

"Great."

This time we sat at the light at Westheimer. I scanned the area with the binoculars. No luck.

"It's like she knew she was being followed," I said.

"You're right. They had to have made the block on one of those little streets."

"Or gone east on Westheimer."

"Even then I think we would've seen them."

"You shot through that first light," I said. "I don't know." I continued to scan. We began to move.

"Say she did go east. Why?" Linda asked.

I lowered the glasses. "To double back," I answered.

"Exactly."

Traffic was thick at the intersection of the Southwest Freeway. Once we broke through, though, we sailed. Linda kept a quick pace and every two or three blocks I felt her tone it down. We didn't want to attract unwanted attention. I saw no sign of the Mercedes through the binoculars, so, by the time we reached University Boulevard, I gave up on the glasses. We knew where they were going.

With our silence, Linda's tension again mounted. It wasn't anything she did. It was the energy I felt. I wanted to touch her arm, rub her shoulders, but I was afraid she'd jump like a firing gun.

Of course, I might've been placing my feelings onto Linda. By the time we hit Del Westview's quiet street, my palms were slick and my shirt was soaked in sweat despite the air-conditioning in the truck being on. Full blast. My heart was pounding black spots against the backs of my eyeballs and my legs felt as if they'd never lifted me in my life. It was that run in the park all over again.

Linda stopped beside a large live oak tree a couple of houses from the powder blue ranch and Del's black Mercedes. The car took up the middle portion of the driveway.

"She parked in the garage yesterday," I commented.

"Really?"

"The only time I saw her was when I peeked in the window."

No sooner had we arrived than the maid left the house and started walking down the street.

"And that's strange," I said.

"What?"

"The maid usually has a ride. A man I took to be her husband picked her up yesterday and dropped her off this morning."

"What are you saying, Neil?"

The old Mexican woman walked by us without so much as a glance.

"It seemed to me they had a routine going."

"And now they've broken it," Linda added.

"The maid's taking the bus."

"Dismissed early?" Linda said, paused, then leaned forward on the steering wheel. "I knew it."

Heading in from the other end of the street, and parking behind the Mercedes, was Ray Westview. Slowly, he climbed out of the car and lumbered up the driveway.

Linda opened her door. "Call Hernandez. Call Gardner. Punch in 911 if you have to, but get the cops over here."

"What are you doing?"

She pulled out her gun.

"And stay here," she added.

Before I could say anything else, Linda hit the street in quick, long strides. The gun was at her hip. Ray Westview was halfway to the front door.

But I knew the hard, scraping sound of Linda's boots against pavement was going to give her away.

25

Ray Westview stumbled as he looked back over his shoulder. The moment or two it took him to recognize Linda was all she needed. Time hung as heavy in the air as the echoing sound of her boot heels. He just stared.

Until he saw the gun.

Then he surprised us both. I had Linda's car phone in hand, trying to get through to Lieutenant Gardner, when Linda caught Westview. She held the gun at her side and pointed the barrel at him. He staggered, hesitated until Linda approached him. Suddenly, like a cornered bear, he turned and swiped at her with one of his thick hands. The right cross hit Linda square in the face and sent her sprawling to the ground. The gun flew deep into the grass.

Linda brought herself to her knees as Westview picked up the revolver. Then he grabbed her by the hair and lifted Linda to her feet. She started to swing at him, but Westview put the gun to Linda's head, then shoved her into the house.

Anger fought its way from my clenched fists to my grinding teeth. I was going to kill him.

Gardner wasn't there, so I quickly told the woman on the other end of the line who I was, whom I was with, and where I was. And I described what had just happened. She flatly told me to slow down, but I simply repeated the address, said it was an emergency, and hung up.

I jumped out of the truck, quietly closed the door, and zigzagged my way to the house. The little .25 had flakes of black tape on it, and I was peeling the sticky stuff off while I ran. I swung to the far side of the cars and came up by the garage. God knew what I was going to do, and I strained so hard listening for sirens that my head hurt.

All was quiet but my heart. The sun washed me with sweat. Hunched over, I crept past one of the curtained windows to the front door. It was slightly ajar. I could hear voices.

"You didn't have to hit C. J.'s baby," Del Westview said.

"Goddamn it, she was pointing a gun at me."

"I'm surprised you could see it."

"What does that mean?" Westview asked his wife.

"You spend so much time inside the bottle it's pitiful," Del told him. "And look at that damn bruise on your face. You have no fight in you. Give me the gun before you hurt someone."

"Me hurt someone? That's funny coming from you."

"Ray," C. J. said, "let me have the gun."

"Take one more step, McDaniels, and I'll finish the job."

"Why'd you send those two thugs after me, Ray? What were you afraid I was going to find? I only took the case to pacify the old man, Ray, and to needle you."

"Ray's business sense is simply amazing," said Del.

"Shut up!"

"Don't tell me to shut up."

"Those two idiots weren't supposed to do anything but follow you. Then they get it in mind that they're going to kill you and blackmail me, say I put a hit out on you if I don't pay them. Assholes didn't even know my real name. But you did me a favor on that score, McDaniels, by taking them out."

I inched the door open. There was a little entryway. I could hear them in the room to my left. A baby started to cry.

"Don't pick him up," Ray barked. "Goddamn it, Del, that kid can't whimper without you mothering it to death. He's going to grow up spoiled."

"He's going to grow up strong," she said.

"Not the way you're treating him."

She didn't respond.

"McDaniels, don't move," he ordered. I heard the gun cock. "Good, that's better."

I listened for, but didn't hear, Linda. The thought that Westview might've hit her again caused the resurging anger to pound through my veins.

The baby stopped crying.

"What are we going to do with these two?" Westview asked.

"I know what we should do," Del replied.

I edged to the doorway. The front room opened onto the back. Del slowly walked from one to the other, carrying the baby. Ray had his back to me about twenty feet away. There was a standing lamp and a large, cushioned chair between us. I couldn't see Linda or C. J.

"Pretty baby," C. J. said.

"McDaniels!"

"I only want to look at the baby," C. J. said, and approached Del. "Pauline Burns sure must've been proud," he added.

"Oh, yes," Del told him. "Too proud."

I was about to take on Westview when I heard Linda.

"Did you give Pauline a little beating, too, before you killed her?" she asked.

"Listen, you little bitch," he said, and moved out of view, "the only place I worked that girl over was in bed."

I was crouched low, and I leaned my back flat against the wall.

"Yes, Ray's very proud of that," Del said, her voice soothing and high-pitched. "He was finally able to father a baby."

"I see," said C. J. "Did Pauline have a choice in the matter?"

"She was well paid, very well paid," Westview stated.

"That was the deal," Del purred. "But then she didn't want to live up to her end, and we couldn't have that. No, we couldn't."

I spied around the corner. Ray was still out of sight. Del was talking to the baby.

"All right, McDaniels, that's enough looking," Westview announced. "Get back over by your kid."

Slowly C. J. walked to the front part of the room.

"So you had Sam Contella do your dirty work and kill Pauline Burns," C. J. said.

Del laughed. "He couldn't kill time."

"She thinks she's making a joke," Ray said. "There is no Sam Contella. That was a name I used to set up the Burns girl and to funnel—" He stopped.

"Go ahead and tell him," Del said. "It doesn't matter."

"I've been stashing money out of the country."

"The old man was right," said C. J. "And Mark Hill."

"Poor Mark," Del said. "Now, there was a man. Much like you, C. J. If he'd only had a stronger heart."

"So it was his heart."

"I didn't lie about that," Del told him.

"What did you lie about?"

"I knew where Pauline Burns was. I left her there. Poor child, but she shouldn't have tried to keep little Cory."

"His name's not Cory," Ray growled.

"We'll see." Del Westview disappeared into the back room.

"You killed Pauline Burns?" Linda said.

"It was very easy," Del replied. "I drove her to that house and shot her. I didn't like her."

Del came back into view. The baby was gone. She was holding a gun.

"The police know about this house," C. J. said. "They know about the baby. Give it up."

"Give it up?!" she cried. "After all I've been through. C. J., you know me better than that. I'm not going to give it up. I'm going to leave town."

"That's right, we are," blurted Westview. "I've got it all planned."

"Plans—your plans!" Del snapped. "It was the same way with our wedding, wasn't it? *Your* plans."

"Shut up."

"You didn't know it, C. J.," she continued, "but I was carrying your baby. In Galveston. I was so scared."

"Oh, Christ," C. J. said. "Why—"

"I tried to tell you, but I couldn't."

"Shut the fuck up, Del!"

"Goddamn you, Ray! The only way I could marry you was to have an abortion."

"I never said that."

"You did, you son of a bitch! You said you would never raise his child."

"I told you I'd take care of you!" Westview said.

"And Daddy would never find out."

"He never did," Westview stated.

"So I went down to Mexico—"

"And I paid for it—"

"And I lost all chances of ever bearing children. You took care of me, all right."

"I protected you." Westview staggered toward her.

"You protected your own interests, your own investment."

"We have a lot of money. We had a good plan. I mean, have a good plan. Now, don't you want to leave?"

"Yes, I want to leave!" she screamed. "Alone."

She raised the gun and fired two deafening shots. I stood quickly, nearly blacked out.

"Oh, my God," Linda said.

I turned the corner, my small gun out. Shaking.

C. J. was bent over Ray's massive, blood-soaked body. Westview was on his back; the shots had gone into his chest. C. J.'s hand was pressing against the man's throat.

"He's dead," he announced. As he stood, he noticed me.

"I hated that son of a bitch," Del said, staring at him. "I hated him for what he did to me. I don't need him anymore. I left town a long time ago and made my mistake by coming back. This time I'm going to do it right."

The baby started crying.

"You're not going to come with me, are you, C. J.?" she asked.

"Del, put the gun down. The baby needs you."

"It could've been our baby," she said.

"Del, the baby needs you."

"I hate you, too, C. J. I hate you for taking me home. You should've left me in Galveston. You should've made me stay with you."

C. J. cautiously stepped toward Del. Linda backed away from Ray's body, away from Del's line of fire. The side of Linda's face was swollen.

"I didn't force you," C. J. said.

"Yes, you did. You forced me to go away."

"I asked you to move in with me, remember?"

"You wouldn't commit," she said.

"I tried."

"No, you didn't. You ran off with that Mexican woman."

"That was years later." Ever so slowly he moved. Del was still holding the gun out in front of her. I had her in my sight. It seemed she didn't even know I was here.

"I love you, C. J."

"Del, the baby's crying. Put the gun down."

"Did you hear me, C. J.? I said I love you."

"Put the gun down. Get the baby."

C. J. was halfway across the room. He put a hand against his lower back.

"But I hate Karla," she said, and looked at Linda. "Karla, I hate you. I'm sorry I have to do this, C. J. But Karla died."

C. J. stepped in her way, paused.

"Don't do this, darling. I have to get little Cory. He's crying."

"Give me the gun." He stretched a hand out, though he was well out of reach. His other hand was still behind his back.

"No, I can't. Daddy will get me out of the country. I have the baby. All I won't have is you."

"Del," C. J. said, reaching.

"I never had you."

"Del?"

"And I don't want you now. Damn, I knew this was going to be hard."

"Drop it," I said loudly.

Startled, Del Westview swung the gun in my direction and fired. Her eyes were wide and fierce.

I felt the impact on my right shoulder. It knocked me back, and I twisted to the floor.

Linda yelled, "No!"

Something was happening to me. My mind was spinning. I smelled wood, tasted copper. My shoulder was wet. There was a trickling. The baby was screaming. Storm clouds of pain began blocking out light. The front door pounded open. Scuffling. I wondered if I was dying.

I heard two more shots before everything went black.

26

The hospital was a mass of groggy, dull, heavy aching pain. No, the hospital wasn't. I was. I was in the hospital waking up, or trying to. There was a bandage wrapped around my shoulder and chest and an IV stuck in my arm that weighed me to the bed. Bright sun illuminated the closed blinds, but I felt cold. I felt alone. After a blink or two, I strained to bring the room into focus.

I had been dreaming. I was jogging. Alone at first, then Susan was there, on Allen Parkway, above the bayou. She came up to hug me. Only she was jogging, too. I'd never known her to exercise a day in her life. Instead of hugging, though, she smiled, grabbed my T-shirt, and began ripping it. I stopped, dumbfounded, and did nothing as she completely tore off the front. The material, clutched in her hand, trembled like a pennant in the wind. A pennant the color of the gray sky. She then pointed at a small, red hole deep in my right shoulder. Perfectly round. Maroon dried blood was a rim. She dug at it. A scarlet fingernail sent jolts of pain into me as if a burr shuttled through my veins. I caught her wrist and pushed her from me. Her look was pure shock. Fair face turning flush. How could I? She stood, blonde hair tussled, green eyes glaring. I backed up, stumbled. Then she was gone. I was alone. Suddenly on my back. The hard, painful run left my body through thick breathing and cold sweat. I stared at the bright, milky sky.

A hand stroked my face.

"You've had a tough week," Linda softly told me.

I forced a smile. She was blurry. "Are you okay?" I asked weakly, then cleared my throat and repeated myself. I wanted to reach up and touch her face, but my arm wouldn't let me.

"I'm fine."

"What time is it?"

"Ten o'clock, Wednesday morning. You've been out for almost two days."

"Am I still in one piece?" I asked.

"Yes, darling."

Linda was running her hand through my hair. Her caress felt good. I closed my eyes.

"I've never been shot before," I said absently.

"I know," she said, and kissed me. "And let's hope you never are again."

"Yes," I agreed, but I felt a coldness, a strange aloneness under her warm touch as I fell back asleep.

Long shadows covered the room when I awoke again. This time I heard a mingling of voices.

"What is this, happy hour?" I asked. "Can't you let a guy get some rest?"

"Oh, you're sounding better," said Linda.

I was able to bring her into focus. Linda sat beside me, took my hand. There was something different from the last time I'd seen her. She'd changed into a rust-colored shirt.

"Neil!" a young woman yelped. And suddenly Candace Littlefield about jumped on top of me.

"You've had a lot of visitors," Linda muttered.

"You big idiot," Candace snapped, "you'll do anything to get out of riding horses."

It took tremendous effort, but I patted Candace on the cheek. Her auburn hair tickled my face, and her green eyes bored into me.

"You know me and horses," I said. "Twelve hundred pounds of stupid."

"Which one?"

"Oh, Candace, give the boy some room," Sondra Anderson said.

Candace straightened, though she kept a hand on my shoulder. She stood opposite Linda, who continued to hold my hand.

Sondra bent down and pecked my cheek. "Dear, this is the first time we've been able to visit, and it wasn't really planned. I mean, well, Candace woke up after having a dream about you and rushed over to the university to get me. Funny, John and I had just given her back her truck keys. Keely came, too, though I don't know where she ran off to."

"Keely?" I asked.

"Right in the middle of class," Sondra said.

I felt Linda squeeze my hand.

"What was your dream, 'baby' sister?" I asked.

"Nothing," she quickly replied. "It was silly."

"I died, huh? Oh, ye of little faith."

"I ain't never seen faith stop a bullet," Candace quipped. "And you've been lucky twice."

I only smiled as I was beginning to feel weak.

"Maybe it's time to go," Linda said. "Neil needs his rest."

I caught Candace's glare. "Have you met Linda?" I asked.

"Yes."

"I'll be fine—" I started to say, when Keely walked in. The tugs at my heart went lovely, dark, and deep. But she, and I now, had promises . . .

"I finally reached your mother," Keely informed me.

"You what?" asked Linda. "I told you I'd take care of that."

"I felt she should know," Keely replied. "I tracked down Robbie Persons and he had her number."

"No one called Mom?" I asked.

"She's coming in on the first flight she can book."

"I didn't want to worry the woman unnecessarily," Linda said. "Did you tell her that Neil's okay?"

"I told her the truth."

"Well, dear, now you can call back and let her know he's pulled out of the coma."

"I think we best go," Sondra piped up. "Neil needs his rest."

"I think that's a good idea," said Linda.

Candace sighed, then kissed me on the cheek. "You still owe me an outing on the horses."

"You got it, kid."

Sondra also pecked me again. "I've got this poem I'm dying for you to read," she said. "Get well so you can return to class."

"Yes, ma'am."

Now it was Keely's turn. She stared hard at me with those light brown eyes.

"Guess I failed the course, didn't I?" I asked.

For a moment Keely said nothing, then suddenly she leaned down, put my face between her hands, softly announced, "Like hell, babe," and kissed me hard on the mouth.

It was sweet and good, but I felt Linda was going to rip my hand off. She carries a gun, I wanted to tell Keely. Then she broke, and without a word, marched out the door with Candace and Sondra following.

Jesus, I thought.

"Jesus, you're going to wrench off my hand," I told Linda.

"Who was she?" she asked.

"A good friend. Oh, for Christ's sake, she's married."

"So were you."

Then in walked C. J. with Lieutenant Gardner. I was saved. They stood at the foot of the bed.

"You're a popular guy," Gardner stated. "People have been in and out of these doors."

"Like who?"

"A couple of guys from your catering company."

"Robbie and Perry," I mumbled. "Anyone else?"

"Only your ex-wife," Linda spoke up. "How'd you ever get hooked up with her? She's a piece of work."

"My kind of luck."

"Well, your luck's changing," Linda stated.

Is it? I wondered, glancing at the tubes and bandages. I thought of Keely's kiss and smiled. "What did Susan want?"

"She was *distraught* about your *condition* and the way you've *totally lost control of your life.* By the way, *Who was I?*"

"What did you say?"

"Your lover. *Oh,* she said, and left."

I should have found the incident amusing, but I didn't. It struck a deep part of my mind, an echo finally coming back. *Goodbye, Susan.*

C. J. coughed. "Son, I guess I owe you another one."

"You don't owe me," I started to say, then caught the look in his eyes. Today, the game face wasn't hiding the deep sorrow. At least not from me.

"What happened after I blacked out?" I asked.

"You didn't leave a very coherent message," Lieutenant Gardner spoke up.

"I did the best I could, considering I was ready to piss my pants."

"Del shot at you twice," C. J. explained. "She tore you up with that first bullet but missed with the second as you went down." He paused. It was as if the heaviness in my body had suddenly spread across the room.

"I shot her," he said. "I had the .38 out from the small of my back before she had the second round off, but she wouldn't listen. She was going to fire a third volley at you. If I'd been younger, if my side hadn't been busted up, I'd have rushed her. I had no choice. Point-blank range. She died before she hit the floor."

"So it's me who owes you," I said.

"She'd have killed Linda and me before I could've gotten the gun out if you hadn't hollered."

"What business did you have going in there unarmed?" Gardner asked. "Then calling attention to yourself?"

I glanced at C. J. His poker face was on. The little .25 had been in my hand. I said nothing about it. Later I would learn that Linda had taken it from me as the police arrived and as Del Westview collapsed to the floor.

"I had to do something," I told the officer.

"The jury's still out on whether you're very brave or very stupid," he said.

"What about the baby?" I asked.

"Willie Burns wants it," C. J. replied, "but Child Protective Services and the courts aren't jumping up and down to give a baby to a hotheaded ex-con. Right now the baby's in a foster home."

I thought about it for a minute. That poor child wasn't a year old and already had two dead mothers. Now, what did Del call him? Cory?

"What's going to happen to Willie?" I asked.

"I put in a word for him," C. J. told me, "for what it's worth. Under the circumstances, he'll probably get another chance as long as he stays in touch with his parole officer.

"As for Caulfield Bedford," he continued, "the company's a mess. There's almost two million bucks that they can't account for. No one's sure where it is."

"Ray's stash?"

"Damn straight. Apparently the cash was laundered out of the country through the dummy company. I reckon that's why Westview set up the front to begin with. Then it came in handy to hide Pauline while she had her baby. Then to cover up her murder."

"But why steal from a company you're going to inherit?" I asked.

"Bedford was working to oust Ray, and he knew it. I reason Westview was determined to get what he figured was owed to him while he could."

"Swiss bank account?"

"My bet would be South America. Argentina, maybe. Easier to make like you're doing oil business with them."

"The old man's been hospitalized," Lieutenant Gardner added, staring at me. I expected him to pop off with some crass comment on the state of old men in my presence. But he didn't. Instead he said, "It's all been too much for him."

I sort of nodded. It wasn't the missing money or the scandal in the company that was doing him in, I thought. And I bet C. J., because of his past relationship with the family, personally took on the burden of telling Caulfield Bedford that his daughter was dead, that he'd killed her.

"Now that you're conscious, I'll send someone around to get an official statement from you," Gardner told me. "Tomorrow."

"No problem."

"And stay away from this guy," Gardner added, jerking a thumb at C. J. "He'll bring you nothing but trouble, which appears to me you've had plenty of in the past year."

"Eventful, huh?"

"You'll finally take the hit for one too many people and find yourself sleeping like a baby—forever. Go back to your poetry."

I flashed Gardner a smile as he left.

"I'm heading out, too," C. J. announced. "I need a cigarette. Neil, the doctor said you'd be able to go home in a couple of days. You'll need some care, so I've arranged—"

"For you to go home with me," Linda interrupted.

C. J. sighed.

"Mama's a great person," Linda continued, "but God

knows I've taken care of you often enough to know what I'm doing."

C. J. drew a long silence out of the room. It was strange, and the drugs I was on must've been potent, because when he finally released a large breath I thought I saw cigarette smoke whispering in the air.

"Whatever," he said, and walked out of the room.

"Is he all right?" I asked Linda.

"No. But he will be."

"He's haunted by the abortion, too, isn't he?"

"Knowing C. J., it's the decisions he made, or didn't make, that he'll have to deal with. He won't talk about it. Or if he does, he'll make it sound like it was a lifetime ago. C. J. is a hard, hard man."

"What does *C. J.* stand for?"

"Cory James."

"Figured," I muttered.

"Del wanted him so badly she didn't want him anymore," Linda said. "In other words, she wanted the C. J. from years ago, the young brawny one. The James Dean. The old C. J. was in the way, hadn't grown old with her, hadn't given her the things she craved."

"So she was going to start over with the baby."

"Clean slate."

I paused, looked up at Linda. "Did he cry when your mother died?"

"That's an odd question. Of course he did."

"Oh." I didn't know why I asked her, except that I couldn't see him crying over Del Westview. Not now. There was just a tremendous pool of sadness locked behind his eyes.

"What are your plans, Neil?" Linda asked.

"Why didn't you try to call my mother?" I asked.

"I told you. I didn't want to worry her."

"You should have."

"Now, you're not going to stew over that, are you?"

"No," I said slowly. I was beginning to hurt inside.

Linda released my hand.

"You're in love with that professor," she said.

"It's not that," I replied.

"You are."

"Linda, I'm going home to my apartment," I said. "I want some time alone."

"I see," she said, and rose from the chair.

"My mom's coming down," I explained. "She'll expect to take care of me."

"Of course."

I can't go from Susan to someone with controlling characteristics like hers, I thought of saying, but couldn't.

"There's fire between us, Neil," Linda stated.

"And we need to let the flames rest to see if there's more," I managed to say. "I think you know—"

"Don't tell me what I know," Linda said to me, turned her back, and walked away.

Linda? I thought.

And the door closed.

In the room, alone, I felt the drugs pressing against my sadness. Perhaps with a clear head I would see the relationship differently. Yes, I comforted myself, perhaps I would.

But I still shivered from Keely's show of emotion. Oh, I was a fool. A bird in hand, and one in marriage.

Before I drifted off, though, I felt someone touch my arm. I forced into focus the image of Candace Littlefield.

"Sondra's going to pick up your mom tonight," she said. "We called from the phone downstairs. When I saw your friend leave, I snuck back up here. I thought I might keep you company for a while. Okay?"

"You're a good kid," I mumbled.

"What?"

I tried again, but the words were no more than the shadow of cigarette smoke.

"Oh, never mind, Neil. Get some rest."

And so I drifted off to sleep, thoughts confused and wild, and I wondered, finally, if this was how a baby felt as he fitfully rocked himself into that lonely, silent cry called life.

If you liked this Neil Marshall mystery, you'll love his debut!

IF WISHES WERE HORSES . . .
by Tim Hemlin

"What a debut! Gourmet cooking and spirited horseflesh combine to make this premiere mystery first at the post!"
—*Meritorious Mysteries*

Please read on for an exciting look at where it all started . . .

Our marriage was reduced to shrapnel. With the impending divorce threatening to add a fatal twist, I got the hell away from Susan and our house in Sharpstown. My '73 Bug chugged with all the heart, soul, and strength I could muster. The culmination of the Fall from Hell. Funny thing. I thought I was leaving murder, not driving into it.

Traffic on the Southwest Freeway was light on a Thursday at midnight. The VW cruised easily, considering that all the worldly possessions I'd made off with were my course notes, textbooks, writing notebooks, and a handful of clothes. Tom Waits growled and lamented appropriately on the tape deck I'd installed. Down and out, smoking a cigarette, and drinking a stout. Sounded good. I had to fight the urge to stop at my favorite pub. As late as it was, I had to get to the one person who would take me in at this hour, Jason Keys.

Jason was my coworker, a little less now than before he'd bought land down toward Pearland and begun breeding horses. He was trying to make a go of it in the horse business and, according to his reports, was beginning to gain notice. I hoped he was in town tonight.

I hit I-45 and the Pierce elevated and curled around the dormant heart of downtown Houston. The sleek buildings were clustered like pieces in a titan's chess game. A minute later I was speeding by the new opera house that was so ugly it made me sad as Pagliacci. I tossed the remains of my cigarette at the edifice and closed in on Jason's place. . . .

A couple of raps—no answer. I tried the door. It was unlocked, so I invited myself in.

"Jason," I called. "It's your drinking buddy."

The only response was the hum of the water filter in the fish tank by the TV. I stuck the ale I brought in the small refrigerator and poked my head behind the curtain that blocked off his sleeping space, but he wasn't there. Horse magazines, books, pads of paper, and pens were stacked on and around a small couch in the living room. A card table took up a chunk of the kitchen, and on a counter was a pot half-full of coffee. There were a couple of throw rugs on the floor and a calendar beside the gun rack against the north wall. I went back outside.

"Jason," I called. "It's me, Neil."

No answer.

Jason had built the stables himself. They were long, lean, and tightly constructed. A weather vane on top creaked in the gentle wind that rose out of the north. As I drew closer, I heard a radio tuned to country music—or almost tuned. The music sounded fuzzy and faded in and out. The smell of hay and manure filled my nostrils. It was an odor I'd always liked.

The stables, which butted the corral, were large enough to house twelve horses. Two lines of six stalls faced each other, and I stepped onto the concrete floor between them. It was then I heard a hard blowing—like steam rising from an old locomotive. Again, I called for Jason.

The sorrel responded. He stuck his head out of the first stall, eyes wide and bulging, nostrils flared, then leaned back. His ears were arched so far forward they almost met in a point. He danced nervously. I walked up to him but didn't touch, fearing he'd take a nip at me. The snorting continued. Two stalls down, the quarter horse did the same thing. I noticed the middle stall was empty, gate open. Jason said he was tending three horses, and I wondered if he was out with the missing thoroughbred. None of the other stalls were occupied.

"How's the colic, guys?" I asked, though my voice didn't sound right. Neither did the lame attempt at a joke. A feeling cold as the day pushed against my ribs.

The blurry sound of Clint Black slid and twanged from the storage area.

"Jason?" I ducked my head as I went through the open door by the second line of stalls. The music grew louder, and the barn doors were open. A sawhorse with a saddle draped across it was overturned. Beyond that an orange cord ran from a light outlet on the ceiling to the radio. But the radio wasn't in its usual place. It was buzzing from a pile of hay with a wooden stool knocked down behind it.

Then I found Jason Keys.

He was lying on his back across sacks of feed, eyes wide open, his chest a river of blood. My knees started to buckle as I knelt beside him. The right side of his head was bashed in. God, no, I thought. Why? When I touched his neck with my trembling fingers, it felt as I feared it would. Cold as the shards of ice stabbing my heart.

IF WISHES WERE HORSES . . .
by Tim Hemlin

TIM HEMLIN

"Tim Hemlin is a welcome new voice
in the mystery field."
—EARL EMERSON

Praise for the novels of
STEPHANIE LAURENS

"Laurens's writing shines."
—*Publishers Weekly*

"In an Amanda Quick-style suspense/romance,
Laurens never loses touch with her characters'
deep emotions or the haunting mystery."
—*Romantic Times BOOKreviews*

"An interesting and absorbing plot...an exciting
and appealing romantic mystery."
—*FreshFiction.com*

"The sensual tension simmers...
and, as always, Laurens delivers the delicious
heat as they fall in love."
—Michelle Buonfiglio, *myLifetime.com*

"Laurens spices up her superbly sensual, elegantly
written love story with a generous measure of
intrigue, and the results are
splendidly entertaining."
—*Booklist*

"A fast-paced, action-packed, historical romance.
Stephanie Laurens has another winner on her hands."
—*The Romance Readers Connection*

"Danger, intrigue and seduction aplenty—
will leave you satisfied yet hungry for more."
—*Romance Reviews Today*

STEPHANIE LAURENS

Four in Hand

HQN™

ISBN-13: 978-0-373-77309-1
ISBN-10:   0-373-77309-9

FOUR IN HAND

Four in Hand

CHAPTER ONE

THE RATTLE OF THE curtain rings sounded like thunder. The head of the huge four-poster bed remained wreathed in shadow yet Max was aware that for some mysterious reason Masterton was trying to wake him. Surely it couldn't be noon already?

Lying prone amid his warm sheets, his stubbled cheek cushioned in softest down, Max contemplated faking slumber. But Masterton knew he was awake. And knew that he knew, so to speak. Sometimes, the damned man seemed to know his thoughts before he did. And he certainly wouldn't go away before Max capitulated and acknowledged him.

Raising his head, Max opened one very blue eye. His terrifyingly correct valet was standing, entirely immobile, plumb in his line of vision. Masterton's face was impassive. Max frowned.

In response to this sign of approaching wrath, Masterton made haste to state his business. Not that it was *his* business, exactly. Only the combined vote of the rest of the senior staff of Delmere House had induced him to disturb His Grace's rest at the unheard-of hour of nine o'clock. He had every reason to know just how dangerous such an undertaking could be. He had been in the service of Max Rotherbridge, Viscount Delmere, for nine years. It was highly unlikely his master's recent elevation to the estate of His Grace the Duke of Twyford had in any way altered his temper. In fact, from what Masterton had seen, his master had had more to try his temper in dealing with his unexpected inheritance than in all the rest of his thirty-four years.

"Hillshaw wished me to inform you that there's a young lady to see you, Your Grace."

It was still a surprise to Max to hear his new title on his servants' lips. He had to curb an automatic reaction to look about him for whomever they were addressing. A lady. His frown deepened. "No." He dropped his head back into the soft pillows and closed his eyes.

"*No,* Your Grace?"

The bewilderment in his valet's voice was unmistakable. Max's head ached. He had been up until dawn. The evening had started badly, when he had felt constrained to attend a ball given by his maternal aunt, Lady Maxwell. He rarely attended such functions. They were too tame for his liking; the languishing sighs his appearance provoked among all the sweet young things were enough to throw even the most hardened reprobate entirely off his stride. And while he had every claim to that title, seducing débutantes was no longer his style. Not at thirty-four.

He had left the ball as soon as he could and repaired to the discreet villa wherein resided his latest mistress. But the beautiful Carmelita had been in a petulant mood. Why were such women invariably so grasping? And why did they imagine he was so besotted that he'd stand for it? They had had an almighty row, which had ended with him giving the luscious ladybird her congé in no uncertain terms.

From there, he had gone to White's, then Boodles. At that discreet establishment, he had found a group of his cronies and together they had managed to while the night away. And most of the morning, too. He had neither won nor lost. But his head reminded him that he had certainly drunk a lot.

He groaned and raised himself on his elbows, the better to fix Masterton with a gaze which, despite his condition, was remarkably lucid. Speaking in the voice of one instructing a dimwit, he explained. "If there's a woman to see me, she can't be a lady. No lady would call here."

Max thought he was stating the obvious but his henchman stared woodenly at the bedpost. The frown, which had temporarily left his master's handsome face, returned.

Silence.

Max sighed and dropped his head on to his hands. "Have you seen her, Masterton?"

"I did manage to get a glimpse of the young lady when Hillshaw showed her into the library, Your Grace."

Max screwed his eyes tightly shut. Masterton's insistence on using the term "young lady" spoke volumes. All of Max's servants were experienced in telling the difference between ladies and the sort of female who might be expected to call at a bachelor's residence. And if both Masterton and Hillshaw insisted the woman downstairs was a young lady, then a young lady she must be. But it was inconceivable that any young lady would pay a nine o'clock call on the most notorious rake in London.

Taking his master's silence as a sign of commitment to the day, Masterton crossed the large chamber to the wardrobe. "Hillshaw mentioned that the young lady, a Miss Twinning, Your Grace, was under the impression she had an appointment with you."

Max had the sudden conviction that this was a nightmare. He rarely made appointments with anyone and certainly not with young ladies for nine o'clock in the morning. And particularly not with unmarried young ladies. "Miss Twinning?" The name rang no bells. Not even a rattle.

"Yes, Your Grace." Masterton returned to the bed, various garments draped on his arm, a deep blue coat lovingly displayed for approval. "The Bath superfine would, I think, be most appropriate?"

Yielding to the inevitable with a groan, Max sat up.

ONE FLOOR BELOW, Caroline Twinning sat calmly reading His Grace of Twyford's morning paper in an armchair by his library hearth. If she felt any qualms over the propriety of her present position, she hid them well. Her charmingly candid countenance was free of all nervousness and, as she scanned a frankly libellous account of a garden party enlivened by the scandalous propensities of the ageing Duke of Cumberland, an engaging smile curved her generous lips. In truth, she was looking forward to her meeting with the Duke. She and her sisters had spent a most enjoyable eighteen months, the wine of freedom a heady tonic after their previously monastic existence. But it was time and more for them to embark on the serious business of securing their futures. To do that, they needs must enter the *ton*, that glittering arena thus far denied them. And, for them, the Duke of Twyford undeniably held the key to that particular door.

Hearing the tread of a masculine stride approach the library door, Caroline raised her head, then smiled confidently. Thank heavens the Duke was so easy to manage.

By the time he reached the ground floor, Max had exhausted every possible excuse for the existence of the mysterious Miss Twinning. He had taken little time to dress, having no need to employ extravagant embellishments to distract attention from his long and powerful frame. His broad shoulders and muscular thighs perfectly suited the prevailing fashion. His superbly cut coats looked as though they had been moulded on to him and his buckskin breeches showed not a crease. The understated waistcoat, perfectly tied cravat and shining top-boots which completed the picture were the envy of many an aspiring exquisite. His hair, black as night, was neatly cropped to frame a dark face on which the years had left nothing more than a trace of worldly cynicism. Disdaining the ornamentation common to the times, His Grace of Twyford wore no ring other than a gold signet on his left hand and displayed no fobs or seals. In spite of this, no one setting eyes on him could imagine he was other than he was— one of the most fashionable and wealthy men in the *ton*.

He entered his library, a slight frown in the depths of his midnight-blue eyes. His attention was drawn by a flash of movement as the young lady who had been calmly reading his copy of the morning *Gazette* in his favourite armchair by the hearth folded the paper and laid it aside, before rising to face him. Max halted, blue eyes suddenly intent, all trace of displeasure vanishing as he surveyed his unexpected visitor. His nightmare had transmogrified into a dream. The vision before him was unquestionably a houri. For a number of moments he remained frozen in rapturous contemplation. Then, his rational mind reasserted itself. Not a houri. Houris did not read the *Gazette.* At least, not in his library at nine o'clock in the morning. From the unruly copper curls clustering around her face to the tips of her tiny slippers, showing tantalisingly from under the simply cut and outrageously fashionable gown, there was nothing with which he could find fault. She was built on generous lines, a tall Junoesque figure, deep-bosomed and wide-hipped, but all in the most perfect proportions. Her apricot silk gown did justice to her ample charms, clinging suggestively to a figure of Grecian delight. When his eyes returned to her face, he had time to take in the straight nose and full lips and the dimple that peeked irrepressibly from one cheek before his gaze was drawn to the finely arched brows and long lashes which framed her large eyes. It was only when he looked into the cool grey-green orbs that he saw the twinkle of amusement lurking there. Unused to provoking such a response, he frowned.

"Who, exactly, are you?" His voice, he was pleased to find, was even and his diction clear.

The smile which had been hovering at the corners of those inviting lips finally came into being, disclosing a row of small pearly teeth. But instead of answering his question, the vision replied, "I was waiting for the Duke of Twyford."

Her voice was low and musical. Mentally engaged in

considering how to most rapidly dispense with the formalities, Max answered automatically. "I am the Duke."

"You?" For one long moment, utter bewilderment was writ large across her delightful countenance.

For the life of her, Caroline could not hide her surprise. How could this man, of all men, be the Duke? Aside from the fact he was far too young to have been a crony of her father's, the gentleman before her was unquestionably a rake. And a rake of the first order, to boot. Whether the dark-browed, harsh-featured face with its aquiline nose and firm mouth and chin or the lazy assurance with which he had entered the room had contributed to her reading of his character, she could not have said. But the calmly arrogant way his intensely blue eyes had roved from the top of her curls all the way down to her feet, and then just as calmly returned by the same route, as if to make sure he had missed nothing, left her in little doubt of what sort of man she now faced. Secure in the knowledge of being under her guardian's roof, she had allowed the amusement she felt on seeing such decided appreciation glow in the deep blue eyes to show. Now, with those same blue eyes still on her, piercingly perceptive, she felt as if the rug had been pulled from beneath her feet.

Max could hardly miss her stunned look. "For my sins," he added in confirmation.

With a growing sense of unease, he waved his visitor to a seat opposite the huge mahogany desk while he moved to take the chair behind it. As he did so, he mentally shook his head to try to clear it of the thoroughly unhelpful thoughts that kept crowding in. Damn Carmelita!

Caroline, rapidly trying to gauge where this latest

disconcerting news left her, came forward to sink into the chair indicated.

Outwardly calm, Max watched the unconsciously graceful glide of her walk, the seductive swing of her hips as she sat down. He would have to find a replacement for Carmelita. His gaze rested speculatively on the beauty before him. Hillshaw had been right. She was unquestionably a lady. Still, that had never stopped him before. And, now he came to look more closely, she was not, he thought, that young. Even better. No rings, which was odd. Another twinge of pain from behind his eyes lent a harshness to his voice. "Who the devil are you?"

The dimple peeped out again. In no way discomposed, she answered, "My name is Caroline Twinning. And, if you really are the Duke of Twyford, then I'm very much afraid I'm your ward."

Her announcement was received in perfect silence. A long pause ensued, during which Max sat unmoving, his sharp blue gaze fixed unwaveringly on his visitor. She bore this scrutiny for some minutes, before letting her brows rise in polite and still amused enquiry.

Max closed his eyes and groaned. "Oh, God."

It had only taken a moment to work it out. The only woman he could not seduce was his own ward. And he had already decided he very definitely wanted to seduce Caroline Twinning. With an effort, he dragged his mind back to the matter at hand. He opened his eyes. Hopefully, she would put his reaction down to natural disbelief. Encountering the grey-green eyes, now even more amused, he was not so sure. "Explain, if you please. Simple language only. I'm not up to unravelling mysteries at the moment."

Caroline could not help grinning. She had noticed twinges of what she guessed to be pain passing spasmodically through the blue eyes. "If your head hurts that much, why don't you try an ice-pack? I assure you I won't mind."

Max threw her a look of loathing. His head felt as if it was splitting, but how dared she be so lost to all propriety as to notice, let alone mention it? Still, she was perfectly right. An ice-pack was exactly what he needed. With a darkling look, he reached for the bell pull.

Hillshaw came in answer to his summons and received the order for an ice-pack without noticeable perturbation. "Now, Your Grace?"

"Of course now! What use will it be later?" Max winced at the sound of his own voice.

"As Your Grace wishes." The sepulchral tones left Max in no doubt of his butler's deep disapproval.

As the door closed behind Hillshaw, Max lay back in the chair, his fingers at his temples, and fixed Caroline with an unwavering stare. "You may commence."

She smiled, entirely at her ease once more. "My father was Sir Thomas Twinning. He was an old friend of the Duke of Twyford—the previous Duke, I imagine."

Max nodded. "My uncle. I inherited the title from him. He was killed unexpectedly three months ago, together with his two sons. I never expected to inherit the estate, so am unfamiliar with whatever arrangements your parent may have made with the last Duke."

Caroline nodded and waited until Hillshaw, delivering the requested ice-pack on a silver salver to his master, withdrew. "I see. When my father died eighteen months ago, my sisters and I were informed that he had left us to the guardianship of the Duke of Twyford."

"Eighteen months ago? What have you been doing since then?"

"We stayed on the estate for a time. It passed to a distant cousin and he was prepared to let us remain. But it seemed senseless to stay buried there forever. The Duke wanted us to join his household immediately, but we were in mourning. I persuaded him to let us go to my late stepmother's family in New York. They'd always wanted us to visit and it seemed the perfect opportunity. I wrote to him when we were in New York, telling him we would call on him when we returned to England and giving him the date of our expected arrival. He replied and suggested I call on him today. And so, here I am."

Max saw it all now. Caroline Twinning was yet another part of his damnably awkward inheritance. Having led a life of unfettered hedonism from his earliest days, a rakehell ever since he came on the town, Max had soon understood that his lifestyle required capital to support it. So he had ensured his estates were all run efficiently and well. The Delmere estates he had inherited from his father were a model of modern estate management. But his uncle Henry had never had much real interest in his far larger holdings. After the tragic boating accident which had unexpectedly foisted on to him the responsibilities of the dukedom of Twyford, Max had found a complete overhaul of all his uncle's numerous estates was essential if they were not to sap the strength from his more prosperous Delmere holdings. The last three months had been spent in constant upheaval, with the old Twyford retainers trying to come to grips with the new Duke and his very different style. For Max, they had been three months of unending work. Only this week, he had finally thought that the end of the worst was in sight. He had packed his long-suffering secretary, Joshua Cummings, off home for a much needed rest. And now, quite clearly, the next chapter in the saga of his Twyford inheritance was about to start.

"You mentioned sisters. How many?"

"My half-sisters, really. There are four of us, altogether."

The lightness of the answer made Max instantly suspicious. "How old?"

There was a noticeable hesitation before Caroline answered, "Twenty, nineteen and eighteen."

The effect on Max was electric. "Good Lord! They didn't accompany you here, did they?"

Bewildered, Caroline replied, "No. I left them at the hotel."

"Thank God for that," said Max. Encountering Caroline's enquiring gaze, he smiled. "If anyone had seen them entering here, it would have been around town in a flash that I was setting up a harem."

The smile made Caroline blink. At his words, her grey eyes widened slightly. She could hardly pretend not to understand. Noticing the peculiar light in the blue eyes as they rested on her, it seemed a very good thing she was the Duke's ward. From her admittedly small understanding of the morals of his type, she suspected her position would keep her safe as little else might.

Unbeknown to her, Max was thinking precisely the same thing. And resolving to divest himself of his latest inherited responsibility with all possible speed. Aside from having no wish whatever to figure as the guardian of four young ladies of marriageable age, he needed to clear the obstacles from his path to Caroline Twinning. It occurred to him that her explanation of her life history had been curiously glib and decidedly short on detail. "Start at the beginning. Who was your mother and when did she die?"

Caroline had come unprepared to recite her history, imagining the Duke to be cognizant of the facts. Still, in the circumstances, she could hardly refuse. "My mother was Caroline Farningham, of the Staffordshire Farninghams."

Max nodded. An ancient family, well-known and well-connected.

Caroline's gaze had wandered to the rows of books lining the shelves behind the Duke. "She died shortly after I was born. I never knew her. After some years, my father married again, this time to the daughter of a local family who were about to leave for the colonies. Eleanor was very good to me and she looked after all of us comfortably, until she died six years ago. Of course, my father was disappointed that he never had a son and he rarely paid any attention to the four of us, so it was all left up to Eleanor."

The more he heard of him, the more Max was convinced that Sir Thomas Twinning had had a screw loose. He had clearly been a most unnatural parent. Still, the others were only Miss Twinning's half-sisters. Presumably they were not all as ravishing as she. It occurred to him that he should ask for clarification on this point but, before he could properly phrase the question, another and equally intriguing matter came to mind.

"Why was it none of you was presented before? If your father was sufficiently concerned to organize a guardian for you, surely the easiest solution would have been to have handed you into the care of husbands?"

Caroline saw no reason not to satisfy what was, after all, an entirely understandable curiosity. "We were never presented because my father disapproved of such…oh, frippery pastimes! To be perfectly honest, I sometimes thought he disapproved of women in general."

Max blinked.

Caroline continued, "As for marriage, he had organized that after a fashion. I was supposed to have married Edgar Mulhall, our neighbour." Involuntarily, her face assumed an expression of distaste.

Max was amused. "Wouldn't he do?"

Caroline's gaze returned to the saturnine face. "You haven't met him or you wouldn't need to ask. He's…" She wrinkled her nose as she sought for an adequate description. "Righteous," she finally pronounced.

At that, Max laughed. "Clearly out of the question."

Caroline ignored the provocation in the blue eyes. "Papa had similar plans for my sisters, only, as he never noticed they were of marriageable age and I never chose to bring it to his attention, nothing came of them either."

Perceiving Miss Twinning's evident satisfaction, Max made a mental note to beware of her manipulative tendencies. "Very well. So much for the past. Now to the future. What was your arrangement with my uncle?"

The grey-green gaze was entirely innocent as it rested on his face. Max did not know whether to believe it or not.

"Well, it was really his idea, but it seemed a perfectly sensible one to me. He suggested we should be presented to the *ton*. I suspect he intended to find us suitable husbands and so bring his guardianship to an end." She paused, thinking. "I'm not aware of the terms of my father's will, but I assume such arrangements terminate should we marry?"

"Very likely," agreed Max. The throbbing in his head had eased considerably. His uncle's plan had much to recommend it, but, personally, he would much prefer not to have any wards at all. And he would be damned if he would have Miss Twinning as his ward—that would cramp his style far too much. There were a few things even reprobates such as he held sacred and guardianship was one.

He knew she was watching him but made no further comment, his eyes fixed frowningly on his blotter as he considered his next move. At last, looking up at her, he said, "I've heard nothing of this until now. I'll have to get my solicitors to sort it out. Which firm handles your affairs?"

"Whitney and White. In Chancery Lane."

"Well, at least that simplifies matters. They handle the Twyford estates as well as my others." He laid the ice-pack down and looked at Caroline, a slight frown in his blue eyes. "Where are you staying?"

"Grillon's. We arrived yesterday."

Another thought occurred to Max. "On what have you been living for the last eighteen months?"

"Oh, we all had money left us by our mothers. We arranged to draw on that and leave our patrimony untouched."

Max nodded slowly. "But who had you in charge? You can't have travelled halfway around the world alone."

For the first time during this strange interview, Max saw Miss Twinning blush, ever so slightly. "Our maid and coachman, who acted as our courier, stayed with us."

The airiness of the reply did not deceive Max. "Allow me to comment, Miss Twinning, as your potential guardian, that such an arrangement will not do. Regardless of what may have been acceptable overseas, such a situation will not pass muster in London." He paused, considering the proprieties for what was surely the first time in his life. "At least you're at Grillon's for the moment. That's safe enough."

After another pause, during which his gaze did not leave Caroline's face, he said, "I'll see Whitney this morning and settle the matter. I'll call on you at two to let you know how things have fallen out." A vision of himself meeting a beautiful young lady and attempting to converse with her within the portals of fashionable Grillon's, under the fascinated gaze of all the other patrons, flashed before his eyes. "On second thoughts, I'll take you for a drive in the Park. That way," he continued in reply to the question in her grey-green eyes, "we might actually get a chance to talk."

He tugged the bell pull and Hillshaw appeared. "Have the carriage brought around. Miss Twinning is returning to Grillon's."

"Yes, Your Grace."

"Oh, no! I couldn't put you to so much trouble," said Caroline.

"My dear child," drawled Max, "my wards would certainly not go about London in hacks. See to it, Hillshaw."

"Yes, Your Grace." Hillshaw withdrew, for once in perfect agreement with his master.

Caroline found the blue eyes, which had quizzed her throughout this exchange, still regarding her, a gently mocking light in their depths. But she was a lady of no little courage and smiled back serenely, unknowingly sealing her fate.

Never, thought Max, had he met a woman so attractive. One way or another, he would break the ties of guardianship. A short silence fell, punctuated by the steady ticking of the long case clock in the corner. Max took the opportunity afforded by Miss Twinning's apparent fascination with the rows of leather-bound tomes at his back to study her face once more. A fresh face, full of lively humour and a brand of calm self-possession which, in his experience, was rarely found in young women. Undoubtedly a woman of character.

His sharp ears caught the sound of carriage wheels in the street. He rose and Caroline perforce rose, too. "Come, Miss Twinning. Your carriage awaits."

Max led her to the front door but forbore to go any further, bowing over her hand gracefully before allowing Hillshaw to escort her to the waiting carriage. The less chance there was for anyone to see him with her the better. At least until he had solved this guardianship tangle.

AS SOON AS the carriage door was shut by the majestic Hillshaw, the horses moved forward at a trot. Caroline lay back against the squabs, her gaze fixed unseeingly on the near-side window as the carriage traversed fashionable London. Bemused, she tried to gauge the effect of the unexpected turn their futures had taken. Imagine having a guardian like that!

Although surprised at being redirected from Twyford House to Delmere House, she had still expected to meet the vague and amenable gentleman who had so readily acquiesced, albeit by correspondence, to all her previous suggestions. Her mental picture of His Grace of Twyford had been of a man in late middle age, bewigged as many of her father's generation were, distinctly past his prime and with no real interest in dealing with four lively young women. She spared a small smile as she jettisoned her preconceived image. Instead of a comfortable, fatherly figure, she would now have to deal with a man who, if first impressions were anything to go by, was intelligent, quick-witted and far too perceptive for her liking. To imagine the new Duke would not know to a nicety how to manage four young women was patently absurd. If she had been forced to express an opinion, Caroline would have said that, with the present Duke of Twyford, managing women was a speciality. Furthermore, given his undoubted experience, she strongly suspected he would be highly resistant to feminine cajoling in any form. A frown clouded her grey-green eyes. She was not entirely sure she approved of the twist their fates had taken. Thinking back over the recent interview, she smiled. He had not seemed too pleased with the idea himself.

For a moment, she considered the possibility of coming to some agreement with the Duke, essentially breaking the guardianship clause of her father's will. But only for a moment. It was true she had never been presented to the *ton* but she had cut her social eyeteeth long ago. While the idea of unlimited freedom to do as they pleased might sound tempting, there was the undeniable fact that she and her half-sisters were heiresses of sorts. Her father, having an extremely repressive notion of the degree of knowledge which could be allowed mere females, had never been particularly forthcoming regarding their eventual state. Yet there had never been any shortage of funds in all the years Caroline could remember. She rather thought they would at least be comfortably dowered. Such being the case, the traps and pitfalls of society, without the protection of a guardian, such as the Duke of Twyford, were not experiences to which she would willingly expose her sisters.

As the memory of a certain glint in His Grace of Twyford's eye and the distinctly determined set of his jaw drifted past her mind's eye, the unwelcome possibility that he might repudiate them, for whatever reasons, hove into view. Undoubtedly, if there was any way to overset their guardianship, His Grace would find it. Unaccountably, she was filled with an inexplicable sense of disappointment.

Still, she told herself, straightening in a purposeful way, it was unlikely there was anything he could do about it. And she rather thought they would be perfectly safe with the new Duke of Twyford, as long as they *were* his wards. She allowed her mind to dwell on the question of whether she really wanted to be safe from the Duke of Twyford for several minutes before giving herself a mental shake. Great heavens! She had only just met the man and here she was, mooning over him like a green girl! She tried to frown but the action dissolved into a sheepish grin at her own susceptibility. Settling more comfortably in the corner of the luxurious carriage, she fell to rehearsing her description of what had occurred in anticipation of her sisters' eager questions.

WITHIN MINUTES of Caroline Twinning's departure from Delmere House, Max had issued a succession of orders, one of which caused Mr. Hubert Whitney, son of Mr. Josiah Whitney, the patriarch of the firm Whitney and White, Solicitors, of Chancery Lane, to present himself at Delmere House just before eleven. Mr. Whitney was a dry, desiccated man of uncertain age, very correctly attired in dusty black. He was his father's son in every way and, now that his sire was no longer able to leave his bed, he attended to all his father's wealthier clients. As Hillshaw showed him into the well-appointed library, he breathed a sigh of relief, not for the first time, that it was Max Rotherbridge who had inherited the difficult Twyford estates. Unknown to Max, Mr. Whitney held him in particular esteem, frequently wishing that others among his clients could be equally straightforward and decisive. It really made life so much easier.

Coming face-to-face with his favourite client, Mr. Whitney was immediately informed that His Grace, the Duke of Twyford, was in no way amused to find he was apparently the guardian of four marriageable young ladies. Mr. Whitney was momentarily at a loss. Luckily, he had brought with him all the current Twyford papers and the Twinning documents were among these. Finding that his employer did not intend to upbraid him for not having informed him of a circumstance which, he was only too well aware, he should have brought forward long ago, he applied himself to assessing the terms of the late Sir Thomas Twinning's will. Having refreshed his memory on its details, he then turned to the late Duke's will.

Max stood by the fire, idly watching. He liked Whitney. He did not fluster and he knew his business.

Finally, Mr. Whitney pulled the gold pince-nez from his face and glanced at his client. "Sir Thomas Twinning predeceased your uncle, and, under the terms of your uncle's will, it's quite clear you inherit all his responsibilities."

Max's black brows had lowered. "So I'm stuck with this guardianship?"

Mr. Whitney pursed his lips. "I wouldn't go so far as to say that. The guardianship could be broken, I fancy, as it's quite clear Sir Thomas did not intend you, personally, to be his daughters' guardian." He gazed at the fire and solemnly shook his head. "No one, I'm sure, could doubt that."

Max smiled wryly.

"However," Mr. Whitney continued, "should you succeed in dissolving the guardianship clause, then the young ladies will be left with no protector. Did I understand you correctly in thinking they are presently in London and plan to remain for the Season?"

It did not need a great deal of intelligence to see where Mr. Whitney's discourse was heading. Exasperated at having his usually comfortably latent conscience pricked into life, Max stalked to the window and stood looking out at the courtyard beyond, hands clasped behind his straight back. "Good God, man! You can hardly think I'm a suitable guardian for four sweet young things!"

Mr. Whitney, thinking the Duke could manage very well if he chose to do so, persevered. "There remains the question of who, in your stead, would act for them."

The certain knowledge of what would occur if he abandoned four inexperienced, gently reared girls to the London scene, to the mercies of well-bred wolves who roamed its streets, crystallised in Max's unwilling mind. This was closely followed by the uncomfortable thought that he was considered the leader of one such pack, generally held to be the most dangerous. He could hardly refuse to be Caroline Twinning's guardian, only to set her up as his mistress. No. There was a limit to what even he could face down. Resolutely thrusting aside the memory, still vivid, of a pair of grey-green eyes, he turned to Mr. Whitney and growled, "All right, dammit! What do I need to know?"

Mr. Whitney smiled benignly and started to fill him in on the Twinning family history, much as Caroline had told it. Max interrupted him. "Yes, I know all that! Just tell me in round figures—how much is each of them worth?"

Mr. Whitney named a figure and Max's brows rose. For a moment, the Duke was entirely bereft of speech. He moved towards his desk and seated himself again.

"Each?"

Mr. Whitney merely inclined his head in assent. When the Duke remained lost in thought, he continued, "Sir Thomas was a very shrewd businessman, Your Grace."

"So it would appear. So each of these girls is an heiress in her own right?"

This time, Mr. Whitney nodded decisively.

Max was frowning.

"Of course," Mr. Whitney went on, consulting the documents on his knee, "you would only be responsible for the three younger girls."

Instantly he had his client's attention, the blue eyes oddly piercing. "Oh? Why is that?"

"Under the terms of their father's will, the Misses Twinning were given into the care of the Duke of Twyford until they attained the age of twenty-five or married. According to my records, I believe Miss Twinning to be nearing her twenty-sixth birthday. So she could, should she wish, assume responsibility for herself."

Max's relief was palpable. But hard on its heels came another consideration. Caroline Twinning had recognised his interest in her—hardly surprising as he had taken no pains to hide it. If she knew he was not her guardian, she would keep him at arm's length. Well, try to, at least. But Caroline Twinning was not a green girl. The aura of quiet self-assurance which clung to her suggested she would not be an easy conquest. Obviously, it would be preferable if she continued to believe she was protected from him by his guardianship. That way, he would have no difficulty in approaching her, his reputation notwithstanding. In fact, the more he thought of it, the more merits he could see in the situation. Perhaps, in this case, he could have his cake and eat it too? He eyed Mr. Whitney. "Miss Twinning knows nothing of the terms of her father's will. At present, she believes herself to be my ward, along with her half-sisters. Is there any pressing need to inform her of her change in status?"

Mr. Whitney blinked owlishly, a considering look suffusing his face as he attempted to unravel the Duke's motives for wanting Miss Twinning to remain as his ward. Particularly after wanting to dissolve the guardianship altogether. Max Rotherbridge did not normally vacillate.

Max, perfectly sensible of Mr. Whitney's thoughts,

put forward the most acceptable excuses he could think of. "For a start, whether she's twenty-four or twenty-six, she's just as much in need of protection as her sisters. Then, too, there's the question of propriety. If it was generally known she was not my ward, it would be exceedingly difficult for her to be seen in my company. And as I'll still be guardian to her sisters, and as they'll be residing in one of my establishments, the situation could become a trifle delicate, don't you think?"

It was not necessary for him to elaborate. Mr. Whitney saw the difficulty clearly enough. It was his turn to frown. "What you say is quite true." Hubert Whitney had no opinion whatever in the ability of the young ladies to manage their affairs. "At present, there is nothing I can think of that requires Miss Twinning's agreement. I expect it can do no harm to leave her in ignorance of her status until she weds."

The mention of marriage brought a sudden check to Max's racing mind but he resolutely put the disturbing notion aside for later examination. He had too much to do today.

Mr. Whitney was continuing, "How do you plan to handle the matter, if I may make so bold as to ask?"

Max had already given the thorny problem of how four young ladies could be presented to the *ton* under his protection, without raising a storm, some thought. "I propose to open up Twyford House immediately. They can stay there. I intend to ask my aunt, Lady Benborough, to stand as the girls' sponsor. I'm sure she'll be only too thrilled. It'll keep her amused for the Season."

Mr. Whitney was acquainted with Lady Benborough. He rather thought it would. A smile curved his thin lips.

The Duke stood, bringing the interview to a close.

Mr. Whitney rose. "That seems most suitable. If there's anything further in which we can assist Your Grace, we'll be only too delighted."

Max nodded in response to this formal statement. As Mr. Whitney bowed, prepared to depart, Max, a past master of social intrigue, saw one last hole in the wall and moved to block it. "If there's any matter you wish to discuss with Miss Twinning, I suggest you do it through me, as if I was, in truth, her guardian. As you handle both our estates, there can really be no impropriety in keeping up appearances. For Miss Twinning's sake."

Mr. Whitney bowed again. "I foresee no problems, Your Grace."

CHAPTER TWO

AFTER MR. WHITNEY LEFT, Max issued a set of rapid and comprehensive orders to his majordomo Wilson. In response, his servants flew to various corners of London, some to Twyford House, others to certain agencies specializing in the hire of household staff to the élite of the *ton*. One footman was despatched with a note from the Duke to an address in Half Moon Street, requesting the favour of a private interview with his paternal aunt, Lady Benborough.

As Max had intended, his politely worded missive intrigued his aunt. Wondering what had prompted such a strange request from her reprehensible nephew, she immediately granted it and settled down to await his coming with an air of pleasurable anticipation.

Max arrived at the small house shortly after noon. He found his aunt attired in a very becoming gown of purple sarsenet with a new and unquestionably modish wig perched atop her commanding visage. Max, bowing elegantly before her, eyed the wig askance.

Augusta Benborough sighed. "Well, I suppose I'll have to send it back, if that's the way you feel about it!"

Max grinned and bent to kiss the proffered cheek. "Definitely not one of your better efforts, Aunt."

She snorted. "Unfortunately, I can hardly claim you know nothing about it. It's the very latest fashion, I'll have you know." Max raised one laconic brow. "Yes, well," continued his aunt, "I dare say you're right. Not quite my style."

As she waited while he disposed his long limbs in a chair opposite the corner of the chaise where she sat, propped up by a pile of colourful cushions, she passed a critical glance over her nephew's elegant figure. How he contrived to look so precise when she knew he cared very little how he appeared was more than she could tell. She had heard it said that his man was a genius. Personally, she was of the opinion it was Max's magnificent physique and dark good looks that carried the day.

"I hope you're going to satisfy my curiosity without a great deal of roundaboutation."

"My dear aunt, when have I ever been other than direct?"

She looked at him shrewdly. "Want a favour, do you? Can't imagine what it is but you'd better be quick about asking. Miriam will be back by one and I gather you'd rather not have her listening." Miriam Alford was a faded spinster cousin of Lady Benborough's who lived with her, filling the post of companion to the fashionable old lady. "I sent her to Hatchard's when I got your note," she added in explanation.

Max smiled. Of all his numerous relatives, his Aunt Benborough, his father's youngest sister, was his favourite. While the rest of them, his mother included, constantly tried to reform him by ringing peals over him, appealing to his sense of what was acceptable, something he steadfastly denied any knowledge of, Augusta

Benborough rarely made any comment on his lifestyle or the numerous scandals this provoked. When he had first come on the town, it had rapidly been made plain to his startled family that in Max they beheld a reincarnation of the second Viscount Delmere. If even half the tales were true, Max's great-grandfather had been a thoroughly unprincipled character, entirely devoid of morals. Lady Benborough, recently widowed, had asked Max to tea and had taken the opportunity to inform him in no uncertain terms of her opinion of his behaviour. She had then proceeded to outline all his faults, in detail. However, as she had concluded by saying that she fully expected her tirade to have no effect whatsoever on his subsequent conduct, nor could she imagine how anyone in their right mind could think it would, Max had borne the ordeal with an equanimity which would have stunned his friends. She had eventually dismissed him with the words, "Having at least had the politeness to hear me out, you may now depart and continue to go to hell in your own fashion and with my good will."

Now a widow of many years' standing, she was still a force to be reckoned with. She remained fully absorbed in the affairs of the *ton* and continued to be seen at all the crushes and every gala event. Max knew she was as shrewd as she could hold together and, above all, had an excellent sense of humour. All in all, she was just what he needed.

"I've come to inform you that, along with all the other encumbrances I inherited from Uncle Henry, I seem to have acquired four wards."

"You?" Lady Benborough's rendering of the word was rather more forceful than Miss Twinning's had been.

Max nodded. "Me. Four young ladies, one, the only one I've so far set eyes on, as lovely a creature as any other likely to be presented this Season."

"Good God! Who was so besotted as to leave four young girls in your care?" If anything, her ladyship was outraged at the very idea. Then, the full impact of the situation struck her. Her eyes widened. "Oh, good lord!" She collapsed against her cushions, laughing uncontrollably.

Knowing this was an attitude he was going to meet increasingly in the next few weeks, Max sighed. In an even tone suggestive of long suffering, he pointed out the obvious. "They weren't left to me but to my esteemed and now departed uncle's care. Mind you, I can't see that he'd have been much use to 'em either."

Wiping the tears from her eyes, Lady Benborough considered this view. "Can't see it myself," she admitted. "Henry always was a slow-top. Who are they?"

"The Misses Twinning. From Hertfordshire." Max proceeded to give her a brief résumé of the life history of the Twinnings, ending with the information that it transpired all four girls were heiresses.

Augusta Benborough was taken aback. "And you say they're beautiful to boot?"

"The one I've seen, Caroline, the eldest, most definitely is."

"Well, if anyone should know it's you!" replied her ladyship testily. Max acknowledged the comment with the slightest inclination of his head.

Lady Benborough's mind was racing. "So, what do you want with me?"

"What I would *like,* dearest Aunt," said Max, with his sweetest smile, "is for you to act as chaperon to the girls and present them to the *ton*." Max paused. His aunt said nothing, sitting quite still with her sharp blue eyes, very like his own, fixed firmly on his face. He continued. "I'm opening up Twyford House. It'll be ready for them tomorrow. I'll stand the nonsense—all of it." Still she said nothing. "Will you do it?"

Augusta Benborough thought she would like nothing better than to be part of the hurly-burly of the marriage game again. But four? All at once? Still, there was Max's backing, and that would count for a good deal. Despite his giving the distinct impression of total un-interest in anything other than his own pleasure, she knew from experience that, should he feel inclined, Max could and would perform feats impossible for those with lesser clout in the fashionable world. Years after the event, she had learned that, when her youngest son had embroiled himself in a scrape so hideous that even now she shuddered to think of it, it had been Max who had rescued him. And apparently for no better reason than it had been bothering her. She still owed him for that.

But there were problems. Her own jointure was not particularly large and, while she had never asked Max for relief, turning herself out in the style he would expect of his wards' chaperon was presently beyond her slender means. Hesitantly, she said, "My own wardrobe…"

"Naturally you'll charge all costs you incur in this business to me," drawled Max, his voice bored as he examined through his quizzing glass a china cat presently residing on his aunt's mantelpiece. He knew perfectly well his aunt managed on a very slim purse but was too wise to offer direct assistance which would, he knew, be resented, not only by the lady herself but also by her pompous elder son.

"Can I take Miriam with me to Twyford House?"

With a shrug, Max assented. "Aside from anything else, she might come in handy with four charges."

"When can I meet them?"

"They're staying at Grillon's. I'm taking Miss Twinning for a drive this afternoon to tell her what I've decided. I'll arrange for them to move to Twyford House tomorrow afternoon. I'll send Wilson to help you and Mrs. Alford in transferring to Mount Street. It would be best, I suppose, if you could make the move in the morning. You'll want to familiarize yourself with the staff and so on." Bethinking himself that it would be wise to have one of his own well-trained staff on hand, he added, "I suppose I can let you have Wilson for a week or two, until you settle in. I suggest you and I meet the Misses Twinning when they arrive—shall we say at three?"

Lady Benborough was entranced by the way her nephew seemed to dismiss complications like opening and staffing a mansion overnight. Still, with the efficient and reliable Wilson on the job, presumably it would be done. Feeling a sudden and unexpected surge of excitement at the prospect of embarking on the Season with a definite purpose in life, she drew a deep breath. "Very well. I'll do it!"

"Good!" Max stood. "I'll send Wilson to call on you this afternoon."

His aunt, already engrossed in the matter of finding husbands for the Twinning chits, looked up. "Have you seen the other three girls?"

Max shook his head. Imagining the likely scene

should they be on hand this afternoon when he called for Miss Twinning, he closed his eyes in horror. He could just hear the *on-dits*. "And I hope to God I don't see them in Grillon's foyer either!"

Augusta Benborough laughed.

WHEN HE CALLED AT Grillon's promptly at two, Max was relieved to find Miss Twinning alone in the foyer, seated on a chaise opposite the door, her bonnet beside her. He was not to know that Caroline had had to exert every last particle of persuasion to achieve this end. And she had been quite unable to prevent her three sisters from keeping watch from the windows of their bedchambers.

As she had expected, she had had to describe His Grace of Twyford in detail for her sisters. Looking up at the figure striding across the foyer towards her, she did not think she had done too badly. What had been hardest to convey was the indefinable air that hung about him—compelling, exciting, it immediately brought to mind a whole range of emotions well-bred young ladies were not supposed to comprehend, let alone feel. As he took her hand for an instant in his own, and smiled down at her in an oddly lazy way, she decided she had altogether underestimated the attractiveness of that sleepy smile. It was really quite devastating.

Within a minute, Caroline found herself on the box seat of a fashionable curricle drawn by a pair of beautiful but restive bays. She resisted the temptation to glance up at the first-floor windows where she knew the other three would be stationed. Max mounted to the driving seat and the diminutive tiger, who had been holding the horses' heads, swung up behind. Then they were off, tacking through the traffic towards Hyde Park.

Caroline resigned herself to silence until the safer precincts of the Park were reached. However, it seemed the Duke was quite capable of conversing intelligently while negotiating the chaos of the London streets.

"I trust Grillon's has met with your approval thus far?"

"Oh, yes. They've been most helpful," returned Caroline. "Were you able to clarify the matter of our guardianship?"

Max was unable to suppress a smile at her directness. He nodded, his attention temporarily claimed by the off-side horse which had decided to take exception to a monkey dancing on the pavement, accompanied by an accordion player.

"Mr. Whitney has assured me that, as I am the Duke of Twyford, I must therefore be your guardian." He had allowed his reluctance to find expression in his tone. As the words left his lips, he realised that the unconventional woman beside him might well ask why he found the role of protector to herself and her sisters so distasteful. He immediately went on the attack. "And, in that capacity, I should like to know how you have endeavoured to come by Parisian fashions?"

His sharp eyes missed little and his considerable knowledge of feminine attire told him Miss Twinning's elegant pelisse owed much to the French. But France was at war with England and Paris no longer the playground of the rich.

Initially stunned that he should know enough to come so close to the truth, Caroline quickly realised the source of his knowledge. A spark of amusement danced in her eyes. She smiled and answered readily, "I assure you we did not run away to Brussels instead of New York."

"Oh, I wasn't afraid of that!" retorted Max, perfectly willing to indulge in plain speaking. "If you'd been in Brussels, I'd have heard of it."

"Oh?" Caroline turned a fascinated gaze on him.

Max smiled down at her.

Praying she was not blushing, Caroline strove to get the conversation back on a more conventional course. "Actually, you're quite right about the clothes, they are Parisian. But not from the Continent. There were two *couturières* from Paris on the boat going to New York. They asked if they could dress us, needing the business to become known in America. It was really most fortunate. We took the opportunity to get quite a lot made up before we returned—we'd been in greys for so long that none of us had anything suitable to wear."

"How did you find American society?"

Caroline reminded herself to watch her tongue. She did not delude herself that just because the Duke was engaged in handling a team of high-couraged cattle through the busy streets of London he was likely to miss any slip she made. She was rapidly learning to respect the intelligence of this fashionable rake. "Quite frankly, we found much to entertain us. Of course, our relatives were pleased to see us and organised a great many outings and entertainments." No need to tell him they had had a riotous time.

"Did the tone of the society meet with your approval?"

He had already told her he would have known if they had been in Europe. Did he have connections in New York? How much could he know of their junketing?

Caroline gave herself a mental shake. How absurd! He had not known of their existence until this morning. "Well, to be sure, it wasn't the same as here. Many more cits and half-pay officers about. And, of course, nothing like the *ton*."

Unknowingly, her answer brought some measure of relief to Max. Far from imagining his new-found wards had been indulging in high living abroad, he had been wondering whether they had any social experience at all. Miss Twinning's reply told him that she, at least, knew enough to distinguish the less acceptable among society's hordes.

They had reached the gates of the Park and turned into the carriage drive. Soon, the curricle was bowling along at a steady pace under the trees, still devoid of any but the earliest leaves. A light breeze lifted the ends of the ribbons on Caroline's hat and playfully danced along the horses' dark manes.

Max watched as Caroline gazed about her with interest. "I'm afraid you'll not see many notables at this hour. Mostly nursemaids and their charges. Later, between three and five, it'll be crowded. The Season's not yet begun in earnest, but by now most people will have returned to town. And the Park is the place to be seen. All the old biddies come here to exchange the latest *on-dits* and all the young ladies promenade along the walks with their beaux."

"I see." Caroline smiled to herself, a secret smile as she imagined how she and her sisters would fit into this scene.

Max saw the smile and was puzzled. Caroline Twinning was decidedly more intelligent than the women with whom he normally consorted. He could not guess her thoughts and was secretly surprised at wanting to know them. Then, he remembered one piece of vital information he had yet to discover. "Apropos of my uncle's plan to marry you all off, satisfy my curiosity, Miss Twinning. What do your sisters look like?"

This was the question she had been dreading. Caroline hesitated, searching for precisely the right words with which to get over the difficult ground. "Well, they've always been commonly held to be well to pass."

Max noted the hesitation. He interpreted her careful phrasing to mean that the other three girls were no more than average. He nodded, having suspected as much, and allowed the subject to drop.

They rounded the lake and he slowed his team to a gentle trot. "As your guardian, I've made certain arrangements for your immediate future." He noticed the grey eyes had flown to his face. "Firstly, I've opened Twyford House. Secondly, I've arranged for my aunt, Lady Benborough, to act as your chaperon for the Season. She's very well-connected and will know exactly how everything should be managed. You may place complete confidence in her advice. You will remove from Grillon's tomorrow. I'll send my man, Wilson, to assist you in the move to Twyford House. He'll call for you at two tomorrow. I presume that gives you enough time to pack?"

Caroline assumed the question to be rhetorical. She was stunned. He had not known they existed at nine this morning. How could he have organised all that since ten?

Thinking he may as well clear all the looming fences while he was about it, Max added, "As for funds, I presume your earlier arrangements still apply. However, should you need any further advances, as I now hold the purse-strings of your patrimonies, you may apply directly to me."

His last statement succeeded in convincing Caroline that it would not be wise to underestimate this Duke. Despite having only since this morning to think about it, he had missed very little. And, as he held the purse-strings, he could call the tune. As she had foreseen, life as the wards of a man as masterful and domineering as the present Duke of Twyford was rapidly proving to be was definitely not going to be as unfettered as they had imagined would be the case with his vague and easily led uncle. There were, however, certain advantages in the changed circumstances and she, for one, could not find it in her to repine.

More people were appearing in the Park, strolling about the lawns sloping down to the river and gathering in small groups by the carriageway, laughing and chatting.

A man of slight stature, mincing along beside the carriage drive, looked up in startled recognition as they passed. He was attired in a bottle-green coat with the most amazing amount of frogging Caroline had ever seen. In place of a cravat, he seemed to be wearing a very large floppy bow around his neck. "Who on earth was that quiz?" she asked.

"That quiz, my dear ward, is none other than Walter Millington, one of the fops. In spite of his absurd clothes, he's unexceptionable enough but he has a sharp tongue so it's wise for young ladies to stay on his right side. Don't laugh at him."

Two old ladies in an ancient landau were staring at them with an intensity which in lesser persons would be considered rude.

Max did not wait to be asked. "And those are the Misses Berry. They're as old as bedamned and know absolutely everyone. Kind souls. One's entirely vague and the other's sharp as needles."

Caroline smiled. His potted histories were entertaining.

A few minutes later, the gates came into view and Max headed his team in that direction. Caroline saw a horseman pulled up by the carriage drive a little way ahead. His face clearly registered recognition of the Duke's curricle and the figure driving it. Then his eyes passed to her and stopped. At five and twenty, Caroline had long grown used to the effect she had on men, particularly certain sorts of men. As they drew nearer, she saw that the gentleman was impeccably attired and had the same rakish air as the Duke. The rider held up a hand in greeting and she expected to feel the curricle slow. Instead, it flashed on, the Duke merely raising a hand in an answering salute.

Amused, Caroline asked, "And who, pray tell, was that?"

Max was thinking that keeping his friends in ignorance of Miss Twinning was going to prove impossible. Clearly, he would be well-advised to spend some time planning the details of this curious seduction, or he might find himself with rather more competition than he would wish. "That was Lord Ramsleigh."

"A friend of yours?"

"Precisely."

Caroline laughed at the repressive tone. The husky sound ran tingling along Max's nerves. It flashed into his mind that Caroline Twinning seemed to understand a great deal more than one might expect from a woman with such a decidedly restricted past. He was prevented from studying her face by the demands of successfully negotiating their exit from the Park.

They were just swinging out into the traffic when an elegant barouche pulled up momentarily beside them, heading into the Park. The thin, middle-aged woman, with a severe, almost horsy countenance, who had been languidly lying against the silken cushions, took one look at the curricle and sat bolt upright. In her face, astonishment mingled freely with rampant curiosity. "Twyford!"

Max glanced down as both carriages started to move again. "My lady." He nodded and then they were swallowed up in the traffic.

Glancing back, Caroline saw the elegant lady remonstrating with her coachman. She giggled. "Who was she?"

"That, my ward, was Sally, Lady Jersey. A name to remember. She is the most inveterate gossip in London. Hence her nickname of Silence. Despite that, she's kindhearted enough. She's one of the seven patronesses of Almack's. You'll have to get vouchers to attend but I doubt that will be a problem."

They continued in companionable silence, threading their way through the busy streets. Max was occupied with imagining the consternation Lady Jersey's sighting of them was going to cause. And there was Ramsleigh, too. A wicked smile hovered on his lips. He rather thought he was going to spend a decidedly amusing evening. It would be some days before news of his guardianship got around. Until then, he would enjoy the speculation. He was certain he would not enjoy the mirth of his friends when they discovered the truth.

"OOOH, CARO! Isn't he magnificent?" Arabella's round eyes, brilliant and bright, greeted Caroline as she entered their parlour.

"Did he agree to be our guardian?" asked the phlegmatic Sarah.

And, "Is he nice?" from the youngest, Lizzie.

All the important questions, thought Caroline with an affectionate smile, as she threw her bonnet aside and subsided into an armchair with a whisper of her stylish skirts. Her three half-sisters gathered around eagerly. She eyed them fondly. It would be hard to find three more attractive young ladies, even though she did say so herself. Twenty-year-old Sarah, with her dark brown hair and dramatically pale face, settling herself on one arm of her chair. Arabella on her other side, chestnut curls rioting around her heart-shaped and decidedly mischievous countenance, and Lizzie, the youngest and quietest of them all, curling up at her feet, her grey-brown eyes shining with the intentness of youth, the light dusting of freckles on the bridge of her nose persisting despite the ruthless application of Denmark lotion, crushed strawberries and every other remedy ever invented.

"Commonly held to be well to pass." Caroline's own words echoed in her ears. Her smile grew. "Well, my loves, it seems we are, incontrovertibly and without doubt, the Duke of Twyford's wards."

"When does he want to meet us?" asked Sarah, ever practical.

"Tomorrow afternoon. He's opening up Twyford House and we're to move in then. He resides at Delmere House, where I went this morning, so the properties will thus be preserved. His aunt, Lady Benborough, is to act as our chaperon—she's apparently well-connected and willing to sponsor us. She'll be there tomorrow."

A stunned silence greeted her news. Then Arabella voiced the awe of all three. "Since ten this morning?"

Caroline's eyes danced. She nodded.

Arabella drew a deep breath. "Is he…masterful?"

"Very!" replied Caroline. "But you'll be caught out, my love, if you think to sharpen your claws on our guardian. He's a deal too shrewd, and experienced besides." Studying the pensive faces around her, she added. "Any flirtation between any of us and Max Rotherbridge would be doomed to failure. As his wards, we're out of court, and he won't stand any nonsense, I warn you."

"Hmm." Sarah stood and wandered to the windows before turning to face her. "So it's as you suspected? He won't be easy to manage?"

Caroline smiled at the thought and shook her head decisively. "I'm afraid, my dears, that any notions we may have had of setting the town alight while in the care of a complaisant guardian have died along with the last Duke." One slim forefinger tapped her full lower lip thoughtfully. "However," she continued, "provided we adhere to society's rules and cause him no trouble, I doubt our new guardian will throw any rub in our way. We did come to London to find husbands, after all. And that," she said forcefully, gazing at the three faces fixed on hers, "is, unless I miss my guess, precisely what His Grace intends us to do."

"So he's agreed to present us so we can find husbands?" asked Lizzie.

Again Caroline nodded. "I think it bothers him, to

have four wards." She smiled in reminiscence, then added, "And from what I've seen of the *ton* thus far, I suspect the present Duke as our protector may well be a distinct improvement over the previous incumbent. I doubt we'll have to fight off the fortune-hunters."

Some minutes ticked by in silence as they considered their new guardian. Then Caroline stood and shook out her skirts. She took a few steps into the room before turning to address her sisters.

"Tomorrow we'll be collected at two and conveyed to Twyford House, which is in Mount Street." She paused to let the implication of her phrasing sink in. "As you love me, you'll dress demurely and behave with all due reticence. No playing off your tricks on the Duke." She looked pointedly at Arabella, who grinned roguishly back. "Exactly so! I think, in the circumstances, we should make life as easy as possible for our new guardian. I feel sure he could have broken the guardianship if he had wished and can only be thankful he chose instead to honour his uncle's obligations. But we shouldn't try him too far." She ended her motherly admonitions with a stern air, deceiving her sisters not at all.

As the other three heads came together, Caroline turned to gaze unseeingly out of the window. A bewitching smile curved her generous lips and a twinkle lit her grey-green eyes. Softly, she murmured to herself, "For I've a definite suspicion he's going to find us very trying indeed!"

THUP, THUP, THUP. The tip of Lady Benborough's thin cane beat a slow tattoo, muffled by the pile of the Aubusson carpet. She was pleasantly impatient, waiting with definite anticipation to see her new charges. Her sharp blue gaze had already taken in the state of the room, the perfectly organised furniture, everything tidy and in readiness. If she had not known it for fact, she would never have believed that, yesterday morn, Twyford House had been shut up, the knocker off the door, every piece of furniture shrouded in Holland covers. Wilson was priceless. There was even a bowl of early crocus on the side-table between the long windows. These stood open, giving access to the neat courtyard, flanked by flowerbeds bursting into colourful life. A marble fountain stood at its centre, a Grecian maiden pouring water never-endingly from an urn.

Her contemplation of the scene was interrupted by a peremptory knock on the street door. A moment later, she heard the deep tones of men's voices and relaxed. Max. She would never get used to thinking of him as Twyford—she had barely become accustomed to him being Viscount Delmere. Max was essentially Max—he needed no title to distinguish him.

The object of her vagaries strode into the room. As always, his garments were faultless, his boots beyond compare. He bowed with effortless grace over her hand, his blue eyes, deeper in shade than her own but alive with the same intelligence, quizzing her. "A vast improvement, Aunt."

It took a moment to realise he was referring to her latest wig, a newer version of the same style she had favoured for the past ten years. She was not sure whether she was pleased or insulted. She compromised and snorted. "Trying to turn me up pretty, heh?"

"I would never insult your intelligence so, ma'am," he drawled, eyes wickedly laughing.

Lady Benborough suppressed an involuntary smile in response. The trouble with Max was that he was such a thorough-going rake that the techniques had flowed into all spheres of his life. He would undoubtedly flirt outrageously with his old nurse! Augusta Benborough snorted again. "Wilson's left to get the girls. He should be back any minute. Provided they're ready, that is."

She watched as her nephew ran a cursory eye over the room before selecting a Hepplewhite chair and elegantly disposing his long length in it.

"I trust everything meets with your approval?"

She waved her hand to indicate the room. "Wilson's been marvellous. I don't know how he does it."

"Neither do I," admitted Wilson's employer. "And the rest of the house?"

"The same," she assured him, then continued, "I've been considering the matter of husbands for the chits. With that sort of money, I doubt we'll have trouble even if they have spots and squint."

Max merely inclined his head. "You may leave the fortune-hunters to me."

Augusta nodded. It was one of the things she particularly appreciated about Max—one never needed to spell things out. The fact that the Twinning girls were his wards would certainly see them safe from the attentions of the less desirable elements. The new Duke of Twyford was a noted Corinthian and a crack shot.

"Provided they're immediately presentable, I thought I might give a small party next week, to start the ball rolling. But if their wardrobes need attention, or they can't dance, we'll have to postpone it."

Remembering Caroline Twinning's stylish dress and her words on the matter, Max reassured her. "And I'd bet a monkey they can dance, too." For some reason, he felt quite sure Caroline Twinning waltzed. It was the only dance he ever indulged in; he was firmly convinced that she waltzed.

Augusta was quite prepared to take Max's word on such matters. If nothing else, his notorious career through the bedrooms and bordellos of England had left him with an unerring eye for all things feminine. "Next week, then," she said. "Just a few of the more useful people and a smattering of the younger crowd."

She looked up to find Max's eye on her.

"I sincerely hope you don't expect to see *me* at this event?"

"Good Lord, no! I want all attention on your wards, not on their guardian!"

Max smiled his lazy smile.

"If the girls are at all attractive, I see no problems at all in getting them settled. Who knows? One of them might snare Wolverton's boy."

"That milksop?" Max's mind rebelled at the vision of the engaging Miss Twinning on the arm of the future Earl of Wolverton. Then he shrugged. After all, he had yet to meet the three younger girls. "Who knows?"

"Do you want me to keep a firm hand on the reins, give them a push if necessary or let them wander where they will?"

Max pondered the question, searching for the right words to frame his reply. "Keep your eye on the three younger girls. They're likely to need some guidance. I haven't sighted them yet, so they may need more than that. But, despite her advanced years, I doubt Miss Twinning will need any help at all."

His aunt interpreted this reply to mean that Miss Twinning's beauty, together with her sizeable fortune, would be sufficient to overcome the stigma of her years. The assessment was reassuring, coming as it did from her reprehensible nephew, whose knowledge was extensive in such matters. As her gaze rested on the powerful figure, negligently at ease in his chair, she reflected that it really was unfair he had inherited only the best from both his parents. The combination of virility, good looks and power of both mind and body was overwhelming; throw the titles in for good measure and it was no wonder Max Rotherbridge had been the target of so many matchmaking mamas throughout his adult life. But he had shown no sign whatever of succumbing to the demure attractions of any débutante. His preference was, always had been, for women of far more voluptuous charms. The litany of his past mistresses attested to his devotion to his ideal. They had all, every last one, been well-endowed. Hardly surprising, she mused. Max was tall, powerful and vigorous. She could not readily imagine any of the delicate debs satisfying his appetites. Her wandering mind dwelt on the subject of his latest *affaire,* aside, of course, from his current *chère amie,* an opera singer, so she had been told. Emma, Lady Mortland, was a widow of barely a year's standing but she had returned to town determined, it seemed, to make up for time lost through her marriage to an ageing peer. If the *on-dits* were true, she had fallen

rather heavily in Max's lap. Looking at the strikingly
handsome face of her nephew, Augusta grinned. Undoubtedly, Lady Mortland had set her cap at a
Duchess's tiara. Deluded woman! Max, for all his air
of unconcern, was born to his position. There was no
chance he would offer marriage to Emma or any of her
ilk. He would certainly avail himself of their proffered
charms. Then when he tired of them, he would dismiss
them, generously rewarding those who had the sense to
play the game with suitable grace, callously ignoring
those who did not.

The sounds of arrival gradually filtered into the
drawing-room. Max raised his head. A spurt of feminine
chatter drifted clearly to their ears. Almost immediately,
silence was restored. Then, the door opened and Millwade,
the new butler, entered to announce, "Miss Twinning."

Caroline walked through the door and advanced into
the room, her sunny confidence cloaking her like bright
sunshine. Max, who had risen, blinked and then strolled
forward to take her hand. He bowed over it, smiling with
conscious charm into her large eyes.

Caroline returned the smile, thoroughly conversant
with its promise. While he was their guardian, she could
afford to play his games. His strong fingers retained their
clasp on her hand as he drew her forward to meet his aunt.

Augusta Benborough's mouth had fallen open at first
sight of her eldest charge. But by the time Caroline
faced her, she had recovered her composure. No wonder
Max had said she would need no help. Great heavens!
The girl was…well, no sense in beating about the
bush—she was devilishly attractive. Sensually so. Responding automatically to the introduction, Augusta

recognised the amused comprehension in the large and friendly grey eyes. Imperceptibly, she relaxed.

"Your sisters?" asked Max.

"I left them in the hall. I thought perhaps…" Caroline's words died on her lips as Max moved to the bell pull. Before she could gather her wits, Millwade was in the room, receiving his instructions. Bowing to the inevitable, Caroline closed her lips on her unspoken excuses. As she turned to Lady Benborough, her ladyship's brows rose in mute question. Caroline smiled and, with a swish of her delicate skirts, sat beside Lady Benborough. "Just watch," she whispered, her eyes dancing.

Augusta Benborough regarded her thoughtfully, then turned her attention to the door. As she did so, it opened again. First Sarah, then Arabella, then Lizzie Twinning entered the room.

A curious hiatus ensued as both Max Rotherbridge and his aunt, with more than fifty years of town bronze between them, stared in patent disbelief at their charges. The three girls stood unselfconsciously, poised and confident, and then swept curtsies, first to Max, then to her ladyship.

Caroline beckoned and they moved forward to be presented, to a speechless Max, who had not moved from his position beside his chair, and then to a flabbergasted Lady Benborough.

As they moved past him to make their curtsy to his aunt, Max recovered the use of his faculties. He closed his eyes. But when he opened them again, they were still there. He was not hallucinating. There they were: three of the loveliest lovelies he had ever set eyes on—four if you counted Miss Twinning. They were scene-stealers, every one—the sort of young women whose appearance suspended conversations, whose passage engendered rampant curiosity, aside from other, less nameable emotions, and whose departure left onlookers wondering what on earth they had been talking about before. All from the same stable, all under one roof. Nominally his. Incredible. And then the enormity, the mind-numbing, all-encompassing reality of his inheritance struck him. One glance into Miss Twinning's grey eyes, brimming with mirth, told him she understood more than enough. His voice, lacking its customary strength and in a very odd register, came to his ears. "Impossible!"

His aunt Augusta collapsed laughing.

CHAPTER THREE

"No!" Max shook his head stubbornly, a frown of quite dramatic proportions darkening his handsome face.

Lady Benborough sighed mightily and frowned back. On recovering her wits, she had sternly repressed her mirth and sent the three younger Twinnings into the courtyard. But after ten minutes of carefully reasoned argument, Max remained adamant. However, she was quite determined her scapegrace nephew would not succeed in dodging his responsibilities. Aside from anything else, the situation seemed set to afford her hours of entertainment and, at her age, such opportunities could not be lightly passed by. Her lips compressed into a thin line and a martial light appeared in her blue eyes.

Max, recognising the signs, got in first. "It's impossible! Just *think* of the talk!"

Augusta's eyes widened to their fullest extent. "Why should you care?" she asked. "Your career to date would hardly lead one to suppose you fought shy of scandal." She fixed Max with a penetrating stare. "Besides, while there'll no doubt be talk, none of it will harm anyone. Quite the opposite. It'll get these girls into the limelight!"

The black frown on Max's face did not lighten.

Caroline wisely refrained from interfering between the two principal protagonists, but sat beside Augusta, looking as innocent as she could. Max's gaze swept over her and stopped on her face. His eyes narrowed. Caroline calmly returned his scrutiny.

There was little doubt in Max's mind that Caroline Twinning had deliberately concealed from him the truth about her sisters until he had gone too far in establishing himself as their guardian to pull back. He felt sure some retribution was owing to one who had so manipulated him but, staring into her large grey-green eyes, was unable to decide which of the numerous and varied punishments his fertile imagination supplied would be the most suitable. Instead, he said, in the tones of one goaded beyond endurance, "'Commonly held to be well to pass', indeed!"

Caroline smiled.

Augusta intervened. "Whatever you're thinking of, Max, it won't do! You're the girls' guardian—you told me so yourself. You cannot simply wash your hands of them. I can see it'll be a trifle awkward for you," her eyes glazed as she thought of Lady Mortland, "but if you don't concern yourself with them, who will?"

Despite his violent response to his first sight of all four Twinning sisters, perfectly understandable in the circumstances, Max had not seriously considered giving up his guardianship of them. His behaviour over the past ten minutes had been more in the nature of an emotional rearguard action in an attempt, which his rational brain acknowledged as futile, to resist the tide of change he could see rising up to swamp his hitherto well-ordered existence. He fired his last shot. "Do you seriously imagine that someone with my reputation will be considered a suitable guardian for four…?" He paused, his eyes on Caroline, any number of highly apt descriptions revolving in his head. "Excessively attractive virgins?" he concluded savagely.

Caroline's eyes widened and her dimple appeared.

"On the contrary!" Augusta answered. "Who better than you to act as their guardian? Odds are you know every ploy ever invented and a few more besides. And if you can't keep the wolves at bay, then no one can. I really don't know why you're creating all this fuss."

Max did not know either. After a moment of silence, he turned abruptly and crossed to the windows giving on to the courtyard. He had known from the outset that this was one battle he was destined to lose. Yet some part of his mind kept suggesting in panic-stricken accents that there must be some other way. He watched as the three younger girls—his wards, heaven forbid!—examined the fountain, prodding and poking in an effort to find the lever to turn it on. They were a breathtaking sight, the varied hues of their shining hair vying with the flowers, their husky laughter and the unconsciously seductive way their supple figures swayed this way and that causing him to groan inwardly. Up to the point when he had first sighted them, the three younger Twinnings had figured in his plans as largely irrelevant entities, easily swept into the background and of no possible consequence to his plans for their elder sister. One glimpse had been enough to scuttle that scenario. He was trapped—a guardian in very truth. And with what the Twinning girls had to offer he would have no choice but to play the role to the hilt. Every man in London with eyes would be after them!

Lady Benborough eyed Max's unyielding back with a frown. Then she turned to the woman beside her. She had already formed a high opinion of Miss Twinning. What was even more to the point, being considerably more than seven, Augusta had also perceived that her reprehensible nephew was far from indifferent to the luscious beauty. Meeting the grey-green eyes, her ladyship raised her brows. Caroline nodded and rose.

Max turned as Caroline laid her hand on his arm. She was watching her sisters, not him. Her voice, when she spoke, was tactfully low. "If it would truly bother you to stand as our guardian, I'm sure we could make some other arrangement." As she finished speaking, she raised her eyes to his.

Accustomed to every feminine wile known to woman, Max nevertheless could see nothing in the lucent grey eyes to tell him whether the offer was a bluff or not. But it only took a moment to realise that if he won this particular argument, if he succeeded in withdrawing as guardian to the Twinning sisters, Caroline Twinning would be largely removed from his orbit. Which would certainly make his seduction of her more difficult, if not impossible. Faced with those large grey-green eyes, Max did what none of the habitués of Gentleman Jackson's boxing salon had yet seen him do. He threw in the towel.

HAVING RESIGNED himself to the inevitable, Max departed, leaving the ladies to become better acquainted. As the street door closed behind him, Lady Benborough turned a speculative glance on Caroline. Her lips twitched. "Very well done, my dear. Clearly you need no lessons in how to manage a man."

Caroline's smile widened. "I've had some experience, I'll admit."

"Well, you'll need it all if you're going to tackle my nephew." Augusta grinned in anticipation. From where she sat, her world looked rosy indeed. Not only did she have four rich beauties to fire off, and unlimited funds to do it with, but, glory of glories, for the first time since he had emerged from short coats her reprehensible nephew was behaving in a less than predictable fashion. She allowed herself a full minute to revel in the wildest of imaginings, before settling down to extract all the pertinent details of their backgrounds and personalities from the Twinning sisters. The younger girls returned when the tea-tray arrived. By the time it was removed, Lady Benborough had satisfied herself on all points of interest and the conversation moved on to their introduction to the *ton*.

"I wonder whether news of your existence has leaked out yet," mused her ladyship. "Someone may have seen you at Grillon's."

"Lady Jersey saw me yesterday with Max in his curricle," said Caroline.

"Did she?" Augusta sat up straighter. "In that case, there's no benefit in dragging our heels. If Silence already has the story, the sooner you make your appearance, the better. We'll go for a drive in the Park tomorrow." She ran a knowledgeable eye over the sisters' dresses. "I must say, your dresses are very attractive. Are they all like that?"

Reassured on their wardrobes, she nodded. "So there's nothing to stop us wading into the fray immediately. Good!" She let her eyes wander over the four faces in front of her, all beautiful yet each with its own allure. Her gaze rested on Lizzie. "You—Lizzie, isn't it? You're eighteen?"

Lizzie nodded. "Yes, ma'am."

"If that's so, then there's no reason for us to be missish," returned her ladyship. "I assume you all wish to find husbands?"

They all nodded decisively.

"Good! At least we're all in agreement over the objective. Now for the strategy. Although your sudden appearance all together is going to cause a riot. I rather think that's going to be the best way to begin. At the very least, we'll be noticed."

"Oh, we're *always* noticed!" returned Arabella, hazel eyes twinkling.

Augusta laughed. "I dare say." From any other young lady, the comment would have earned a reproof. However, it was impossible to deny the Twinning sisters were rather more than just beautiful, and as they were all more than green girls it was pointless to pretend they did not fully comprehend the effect they had on the opposite sex. To her ladyship's mind, it was a relief not to have to hedge around the subject.

"Aside from anything else," she continued thoughtfully, "your public appearance as the Duke of Twyford's wards will make it impossible for Max to renege on his decision." Quite why she was so very firmly set on Max fulfilling his obligations she could not have said. But his guardianship would keep him in contact with Miss Twinning. And that, she had a shrewd suspicion, would be a very good thing.

THEIR DRIVE in the Park the next afternoon was engineered by the experienced Lady Benborough to be tantalisingly brief. As predicted, the sight of four ravishing females in the Twyford barouche caused an immediate impact. As the carriage sedately bowled along the avenues, heads rapidly came together in the carriages they passed. Conversations between knots of elegant gentlemen and the more dashing of ladies who had descended from their carriages to stroll about the well-tended lawns halted in midsentence as all eyes turned to follow the Twyford barouche.

Augusta, happily aware of the stir they were causing, sat on the maroon leather seat and struggled to keep the grin from her face. Her charges were attired in a spectrum of delicate colours, for all the world like a posy of gorgeous blooms. The subtle peach of Caroline's round gown gave way to the soft turquoise tints of Sarah's. Arabella had favoured a gown of the most delicate rose muslin while Lizzie sat, like a quiet bluebell, nodding happily amid her sisters. In the soft spring sunshine, they looked like refugees from the fairy kingdom, too exquisite to be flesh and blood. Augusta lost her struggle and grinned widely at her fanciful thoughts. Then her eyes alighted on a landau drawn up to the side of the carriage-way. She raised her parasol and tapped her coachman on the shoulder. "Pull up over there."

Thus it happened that Emily, Lady Cowper and Maria, Lady Sefton, enjoying a comfortable cose in the afternoon sunshine, were the first to meet the Twinning sisters. As the Twyford carriage drew up, the eyes of both experienced matrons grew round.

Augusta noted their response with satisfaction. She seized the opportunity to perform the introductions, ending with, "Twyford's wards, you know."

That information, so casually dropped, clearly

stunned both ladies. *"Twyford's?"* echoed Lady Sefton. Her mild eyes, up to now transfixed by the spectacle that was the Twinning sisters, shifted in bewilderment to Lady Benborough's face. "How on *earth…?*"

In a few well-chosen sentences, Augusta told her. Once their ladyships had recovered from their amusement, both at once promised vouchers for the girls to attend Almack's.

"My dear, if your girls attend, we'll have to lay on more refreshments. The gentlemen will be there in droves," said Lady Cowper, smiling in genuine amusement.

"Who knows? We might even prevail on Twyford himself to attend," mused Lady Sefton.

While Augusta thought that might be stretching things a bit far, she was thankful for the immediate backing her two old friends had given her crusade to find four fashionable husbands for the Twinnings. The carriages remained together for some time as the two patronesses of Almack's learned more of His Grace of Twyford's wards. Augusta was relieved to find that all four girls could converse with ease. The two younger sisters prettily deferred to the elder two, allowing the more experienced Caroline, ably seconded by Sarah, to dominate the responses.

When they finally parted, Augusta gave the order to return to Mount Street. "Don't want to rush it," she explained to four enquiring glances. "Much better to let them come to us."

TWO DAYS LATER, the *ton* was still reeling from the discovery of the Duke of Twyford's wards. Amusement, from the wry to the ribald, had been the general reaction.

Max had gritted his teeth and borne it, but the persistent demands of his friends to be introduced to his wards sorely tried his temper. He continued to refuse all such requests. He could not stop their eventual acquaintance but at least he did not need directly to foster it. Thus, it was in a far from benign mood that he prepared to depart Delmere House on that fine April morning, in the company of two of his particular cronies, Lord Darcy Hamilton and George, Viscount Pilborough.

As they left the parlour at the rear of the house and entered the front hallway, their conversation was interrupted by a knock on the street door. They paused in the rear of the hall as Hillshaw moved majestically past to answer it.

"I'm not at home, Hillshaw," said Max.

Hillshaw regally inclined his head. "Very good, Your Grace."

But Max had forgotten that Hillshaw had yet to experience the Misses Twinning *en masse*. Resistance was impossible and they came swarming over the threshold, in a frothing of lace and cambrics, bright smiles, laughing eyes and dancing curls.

The girls immediately spotted the three men, standing rooted by the stairs. Arabella reached Max first. "Dear guardian," she sighed languishingly, eyes dancing, "are you well?" She placed her small hand on his arm.

Sarah, immediately behind, came to his other side. "We hope you are because we want to ask your permission for something." She smiled matter-of-factly up at him.

Lizzie simply stood directly in front of him, her huge eyes trained on his face, a smile she clearly knew to be winning suffusing her countenance. "Please?"

Max raised his eyes to Hillshaw, still standing dumb by the door. The sight of his redoubtable henchman rolled up by a parcel of young misses caused his lips to twitch. He firmly denied the impulse to laugh. The Misses Twinning were outrageous already and needed no further encouragement. Then his eyes met Caroline's.

She had hung back, watching her sisters go through their paces, but as his eyes touched her, she moved forward, her hand outstretched. Max, quite forgetting the presence of all the others, took it in his.

"Don't pay any attention to them, Your Grace; I'm afraid they're sad romps."

"Not *romps,* Caro," protested Arabella, eyes fluttering over the other two men, standing mesmerized just behind Max.

"It's just that we heard it was possible to go riding in the Park but Lady Benborough said we had to have your permission," explained Sarah.

"So, here we are and can we?" asked Lizzie, big eyes beseeching.

"No," said Max, without further ado. As his aunt had observed, he knew every ploy. And the opportunities afforded by rides in the Park, where chaperons could be present but sufficiently remote, were endless. The first rule in a seduction was to find the opportunity to speak alone to the lady in question. And a ride in the Park provided the perfect setting.

Caroline's fine brows rose at his refusal. Max noticed that the other three girls turned to check their elder sister's response before returning to the attack.

"Oh, you can't mean that! How shabby!"

"Why on earth not?"

"We all ride well. I haven't been out since we were home."

Both Arabella and Sarah turned to the two gentlemen still standing behind Max, silent auditors to the extraordinary scene. Arabella fixed Viscount Pilborough with pleading eyes. "Surely there's nothing unreasonable in such a request?" Under the Viscount's besotted gaze, her lashes fluttered almost imperceptibly, before her lids decorously dropped, veiling those dancing eyes, the long lashes brushing her cheeks, delicately stained with a most becoming blush.

The Viscount swallowed. "Why on earth not, Max? Not an unreasonable request at all. Your wards would look very lovely on horseback."

Max, who was only too ready to agree on how lovely his wards would look in riding habits, bit back an oath. Ignoring Miss Twinning's laughing eyes, he glowered at the hapless Viscount.

Sarah meanwhile had turned to meet the blatantly admiring gaze of Lord Darcy. Not as accomplished a flirt as Arabella, she could nevertheless hold her own, and she returned his warm gaze with a serene smile. "Is there any real reason why we shouldn't ride?"

Her low voice, cool and strangely musical, made Darcy Hamilton wish there were far fewer people in Max's hall. In fact, his fantasies would be more complete if they were not in Max's hall at all. He moved towards Sarah and expertly captured her hand. Raising it to his lips, he smiled in a way that had thoroughly seduced more damsels than he cared to recall. He could well understand why Max did not wish his wards to ride. But, having met this Twinning sister, there was no way in the world he was going to further his friend's ambition.

His lazy drawl reached Max's ears. "I'm very much afraid, Max, dear boy, that you're going to have to concede. The opposition is quite overwhelming."

Max glared at him. Seeing the determination in his lordship's grey eyes and understanding his reasons only too well, he knew he was outnumbered on all fronts. His eyes returned to Caroline's face to find her regarding him quizzically. "Oh, very well!"

Her smile warmed him and at the prompting lift of her brows he introduced his friends, first to her, and then to her sisters in turn. The chattering voices washed over him, his friends' deeper tones running like a counterpoint in the cacophony. Caroline moved to his side.

"You're not seriously annoyed by us riding, are you?"

He glanced down at her. The stern set of his lips reluctantly relaxed. "I would very much rather you did not. However," he continued, his eyes roving to the group of her three sisters and his two friends, busy with noisy plans for their first ride that afternoon, "I can see that's impossible."

Caroline smiled. "We won't come to any harm, I assure you."

"Allow me to observe, Miss Twinning, that gallivanting about the London *ton* is fraught with rather more difficulty than you would have encountered in American society, nor yet within the circle to which you were accustomed in Hertfordshire."

A rich chuckle greeted his warning. "Fear not, dear guardian," she said, raising laughing eyes to his. Max noticed the dimple, peeking irrepressibly from beside her soft mouth. "We'll manage."

NATURALLY, MAX FELT obliged to join the riding party that afternoon. Between both his and Darcy Hamilton's extensive stables, they had managed to assemble suitable mounts for the four girls. Caroline had assured him that, like all country misses, they could ride very well. By the time they gained the Park, he had satisfied himself on that score. At least he need not worry over them losing control of the frisky horses and being thrown. But, as they were all as stunning as he had feared they would be, elegantly gowned in perfectly cut riding habits, his worries had not noticeably decreased.

As they ambled further into the Park, by dint of the simple expedient of reining in his dappled grey, he dropped to the rear of the group, the better to keep the three younger girls in view. Caroline, riding by his side, stayed with him. She threw him a laughing glance but made no comment.

As he had expected, they had not gone more than two hundred yards before their numbers were swelled by the appearance of Lord Tulloch and young Mr. Mitchell. But neither of these gentlemen seemed able to interrupt the rapport which, to Max's experienced eye, was developing with alarming rapidity between Sarah Twinning and Darcy Hamilton. Despite his fears, he grudgingly admitted the Twinning sisters knew a trick or two. Arabella flirted outrageously but did so with all gentlemen, none being able to claim any special consideration. Lizzie attracted the quieter men and was happy to converse on the matters currently holding the interest of the *ton*. Her natural shyness and understated youth, combined with her undeniable beauty, was a heady tonic for these more sober gentlemen. As they ventured deeper into the Park, Max was relieved to find Sarah giving Darcy no opportunity to lead her apart. Gradually, his watchfulness relaxed. He turned to Caroline.

"Have you enjoyed your first taste of life in London?"

"Yes, thank you," she replied, grey eyes smiling. "Your aunt has been wonderful. I can't thank you enough for all you've done."

Max's brow clouded. As it happened, the last thing he wanted was her gratitude. Here he was, thinking along lines not grossly dissimilar from Darcy's present preoccupation, and the woman chose to thank him. He glanced down at her as she rode beside him, her face free of any worry, thoroughly enjoying the moment. Her presence was oddly calming.

"What plans do you have for the rest of the week?" he asked.

Caroline was slightly surprised by his interest but replied readily. "We've been driving in the Park every afternoon except today. I expect we'll continue to appear, although I rather think, from now on, it will be on horseback." She shot him a measuring glance to see how he would take that. His face was slightly grim but he nodded in acceptance. "Last evening, we went to a small party given by Lady Malling. Your aunt said there are a few more such gatherings in the next week which we should attend, to give ourselves confidence in society."

Max nodded again. From the corner of his eye, he saw Sarah avoid yet another of Darcy's invitations to separate from the group. He saw the quick frown which showed fleetingly in his friend's eyes. Serve him right if the woman drove him mad. But, he knew, Darcy was made of sterner stuff. The business of keeping his wards out of the arms of his friends was going to be deucedly tricky. Returning to contemplation of Miss Twinning's delightful countenance, he asked, "Has Aunt Augusta got you vouchers for Almack's yet?"

"Yes. We met Lady Sefton and Lady Cowper on our first drive in the Park."

Appreciating his aunt's strategy, Max grinned. "Trust Aunt Augusta."

Caroline returned his smile. "She's been very good to us."

Thinking that the unexpected company of four lively young women must have been a shock to his aunt's system, Max made a mental note to do anything in his power to please his aunt Benborough.

They had taken a circuitous route through the Park and only now approached the fashionable precincts. The small group almost immediately swelled to what, to Max, were alarming proportions, with every available gentleman clamouring for an introduction to his beautiful wards. But, to his surprise, at a nod from Caroline, the girls obediently brought their mounts closer and refused every attempt to draw them further from his protective presence. To his astonishment, they all behaved with the utmost decorum, lightened, of course, by their natural liveliness but nevertheless repressively cool to any who imagined them easy targets. Despite his qualms, he was impressed. They continued in this way until they reached the gates of the Park, by which time the group had dwindled to its original size and he could relax again.

He turned to Caroline, still by his side. "Can you guarantee they'll always behave so circumspectly, or was that performance purely for my benefit?" As her laughing eyes met his, he tried to decide whether they were greeny-grey or greyish-green. An intriguing question.

"Oh, we're experienced enough to know which way to jump, I assure you," she returned. After a pause, she continued, her voice lowered so only he could hear. "In the circumstances, we would not willingly do anything to bring disrepute on ourselves. We are very much aware of what we owe to you and Lady Benborough."

Max knew he should be pleased at this avowal of good intentions. Instead, he was aware of a curious irritation. He would certainly do everything in his power to reinforce her expressed sentiment with respect to the three younger girls, but to have Caroline Twinning espousing such ideals was not in keeping with his plans. Somehow, he was going to have to convince her that adherence to all the social strictures was not the repayment he, at least, would desire. The unwelcome thought that, whatever the case, she might now consider herself beholden to him, and would, therefore, grant him his wishes out of gratitude, very nearly made him swear aloud. His horse jibbed at the suddenly tightened rein and he pushed the disturbing thought aside while he dealt with the grey. Once the horse had settled again, he continued by Caroline's side as they headed back to Mount Street, a distracted frown at the back of his dark blue eyes.

AUGUSTA BENBOROUGH flicked open her fan and plied it vigorously. Under cover of her voluminous skirts, she slipped her feet free of her evening slippers. She had forgotten how stifling the small parties, held in the run-up to the Season proper, could be. Every bit as bad as the crushes later in the Season. But there, at least, she would have plenty of her own friends to gossip with. The mothers and chaperons of the current batch of débutantes were a generation removed from her own and at these small parties they were generally the only older members present. Miriam Alford had elected to remain at Twyford House this evening, which left Augusta with little to do but watch her charges. And even that, she mused to herself, was not exactly riveting entertainment.

True, Max was naturally absent, which meant her primary interest in the entire business was in abeyance. Still, it was comforting to find Caroline treating all the gentlemen who came her way with the same unfailing courtesy and no hint of partiality. Arabella, too, seemed to be following that line, although, in her case, the courtesy was entirely cloaked in a lightly flirtatious manner. In any other young girl, Lady Benborough would have strongly argued for a more demure style. But she had watched Arabella carefully. The girl had quick wits and a ready tongue. She never stepped beyond what was acceptable, though she took delight in sailing close to the wind. Now, convinced that no harm would come of Arabella's artful play, Augusta nodded benignly as that young lady strolled by, accompanied by the inevitable gaggle of besotted gentlemen.

One of their number was declaiming,

"'My dearest flower,
More beautiful by the hour,
To you I give my heart.'"

Arabella laughed delightedly and quickly said, "My dear sir, I beg you spare my blushes! Truly, your verses do me more credit than I deserve. But surely, to do them justice, should you not set them down on parchment?" Anything was preferable to having them said aloud.

The budding poet, young Mr. Rawlson, beamed. "*Nothing* would give me greater pleasure, Miss Arabella. I'll away and transcribe them immediately. And dedicate them to your inspiration!" With a flourishing bow, he departed precipitately, leaving behind a silence pregnant with suppressed laughter.

This was broken by a snigger from Lord Shannon. "Silly puppy!"

As Mr. Rawlson was a year or two older than Lord Shannon, who himself appeared very young despite his attempts to ape the Corinthians, this comment itself caused some good-natured laughter.

"Perhaps, Lord Shannon, you would be so good as to fetch me some refreshment?" Arabella smiled sweetly on the hapless youngster. With a mutter which all interpreted to mean he was delighted to be of service to one so fair, the young man escaped.

With a smile, Arabella turned to welcome Viscount Pilborough to her side.

Augusta's eyelids drooped. The temperature in the room seemed to rise another degree. The murmuring voices washed over her. Her head nodded. With a start, she shook herself awake. Determined to keep her mind active for the half-hour remaining, she sought out her charges. Lizzie was chattering animatedly with a group of débutantes much her own age. The youngest Twinning was surprisingly innocent, strangely unaware of her attractiveness to the opposite sex, still little more than a schoolgirl at heart. Lady Benborough smiled.

Lizzie would learn soon enough; let her enjoy her girlish gossiping while she might.

A quick survey of the room brought Caroline to light, strolling easily on the arm of the most eligible Mr. Willoughby.

"It's so good of you to escort your sister to these parties, sir. I'm sure Miss Charlotte must be very grateful." Caroline found conversation with the reticent Mr. Willoughby a particular strain.

A faint smile played at the corners of Mr. Willoughby's thin lips. "Indeed, I believe she is. But really, there is very little to it. As my mother is so delicate as to find these affairs quite beyond her, it would be churlish of me indeed to deny Charlotte the chance of becoming more easy in company before she is presented."

With grave doubts over how much longer she could endure such ponderous conversation without running amok, Caroline seized the opportunity presented by passing a small group of young ladies, which included the grateful Charlotte, to stop. The introductions were quickly performed.

As she stood conversing with a Miss Denbright, an occupation which required no more than half her brain, Caroline allowed her eyes to drift over the company. Other than Viscount Pilborough, who was dangling after Arabella in an entirely innocuous fashion, and Darcy Hamilton, who was pursuing Sarah in a far more dangerous way, there was no gentleman in whom she felt the least interest. Even less than her sisters did she need the opportunity of the early parties to gain confidence. Nearly eighteen months of social consorting in the ball-

rooms and banquet halls in New York had given them
all a solid base on which to face the London *ton*. And
even more than her sisters, Caroline longed to get on
with it. Time, she felt, was slipping inexorably by. Still,
there were only four more days to go. And then, surely
their guardian would reappear? She had already discovered that no other gentleman's eyes could make her feel
quite the same breathless excitement as the Duke of
Twyford's did. He had not called on them since that first
ride in the Park, a fact which had left her with a wholly
resented feeling of disappointment. Despite the
common sense on which she prided herself, she had
formed an irritating habit of comparing all the men she
met with His domineering Grace and inevitably found
them wanting. Such foolishness would have to stop.
With a small suppressed sigh, she turned a charming
smile on Mr. Willoughby, wishing for the sixteenth time
that his faded blue eyes were of a much darker hue.

Satisfied that Caroline, like Lizzie and Arabella,
needed no help from her, Lady Benborough moved her
gaze on, scanning the room for Sarah's dark head. When
her first survey drew no result, she sat up straighter, a
slight frown in her eyes. Darcy Hamilton was here,
somewhere, drat him. He had attended every party they
had been to this week, a fact which of itself had already
drawn comment. His attentions to Sarah were becoming
increasingly marked. Augusta knew all the Hamiltons.
She had known Darcy's father and doubted not the truth
of the 'like father, like son' adage. But surely Sarah was
too sensible to... She wasted no time in completing that
thought but started a careful, methodical and entirely
well-disguised visual search. From her present position,

on a slightly raised dais to one side, she commanded a view of the whole room. Her gaze passed over the alcove set in the wall almost directly opposite her but then returned, caught by a flicker of movement within the shadowed recess.

There they were, Sarah and, without doubt, Darcy Hamilton. Augusta could just make out the blur of colour that was Sarah's green dress. How typical of Darcy. They were still in the room, still within sight, but, in the dim light of the alcove, almost private. As her eyes adjusted to the poor light, Augusta saw to her relief that, despite her fears and Darcy's reputation, they were merely talking, seated beside one another on a small settee. Still, to her experienced eye, there was a degree of familiarity in their pose, which, given that it must be unconscious, was all too revealing. With a sigh, she determined to have a word, if not several words, with Sarah, regarding the fascinations of men like Darcy Hamilton. She would have to do it, for Darcy's proclivities were too well-known to doubt.

She watched as Darcy leaned closer to Sarah.

"My dear," drawled Darcy Hamilton, "do you have any idea of the temptation you pose? Or the effect beauty such as yours has on mere men?"

His tone was lazy and warm, with a quality of velvety smoothness which fell like a warm cloak over Sarah's already hypersensitized nerves. He had flung one arm over the back of the settee and long fingers were even now twining in the soft curls at her nape. She knew she should move but could not. The sensations rippling down her spine were both novel and exhilarating. She was conscious of a ludicrous desire to snuggle into that

warmth, to invite more soft words. But the desire which
burned in his lordship's grey eyes was already frighteningly intense. She determinedly ignored the small
reckless voice which urged her to encourage him and
instead replied, "Why, no. Of course not."

Darcy just managed to repress a snort of disgust.
Damn the woman! Her voice had held not the thread of
a quaver. Calm and steady as a rock when his own pulses
were well and truly racing. He simply did not believe
it. He glanced down into her wide brown eyes, guileless as ever, knowing that his exasperation was showing.
For a fleeting instant, he saw a glimmer of amusement
and, yes, of triumph in the brown depths. But when he
looked again, the pale face was once again devoid of
emotion. His grey eyes narrowed.

Sarah saw his intent look and immediately dropped
her eyes.

Her action confirmed Darcy's suspicions. By God,
the chit was playing with him! The fact that Sarah could
only be dimly aware of the reality of the danger she was
flirting with was buried somewhere in the recesses of his
mind. But, like all the Hamiltons, for him, desire could
easily sweep aside all reason. In that instant, he determined he would have her, no matter what the cost. Not
here, not now—neither place nor time was right. But
some time, somewhere, Sarah Twinning would be his.

Augusta's attention was drawn by the sight of a
mother gathering her two daughters and preparing to
depart. As if all had been waiting for this signal, it
suddenly seemed as if half the room was on their way.
With relief, she turned to see Darcy lead Sarah from the
alcove and head in her direction. As Caroline ap-

proached, closely followed by Lizzie and Arabella, Augusta Benborough wriggled her aching toes back into her slippers and rose. It was over. And in four days' time the Season would begin. As she smiled benignly upon the small army of gentlemen who had escorted her charges to her side, she reminded herself that, with the exception of Darcy Hamilton, there was none present tonight who would make a chaperon uneasy. Once in wider society, she would have no time to be bored. The Twinning sisters would certainly see to that.

CHAPTER FOUR

EMMA, LADY MORTLAND, thought Max savagely, had no right to the title. He would grant she was attractive, in a blowsy sort of way, but her conduct left much to be desired. She had hailed him almost as soon as he had entered the Park. He rarely drove there except when expediency demanded. Consequently, her ladyship had been surprised to see his curricle, drawn by his famous match bays, advancing along the avenue. He had been forced to pull up or run the silly woman down. The considerable difficulty in conversing at any length with someone perched six feet and more above you, particularly when that someone displayed the most blatant uninterest, had not discouraged Lady Mortland. She had done her best to prolong the exchange in the dim hope, Max knew, of gaining an invitation to ride beside him. She had finally admitted defeat and archly let him go, but not before issuing a thickly veiled invitation which he had had no compunction in declining. As she had been unwise enough to speak in the hearing of two gentlemen of her acquaintance, her resulting embarrassment was entirely her own fault. He knew she entertained hopes, totally unfounded, of becoming his Duchess. Why she should imagine he would consider taking a woman with the morals of an alley cat to wife was beyond him.

As he drove beneath the trees, he scanned the carriages that passed, hoping to find his wards. He had not seen them since that first ride in the Park, a feat of self-discipline before which any other he had ever accomplished in his life paled into insignificance. Darcy Hamilton had put the idea into his head. His friend had returned with him to Delmere House after that first jaunt, vociferous in his complaints of the waywardness of Sarah Twinning. The fact that she was Max's ward had not subdued him in the least. Max had not been surprised; Darcy could be ruthlessly singleminded when hunting. It had been Darcy who had suggested that a short absence might make the lady more amenable and had departed with the firm resolve to give the Twinning girls the go-by for at least a week.

That had been six days ago. The Season was about to get under way and it was time to reacquaint himself with his wards. Having ascertained that their horses had not left his stable, he had had the bays put to and followed them to the Park. He finally spied the Twyford barouche drawn up to the side of the avenue. He pulled up alongside.

"Aunt Augusta," he said as he nodded to her. She beamed at him, clearly delighted he had taken the trouble to find them. His gaze swept over the other occupants of the carriage in an appraising and approving manner, then came to rest on Miss Twinning. She smiled sunnily back at him. Suddenly alert, Max's mind returned from where it had wandered and again counted heads. There was a total of five in the carriage but

Miriam Alford was there, smiling vaguely at him. Which meant one of his wards was missing. He quelled the urge to immediately question his aunt, telling himself there would doubtless be some perfectly reasonable explanation. Perhaps one was merely unwell. His mind reverted to its main preoccupation.

Responding automatically to his aunt's social chatter, he took the first opportunity to remark, "But I can't keep my horses standing, ma'am. Perhaps Miss Twinning would like to come for a drive?"

He was immediately assured that Miss Twinning would and she descended from the carriage. He reached down to help her up beside him and they were off.

Caroline gloried in the brush of the breeze on her face as the curricle bowled along. Even reined in to the pace accepted in the Park, it was still infinitely more refreshing than the funereal plod favoured by Lady Benborough. That was undoubtedly the reason her spirits had suddenly soared. Even the sunshine seemed distinctly brighter.

"Not riding today?" asked Max.

"No. Lady Benborough felt we should not entirely desert the matrons."

Max smiled. "True enough. It don't do to put people's backs up unnecessarily."

Caroline turned to stare at him. "Your philosophy?" Augusta had told her enough of their guardian's past to realise this was unlikely.

Max frowned. Miss Caroline Twinning was a great deal too knowing. Unprepared to answer her query, he changed the subject. "Where's Sarah?"

"Lord Darcy took her up some time ago. Maybe we'll see them as we go around?"

Max suppressed the curse which rose to his lips. How many friends was he going to have left by the end of this Season? Another thought occurred. "Has she been seeing much of him?"

A deep chuckle answered this and his uneasiness grew. "If you mean has he taken to haunting us, no. On the other hand, he seems to have the entrée to all the salons we've attended this week."

He should, he supposed, have anticipated his friend's duplicity. Darcy was, after all, every bit as experienced as he. Still, it rankled. He would have a few harsh words to say to his lordship when next they met. "Has he been…particularly attentive towards her?"

"No," she replied in a careful tone, "not in any unacceptable way."

He looked his question and she continued, "It's just that she's the only lady he pays any attention to at all. If he's not with Sarah, he either leaves or retires to the card tables or simply watches her from a distance."

The description was so unlike the Darcy Hamilton he knew that it was on the tip of his tongue to verify they were talking about the same man. A sneaking suspicion that Darcy might, just might, be seriously smitten awoke in his mind. One black brow rose.

They paused briefly to exchange greetings with Lady Jersey, then headed back towards the barouche. Coming to a decision, Max asked, "What's your next major engagement?"

"Well, we go to the first of Almack's balls tomorrow, then it's the Billingtons' ball the next night."

The start of the Season proper. But there was no way he was going to cross the threshold of Almack's. He had not been near the place for years. Tender young virgins were definitely not on his menu these days. He did not equate that description with Miss Twinning. Nor, if it came to that, to her sisters. Uncertain what to do for the best, he made no response to the information, merely inclining his head to show he had heard.

Caroline was silent as the curricle retraced its journey. Max's questions had made her uneasy. Lord Darcy was a particular friend of his—surely Sarah was in no real danger with him? She stifled a small sigh. Clearly, their guardian's attention was wholly concentrated on their social performance. Which, of course, was precisely what a guardian should be concerned with. Why, then, did she feel such a keen sense of disappointment?

They reached the barouche to find Sarah already returned. One glance at her stormy countenance was sufficient to answer Max's questions. It seemed Darcy's plans had not prospered. Yet.

As he handed Caroline to the ground and acknowledged her smiling thanks, it occurred to him she had not expressed any opinion or interest in his week-long absence. So much for that tactic. As he watched her climb into the barouche, shapely ankles temporarily exposed, he realised he had made no headway during their interlude. Her sister's affair with his friend had dominated his thoughts. Giving his horses the office, he grimaced to himself. Seducing a young woman while acting as guardian to her three younger sisters was clearly going to be harder going than he had imagined.

CLIMBING THE STEPS to Twyford House the next evening, Max was still in two minds over whether he was doing the right thing. He was far too wise to be overly attentive to Caroline, yet, if he did not make a push to engage her interest, she would shortly be the object of the attentions of a far larger circle of gentlemen, few of whom would hesitate to attend Almack's purely because they disliked being mooned over by very young women. He hoped, in his capacity as their guardian, to confine his attentions to the Twinning sisters and so escape the usual jostle of matchmaking mamas. They should have learned by now that he was not likely to succumb to their daughters' vapid charms. Still, he was not looking forward to the evening.

If truth were told, he had been hearing about his wards on all sides for the past week. They had caught the fancy of the *ton,* starved as it was of novelty. And their brand of beauty always had attraction. But what he had not heard was worrying him more. There had been more than one incident when, entering a room, he had been aware of at least one conversation abruptly halted, then smoothly resumed. Another reason to identify himself more closely with his wards. He reminded himself that three of them were truly his responsibility and, in the circumstances, the polite world would hold him responsible for Miss Twinning as well. His duty was clear.

Admitted to Twyford House, Max paused to exchange a few words with Millwade. Satisfied that all was running smoothly, he turned and stopped, all thought deserting him. Transfixed, he watched the Twinning sisters descend the grand staircase. Seen together, gorgeously garbed for the ball, they were quite the most heart-stopping sight he had beheld in many a

year. His eyes rested with acclaim on each in turn, but
stopped when they reached Caroline. The rest of the
company seemed to dissolve in a haze as his eyes
roamed appreciatively over the clean lines of her eau-
de-Nil silk gown. It clung suggestively to her ripe figure,
the neckline scooped low over her generous breasts.
His hands burned with the desire to caress those tantal-
ising curves. Then his eyes locked with hers as she
crossed the room to his side, her hand extended to him.
Automatically, he took it in his. Then she was speaking,
smiling up at him in her usual confiding way.

"Thank you for coming. I do hope you'll not be too
bored by such tame entertainment." Lady Benborough,
on receiving Max's curt note informing them of his intention to accompany them to Almack's, had crowed
with delight. When she had calmed, she had explained
his aversion to the place. So it was with an unexpected
feeling of guilt that Caroline had come forward to
welcome him. But, gazing into his intensely blue eyes,
she could find no trace of annoyance or irritation.
Instead, she recognised the same emotion she had
detected the very first time they had met. To add to her
confusion, he raised her hand to his lips, his eyes warm
and entirely too knowing.

"Do you know, I very much doubt that I'll be bored
at all?" her guardian murmured wickedly.

Caroline blushed vividly. Luckily, this was missed by
all but Max in the relatively poor light of the hall and
the bustle as they donned their cloaks. Both Lady Benborough and Miriam Alford were to go, cutting the odds
between chaperons and charges. Before Max's interven-
tion, the coach would have had to do two trips to King

Street. Now, Caroline found that Augusta and Mrs.
Alford, together with Sarah and Arabella, were to go in
the Twyford coach while she and Lizzie were to travel
with Max. Suddenly suspicious of her guardian's intentions, she was forced to accept the arrangement with
suitable grace. As Max handed her into the carriage and
saw her settled comfortably, she told herself she was a
fool to read into his behaviour anything other than an
attempt to trip her up. He was only amusing himself.

As if to confirm her supposition, the journey was un-
remarkable and soon they were entering the hallowed
precincts of the Assembly Rooms. The sparsely furnished halls were already well filled with the usual mix
of débutantes and unmarried young ladies, carefully
chaperoned by their mamas in the hope of finding a
suitable connection among the unattached gentlemen
strolling through the throng. It was a social club to
which it was necessary to belong. And it was clear from
their reception that, at least as far as the gentlemen were
concerned, the Twinning sisters definitely belonged. To
Max's horror, they were almost mobbed.

He stood back and watched the sisters artfully
manage their admirers. Arabella had the largest court
with all the most rackety and dangerous blades. A more
discerning crowd of eminently eligible gentlemen had
formed around Sarah while the youthful Lizzie had
gathered all the more earnest of the younger men to her.
But the group around Caroline drew his deepest consideration. There were more than a few highly dangerous
roués in the throng gathered about her but all were experienced and none was likely to attempt anything scandalous without encouragement. As he watched, it

became clear that all four girls had an innate ability to choose the more acceptable among their potential partners. They also had the happy knack of dismissing the less favoured with real charm, a not inconsiderable feat. The more he watched, the more intrigued Max became. He was about to seek clarification from his aunt, standing beside him, when that lady very kindly answered his unspoken query.

"You needn't worry, y'know. Those girls have got heads firmly on their shoulders. Ever since they started going about, I've been bombarded with questions on who's eligible and who's not. Even Arabella, minx that she is, takes good care to know who she's flirting with."

Max looked his puzzlement.

"Well," explained her ladyship, surprised by his obtuseness, "they're all set on finding husbands, of course!" She glanced up at him, eyes suddenly sharp, and added, "I should think you'd be thrilled—it means they'll be off your hands all the sooner."

"Yes. Of course," Max answered absently.

He stayed by his wards until they were claimed for the first dance. His sharp eyes had seen a number of less than desirable gentlemen approach the sisters, only to veer away as they saw him. If nothing else, his presence had achieved that much.

Searching through the crowd, he finally spotted Darcy Hamilton disappearing into one of the salons where refreshments were laid out.

"Going to give them the go-by for at least a week, huh?" he growled as he came up behind Lord Darcy.

Darcy choked on the lemonade he had just drunk.

Max gazed in horror at the glass in his friend's hand. "No! Bless me, Darcy! You turned temperate?"

Darcy grimaced. "Have to drink something and seemed like the best of a bad lot." His wave indicated the unexciting range of beverages available. "Thirsty work, getting a dance with one of your wards."

"Incidentally—" intoned Max in the manner of one about to pass judgement.

But Darcy held up his hand. "No. Don't start. I don't need any lectures from you on the subject. And you don't need to bother, anyway. Sarah Twinning has her mind firmly set on marriage and there's not a damned thing I can do about it."

Despite himself, Max could not resist a grin. "No luck?"

"None!" replied Darcy, goaded. "I'm almost at the stage of considering offering for her but I can't be sure she wouldn't reject me, and *that* I couldn't take."

Max, picking up a glass of lemonade himself, became thoughtful.

Suddenly, Darcy roused himself. "Do you know what she told me yesterday? Said I spent too much time on horses and not enough on matters of importance. *Can* you believe it?"

He gestured wildly and Max nearly hooted with laughter. Lord Darcy's stables were known the length and breadth of England as among the biggest and best producers of quality horseflesh.

"I very much doubt that she appreciates your interest in the field," Max said placatingly.

"Humph," was all his friend vouchsafed.

After a pause, Darcy laid aside his glass. "Going to

find Maria Sefton and talk her into giving Sarah permission to waltz with me. One thing she won't be able to refuse." With a nod to Max, he returned to the main hall.

For some minutes, Max remained as he was, his abstracted gaze fixed on the far wall. Then, abruptly, he replaced his glass and followed his friend.

"YOU WANT ME to give *your ward* permission to waltz with you?" Lady Jersey repeated Max's request, clearly unable to decide whether it was as innocuous as he represented or whether it had an ulterior motive concealed within and if so, what.

"It's really not such an odd request," returned Max, unperturbed. "She's somewhat older than the rest and, as I'm here, it seems appropriate."

"Hmm." Sally Jersey simply did not believe there was not more to it. She had been hard-pressed to swallow her astonishment when she had seen His Grace of Twyford enter the room. And she was even more amazed that he had not left as soon as he had seen his wards settled. But he was, after all, Twyford. And Delmere and Rotherbridge, what was more. So, if he wanted to dance with his ward… She shrugged. "Very well. Bring her to me. If you can separate her from her court, that is."

Max smiled in a way that reminded Lady Jersey of the causes of his reputation. "I think I'll manage," he drawled, bowing over her hand.

CAROLINE WAS surprised that Max had remained at the Assembly Rooms for so long. She lost sight of him for a while, and worked hard at forcing herself to pay attention to her suitors, for it was only to be expected their guardian would seek less tame entertainment elsewhere. But then his tall figure reappeared at the side of the room. He seemed to be scanning the multitude, then, over a sea of heads, his eyes met hers. Caroline fervently hoped the peculiar shock which went through her was not reflected in her countenance. After a moment, unobtrusively, he made his way to her side.

Under cover of the light flirtation she was engaged in with an ageing baronet, Caroline was conscious of the sudden acceleration of her heartbeat and the constriction that seemed to be affecting her breathing. Horrendously aware of her guardian's blue eyes, she felt her nervousness grow as he approached despite her efforts to remain calm.

But, when he gained her side and bowed over her hand in an almost bored way, uttering the most commonplace civilities and engaging her partner in a discussion of some sporting event, the anticlimax quickly righted her mind for her.

Quite how it was accomplished she could not have said, but Max succeeded in excusing them to her court, on the grounds that he had something to discuss with his ward. Finding herself on his arm, strolling apparently randomly down the room, she turned to him and asked, "What was it you wished to say to me?"

He glanced down at her and she caught her breath. That devilish look was back in his eyes as they rested on her, warming her through and through. What on earth was he playing at?

"Good heavens, my ward. And I thought you up to all the rigs. Don't you know a ruse when you hear it?"

The tones of his voice washed languorously over Caroline, leaving a sense of relaxation in their wake. She made a grab for her fast-disappearing faculties. Interpreting his remark to mean that his previously bored attitude had also been false, Caroline was left wondering what the present reality meant. She made a desperate bid to get their interaction back on an acceptable footing. "Where are we going?"

Max smiled. "We're on our way to see Lady Jersey."

"Why?"

"Patience, sweet Caroline," came the reply, all the more outrageous for its tone. "All will be revealed forthwith."

They reached Lady Jersey's side where she stood just inside the main room.

"There you are, Twyford!"

The Duke of Twyford smoothly presented his ward. Her ladyship's prominent eyes rested on the curtsying Caroline, then, as the younger woman rose, widened with a suddenly arrested expression. She opened her mouth to ask the question burning the tip of her tongue but caught His Grace's eye and, reluctantly swallowing her curiosity, said, "My dear Miss Twinning. Your guardian has requested you to be given permission to waltz and I have no hesitation in granting it. And, as he is here, I present the Duke as a suitable partner."

With considerable effort, Caroline managed to school her features to impassivity. Luckily, the musicians struck up at that moment, so that she barely had time to murmur her thanks to Lady Jersey before Max swept her on to the floor, leaving her ladyship, intrigued, staring after them.

Caroline struggled to master the unnerving sensation

of being in her guardian's arms. He was holding her closer than strictly necessary, but, as they twirled down the room, she realised that to everyone else they presented a perfect picture of the Duke of Twyford doing the pretty by his eldest ward. Only she was close enough to see the disturbing glint in his blue eyes and hear the warmth in his tone as he said, "My dear ward, what a very accomplished dancer you are. Tell me, what other talents do you have that I've yet to sample?"

For the life of her, Caroline could not tear her eyes from his. She heard his words and understood their meaning but her brain refused to react. No shock, no scandalized response came to her lips. Instead, her mind was completely absorbed with registering the unbelievable fact that, despite their relationship of guardian and ward, Max Rotherbridge had every intention of seducing her. His desire was clear in the heat of his blue, blue gaze, in the way his hand at her back seemed to burn through the fine silk of her gown, in the gentle caress of his long fingers across her knuckles as he twirled her about the room under the long noses of the biggest gossips in London.

Mesmerized, she had sufficient presence of mind to keep a gentle smile fixed firmly on her face but her thoughts were whirling even faster than her feet. With a superhuman effort, she forced her lids to drop, screening her eyes from his. "Oh, we Twinnings have many accomplishments, dear guardian." To her relief, her voice was clear and untroubled. "But I'm desolated to have to admit that they're all hopelessly mundane."

A rich chuckle greeted this. "Permit me to tell you, my ward, that, for the skills I have in mind, your qualifi-

cations are more than adequate." Caroline's eyes flew
to his. She could hardly believe her ears. But Max continued before she could speak, his blue eyes holding
hers, his voice a seductive murmur. "And while you
naturally lack experience, I assure you that can easily,
and most enjoyably, be remedied."

It was too much. Caroline gave up the struggle to
divine his motives and made a determined bid to rein-
stitute sanity. She smiled into the dark face above hers
and said, quite clearly, "This isn't happening."

For a moment, Max was taken aback. Then, his sense
of humour surfaced. "No?"

"Of course not," Caroline calmly replied. "You're
my guardian and I'm your ward. Therefore, it is simply
not possible for you to have said what you just did."

Studying her serene countenance, Max recognised
the strategy and reluctantly admired her courage for
adopting it. As things stood, it was not an easy defence
for him to overcome. Reading in the grey-green eyes a
determination not to be further discomposed, Max, too
wise to push further, gracefully yielded.

"So what do you think of Almack's?" he asked.

Relieved, Caroline took the proffered olive branch
and their banter continued on an impersonal level.

At the end of the dance, Max suavely surrendered her
to her admirers, but not without a glance which, if she
had allowed herself to think about it, would have made
Caroline blush. She did not see him again until it was
time for them to quit the Assembly Rooms. In order to
survive the evening, she had sternly refused to let her
mind dwell on his behaviour. Consequently, it had not
occurred to her to arrange to exchange her place in her

guardian's carriage for one in the Twyford coach. When Lizzie came to tug at her sleeve with the information that the others had already left, she perceived her error. But the extent of her guardian's foresight did not become apparent until they were halfway home.

She and Max shared the forward facing seat with Lizzie curled up in a corner opposite them. On departing King Street, they preserved a comfortable silence— due to tiredness in Lizzie's case, from being too absorbed with her thoughts in her case and, as she suddenly realised, from sheer experience in the case of her guardian.

They were still some distance from Mount Street when, without warning, Max took her hand in his. Surprised, she turned to look up at him, conscious of his fingers moving gently over hers. Despite the darkness of the carriage, his eyes caught hers. Deliberately, he raised her hand and kissed her fingertips. A delicious tingle raced along Caroline's nerves, followed by a second of increased vigour as he turned her hand over and placed a lingering kiss on her wrist. But they were nothing compared to the galvanising shock that hit her when, without giving any intimation of his intent, he bent his head and his lips found hers.

From Max's point of view, he was behaving with admirable restraint. He knew Lizzie was sound asleep and that his manipulative and normally composed eldest ward was well out of her depth. Yet he reined in his desires and kept the kiss light, his lips moving gently over hers, gradually increasing the pressure until she parted her lips. He savoured the warm sweetness of her mouth, then, inwardly smiling at the response she had been unable to hide, he withdrew and watched as her eyes slowly refocused.

Caroline, eyes round, looked at him in consternation. Then her shocked gaze flew to Lizzie, still curled in her corner.

"Don't worry. She's sound asleep." His voice was deep and husky in the dark carriage.

Caroline, stunned, felt oddly reassured by the sound. Then she felt the carriage slow.

"And you're safe home," came the gently mocking voice.

In a daze, Caroline helped him wake Lizzie and then Max very correctly escorted them indoors, a smile of wicked contentment on his face.

ARABELLA STIFLED a wistful sigh and smiled brightly at the earnest young man who was guiding her around the floor in yet another interminable waltz. It had taken only a few days of the Season proper for her to sort through her prospective suitors. And come to the unhappy conclusion that none matched her requirements. The lads were too young, the men too old. There seemed to be no one in between. Presumably many were away with Wellington's forces, but surely there were those who could not leave the important business of keeping England running? And surely not all of them were old? She could not describe her ideal man, yet was sure she would instantly know when she met him. She was convinced she would feel it, like a thunderbolt from the blue. Yet no male of her acquaintance increased her heartbeat one iota.

Keeping up a steady and inconsequential conversa-

tion with her partner, something she could do half
asleep, Arabella sighted her eldest sister, elegantly
waltzing with their guardian. Now there was a coil.
There was little doubt in Arabella's mind of the cause
of Caroline's bright eyes and slightly flushed countenance. She looked radiant. But could a guardian marry
his ward? Or, more to the point, was their guardian
intent on marriage or had he some other arrangement in
mind? Still, she had complete faith in Caroline. There
had been many who had worshipped at her feet with
something other than matrimony in view, yet her eldest
sister had always had their measure. True, none had
affected her as Max Rotherbridge clearly did. But
Caroline knew the ropes, few better.

"I'll escort you back to Lady Benborough."

The light voice of her partner drew her thoughts back
to the present. With a quick smile, Arabella declined. "I
think I've torn my flounce. I'll just go and pin it up.
Perhaps you could inform Lady Benborough that I'll
return immediately?" She smiled dazzlingly upon the
young man. Bemused, he bowed and moved away into
the crowd. Her flounce was perfectly intact but she
needed some fresh air and in no circumstances could she
have borne another half-hour of that particular young
gentleman's serious discourse.

She started towards the door, then glanced back to
see Augusta receive her message without apparent perturbation. Arabella turned back to the door and immediately collided with a chest of quite amazing
proportions.

"Oh!"

For a moment, she thought the impact had winded

her. Then, looking up into the face of the mountain she had met, she realised it wasn't that at all. It was the thunderbolt she had been waiting for.

Unfortunately, the gentleman seemed unaware of this momentous happening. "My apologies, m'dear. Didn't see you there."

The lazy drawl washed over Arabella. He was tall, very tall, and seemed almost as broad, with curling blond hair and laughing hazel eyes. He had quite the most devastating smile she had ever seen. Her knees felt far too weak to support her if she moved, so she stood still and stared, mouthing she knew not what platitudes.

The gentleman seemed to find her reaction amusing. But, with a polite nod and another melting smile, he was gone.

Stunned, Arabella found herself standing in the doorway staring at his retreating back. Sanity returned with a thump. Biting back a far from ladylike curse, she swept out in search of the withdrawing-room. The use of a borrowed fan and the consumption of a glass of cool water helped to restore her outward calm. Inside, her resentment grew.

No gentleman simply excused himself and walked away from her. That was her role. Men usually tried to stay by her side as long as possible. Yet this man had seemed disinclined to linger. Arabella was not vain but wondered what was more fascinating than herself that he needs must move on so abruptly. Surely he had felt that strange jolt just as she had? Maybe he wasn't a ladies' man? But no. The memory of the decided appreciation which had glowed so warmly in his hazel eyes put paid to that idea. And, now she came to think of it, the comprehensive glance which had roamed suggestively over most of her had been decidedly impertinent.

Arabella returned to the ballroom determined to bring her large gentleman to heel, if for no better reason than to assure herself she had been mistaken in him. But frustration awaited her. He was not there. For the rest of the evening, she searched the throng but caught no glimpse of her quarry. Then, just before the last dance, another waltz, he appeared in the doorway from the card-room.

Surrounded by her usual court, Arabella was at her effervescent best. Her smile was dazzling as she openly debated, laughingly teasing, over who to bestow her hand on for this last dance. Out of the corner of her eye, she watched the unknown gentleman approach. And walk past her to solicit the hand of a plain girl in an outrageously overdecorated pink gown.

Arabella bit her lip in vexation but managed to conceal it as severe concentration on her decision. As the musicians struck up, she accepted handsome Lord Tulloch as her partner and studiously paid him the most flattering attention for the rest of the evening.

CHAPTER FIVE

MAX WAS WORRIED. Seriously worried. Since that first night at Almack's, the situation between Sarah Twinning and Darcy Hamilton had rapidly deteriorated to a state which, from experience, he knew was fraught with danger. As he watched Sarah across Lady Overton's ballroom, chatting with determined avidity to an eminently respectable and thoroughly boring young gentleman, his brows drew together in a considering frown. If, at the beginning of his guardianship, anyone had asked him where his sympathies would lie, with the Misses Twinning or the gentlemen of London, he would unhesitatingly have allied himself with his wards, on the grounds that four exquisite but relatively inexperienced country misses would need all the help they could get to defend their virtue successfully against the highly knowledgeable rakes extant within the *ton*. Now, a month later, having gained first-hand experience of the tenacious perversity of the Twinning sisters, he was not so sure.

His behaviour with Caroline on the night of their first visit to Almack's had been a mistake. How much of a mistake had been slowly made clear to him over the succeeding weeks. He was aware of the effect he had on her, had been aware of it from the first time he had seen

her in his library at Delmere House. But in order to
make any use of that weapon, he had to have her to
himself. A fact, unfortunately, that she had worked out
for herself. Consequently, whenever he approached her,
he found her surrounded either by admirers who had
been given too much encouragement for him to dismiss
easily or one or more of her far too perceptive sisters.
Lizzie, it was true, was not attuned to the situation
between her eldest sister and their guardian. But he had
unwisely made use of her innocence, to no avail as it
transpired, and was now unhappily certain he would get
no further opportunity by that route. Neither Arabella
nor Sarah was the least bit perturbed by his increasingly
blatant attempts to be rid of them. He was sure that, if
he was ever goaded into ordering them to leave their
sister alone with him, they would laugh and refuse. And
tease him unmercifully about it, what was more. He
had already had to withstand one episode of Arabella's
artful play, sufficiently subtle, thank God, so that the
others in the group had not understood her meaning.

His gaze wandered to where the third Twinning sister
held court, seated on a chaise surrounded by ardent
swains, her huge eyes wickedly dancing with mischief.
As he watched, she tossed a comment to one of the
circle and turned, her head playfully tilted, to throw a
glance of open invitation into the handsome face of a
blond giant standing before her. Max stiffened. Hell
and the devil! He would have to put a stop to that game,
and quickly. He had no difficulty in recognising the
large frame of Hugo, Lord Denbigh. Although a few
years younger than himself, in character and accomplishments there was little to choose between them.

Under his horrified gaze, Hugo took advantage of a momentary distraction which had succeeded in removing attention temporarily from Arabella to lean forward and whisper something, Max could guess what, into her ear. The look she gave him in response made Max set his jaw grimly. Then, Hugo extended one large hand and Arabella, adroitly excusing herself to her other admirers, allowed him to lead her on to the floor. A waltz was just starting up.

Knowing there was only so much Hugo could do on a crowded ballroom floor, Max made a resolution to call on his aunt and wards on the morrow, firmly determined to acquaint them with his views on encouraging rakes. Even as the idea occurred, he groaned. How on earth could he tell Arabella to cease her flirtation with Hugo on the grounds he was a rake when he was himself trying his damnedest to seduce her sister and his best friend was similarly occupied with Sarah? He had known from the outset that this crazy situation would not work.

Reminded of what had originally prompted him to stand just inside the door between Lady Overton's ballroom and the salon set aside for cards and quietly study the company, Max returned his eyes to Sarah Twinning. Despite her assured manner, she was on edge, her hands betraying her nervousness as they played with the lace on her gown. Occasionally, her eyes would lift fleetingly to the door behind him. While to his experienced eye she was not looking her best, Darcy, ensconced in the card-room, was looking even worse. He had been drinking steadily throughout the evening and, although far from drunk, was fast attaining a dangerous state. Suffering from Twinning-induced frustration himself, Max could readily sympathise. He sincerely hoped his pursuit of the eldest Miss Twinning would not bring him so low. His friendship with Darcy Hamilton stretched back over fifteen years. In all that time he had never seen his friend so affected by the desire of a particular woman. Like himself, Darcy was an experienced lover who liked to keep his affairs easy and uncomplicated. If a woman proved difficult, he was much more likely to shrug and, with a smile, pass on to greener fields. But with Sarah Twinning, he seemed unable to admit defeat.

The thought that he himself had no intention of letting the elder Miss Twinning escape and was, even now, under the surface of his preoccupation with his other wards, plotting to get her into his arms, and, ultimately, into his bed, surfaced to shake his self-confidence. His black brows rose a little, in self-mockery. One could hardly blame the girls for keeping them at arm's length. The Twinning sisters had never encouraged them to believe they were of easy virtue, nor that they would accept anything less than marriage. Their interaction, thus far, had all been part of the game. By rights, it was they, the rakes of London, who should now acknowledge the evident truth that, despite their bountiful attractions, the Twinnings were virtuous females in search of husbands. And, having acknowledged that fact, to desist from their pursuit of the fair ladies. Without conscious thought on his part, his eyes strayed to where Caroline stood amid a group, mostly men, by the side of the dance floor. She laughed and responded to some comment, her copper curls gleaming like rosy gold in the bright light thrown down by the chandeliers.

As if feeling his gaze, she turned and, across the intervening heads, their eyes met. Both were still. Then, she smoothly turned back to her companions and Max, straightening his shoulders, moved further into the crowd. The trouble was, he did not think that he, any more than Darcy, could stop.

Max slowly passed through the throng, stopping here and there to chat with acquaintances, his intended goal his aunt, sitting in a blaze of glorious purple on a chaise by the side of the room. But before he had reached her, a hand on his arm drew him around to face the sharp features of Emma Mortland.

"Your Grace! It's been such an age since we've… talked." Her ladyship's brown eyes quizzed him playfully.

Her arch tone irritated Max. It was on the tip of his tongue to recommend she took lessons in flirting from Arabella before she tried her tricks on him. Instead, he took her hand from his sleeve, bowed over it and pointedly returned to her, "As you're doubtless aware, Emma, I have other claims on my time."

His careless use of her first name was calculated to annoy but Lady Mortland, having seen his absorption with his wards, particularly his eldest ward, over the past weeks, was fast coming to the conclusion that she should do everything in her power to bring Twyford to his knees or that tiara would slip through her fingers. As she was a female of little intelligence, she sincerely believed the attraction that had brought Max Rotherbridge to her bed would prove sufficient to induce him to propose. Consequently, she coyly glanced up at him through her long fair lashes and sighed sympathetically.

"Oh, my dear, *I know*. I do *feel* for you. This business of being guardian to four country girls must be such a bore to you. But surely, as a diversion, you could manage to spare us some few hours?"

Not for the first time, Max wondered where women such as Emma Mortland kept their intelligence. In their pockets? One truly had to wonder. As he looked down at her, his expression unreadable, he realized that she was a year or so younger than Caroline. Yet, from the single occasion on which he had shared her bed, he knew the frills and furbelows she favoured disguised a less than attractive figure, lacking the curves that characterized his eldest ward. And Emma Mortland's energies, it seemed, were reserved for scheming. He had not been impressed. As he knew that a number of gentlemen, including Darcy Hamilton, had likewise seen her sheets, he was at a loss to understand why she continued to single him out. A caustic dismissal was about to leave his lips when, amid a burst of hilarity from a group just behind them, he heard the rich tones of his eldest ward's laugh.

On the instant, a plan, fully formed, came into his head and, without further consideration, he acted. He allowed a slow, lazy smile to spread across his face. "How well you read me, my sweet," he drawled to the relieved Lady Mortland. Encouraged, she put her hand tentatively on his arm. He took it in his hand, intending to raise it to his lips, but to his surprise he could not quite bring himself to do so. Instead, he smiled meaningfully into her eyes. With an ease born of countless hours of practice, he instituted a conversation of the risqué variety certain to appeal to Lady Mortland. Soon, he had her gaily laughing and flirting freely with her eyes and her fan. Deliberately, he turned to lead her on to the floor for the waltz just commencing, catching, as he did, a look of innocent surprise on Caroline's face.

Grinning devilishly, Max encouraged Emma to the limits of acceptable flirtation. Then, satisfied with the scene he had created, as they circled the room, he raised his head to see the effect the sight of Lady Mortland in his arms was having on Caroline. To his chagrin, he discovered his eldest ward was no longer standing where he had last seen her. After a frantic visual search, during which he ignored Emma entirely, he located Caroline, also dancing, with the highly suitable Mr. Willoughby. That same Mr. Willoughby who, he knew, was becoming very particular in his attentions. Smothering a curse, Max half-heartedly returned his attention to Lady Mortland.

He had intended to divest himself of the encumbrance of her ladyship as soon as the dance ended but, as the music ceased, he realized they were next to Caroline and her erstwhile partner. Again, Emma found herself the object of Max's undeniable, if strangely erratic charm. Under its influence, she blossomed and bloomed. Max, with one eye on Caroline's now unreadable countenance, leaned closer to Emma to whisper an invitation to view the beauties of the moonlit garden. As he had hoped, she crooned her delight and, with an air of anticipated pleasure, allowed him to escort her through the long windows leading on to the terrace.

"COUNT ME OUT." Darcy Hamilton threw his cards on to the table and pushed back his chair. None of the other players was surprised to see him leave. Normally an excellent player, tonight his lordship had clearly had his mind elsewhere. And the brandy he had drunk was hardly calculated to improve matters, although his gait, as he headed for the ballroom, was perfectly steady.

In the ballroom, Darcy paused to glance about. He saw the musicians tuning up and then sighted his prey.

Almost as if she sensed his approach, Sarah turned as he came up to her. The look of sudden wariness that came into her large eyes pricked his conscience and, consequently, his temper. "My dance, I think."

It was not, as he well knew, but before she could do more than open her mouth to deny him Darcy had swept her on to the floor.

They were both excellent dancers and, despite their current difficulties, they moved naturally and easily together. Which was just as well, as their minds were each completely absorbed in trying to gauge the condition of the other. Luckily, they were both capable of putting on a display of calmness which succeeded in deflecting the interest of the curious.

Sarah, her heart, as usual, beating far too fast, glanced up under her lashes at the handsome face above her, now drawn and slightly haggard. Her heart sank. She had no idea what the outcome of this strange relationship of theirs would be, but it seemed to be causing both of them endless pain. Darcy Hamilton filled her thoughts, day in, day out. But he had steadfastly refused to speak of marriage, despite the clear encouragement she had given him to do so. He had side-stepped her invitations, offering, instead, to introduce her to a vista of illicit delights whose temptation was steadily increasing with time. But she could not, would not accept. She would give anything in the world to be his wife but had no ambition to be his mistress. Lady Benborough had, with all kindness, dropped her a hint that he was very likely a confirmed bachelor, too wedded to his equestrian interests to be bothered with a wife and family, satisfied instead with mistresses and the occasional *affaire*. Surreptitiously studying his rigid and unyielding face, she could find no reason to doubt Augusta's assessment. If that was so, then their association must end. And the sooner the better, for it was breaking her heart.

Seeing her unhappiness reflected in the brown pools of her eyes, Darcy inwardly cursed. There were times he longed to hurt her, in retribution for the agony she was putting him through, but any pain she felt seemed to rebound, ten times amplified, back on him. He was, as Lady Benborough had rightly surmised, well satisfied with his bachelor life. At least, he had been, until he had met Sarah Twinning. Since then, nothing seemed to be right any more. Regardless of the response he knew he awoke in her, she consistently denied any interest in the delightful pleasures he was only too willing to introduce her to. Or rather, held the prospect of said pleasures like a gun at his head, demanding matrimony. He would be damned if he would yield to such tactics. He had long ago considered matrimony, the state of, in a calm and reasoned way, and had come to the conclusion that it held few benefits for him. The idea of being driven, forced, pushed into taking such a step, essentially by the strength of his own raging desires, horrified him, leaving him annoyed beyond measure, principally with himself, but also, unreasonably he knew, with the object of said desires. As the music slowed and halted, he looked down at her lovely face and determined to give her one last chance to capitulate. If she remained adamant, he would have to leave London until the end of the Season. He was quite sure he could not bear the agony any longer.

As Sarah drew away from him and turned towards the room, Darcy drew her hand through his arm and deftly steered her towards the long windows leading on to the terrace. As she realized his intention, she hung back. With a few quick words, he reassured her. "I just want to talk to you. Come into the garden."

Thus far, Sarah had managed to avoid being totally private with him, too aware of her inexperience to chance such an interview. But now, looking into his pale grey eyes and seeing her own unhappiness mirrored there, she consented with a nod and they left the ballroom.

A stone terrace extended along the side of the house, the balustrade broken here and there by steps leading down to the gardens. Flambeaux placed in brackets along the walls threw flickering light down into the avenues and any number of couples could be seen, walking and talking quietly amid the greenery.

Unhurriedly, Darcy led her to the end of the terrace and then down the steps into a deserted walk. They both breathed in the heady freshness of the night air, calming their disordered senses and, without the need to exchange words, each drew some measure of comfort from the other's presence. At the end of the path, a secluded summer-house stood, white paintwork showing clearly against the black shadows of the shrubbery behind it.

As Darcy had hoped, the summer-house was deserted. The path leading to it was winding and heavily screened. Only those who knew of its existence would be likely to find it. He ushered Sarah through the narrow door and let it fall quietly shut behind them. The moonlight slanted through the windows, bathing the room in silvery tints. Sarah stopped in the middle of the circular floor and turned to face him. Darcy paused, trying to decide where to start, then crossed to stand before her, taking her hands in his. For some moments, they stood thus, the rake and the maid, gazing silently into each other's eyes. Then Darcy bent his head and his lips found hers.

Sarah, seduced by the setting, the moonlight and the man before her, allowed him to gather her, unresisting, into his arms. The magic of his lips on hers was a more potent persuasion than any she had previously encountered. Caught by a rising tide of passion, she was drawn, helpless and uncaring, beyond the bounds of thought. Her lips parted and gradually the kiss deepened until, with the moonlight washing in waves over them, he stole her soul.

It was an unintentionally intimate caress which abruptly shook the stars from her eyes and brought her back to earth with an unsteady bump. Holding her tightly within one arm, Darcy had let his other hand slide, gently caressing, over her hip, intending to draw her more firmly against him. But the feel of his hand, scorching through her thin evening dress, sent shock waves of such magnitude through Sarah's pliant body that she pulled back with a gasp. Then, as horrified realization fell like cold water over her heated flesh, she tore herself from his arms and ran.

For an instant, Darcy, stunned both by her response and by her subsequent reaction, stood frozen in the middle of the floor. A knot of jonquil ribbon from Sarah's dress had caught on the button of his cuff and impatiently he shook it free, then watched, fascinated, as it floated to the ground. The banging of the wooden door against its frame had stilled. Swiftly, he crossed the floor and, opening the door, stood in the aperture, listening to her footsteps dying in the spring night. Then, smothering a curse, he followed.

Sarah instinctively ran away from the main house, towards the shrubbery which lay behind the summerhouse. She did not stop to think or reason, but just ran. Finally, deep within the tall clipped hedges and the looming bushes, her breath coming in gasps, she came to a clearing, a small garden at the centre of the shrubbery. She saw a marble bench set in an arbour. Thankfully, she sank on to it and buried her face in her hands.

Darcy, following, made for the shrubbery, her hurrying footsteps echoing hollowly on the gravel walks giving him the lead. But once she reached the grassed avenues between the high hedges, her feet made no sound. Penetrating the dark alleys, he was forced to go slowly, checking this way and that to make sure he did not pass her by. So quite fifteen minutes had passed before he reached the central garden and saw the dejected figure huddled on the bench.

In that time, sanity of sorts had returned to Sarah's mind. Her initial horror at her weakness had been replaced by the inevitable reaction. She was angry. Angry at herself, for being so weak that one kiss could overcome all her defences; angry at Darcy, for having engineered that little scene. She was busy whipping up the necessary fury to face the prospect of not seeing him ever again, when he materialized at her side. With a gasp, she came to her feet.

Relieved to find she was not crying, as he had thought, Darcy immediately caught her hand to prevent her flying from him again.

Stung by the shock his touch always gave her, intensified now, she was annoyed to discover, Sarah tried to pull her hand away. When he refused to let her go, she said, her voice infused with an iciness designed to freeze, "Kindly release me, Lord Darcy."

On hearing her voice, Darcy placed the emotion that was holding her so rigid. The knowledge that she was angry, nay, furious, did nothing to improve his own temper, stirred to life by her abrupt flight. Forcing his voice to a reasonableness he was far from feeling, he said, "If you'll give me your word you'll not run away from me, I'll release you."

Sarah opened her mouth to inform him she would not so demean herself as to run from him when the knowledge that she just had, and might have reason to do so again, hit her. She remained silent. Darcy, accurately reading her mind, held on to her hand.

After a moment's consideration, he spoke. "I had intended, my dear, to speak to you of our…curious relationship."

Sarah, breathing rapidly and anxious to end the interview, immediately countered, "I really don't think there's anything to discuss."

A difficult pause ensued, then, "So you would deny there's anything between us?"

The bleakness in his voice shook her, but she determinedly put up her chin, turning away from him as far as their locked hands would allow. "Whatever's between us is neither here nor there," she said, satisfied with the lightness she had managed to bring to her tone.

Her satisfaction was short-lived. Taking advantage of her movement, Darcy stepped quickly behind her, the hand still holding hers reaching across her, his arm wrapping around her waist and drawing her hard against him. His other hand came to rest on her shoulder, holding her still. He knew the shock it would give her, to feel his body against hers, and heard with grim satisfaction the hiss of her indrawn breath.

Sarah froze, too stunned to struggle, the sensation of his hard body against her back, his arm wound like steel about her waist, holding her fast, driving all rational thought from her brain. Then his breath wafted the curls around her ear. His words came in a deep and husky tone, sending tingling shivers up and down her spine.

"Well, sweetheart, there's very little between us now. So, perhaps we can turn our attention to our relationship?"

Sarah, all too well aware of how little there was between them, wondered in a moment of startling lucidity how he imagined that would improve her concentration. But Darcy's attention had already wandered. His lips were very gently trailing down her neck, creating all sorts of marvellous sensations which she tried very hard to ignore.

Then, he gave a deep chuckle. "As I've been saying these weeks past, my dear, you're wasted as a virgin. Now, if you were to become my mistress, just think of all the delightful avenues we could explore."

"I don't want to become your mistress!" Sarah almost wailed, testing the arm at her waist and finding it immovable.

"No?" came Darcy's voice in her ear. She had the impression he considered her answer for a full minute before he continued, "Perhaps we should extend your education a trifle, my dear. So you fully appreciate what you're turning down. We wouldn't want you to make the wrong decision for lack of a few minutes' instruction, would we?"

Sarah had only a hazy idea of what he could mean but his lips had returned to her throat, giving rise to those strangely heady swirls of pleasure that washed through her, sapping her will. "Darcy, stop! You know you shouldn't be doing this!"

He stilled. "Do I?"

Into the silence, a nightingale warbled. Sarah held her breath.

But, when Darcy spoke again, the steel threading his voice, so often sensed yet only now recognised, warned her of the futility of missish pleas.

"Yes. You're right. I know I shouldn't." His lips moved against her throat, a subtle caress. "But what I want to do is make love to you. As you won't allow that, then this will have to do for now."

Sarah, incapable of further words, simply shook her head, powerless to halt the spreading fires he was so skilfully igniting.

Afterwards, Darcy could not understand how it had happened. He was as experienced with women as Max and had never previously lost control as he did that night. He had intended to do no more than reveal to the

perverse woman her own desires and give her some
inkling of the pleasures they could enjoy together.
Instead, her responses were more than he had bargained
for and his own desires stronger than he had been
prepared to admit. Fairly early in the engagement, he
had turned her once more into his arms, so he could
capture her lips and take the lesson further. And further
it had certainly gone, until the moon sank behind the
high hedges and left them in darkness.

HOW THE HELL WAS HE to get rid of her? Max, Lady
Mortland on his arm, had twice traversed the terrace. He
had no intention of descending to the shadowy avenues.
He had no intention of paying any further attention to
Lady Mortland at all. Lady Mortland, on the other hand,
was waiting for his attentions to begin and was rather
surprised at his lack of ardour in keeping to the terrace.

They were turning at the end of the terrace, when
Max, glancing along, saw Caroline come out of the
ballroom, alone, and walk quickly to the balustrade and
peer over. She was clearly seeking someone. Emma
Mortland, prattling on at his side, had not seen her. With
the reflexes necessary for being one of the more successful rakes in the *ton,* Max whisked her ladyship back
into the ballroom via the door they were about to pass.

Finding herself in the ballroom once more, with the
Duke of Twyford bowing over her hand in farewell,
Lady Mortland put a hand to her spinning head. "Oh!
But surely…"

"A guardian is never off duty for long, my dear,"
drawled Max, about to move off.

"Perhaps I'll see you in the Park, tomorrow?" asked

Emma, convinced his departure had nothing to do with inclination.

Max smiled. "Anything's possible."

He took a circuitous route around the ballroom and exited through the same door he had seen his ward use. Gaining the terrace, he almost knocked her over as she returned to the ballroom, looking back over her shoulder towards the gardens.

"Oh!" Finding herself unexpectedly in her guardian's arms temporarily suspended Caroline's faculties.

From her face, Max knew she had not been looking for him. He drew her further into the shadows of the terrace, placing her hand on his arm and covering it comfortingly with his. "What is it?"

Caroline could not see any way of avoiding telling him. She fell into step beside him, unconsciously following his lead. "Sarah. Lizzie saw her leave the ballroom with Lord Darcy. More than twenty minutes ago. They haven't returned."

In the dim light, Max's face took on a grim look. He had suspected there would be trouble. He continued strolling towards the end of the terrace. "I know where they'll be. There's a summer-house deeper in the gardens. I think you had better come with me."

Caroline nodded and, unobtrusively, they made their way to the summer-house.

Max pushed open the door, then frowned at the empty room. He moved further in and Caroline followed. "Not here?"

Max shook his head, then bent to pick up a knot of ribbon from the floor.

Caroline came to see and took it from him. She

crossed to the windows, turning the small cluster this way and that to gauge the colour.

"Is it hers?" asked Max as he strolled to her side.

"Yes. I can't see the colour well but I know the knot. It's a peculiar one. I made it myself."

"So they were here."

"But where are they now?"

"Almost certainly on their way back to the house," answered Max. "There's nowhere in this garden suitable for the purpose Darcy would have in mind. Presumably, your sister convinced him to return to more populated surroundings." He spoke lightly, but, in truth, was puzzled. He could not readily imagine Sarah turning Darcy from his purpose, not in his present mood, not in this setting. But he was sure there was nowhere else they could go.

"Well, then," said Caroline, dusting the ribbon, "we'd better go back, too."

"In a moment," said Max.

His tone gave Caroline an instant's warning. She put out a hand to fend him off. "No! This is *absurd*—you know it is."

Despite her hand, Max succeeded in drawing her into his arms, holding her lightly. "Absurd, is it? Well, you just keep on thinking how absurd it is, while I enjoy your very sweet lips." And he proceeded to do just that.

As his lips settled over hers, Caroline told herself she should struggle. But, for some mystical reason, her body remained still, her senses turned inward by his kiss. Under gentle persuasion, her lips parted and, with a thrill, she felt his gentle exploration teasing her senses, somehow drawing her deeper. Time seemed suspended and she felt her will weakening as she melted into his arms and they locked around her.

Max's mind was ticking in double time, evaluating the amenities of the summer-house and estimating how long they could remain absent from the ballroom. He decided neither answer was appropriate. Seduction was an art and should not be hurried. Besides, he doubted his eldest ward was quite ready to submit yet. Reluctantly, he raised his head and grinned wolfishly at her. "Still absurd?"

Caroline's wits were definitely not connected. She simply stared at him uncomprehendingly.

In face of this response, Max laughed and, drawing her arm through his, steered her to the door. "I think you're right. We'd better return."

SANITY RETURNED to Sarah's mind like water in a bucket, slowing filling from a dripping tap, bit by bit, until it was full. For one long moment, she allowed her mind to remain blank, savouring the pleasure of being held so gently against him. Then, the world returned and demanded her response. She struggled to sit up and was promptly helped to her feet. She checked her gown and found it perfectly tidy, bar one knot of ribbon on her sleeve which seemed to have gone missing.

Darcy, who had returned to earth long before, had been engaged in some furious thinking. But, try as he might, he could not imagine how she would react. Like Max, it had been a long time since young virgins had been his prey. As she stood, he tried to catch a glimpse of her face in the dim light but she perversely kept it averted. In the end, he caught her hands and drew her to stand before him. "Sweetheart, are you all right?"

Strangely enough, it was the note of sincerity in his voice which snapped Sarah's control. Her head came up and, even in the darkness, her eyes flashed fire. "Of course I'm not all right! How *dare* you take advantage of me?"

She saw Darcy's face harden at her words and, in fury at his lack of comprehension, she slapped him.

For a minute, absolute silence reigned. Then a sob broke from Sarah as she turned away, her head bent to escape the look on Darcy's face.

Darcy, slamming a door on his emotions, so turbulent that even he had no idea what he felt, moved to rescue them both. In a voice totally devoid of all feeling, he said, "We had better get back to the house."

In truth, neither had any idea how long they had been absent. In silence, they walked side by side, careful not to touch each other, until, eventually, the terrace was reached. Sarah, crying but determined not to let the tears fall, blinked hard, then mounted the terrace steps by Darcy's side. At the top, he turned to her. "It would be better, I think, if you went in first."

Sarah, head bowed, nodded and went.

CAROLINE AND MAX regained the ballroom and both glanced around for their party. Almost immediately, Lizzie appeared by her sister's side on the arm of one of her youthful swains. She prettily thanked him and dismissed him before turning to her sister and their guardian. "Sarah came back just after you left to look for her. She and Lady Benborough and Mrs. Alford have gone home."

"Oh?" It was Max's voice which answered her. "Why?"

Lizzie cast a questioning look at Caroline and received a nod in reply. "Sarah was upset about something."

Max was already scanning the room when Lizzie's voice reached him. "Lord Darcy came in a little while after Sarah. He's left now, too."

With a sigh, Max realized there was nothing more to be done that night. They collected Arabella and departed Overton House, Caroline silently considering Sarah's problem and Max wondering if he was going to have to wait until his friend solved his dilemma before he would be free to settle his own affairs.

CHAPTER SIX

MAX TOOK A LONG SIP of his brandy and savoured the smooth warmth as it slid down his throat. He stretched his legs to the fire. The book he had been trying to reach rested open, on his thighs, one strong hand holding it still. He moved his shoulders slightly, settling them into the comfort of well padded leather and let his head fall back against the chair.

It was the first night since the beginning of the Season that he had had a quiet evening at home. And he needed it. Who would have thought his four wards would make such a drastic change in a hitherto well-ordered existence? Then he remembered. He had. But he had not really believed his own dire predictions. And the only reason he was at home tonight was because Sarah, still affected by her brush with Darcy the night before, had elected to remain at home and Caroline had stayed with her. He deemed his aunt Augusta and Miriam Alford capable of chaperoning the two younger girls between them. After the previous night, it was unlikely they would allow any liberties.

Even now, no one had had an accounting of what had actually taken place between Darcy and Sarah. But, knowing Darcy, his imagination had supplied a quantity

of detail. He had left Delmere House at noon that day
with the full intention of running his lordship to earth
and demanding an explanation. He had finally found
him at Manton's Shooting Gallery, culping wafer after
wafer with grim precision. One look at his friend's face
had been enough to cool his temper. He had patiently
waited until Darcy, having dispatched all the wafers
currently in place, had thrown the pistol down with an
oath and turned to him.

"Don't ask!"

So he had preserved a discreet silence on the subject
and together they had rolled about town, eventually
ending in Cribb's back parlour, drinking Blue Ruin.
Only then had Darcy reverted to the topic occupying
both their minds. "I'm leaving town."

"Oh?"

His lordship had run a hand through his perfectly cut
golden locks, disarranging them completely, in a gesture
Max had never, in all their years together, seen him use.
"Going to Leicestershire. I need a holiday."

Max had nodded enigmatically. Lord Darcy's principal estates lay in Leicestershire and always, due to the
large number of horses he raised, demanded attention.
But in general, his lordship managed to run his business
affairs quite comfortably from town.

"No, by God! I've got a better idea. I'll go to Ireland.
It's further away."

As Max knew, Lord Darcy's brother resided on the
family estates in Ireland. Still, he had said nothing, patiently waiting for what he had known would come.

Darcy had rolled his glass between his hands, studying
the swirling liquid with apparent interest. "About Sarah."

"Mmm?" Max had kept his own eyes firmly fixed on his glass.

"I didn't."

"Oh?"

"No. But I'm not entirely sure she knows what happened." Darcy had drained his glass, using the opportunity to watch Max work this out.

Finally, comprehension had dawned. A glimmer of a smile had tugged at the corners of His Grace of Twyford's mouth. "Oh."

"Precisely. I thought I'd leave it in your capable hands."

"Thank you!" Max had replied. Then he had groaned and dropped his head into his hands. "How the hell do you imagine I'm going to find out what she believes and then explain it to her if she's wrong?" His mind had boggled at the awful idea.

"I thought you might work through Miss Twinning," Darcy had returned, grinning for the first time that day.

Relieved to see his friend smile, even at his expense, Max had grinned back. "I've not been pushing the pace quite as hard as you. Miss Twinning and I have some way to go before we reach the point where such intimate discussion would be permissible."

"Oh, well," Darcy had sighed. "I only hope you have better luck than I."

"Throwing in the towel?"

Darcy had shrugged. "I wish I knew." A silence had ensued which Darcy eventually broke. "I've got to get away."

"How long will you be gone?"

Another shrug. "Who knows? As long as it takes, I suppose."

He had left Darcy packing at Hamilton House and returned to the comfort of his own home to spend a quiet evening in contemplation of his wards. Their problems should really not cause surprise. At first sight, he had known what sort of men the Twinning girls would attract. And there was no denying they responded to such men. Even Arabella seemed hell-bent on tangling with rakes. Thankfully, Lizzie seemed too quiet and gentle to take the same road—three rakes in any family should certainly be enough.

Family? The thought sobered him. He sat, eyes on the flames leaping in the grate, and pondered the odd notion.

His reverie was interrupted by sounds of an arrival. He glanced at the clock and frowned. Too late for callers. What now? He reached the hall in time to see Hillshaw and a footman fussing about the door.

"Yes, it's all right, Hillshaw, I'm not an invalid, you know!"

The voice brought Max forward. "Martin!"

The tousled brown head of Captain Martin Rotherbridge turned to greet his older brother. A winning grin spread across features essentially a more boyish version of Max's own. "Hello, Max. I'm back, as you see. Curst Frenchies put a hole in my shoulder."

Max's gaze fell to the bulk of bandaging distorting the set of his brother's coat. He clasped the hand held out to him warmly, his eyes raking the other's face. "Come into the library. Hillshaw?"

"Yes, Your Grace. I'll see to some food."

When they were comfortably ensconced by the fire, Martin with a tray of cold meat by his side and a large balloon of his brother's best brandy in his hand, Max asked his questions.

"No, you're right," Martin answered to one of these. "It wasn't just the wound, though that was bad enough. They tell me that with rest it'll come good in time." Max waited patiently. His brother fortified himself before continuing. "No. I sold out simply because, now the action's over, it's deuced boring over there. We sit about and play cards half the day. And the other half, we just sit and reminisce about all the females we've ever had." He grinned at his brother in a way Caroline, for one, would have recognised. "Seemed to me I was running out of anecdotes. So I decided to come home and lay in a fresh stock."

Max returned his brother's smile. Other than the shoulder wound, Martin was looking well. The difficult wound and slow convalescence had not succeeded in erasing the healthy glow from outdoor living which burnished his skin and, although there were lines present which had not been there before, these merely seemed to emphasize the fact that Martin Rotherbridge had seen more than twenty-five summers and was an old hand in many spheres. Max was delighted to hear he had returned to civilian life. Aside from his genuine concern for a much loved sibling, Martin was now the heir to the Dukedom of Twyford. While inheriting the Delmere holdings, with which he was well-acquainted, would have proved no difficulty to Martin, the Twyford estates were a different matter. Max eyed the long, lean frame stretched out in the chair before him and wondered where to begin. Before he had decided, Martin asked, "So how do you like being 'Your Grace'?"

In a few pithy sentences, Max told him. He then

embarked on the saga of horrors examination of his uncle's estate had revealed, followed by a brief description of their present circumstances. Seeing the shadow of tiredness pass across Martin's face, he curtailed his report, saying instead, "Time for bed, stripling. You're tired."

Martin started, then grinned sleepily at Max's use of his childhood tag. "What? Oh, yes. I'm afraid I'm not up to full strength yet. And we've been travelling since first light."

Max's hand at his elbow assisted him to rise from the depth of the armchair. On his feet, Martin stretched and yawned. Seen side by side, the similarity between the brothers was marked. Max was still a few inches taller and his nine years' seniority showed in the heavier musculature of his chest and shoulders. Other than that, the differences were few—Martin's hair was a shade lighter than Max's dark mane and his features retained a softness Max's lacked, but the intensely blue eyes of the Rotherbridges shone in both dark faces.

Martin turned to smile at his brother. "It's good to be home."

"GOOD MORNING. Hillshaw, isn't it? I'm Lizzie Twinning. I've come to return a book to His Grace."

Although he had only set eyes on her once before, Hillshaw remembered his master's youngest ward perfectly. As she stepped daintily over the threshold of Delmere House, a picture in a confection of lilac muslin, he gathered his wits to murmur, "His Grace is not presently at home, miss. Perhaps his secretary, Mr. Cummings, could assist you." Hillshaw rolled one majestic eye toward a hovering footman who immedi-

ately, if reluctantly, disappeared in the direction of the
back office frequented by the Duke's secretary.

Lizzie, allowing Hillshaw to remove her half-cape,
looked doubtful. But all she said was, "Wait here for me,
Hennessy. I shan't be long." Her maid, who had dutifully followed her in, sat primly on the edge of a chair
by the wall and, under the unnerving stare of Hillshaw,
lowered her round-eyed gaze to her hands.

Immediately, Mr. Joshua Cummings came hurrying
forward from the dimness at the rear of the hall. "Miss
Lizzie? I'm afraid His Grace has already left the house,
but perhaps I may be of assistance?" Mr. Cummings was
not what one might expect of a nobleman's secretary.
He was of middle age and small and round and pale,
and, as Lizzie later informed her sisters, looked as if he
spent his days locked away perusing dusty papers. In a
sense, he did. He was a single man and, until taking his
present post, had lived with his mother on the Rotherbridge estate in Surrey. His family had long been associated with the Rotherbridges and he was sincerely
devoted to that family's interests. Catching sight of the
book in Lizzie's small hand, he smiled. "Ah, I see you
have brought back Lord Byron's verses. Perhaps you'd
like to read his next book? Or maybe one of Mrs.
Linfield's works would be more to your taste?"

Lizzie smiled back. On taking up residence at
Twyford House, the sisters had been disappointed to
find that, although extensive, the library there did not
hold any of the more recent fictional works so much discussed among the *ton*. Hearing of their complaint, Max
had revealed that his own library did not suffer from this
deficiency and had promised to lend them any books

they desired. But, rather than permit the sisters free rein in a library that also contained a number of works less suitable for their eyes, he had delegated the task of looking out the books they wanted to his secretary. Consequently, Mr. Cummings felt quite competent to deal with the matter at hand.

"If you'd care to wait in the drawing room, miss?" Hillshaw moved past her to open the door. With another dazzling smile, Lizzie handed the volume she carried to Mr. Cummings, informing him in a low voice that one of Mrs. Linfield's novels would be quite acceptable, then turned to follow Hillshaw. As she did so, her gaze travelled past the stately butler to rest on the figure emerging from the shadow of the library door. She remained where she was, her grey-brown eyes growing rounder and rounder, as Martin Rotherbridge strolled elegantly forward.

After the best night's sleep he had had in months, Martin had felt ready to resume normal activities but, on descending to the breakfast parlour, had discovered his brother had already left the house to call in at Tattersall's. Suppressing the desire to pull on his coat and follow, Martin had resigned himself to awaiting Max's return, deeming it wise to inform his brother in person that he was setting out to pick up the reins of his civilian existence before he actually did so. Knowing his friends, and their likely reaction to his reappearance among them, he was reasonably certain he would not be returning to Delmere House until the following morning. And he knew Max would worry unless he saw for himself that his younger brother was up to it. So, with a grin for his older brother's affection, he had settled in the library to read the morning's news sheets. But, after months of semi-invalidism, his returning health naturally gave rise to returning spirits. Waiting patiently was not easy. He had been irritably pacing the library when his sharp ears had caught the sound of a distinctly feminine voice in the hall. Intrigued, he had gone to investigate.

Setting eyes on the vision gracing his brother's hall, Martin's immediate thought was that Max had taken to allowing his ladybirds to call at his house. But the attitudes of Hillshaw and Cummings put paid to that idea. The sight of a maid sitting by the door confirmed his startled perception that the vision was indeed a young lady. His boredom vanishing like a cloud on a spring day, he advanced.

Martin allowed his eyes to travel, gently, so as not to startle her, over the delicious figure before him. Very nice. His smile grew. The silence around him penetrated his mind, entirely otherwise occupied. "Hillshaw, I think you'd better introduce us."

Hillshaw almost allowed a frown to mar his impassive countenance. But he knew better than to try to avoid the unavoidable. Exchanging a glance of fellow feeling with Mr. Cummings, he obliged in sternly disapproving tones. "Captain Martin Rotherbridge, Miss Lizzie Twinning. The young lady is His Grace's youngest ward, sir."

With a start, Martin's gaze, which had been locked with Lizzie's, flew to Hillshaw's face. "Ward?" He had not been listening too well last night when Max had been telling him of the estates, but he was sure his brother had not mentioned any wards.

With a thin smile, Hillshaw inclined his head in assent.

Lizzie, released from that mesmerising gaze, spoke up, her soft tones a dramatic contrast to the masculine voices. "Yes. My sisters and I are the Duke's wards, you know." She held out her hand. "How do you do? I didn't know the Duke had a brother. I've only dropped by to exchange some books His Grace lent us. Mr. Cummings was going to take care of it."

Martin took the small gloved hand held out to him and automatically bowed over it. Straightening, he moved to her side, placing her hand on his arm and holding it there. "In that case, Hillshaw's quite right. You should wait in the drawing-room." The relief on Hillshaw's and Mr. Cummings's faces evaporated at his next words. "And I'll keep you company."

As Martin ushered Lizzie into the drawing-room and pointedly shut the door in Hillshaw's face, the Duke's butler and secretary looked at each other helplessly. Then Mr. Cummings scurried away to find the required books, leaving Hillshaw to look with misgiving at the closed door of the drawing-room.

Inside, blissfully unaware of the concern she was engendering in her guardian's servants, Lizzie smiled trustingly up at the source of that concern.

"Have you been my brother's ward for long?" Martin asked.

"Oh, no!" said Lizzie. Then, "That is, I suppose, yes." She looked delightfully befuddled and Martin could not suppress a smile. He guided her to the chaise and, once she had settled, took the chair opposite her so that he could keep her bewitching face in full view.

"It depends, I suppose," said Lizzie, frowning in her effort to gather her wits, which had unaccountably scat-

tered, "on what you'd call long. Our father died eighteen
months ago, but then the other Duke—your uncle, was
he not?—was our guardian. But when we came back
from America, your brother had assumed the title. So
then he was our guardian."

Out of this jumbled explanation, Martin gleaned
enough to guess the truth. "Did you enjoy America?
Were you there long?"

Little by little his questions succeeded in their aim and
in short order, Lizzie had relaxed completely and was conversing in a normal fashion with her guardian's brother.

Listening to her description of her home, Martin
shifted, trying to settle his shoulder more comfortably.
Lizzie's sharp eyes caught the awkward movement and
descried the wad of bandaging cunningly concealed
beneath his coat.

"You're injured!" She leaned forward in concern.
"Does it pain you dreadfully?"

"No, no. The enemy just got lucky, that's all. Soon
be right as rain, I give you my word."

"You were in the army?" Lizzie's eyes had grown
round. "Oh, please tell me all about it. It must have
been so exciting!"

To Martin's considerable astonishment, he found
himself recounting for Lizzie's benefit the horrors of the
campaign and the occasional funny incident which had
enlivened their days. She did not recoil but listened
avidly. He had always thought he was a dab hand at
interrogation but her persistent questioning left him
reeling. She even succeeded in dragging from him the
reason he had yet to leave the house. Her ready
sympathy, which he had fully expected to send him

running, enveloped him instead in a warm glow, a sort of prideful care which went rapidly to his head.

Then Mr. Cummings arrived with the desired books. Lizzie took them and laid them on a side-table beside her, patently ignoring the Duke's secretary who was clearly waiting to escort her to the front door. With an ill-concealed grin, Martin dismissed him. "It's all right, Cummings. Miss Twinning has taken pity on me and decided to keep me entertained until my brother returns."

Lizzie, entirely at home, turned a blissful smile on Mr. Cummings, leaving that gentleman with no option but to retire.

AN HOUR LATER, Max crossed the threshold to be met by Hillshaw, displaying, quite remarkably, an emotion very near agitation. This was instantly explained. "Miss Lizzie's here. In the drawing-room with Mr. Martin."

Max froze. Then nodded to his butler. "Very good, Hillshaw." His sharp eyes had already taken in the bored face of the maid sitting in the shadows. Presumably, Lizzie had been here for some time. His face was set in grim lines as his hand closed on the handle of the drawing-room door.

The sight which met his eyes was not at all what he had expected. As he shut the door behind him, Martin's eyes lifted to his, amused understanding in the blue depths. He was seated in an armchair and Lizzie occupied the nearest corner of the chaise. She was presently hunched forward, pondering what lay before her on a small table drawn up between them. As Max rounded the chaise, he saw to his stupefaction that they were playing checkers.

Lizzie looked up and saw him. "Oh! You're back. I was just entertaining your brother until you returned." Max blinked but Lizzie showed no consciousness of the implication of her words and he discarded the notion of enlightening her.

Then Lizzie's eyes fell on the clock on the mantel-shelf. "Oh, dear! I didn't realize it was so late. I must go. Where are those books Mr. Cummings brought?"

Martin fetched them for her and, under the highly sceptical gaze of his brother, very correctly took leave of her. Max, seeing the expression in his brother's eyes as they rested on his youngest ward, almost groaned aloud. This was really too much.

Max saw Lizzie out, then returned to the library. But before he could launch into his inquisition, Martin got in first. "You didn't tell me you had inherited four wards."

"Well, I have," said Max, flinging himself into an armchair opposite the one his brother had resumed.

"Are they all like that?" asked Martin in awe.

Max needed no explanation of what "that" meant. He answered with a groan, "Worse!"

Eyes round, Martin did not make the mistake of imagining the other Twinning sisters were antidotes. His gaze rested on his brother for a moment, then his face creased into a wide smile. "Good lord!"

Max brought his blue gaze back from the ceiling and fixed it firmly on his brother. "Precisely. That being so, I suggest you revise the plans you've been making for Lizzie Twinning."

Martin's grin, if anything, became even broader. "Why so? It's you who's their guardian, not I. Besides, you don't seriously expect me to believe that, if our situations were reversed, you'd pay any attention to such restrictions?" When Max frowned, Martin continued. "Anyway, good heavens, you must have seen it for yourself. She's like a ripe plum, ready for the picking." He stopped at Max's raised hand.

"Permit me to fill you in," drawled his older brother. "For a start, I've nine years on you and there's nothing about the business you know that I don't. However, quite aside from that, I can assure you the Twinning sisters, ripe though they may be, are highly unlikely to fall into anyone's palms without a prior proposal of marriage."

A slight frown settled over Martin's eyes. Not for a moment did he doubt the accuracy of Max's assessment. But he had been strongly attracted to Lizzie Twinning and was disinclined to give up the idea of converting her to his way of thinking. He looked up and blue eyes met blue. "Really?"

Max gestured airily. "Consider the case of Lord Darcy Hamilton." Martin looked his question. Max obliged. "Being much taken with Sarah, the second of the four, Darcy's been engaged in storming her citadel for the past five weeks and more. No holds barred, I might add. And the outcome you ask? As of yesterday, he's retired to his estates, to lick his wounds and, unless I miss my guess, to consider whether he can stomach the idea of marriage."

"Good lord!" Although only peripherally acquainted with Darcy Hamilton, Martin knew he was one of Max's particular friends and that his reputation in matters involving the fairer sex was second only to Max's own.

"Exactly," nodded Max. "Brought low by a chit of a

girl. So, brother dear, if it's your wish to tangle with any Twinnings, I suggest you first decide how much you're willing to stake on the throw."

As he pondered his brother's words, Martin noticed that Max's gaze had become abstracted. He only just caught the last words his brother said, musing, almost to himself. "For, brother mine, it's my belief the Twinnings eat rakes for breakfast."

THE COACH SWAYED as it turned a corner and Arabella clutched the strap swinging by her head. As equilibrium returned, she settled her skirts once more and glanced at the other two occupants of the carriage. The glow from a street lamp momentarily lit the interior of the coach, then faded as the four horses hurried on. Arabella grinned into the darkness.

Caroline had insisted that she and not Lizzie share their guardian's coach. One had to wonder why. Too often these days, her eldest sister had the look of the cat caught just after it had tasted the cream. Tonight, that look of guilty pleasure, or, more specifically, the anticipation of guilty pleasure, was marked.

She had gone up to Caroline's room to hurry her sister along. Caroline had been sitting, staring at her reflection in the mirror, idly twisting one copper curl to sit more attractively about her left ear.

"Caro? Are you ready? Max is here."

"Oh!" Caroline had stood abruptly, then paused to cast one last critical glance over her pale sea-green dress, severely styled as most suited her ample charms, the neckline daringly *décolleté*. She had frowned, her fingers straying to the ivory swell of her breasts. "What do you think, Bella? Is it too revealing? Perhaps a piece of lace might make it a little less…?"

"Attractive?" Arabella had brazenly supplied. "To be perfectly frank, I doubt our guardian would approve a fichu."

The delicate blush that had appeared on Caroline's cheeks had been most informative. But, "Too true," was all her sister had replied.

Arabella looked across the carriage once more and caught the gleam of warm approval that shone in their guardian's eyes as they rested on Caroline. It was highly unlikely that the conservative Mr. Willoughby was the cause of her sister's blushes. That being so, what game was the Duke of Twyford playing? And, even more to the point, was Caro thinking of joining in?

Heaven knew, they had had a close enough call with Sarah and Lord Darcy. Nothing had been said of Sarah's strange affliction, yet they were all close enough for even the innocent Lizzie to have some inkling of the root cause. And while Max had been the soul of discretion in speaking privately to Caroline and Sarah in the hall before they had left, it was as plain as a pikestaff the information he had imparted had not included news of a proposal. Sarah's pale face had paled further. But the Twinnings were made of stern stuff and Sarah had shaken her head at Caro's look of concern.

The deep murmur of their guardian's voice came to her ears, followed by her sister's soft tones. Arabella's big eyes danced. She could not make out their words but those tones were oh, so revealing. But if Sarah was in deep waters and Caro was hovering on the brink, she, to her chagrin, had not even got her toes wet yet.

Arabella frowned at the moon, showing fleetingly between the branches of a tall tree. Hugo, Lord Denbigh. The most exasperating man she had ever met. She would give anything to be able to say she didn't care a button for him. Unfortunately, he was the only man who could make her tingle just by looking at her.

Unaware that she was falling far short of Caroline's expectations, Arabella continued to gaze out of the window, absorbed in contemplation of the means available for bringing one large gentleman to heel.

THE HEAVY TWYFORD coach lumbered along in the wake of the sleek Delmere carriage. Lady Benborough put up a hand to right her wig, swaying perilously as they rounded a particularly sharp corner. For the first time since embarking on her nephew's crusade to find the Twinning girls suitable husbands, she felt a twinge of nervousness. She was playing with fire and she knew it. Still, she could not regret it. The sight of Max and Caroline together in the hall at Twyford House had sent a definite thrill through her old bones. As for Sarah, she doubted not that Darcy Hamilton was too far gone to desist, resist and retire. True, he might not know it yet, but time would certainly bring home to him the penalty he would have to pay to walk away from the snare. Her shrewd blue eyes studied the pale face opposite her. Even in the dim light, the strain of the past few days was evident. Thankfully, no one outside their party had been aware of that contretemps. So, regardless of what Sarah herself believed, Augusta had no qualms. Sarah was home safe; she could turn her attention elsewhere.

Arabella, the minx, had picked a particularly difficult nut to crack. Still, she could hardly fault the girl's taste. Hugo Denbigh was a positive Adonis, well-born, well-heeled and easy enough in his ways. Unfortunately, he was so easy to please that he seemed to find just as much pleasure in the presence of drab little girls as he derived from Arabella's rather more scintillating company. Gammon, of course, but how to alert Arabella to that fact? Or would it be more to the point to keep quiet and allow Hugo a small degree of success? As her mind drifted down that particular path, Augusta suddenly caught herself up and had the grace to look sheepish. What appalling thoughts for a chaperon!

Her gaze fell on Lizzie, sweet but far from demure in a gown of delicate silver gauze touched with colour in the form of embroidered lilacs. A soft, introspective smile hovered over her classically moulded lips. Almost a smile of anticipation. Augusta frowned. Had she missed something?

Mentally reviewing Lizzie's conquests, Lady Benborough was at a loss to account for the suppressed excitement evident, now she came to look more closely, in the way the younger girl's fingers beat an impatient if silent tattoo on the beads of her reticule. Clearly, whoever he was would be at the ball. She would have to watch her youngest charge like a hawk. Lizzie was too young, in all conscience, to be allowed the licence her more worldly sisters took for granted.

Relaxing back against the velvet squabs, Augusta smiled. Doubtless she was worrying over nothing. Lizzie might have the Twinning looks but surely she was too serious an innocent to attract the attentions of a rake? Three rakes she might land, the Twinnings being the perfect bait, but a fourth was bound to be wishful thinking.

CHAPTER SEVEN

MARTIN PUZZLED OVER Max's last words on the Twinnings but it was not until he met the sisters that evening, at Lady Montacute's drum, that he divined what had prompted his brother to utter them. He had spent the afternoon dropping in on certain old friends, only to be, almost immediately, bombarded with requests for introductions to the Twinnings. He had come away with the definite impression that the best place to be that evening would be wherever the Misses Twinning were destined. His batman and valet, Jiggins, had turned up the staggering information that Max himself usually escorted his wards to their evening engagements. Martin had found this hard to credit, but when, keeping an unobtrusive eye on the stream of arrivals from a vantage-point beside a potted palm in Lady Montacute's ballroom, he had seen Max arrive surrounded by Twinning sisters, he had been forced to accept the crazy notion as truth. When the observation that the fabulous creature on his brother's arm was, in fact, his eldest ward finally penetrated his brain all became clear.

Moving rapidly to secure a dance with Lizzie, who smiled up at him with flattering welcome, Martin was close enough to see the expression in his brother's eyes as he bent to whisper something in Miss Twinning's ear, prior to relinquishing her to the attention of the circle forming about her. His brows flew and he pursed his lips in surprise. As his brother's words of that morning returned to him, he grinned. How much was Max prepared to stake?

For the rest of the evening, Martin watched and plotted and planned. He used his wound as an excuse not to dance, which enabled him to spend his entire time studying Lizzie Twinning. It was an agreeable pastime. Her silvery dress floated about her as she danced and the candlelight glowed on her sheening brown curls. With her natural grace, she reminded him of a fairy sprite, except that he rather thought such mythical creatures lacked the fulsome charms with which the Twinning sisters were so well-endowed. Due to his experienced foresight, Lizzie accommodatingly returned to his side after every dance, convinced by his chatter of the morning that he was in dire need of cheering up. Lady Benborough, to whom he had dutifully made his bow, had snorted in disbelief at his die-away airs but had apparently been unable to dissuade Lizzie's soft heart from bringing him continual succour. By subtle degrees, he sounded her out on each of her hopeful suitors and was surprised at his own relief in finding she had no special leaning towards any.

He started his campaign in earnest when the musicians struck up for the dance for which he *had* engaged her. By careful manoeuvring, they were seated in a sheltered alcove, free for the moment of her swains. Schooling his features to grave disappointment, he said, "Dear Lizzie. I'm so sorry to disappoint you, but…" He let his voice fade away weakly.

Lizzie's sweet face showed her concern. "Oh! Do you not feel the thing? Perhaps I can get Mrs. Alford's smelling salts for you?"

Martin quelled the instinctive response to react to her suggestion in too forceful a manner. Instead, he waved aside her words with one limp hand. "No! No! Don't worry about me. I'll come about shortly." He smiled forlornly at her, allowing his blue gaze to rest, with calculated effect, on her grey-brown eyes. "But maybe you'd like to get one of your other beaux to dance with you? I'm sure Mr. Mallard would be only too thrilled." He made a move as if to summon this gentleman, the most assiduous of her suitors.

"Heavens, no!" exclaimed Lizzie, catching his hand in hers to prevent the action. "I'll do no such thing. If you're feeling poorly then of course I'll stay with you." She continued to hold his hand and, for his part, Martin made no effort to remove it from her warm clasp.

Martin closed his eyes momentarily, as if fighting off a sudden faintness. Opening them again, he said, "Actually, I do believe it's all the heat and noise in here that's doing it. Perhaps if I went out on to the terrace for a while, it might clear my head."

"The very thing!" said Lizzie, jumping up.

Martin, rising more slowly, smiled down at her in a brotherly fashion. "Actually, I'd better go alone. Someone might get the wrong idea if we both left."

"Nonsense!" said Lizzie, slightly annoyed by his implication that such a conclusion could, of course, have no basis in fact. "Why should anyone worry? We'll only be a few minutes and anyway, I'm your brother's ward, after all."

Martin made some small show of dissuading her, which, as he intended, only increased her resolution to accompany him. Finally, he allowed himself to be bullied on to the terrace, Lizzie's small hand on his arm, guiding him.

As supper time was not far distant, there were only two other couples on the shallow terrace, and within minutes both had returned to the ballroom. Martin, food very far from his mind, strolled down the terrace, apparently content to go where Lizzie led. But his sharp soldier's eyes had very quickly adjusted to the moonlight. After a cursory inspection of the surroundings, he allowed himself to pause dramatically as they neared the end of the terrace. "I really think..." He waited a moment, as if gathering strength, then continued, "I really think I should sit down."

Lizzie looked around in consternation. There were no benches on the terrace, not even a balustrade.

"There's a seat under that willow, I think," said Martin, gesturing across the lawn.

A quick glance from Lizzie confirmed this observation. "Here, lean on me," she said. Martin obligingly draped one arm lightly about her shoulders. As he felt her small hands gripping him about his waist, a pang of guilt shook him. She really was so trusting. A pity to destroy it.

They reached the willow and brushed through the long strands which conveniently fell back to form a curtain around the white wooden seat. Inside the chamber so formed, the moonbeams danced, sprinkling sufficient light to lift the gloom and allow them to see. Martin sank on to the seat with a convincing show of weakness. Lizzie subsided in a susurration of silks beside him, retaining her clasp on his hand and half turning the better to look into his face.

The moon was behind the willow and one bright beam shone through over Martin's shoulder to fall gently on Lizzie's face. Martin's face was in shadow, so Lizzie, smiling confidingly up at him, could only see that he was smiling in return. She could not see the expression which lit his blue eyes as they devoured her delicate face, then dropped boldly to caress the round swell of her breasts where they rose and fell invitingly below the demurely scooped neckline of her gown. Carefully, Martin turned his hand so that now he was holding her hand, not she his. Then he was still.

After some moments, Lizzie put her head on one side and softly asked, "Are you all right?"

It was on the tip of Martin's tongue to answer truthfully. No, he was not all right. He had brought her out here to commence her seduction and now some magical power was holding him back. What was the matter with him? He cleared his throat and answered huskily, "Give me a minute."

A light breeze wafted the willow leaves and the light shifted. Lizzie saw the distracted frown which had settled over his eyes. Drawing her hand from his, she reached up and gently ran her fingers over his brow, as if to smooth the frown away. Then, to Martin's intense surprise, she leaned forward and, very gently, touched her lips to his.

As she drew away, Lizzie saw to her dismay that, if Martin had been frowning before, he was positively scowling now. "Why did you do that?" he asked, his tone sharp.

Even in the dim light he could see her confusion. "Oh, dear! I'm s…so sorry. Please excuse me! I shouldn't have done that."

"Damn right, you shouldn't have," Martin growled. His hand, which had fallen to the bench, was clenched hard with the effort to remain still and not pull the damn woman into his arms and devour her. He realized she had not answered his question. "But why did you?"

Lizzie hung her head in contrition. "It's just that you looked…well, so troubled. I just wanted to help." Her voice was a small whisper in the night.

Martin sighed in frustration. That sort of help he could do without.

"I suppose you'll think me very forward, but…" This time, her voice died away altogether.

What Martin did think was that she was adorable and he hurt with the effort to keep his hands off her. Now he came to think of it, while he had not had a headache when they came out to the garden, he certainly had one now. Repressing the desire to groan aloud, he straightened. "We'd better get back to the ballroom. We'll just forget the incident." As he drew her to her feet and placed her hand on his arm, an unwelcome thought struck him. "You don't go around kissing other men who look troubled, do you?"

The surprise in her face was quite genuine. "No! Of course not!"

"Well," said Martin, wondering why the information so thrilled him, "just subdue any of these sudden impulses of yours. Except around me, of course. I dare say it's perfectly all right with me, in the circumstances. You are my brother's ward, after all."

Lizzie, still stunned by her forward behaviour, and the sudden impulse that had driven her to it, smiled trustingly up at him.

CAROLINE SMILED her practised smile and wished, for at least the hundredth time, that Max Rotherbridge were not their guardian. At least, she amended, not *her* guardian. He was proving a tower of strength in all other respects and she could only be grateful, both for his continuing support and protection, as well as his experienced counsel over the affair of Sarah and Lord Darcy. But there was no doubt in her mind that her own confusion would be immeasurably eased by dissolution of the guardianship clause which tied her so irrevocably to His Grace of Twyford.

While she circled the floor in the respectful arms of Mr. Willoughby who, she knew, was daily moving closer to a declaration despite her attempts to dampen his confidence, she was conscious of a wish that it was her guardian's far less gentle clasp she was in. Mr. Willoughby, she had discovered, was worthy. Which was almost as bad as righteous. She sighed and covered the lapse with a brilliant smile into his mild eyes, slightly below her own. It was not that she despised short men, just that they lacked the ability to make her feel delicate and vulnerable, womanly, as Max Rotherbridge certainly could. In fact, the feeling of utter helplessness that seemed to overcome her every time she found herself in his powerful arms was an increasing concern.

As she and her partner turned with the music, she sighted Sarah, dancing with one of her numerous court, trying, not entirely successfully, to look as if she was enjoying it. Her heart went out to her sister. They had stayed at home the previous night and, in unusual privacy, thrashed out the happenings of the night before. While Sarah skated somewhat thinly over certain aspects, it had been clear that she, at least, knew her heart. But Max had taken the opportunity of a few minutes' wait in the hall at Twyford House to let both herself and Sarah know, in the most subtle way, that Lord Darcy had left town for his estates. She swallowed another sigh and smiled absently at Mr. Willoughby.

As the eldest, she had, in recent years, adopted the role of surrogate mother to her sisters. One unfortunate aspect of that situation was that she had no one to turn to herself. If the gentleman involved had been anyone other than her guardian, she would have sought advice from Lady Benborough. In the circumstances, that avenue, too, was closed to her. But, after that interlude in the Overtons's summer-house, she was abysmally aware that she needed advice. All he had to do was to take her into his arms and her well-ordered defences fell flat. And his kiss! The effect of that seemed totally to disorder her mind, let alone her senses. She had not yet fathomed what, exactly, he was about, yet it seemed inconceivable that he would seduce his own ward. Which fact, she ruefully admitted, but only to herself when at her most candid, was at the seat of her desire to no longer be his ward.

It was not that she had any wish to join the *demi-monde*. But face facts she must. She was nearly twenty-six and she knew what she wanted. She wanted Max Rotherbridge. She knew he was a rake and, if she had not instantly divined his standing as soon as she had laid eyes on him, Lady Benborough's forthright remarks on the subject left no room for doubt. But every tiny particle of her screamed that he was the one. Which was why she was calmly dancing with each of her most ardent suitors, careful not to give any one of them the slightest encouragement, while waiting for her guardian to claim her for the dance before supper. On their arrival in the overheated ballroom, he had, in a sensual murmur that had wafted the curls over her ear and sent shivery tingles all the way down her spine, asked her to hold that waltz for him. She looked into Mr. Willoughby's pale eyes. And sighed.

"SIR MALCOLM, I do declare you're flirting with me!" Desperation lent Arabella's bell-like voice a definite edge. Using her delicate feather fan to great purpose, she flashed her large eyes at the horrendously rich but essentially dim-witted Scottish baronet, managing meanwhile to keep Hugo, Lord Denbigh, in view. Her true prey was standing only feet away, conversing amiably with a plain matron with an even plainer daughter. What was the matter with him? She had tried every trick she knew to bring the great oaf to her tiny feet, yet he persistently drifted away. He would be politely attentive but seemed incapable of settling long enough even to be considered one of her court. She had kept the supper waltz free, declaring it to be taken to all her suitors, convinced he would ask her for that most favoured dance. But now, with supper time fast approaching, she suddenly found herself facing the prospect of having no partner at all. Her eyes flashing, she turned in welcome to Mr. Pritchard and Viscount Molesworth.

She readily captivated both gentlemen, skilfully steering clear of any lapse of her own rigidly imposed standards. She was an outrageous flirt, she knew, but a discerning flirt, and she had long made it her policy never to hurt anyone with her artless chatter. She enjoyed the occupation but it had never involved her heart. Normally, her suitors happily fell at her feet without the slightest assistance from her. But, now that she had at last found someone she wished to attract, she had, to her horror, found she had less idea of how to draw a man to her side than plainer girls who had had to learn the art.

To her chagrin, she saw the musicians take their places on the rostrum. There was only one thing to do. She smiled sweetly at the three gentlemen around her. "My dear sirs," she murmured, her voice mysteriously low, "I'm afraid I must leave you. No! Truly. Don't argue." Another playful smile went around. "Until later, Sir Malcolm, Mr. Pritchard, my lord." With a nod and a mysterious smile she moved away, leaving the three gentlemen wondering who the lucky man was.

Slipping through the crowd, Arabella headed for the exit to the ballroom. Doubtless there would be an ante-chamber somewhere where she could hide. She was not hungry anyway. She timed her exit to coincide with the movement of a group of people across the door, making it unlikely that anyone would see her retreat. Once in the passage, she glanced about. The main stairs lay directly in front of her. She glanced to her left in time to see two ladies enter one of the rooms. The last thing she needed was the endless chatter of a withdrawing-room. She turned purposefully to her right. At the end of the dimly

lit corridor, a door stood open, light from the flames of
a hidden fire flickering on its panels. She hurried down
the corridor and, looking in, saw a small study. It was
empty. A carafe and glasses set in readiness on a small
table suggested it was yet another room set aside for the
use of guests who found the heat of the ballroom too
trying. With a sigh of relief, Arabella entered. After
some consideration, she left the door open.

She went to the table and poured herself a glass of
water. As she was replacing the glass, she heard voices
approaching. Her eyes scanned the room and lit on the
deep window alcove; the curtain across it, if fully drawn,
would make it a small room. On the thought, she was
through, drawing the heavy curtain tightly shut.

In silence, her heart beating in her ears, she listened
as the voices came nearer and entered the room, going
towards the fire. She waited a moment, breathless, but
no one came to the curtain. Relaxing, she turned. And
almost fell over the large pair of feet belonging to the
gentleman stretched at his ease in the armchair behind
the curtain.

"Oh!" Her hand flew to her lips in her effort to
smother the sound. "What are you doing here?" she
whispered furiously.

Slowly, the man turned his head towards her. He
smiled. "Waiting for you, my dear."

Arabella closed her eyes tightly, then opened them
again but he was still there. As she watched, Lord
Denbigh unfurled his long length and stood, magnificent and, suddenly, to Arabella at least, oddly intimidating, before her. In the light of the full moon
spilling through the large windows, his tawny eyes

roved appreciatively over her. He caught her small hand in his and raised it to his lips. "I didn't think you'd be long."

His lazy tones, pitched very low, washed languidly over Arabella. With a conscious effort, she tried to break free of their hypnotic hold. "How could you know I was coming here? *I* didn't."

"Well," he answered reasonably, "I couldn't think where else you would go, if you didn't have a partner for the supper waltz."

He *knew!* In the moonlight, Arabella's fiery blush faded into more delicate tints but the effect on her temper was the same. "You oaf!" she said in a fierce whisper, aiming a stinging slap at the grin on his large face. But the grin grew into a smile as he easily caught her hand and drew it down and then behind her, drawing her towards him. He captured her other hand as well and imprisoned that in the same large hand behind her back.

"Lord Denbigh! Let me go!" Arabella pleaded, keeping her voice low for fear the others beyond the curtain would hear. How hideously embarrassing to be found in such a situation. And now she had another problem. What was Hugo up to? As her anger drained, all sorts of other emotions came to the fore. She looked up, her eyes huge and shining in the moonlight, her lips slightly parted in surprise.

Hugo lifted his free hand and one long finger traced the curve of her full lower lip.

Even with only the moon to light his face, Arabella saw the glimmer of desire in his eyes. "Hugo, let me go. Please?"

He smiled lazily down at her. "In a moment, sweetheart. After I've rendered you incapable of scratching my eyes out."

His fingers had taken hold of her chin and he waited to see the fury in her eyes before he chuckled and bent his head until his lips met hers.

Arabella had every intention of remaining aloof from his kisses. Damn him—he'd tricked her! She tried to whip up her anger, but all she could think of was how wonderfully warm his lips felt against hers. And what delicious sensations were running along her nerves. Everywhere. Her body, entirely of its own volition, melted into his arms.

She felt, rather than heard, his deep chuckle as his arms shifted and tightened about her. Finding her hands free and resting on his shoulders, she did not quite know what to do with them. Box his ears? In the end, she twined them about his neck, holding him close.

When Hugo finally lifted his head, it was to see the stars reflected in her eyes. He smiled lazily down at her. "Now you have to admit that's more fun than waltzing."

Arabella could think of nothing to say.

"No quips?" he prompted.

She blushed slightly. "We should be getting back." She tried to ease herself from his embrace but his arms moved not at all.

Still smiling in that sleepy way, he shook his head. "Not yet. That was just the waltz. We've supper to go yet." His lips lightly brushed hers. "And I'm ravenously hungry."

Despite the situation, Arabella nearly giggled at the boyish tone. But she became much more serious when his lips returned fully to hers, driving her into far deeper waters than she had ever sailed before.

But he was experienced enough to correctly gauge her limits, to stop just short and retreat, until they were sane again. Later, both more serious than was their wont, they returned separately to the ballroom.

DESPITE HER STRATEGIES, Arabella was seen as she slipped from the ballroom. Max, returning from the card-room where he had been idly passing his time until he could, with reasonable excuse, gravitate to the side of his eldest ward, saw the bright chestnut curls dip through the doorway and for an instant had thought that Caroline was deserting him. But his sharp ears had almost immediately caught the husky tone of her laughter from a knot of gentlemen near by and he realised it must have been Arabella, most like Caroline in colouring, whom he had seen.

But he had more serious problems on his mind than whether Arabella had torn her flounce. His pursuit of the luscious Miss Twinning, or, rather, the difficulties which now lay in his path to her, were a matter for concern. The odd fact that he actually bothered to dance with his eldest ward had already been noted. As there were more than a few ladies among the *ton* who could give a fairly accurate description of his preferences in women, the fact that Miss Twinning's endowments brought her very close to his ideal had doubtless not been missed. However, he cared very little for the opinions of others and foresaw no real problem in placating the *ton* after the deed was done. What was troubling him was the un-expected behaviour of the two principals in the affair, Miss Twinning and himself.

With respect to his prey, he had miscalculated on

two counts. Firstly, he had imagined it would take a con-
certed effort to seduce a twenty-five-year-old woman
who had lived until recently a very retired life. Instead,
from the first, she had responded so freely that he had
almost lost his head. He was too experienced not to
know that it would take very little of his persuasion to
convince her to overthrow the tenets of her class and
come to him. It irritated him beyond measure that the
knowledge, far from spurring him on to take immediate advantage of her vulnerability, had made him pause
and consider, in a most disturbing way, just what he was
about. His other mistake had been in thinking that, with
his intensive knowledge of the ways of the *ton,* he would
have no difficulty in using his position as her guardian
to create opportunities to be alone with Caroline.
Despite—or was it because of?—her susceptibility
towards him, she seemed able to avoid his planned tête-
à-têtes with ease and, with the exception of a few occasions associated with some concern over one or other
of her sisters, had singularly failed to give him the opportunities he sought. And seducing a woman whose
mind was filled with worry over one of her sisters was
a task he had discovered to be beyond him.

He had, of course, revised his original concept of
what role Caroline was to play in his life. However, he
was fast coming to the conclusion that he would have
to in some way settle her sisters' affairs before either he
or Caroline would have time to pursue their own desti-
nies. But life, he was fast learning, was not all that
simple. In the circumstances, the *ton* would expect Miss
Twinning's betrothal to be announced before that of her
sisters. And he was well aware he had no intention of

giving his permission for any gentleman to pay his addresses to Miss Twinning. As he had made no move to clarify for her the impression of his intentions he had originally given her, he did not delude himself that she might not accept some man like Willoughby, simply to remove herself from the temptation of her guardian. Yet if he told her she was not his ward, she would undoubtedly be even more vigilant with respect to himself and, in all probability, even more successful in eluding him.

There was, of course, a simple solution. But he had a perverse dislike of behaving as society dictated. Consequently, he had formed no immediate intention of informing Caroline of his change of plans. There was a challenge, he felt, in attempting to handle their relationship his way. Darcy had pushed too hard and too fast and, consequently, had fallen at the last fence. He, on the other hand, had no intention of rushing things. Timing was everything in such a delicate matter as seduction.

The congestion of male forms about his eldest ward brought a slight frown to his face. But the musicians obligingly placed bow to string, allowing him to extricate her from their midst and sweep her on to the floor.

He glanced down into her grey-green eyes and saw his own pleasure in dancing with her reflected there. His arm tightened slightly and her attention focused. "I do hope your sisters are behaving themselves?"

Caroline returned his weary question with a smile. "Assuming your friends are doing likewise, I doubt there'll be a problem."

Max raised his brows. So she knew at least a little of what had happened. After negotiating a difficult turn to avoid old Major Brumidge and his similarly ancient

partner, he jettisoned the idea of trying to learn more of
Sarah's thoughts in favour of spiking a more specific gun.
"Incidently, apropos of your sisters' and your own fell
intent, what do you wish me to say to the numerous beaux
who seem poised to troop up the steps of Delmere House?"

He watched her consternation grow as she grappled
with the sticky question. He saw no reason to tell her
that, on his wards' behalf, he had already turned down
a number of offers, none of which could be considered
remotely suitable. He doubted they were even aware of
the interest of the gentlemen involved.

Caroline, meanwhile, was considering her options. If
she was unwise enough to tell him to permit any acceptable gentlemen to address them, they could shortly be
bored to distraction with the task of convincing said gentlemen that their feelings were not reciprocated. On the
other hand, giving Max Rotherbridge a free hand to choose
their husbands seemed equally unwise. She temporized.
"Perhaps it would be best if we were to let you know if
we anticipated receiving an offer from any particular gentleman that we would wish to seriously consider."

Max would have applauded if his hands had not been
so agreeably occupied. "A most sensible suggestion, my
ward. Tell me, how long does it take to pin up a flounce?"

Caroline blinked at this startling question.

"The reason I ask," said Max as they glided to a halt,
"is that Arabella deserted the room some minutes before
the music started and, as far as I can see, has yet to return."

A frown appeared in Caroline's fine eyes but, in def-
erence to the eyes of others, she kept her face free of
care and her voice light. "Can you see if Lord Denbigh
is in the room?"

Max did not need to look. "Not since I entered it." After a pause, he asked, "Is she seriously pursuing that line? If so, I fear she'll all too soon reach point non plus."

Caroline followed his lead as he offered her his arm and calmly strolled towards the supper-room. A slight smile curled her lips as, in the increasing crowd, she leaned closer to him to answer. "With Arabella, it's hard to tell. She seems so obvious, with her flirting. But that's really all superficial. In reality, she's rather reticent about such things."

Max smiled in reply. Her words merely confirmed his own reading of Arabella. But his knowledge of the relationship between Caroline and her sisters prompted him to add, "Nevertheless, you'd be well-advised to sound her out on that score. Hugo Denbigh, when all is said and done, is every bit as dangerous as…" He paused to capture her eyes with his own before, smiling in a devilish way, he continued, "I am."

Conscious of the eyes upon them, Caroline strove to maintain her composure. "How very…reassuring, to be sure," she managed.

The smile on Max's face broadened. They had reached the entrance of the supper-room and he paused in the doorway to scan the emptying ballroom. "If she hasn't returned in ten minutes, we'll have to go looking. But come, sweet ward, the lobster patties await."

With a flourish, Max led her to a small table where they were joined, much to his delight, by Mr. Willoughby and a plain young lady, a Miss Spence. Mr. Willoughby's transparent intention of engaging the delightful Miss Twinning in close converse, ignoring the undemanding Miss Spence and Miss Twinning's guardian, proved to be rather more complicated than Mr. Willoughby, for one, had imagined. Under the subtle hand of His Grace of Twyford, Mr. Willoughby found himself the centre of a general discussion on philosophy. Caroline listened in ill-concealed delight as Max blocked every move poor Mr. Willoughby made to polarise the conversation. It became apparent that her guardian understood only too well Mr. Willoughby's state and she found herself caught somewhere between embarrassment and relief. In the end, relief won the day.

Eventually, routed, Mr. Willoughby rose, ostensibly to return Miss Spence to her parent. Watching his retreat with laughing eyes, Caroline returned her gaze to her guardian, only to see him look pointedly at the door from the ballroom. She glanced across and saw Arabella enter, slightly flushed and with a too-bright smile on her lips. She made straight for the table where Sarah was sitting with a number of others and, with her usual facility, merged with the group, laughing up at the young man who leapt to his feet to offer her his chair.

Caroline turned to Max, a slight frown in her eyes, to find his attention had returned to the door. She followed his gaze and saw Lord Denbigh enter.

To any casual observer, Hugo was merely coming late to the supper-room, his languid gaze and sleepy smile giving no hint of any more pressing emotion than to discover whether there were any lobster patties left. Max Rotherbridge, however, was a far from casual observer. As he saw the expression in his lordship's heavy-lidded eyes as they flicked across the room to where Arabella sat, teasing her company unmercifully,

His Grace of Twyford's black brows rose in genuine astonishment. Oh, God! Another one?

RESIGNED TO YET another evening spent with no progress in the matter of his eldest ward, Max calmly escorted her back to the ballroom and, releasing her to the attentions of her admirers, not without a particularly penetrating stare at two gentlemen of dubious standing who had had the temerity to attempt to join her circle, he prepared to quit the ballroom. He had hoped to have persuaded Miss Twinning to view the moonlight from the terrace. There was a useful bench he knew of, under a concealing willow, which would have come in handy. However, he had no illusions concerning his ability to make love to a woman who was on tenterhooks over the happiness of not one but two sisters. So he headed for the card-room.

On his way, he passed Arabella, holding court once again in something close to her usual style. His blue gaze searched her face. As if sensing his regard, she turned and saw him. For a moment, she looked lost. He smiled encouragingly. After a fractional pause, she flashed her brilliant smile back and, putting up her chin, turned back to her companions, laughing at some comment.

Max moved on. Clearly, Caroline did have another problem on her hands. He paused at the entrance to the card-room and, automatically, scanned the packed ballroom. Turning, he was about to cross the threshold when a disturbing thought struck him. He turned back to the ballroom.

"Make up your mind! Make up your mind! Oh, it's you, Twyford. What are you doing at such an occasion? Hardly your style these days, what?"

Excusing himself to Colonel Weatherspoon, Max moved out of the doorway and checked the room again. Where was Lizzie? He had not seen her at supper, but then again he had not looked. He had mentally dubbed her the baby of the family but his rational mind informed him that she was far from too young. He was about to cross the room to where his aunt Augusta sat, resplendent in bronze bombazine, when a movement by the windows drew his eyes.

Lizzie entered from the terrace, a shy and entirely guileless smile on her lips. Her small hand rested with easy assurance on his brother's arm. As he watched, she turned and smiled up at Martin, a look so full of trust that a newborn lamb could not have bettered it. And Martin, wolf that he was, returned the smile readily.

Abruptly, Max turned on his heel and strode into the card-room. He needed a drink.

CHAPTER EIGHT

ARABELLA SWATTED at the bumble-bee blundering noisily by her head. She was lying on her stomach on the stone surround of the pond in the courtyard of Twyford House, idly trailing her fingers in the cool green water. Her delicate mull muslin, petal-pink in hue, clung revealingly to her curvaceous form while a straw hat protected her delicate complexion from the afternoon sun. Most other young ladies in a similar pose would have looked childish. Arabella, with her strangely wistful air, contrived to look mysteriously enchanting.

Her sisters were similarly at their ease. Sarah was propped by the base of the sundial, her *bergère* hat shading her face as she threaded daisies into a chain. The dark green cambric gown she wore emphasized her arrestingly pale face, dominated by huge brown eyes, darkened now by the hint of misery. Lizzie sat beside the rockery, poking at a piece of embroidery with a noticeable lack of enthusiasm. Her sprigged mauve muslin proclaimed her youth yet its effect was ameliorated by her far from youthful figure.

Caroline watched her sisters from her perch in a cushioned hammock strung between two cherry trees. If her guardian could have seen her, he would undoubtedly have approved of the simple round gown of particularly fine amber muslin she had donned for the warm day. The fabric clung tantalizingly to her mature figure while the neckline revealed an expanse of soft ivory breasts.

The sisters had gradually drifted here, one by one, drawn by the warm spring afternoon and the heady scents rising from the rioting flowers which crammed the beds and overflowed on to the stone flags. The period between luncheon and the obligatory appearance in the Park was a quiet time they were coming increasingly to appreciate as the Season wore on. Whenever possible, they tended to spend it together, a last vestige, Caroline thought, of the days when they had only had each other for company.

Sarah sighed. She laid aside her hat and looped the completed daisy chain around her neck. Cramming her headgear back over her dark curls, she said, "Well, what are we going to do?"

Three pairs of eyes turned her way. When no answer was forthcoming, she continued, explaining her case with all reasonableness, "Well, we can't go on as we are, can we? None of us is getting anywhere."

Arabella turned on her side better to view her sisters. "But what can we do? In your case, Lord Darcy's not even in London."

"True," returned the practical Sarah. "But it's just occurred to me that he must have friends still in London. Ones who would write to him, I mean. Other than our guardian."

Caroline grinned. "Whatever you do, my love, kindly explain all to me before you set the *ton* ablaze. I don't think I could stomach our guardian demanding an explanation and not having one to give him."

Sarah chuckled. "Has he been difficult?"

But Caroline would only smile, a secret smile of which both Sarah and Arabella took due note.

"He hasn't said anything about me, has he?" came Lizzie's slightly breathless voice. Under her sisters' gaze, she blushed. "About me and Martin," she mumbled, suddenly becoming engrossed in her *petit point*.

Arabella laughed. "Artful puss. As things stand, you're the only one with all sails hoisted and a clear wind blowing. The rest of us are becalmed, for one reason or another."

Caroline's brow had furrowed. "Why do you ask? Has Max given you any reason to suppose he disapproves?"

"Well," temporized Lizzie, "he doesn't seem entirely…happy, about us seeing so much of each other."

Her attachment to Martin Rotherbridge had progressed in leaps and bounds. Despite Max's warning and his own innate sense of danger, Martin had not been able to resist the temptation posed by Lizzie Twinning. From that first undeniably innocent kiss he had, by subtle degrees, led her to the point where, finding herself in his arms in the gazebo in Lady Malling's garden, she had permitted him to kiss her again. Only this time, it had been Martin leading the way. Lizzie, all innocence, had been thoroughly enthralled by the experience and stunned by her own response to the delightful sensations it had engendered. Unbeknownst to her, Martin Rotherbridge had been stunned, too.

Belatedly, he had tried to dampen his own increasing desires, only to find, as his brother could have told him, that that was easier imagined than accomplished. Abstinence had only led to intemperance. In the end, he had capitulated and returned to spend every moment possible at Lizzie's side, if not her feet.

Lizzie was right in her assessment that Max disapproved of their association but wrong in her idea of the cause. Only too well-acquainted with his brother's character, their guardian entertained a grave concern that the frustrations involved in behaving with decorum in the face of Lizzie Twinning's bounteous temptations would prove overwhelming long before Martin was brought to admit he was in love with the chit. His worst fears had seemed well on the way to being realized when he had, entirely unintentionally, surprised them on their way back to the ballroom. His sharp blue eyes had not missed the glow in Lizzie's face. Consequently, the look he had directed at his brother, which Lizzie had intercepted, had not been particularly encouraging. She had missed Martin's carefree response.

Caroline, reasonably certain of Max's thoughts on the matter, realized these might not be entirely clear to Lizzie. But how to explain Max's doubts of his own brother to the still innocent Lizzie? Despite the fact that only a year separated her from Arabella, the disparity in their understandings, particularly with respect to the male of the species, was enormous. All three elder Twinnings had inherited both looks and dispositions from their father's family, which in part explained his aversion to women. Thomas Twinning had witnessed firsthand the dance his sisters had led all the men of their acquaintance before finally settling in happily wedded bliss. The strain on his father and himself had been considerable. Consequently, the discovery that his daughters were entirely from the same mould had prompted him to immure them in rural seclusion. Lizzie, however, had only inherited the Twinning looks, her gentle and often quite stubborn innocence deriving from the placid Eleanor. Viewing the troubled face of her youngest half-sister, Caroline decided the time had come to at least try to suggest to Lizzie's mind that there was often more to life than the strictly obvious. Aside from anything else, this time, she had both Sarah and Arabella beside her to help explain.

"I rather think, my love," commenced Caroline, "that it's not that Max would disapprove of the connection. His concern is more for your good name."

Lizzie's puzzled frown gave no indication of lightening. "But why should my being with his brother endanger my good name?"

Sarah gave an unladylike snort of laughter. "Oh, Lizzie, love! You're going to have to grow up, my dear. Our guardian's concerned because he knows what his brother's like and that, generally speaking, young ladies are not safe with him."

The effect of this forthright speech on Lizzie was galvanizing. Her eyes blazed in defence of her absent love. "Martin's not like that at all!"

"Oh, sweetheart, you're going to have to open your eyes!" Arabella bought into the discussion, sitting up the better to do so. "He's not only 'like that,' Martin Rotherbridge has made a career specializing in being 'like that.' He's a rake. The same as Hugo and Darcy Hamilton, too. And, of course, the greatest rake of them all is our dear guardian, who has his eye firmly set on Caro here. Rakes and Twinnings go together, I'm afraid. We attract them and they—" she put her head on one side, considering her words "—well, they attract us. It's no earthly good disputing the evidence."

Seeing the perturbation in Lizzie's face, Caroline sought to reassure her. "That doesn't mean that the end result is not just the same as if they were more conservative. It's just that, well, it very likely takes longer for such men to accept the…the desirability of marriage." Her eyes flicked to Sarah who, head bent and eyes intent on her fingers, was plaiting more daisies. "Time will, I suspect, eventually bring them around. The danger is in the waiting."

Lizzie was following her sister's discourse with difficulty. "But Martin's never…well, you know, tried to make love to me."

"Do you mean to say he's never kissed you?" asked Arabella in clear disbelief.

Lizzie blushed. "Yes. But I kissed him first."

"Lizzie!" The startled exclamation was drawn from all three sisters who promptly thereafter fell about laughing. Arabella was the last to recover. "Oh, my dear, you're more a Twinning than we'd thought!"

"Well, it was nice, I thought," said Lizzie, fast losing her reticence in the face of her sisters' teasing. "Anyway, what am I supposed to do? Avoid him? That wouldn't be much fun. And I don't think I could stop him kissing me, somehow. I rather like being kissed."

"It's not the kissing itself that's the problem," stated Sarah. "It's what comes next. And that's even more difficult to stop."

"Very true," confirmed Arabella, studying her slippered toes. "But if you want lessons in how to hold a rake at arm's length you shouldn't look to me. Nor to Sarah either. It's only Caro who's managed to hold her own so far." Arabella's eyes started to dance as they rested on her eldest sister's calm face. "But, I suspect, that's only because our dear guardian is playing a deep game."

Caroline blushed slightly, then reluctantly smiled. "Unfortunately, I'm forced to agree with you."

A silence fell as all four sisters pondered their rakes. Eventually, Caroline spoke. "Sarah, what are you planning?"

Sarah wriggled her shoulders against the sundial's pedestal. "Well, it occurred to me that perhaps I should make some effort to bring things to a head. But if I did the obvious, and started wildly flirting with a whole bevy of gentlemen, then most likely I'd only land myself in the suds. For a start, Darcy would very likely not believe it and I'd probably end with a very odd reputation. I'm not good at it, like Bella."

Arabella put her head on one side, the better to observe her sister. "I could give you lessons," she offered.

"No," said Caroline. "Sarah's right. It wouldn't wash." She turned to Lizzie to say, "Another problem, my love, is that rakes know all the tricks, so bamming them is very much harder."

"Too true," echoed Arabella. She turned again to Sarah. "But if not that, what, then?"

A wry smile touched Sarah's lips. "I rather thought the pose of the maiden forlorn might better suit me. Nothing too obvious, just a subtle withdrawing. I'd still go to all the parties and balls, but I'd just become quieter and ever so gradually, let my...what's the word, Caro? My despair? My broken heart? Well, whatever it is, show through."

Her sisters considered her plan and found nothing to criticise. Caroline summed up their verdict. "In truth, my dear, there's precious little else you could do."

Sarah's eyes turned to Arabella. "But what are you going to do about Lord Denbigh?"

Arabella's attention had returned to her toes. She wrinkled her pert nose. "I really don't know. I can't make him jealous; as Caro said, he knows all those tricks. And the forlorn act would not do for me."

Arabella had tried every means possible to tie down the elusive Hugo but that large gentleman seemed to view her attempts with sleepy humour, only bestirring himself to take advantage of any tactical error she made. At such times, as Arabella had found to her confusion and consternation, he could move with ruthless efficiency. She was now very careful not to leave any opening he could exploit to be private with her.

"Why not try...?" Caroline broke off, suddenly assailed by a twinge of guilt at encouraging her sisters in their scheming. But, under the enquiring gaze of Sarah and Arabella, not to mention Lizzie, drinking it all in, she mentally shrugged and continued. "As you cannot convince him of your real interest in any other gentleman, you'd be best not to try, I agree. But you could let him understand that, as he refused to offer marriage, and you, as a virtuous young lady, are prevented from accepting any other sort of offer, then, with the utmost reluctance and the deepest regret, you have been forced to turn aside and consider accepting the attentions of some other gentleman."

Arabella stared at her sister. Then, her eyes started

to dance. "Oh, Caro!" she breathed. "What a perfectly marvellous plan!"

"Shouldn't be too hard for you to manage," said Sarah. "Who are the best of your court for the purpose? You don't want to raise any overly high expectations on their parts but you've loads of experience in playing that game."

Arabella was already deep in thought. "Sir Humphrey Bullard, I think. And Mr. Stone. They're both sober enough and in no danger of falling in love with me. They're quite coldly calculating in their approach to matrimony; I doubt they have hearts to lose. They both want an attractive wife, preferably with money, who would not expect too much attention from them. To their minds, I'm close to perfect but to scramble for my favours would be beneath them. They should be perfect for my charade."

Caroline nodded. "They sound just the thing."

"Good! I'll start tonight," said Arabella, decision burning in her huge eyes.

"But what about you, Caro?" asked Sarah with a grin. "We've discussed how the rest of us should go on, but you've yet to tell us how you plan to bring our dear guardian to his knees."

Caroline smiled, the same gently wistful smile that frequently played upon her lips these days. "If I knew that, my dears, I'd certainly tell you." The last weeks had seen a continuation of the unsatisfactory relationship between His Grace of Twyford and his eldest ward. Wary of his ability to take possession of her senses should she give him the opportunity, Caroline had consistently avoided his invitations to dally alone with him.

Indeed, too often in recent times her mind had been
engaged in keeping a watchful eye over her sisters,
something their perceptive guardian seemed to understand. She could not fault him for his support and was
truly grateful for the understated manner in which he
frequently set aside his own inclinations to assist her in
her concern for her siblings. In fact, it had occurred to
her that, far from being a lazy guardian, His Grace of
Twyford was very much *au fait* with the activities of
each of his wards. Lately, it had seemed to her that her
sisters' problems were deflecting a considerable amount
of his energies from his pursuit of herself. So, with a
twinkle in her eyes, she said, "If truth be told, the best
plan I can think of to further my own ends is to assist
you all in achieving your goals as soon as may be. Once
free of you three, perhaps our dear guardian will be
able to concentrate on me."

IT WAS LIZZIE who initiated the Twinning sisters' friendship with the two Crowbridge girls, also being presented that year. The Misses Crowbridge, Alice and
Amanda, were very pretty young ladies in the manner
which had been all the rage until the Twinnings came
to town. They were pale and fair, as ethereal as the
Twinnings were earthy, as fragile as the Twinnings were
robust, and, unfortunately for them, as penniless as the
Twinnings were rich. Consequently, the push to find
well-heeled husbands for the Misses Crowbridge had
not prospered.

Strolling down yet another ballroom, Lady Mott's as
it happened, on the arm of Martin, of course, Lizzie had
caught the sharp words uttered by a large woman of

horsey mien to a young lady, presumably her daughter, sitting passively at her side. "Why can't you two be like that? Those girls simply walk off with any man they fancy. All it needs is a bit of push. But you and Alice..." The rest of the tirade had been swallowed up by the hubbub around them. But the words returned to Lizzie later, when, retiring to the withdrawing-room to mend her hem which Martin very carelessly had stood upon, she found the room empty except for the same young lady, huddled in a pathetic bundle, trying to stifle her sobs.

As a kind heart went hand in hand with Lizzie's innocence, it was not long before she had befriended Amanda Crowbridge and learned of the difficulty facing both Amanda and Alice. Lacking the Twinning sisters' confidence and abilities, the two girls, thrown without any preparation into the heady world of the *ton,* found it impossible to converse with the elegant gentlemen, becoming tongue-tied and shy, quite unable to attach the desired suitors. To Lizzie, the solution was obvious.

Both Arabella and Sarah, despite having other fish to fry, were perfectly willing to act as tutors to the Crowbridge girls. Initially, they agreed to this more as a favour to Lizzie than from any more magnanimous motive, but as the week progressed they became quite absorbed with their protégées. For the Crowbridge girls, being taken under the collective wing of the three younger Twinnings brought a cataclysmic change to their social standing. Instead of being left to decorate the wall, they now spent their time firmly embedded amid groups of chattering young people. Drawn ruthlessly into conversations by the artful Arabella or Sarah at her most prosaic, they discovered that talking to the swells of the *ton* was not, after all, so very different from conversing with the far less daunting lads at home. Under the steady encouragement provided by the Twinnings, the Crowbridge sisters slowly unfurled their petals.

Caroline and His Grace of Twyford watched the growing friendship from a distance and were pleased to approve, though for very different reasons. Having ascertained that the Crowbridges were perfectly acceptable acquaintances, although their mother, for all her breeding, was, as Lady Benborough succinctly put it, rather too pushy, Caroline was merely pleased that her sisters had found some less than scandalous distraction from their romantic difficulties. Max, on the other hand, was quick to realize that with the three younger girls busily engaged in this latest exploit, which kept them safely in the ballrooms and salons, he stood a much better chance of successfully spending some time, in less populated surroundings, with his eldest ward.

In fact, as the days flew past, his success in his chosen endeavour became so marked that Caroline was forced openly to refuse any attempt to detach her from her circle. She had learned that their relationship had become the subject of rampant speculation and was now seriously concerned at the possible repercussions, for herself, for her sisters and for him. Max, reading her mind with consummate ease, paid her protestations not the slightest heed. Finding herself once more in His Grace's arms and, as usual, utterly helpless, Caroline was moved to remonstrate. "What on earth do you expect to accomplish by all this? I'm your *ward,* for heaven's sake!"

A deep chuckle answered her. Engaged in tracing her

left brow, first with one long finger, then with his lips, Max had replied, "Consider your time spent with me as an educational experience, sweet Caro. As Aunt Augusta was so eager to point out," he continued, transferring his attention to her other brow, "who better than your guardian to demonstrate the manifold dangers to be met with among the *ton?*"

She was prevented from telling him what she thought of his reasoning, in fact, was prevented from thinking at all, when his lips moved to claim hers and she was swept away on a tide of sensation she was coming to appreciate all too well. Emerging, much later, pleasantly witless, she found herself the object of His Grace's heavy-lidded blue gaze. "Tell me, my dear, if you were not my ward, would you consent to be private with me?"

Mentally adrift, Caroline blinked in an effort to focus her mind. For the life of her she could not understand his question, although the answer seemed clear enough. "Of course not!" she lied, trying unsuccessfully to ease herself from his shockingly close embrace.

A slow smile spread across Max's face. As the steel bands around her tightened, Caroline was sure he was laughing at her.

Another deep chuckle, sending shivers up and down her spine, confirmed her suspicion. Max bent his head until his lips brushed hers. Then, he drew back slightly and blue eyes locked with grey. "In that case, sweet ward, you have some lessons yet to learn."

Bewildered, Caroline would have asked for enlightenment but, reading her intent in her eyes, Max avoided her question by the simple expedient of kissing her again. Irritated by his cat-and-mouse tactics, Caroline tried to withdraw from participation in this strange game whose rules were incomprehensible to her. But she quickly learned that His Grace of Twyford had no intention of letting her backslide. Driven, in the end, to surrender to the greater force, Caroline relaxed, melting into his arms, yielding body, mind and soul to his experienced conquest.

IT WAS AT Lady Richardson's ball that Sir Ralph Keighly first appeared as a cloud on the Twinnings's horizon. Or, more correctly, on the Misses Crowbridge's horizon, although by that stage, it was much the same thing. Sir Ralph, with a tidy estate in Gloucestershire, was in London to look for a wife. His taste, it appeared, ran to sweet young things of the type personified by the Crowbridge sisters, Amanda Crowbridge in particular. Unfortunately for him, Sir Ralph was possessed of an overwhelming self-conceit combined with an unprepossessing appearance. He was thus vetoed on sight as beneath consideration by the Misses Crowbridge and their mentors.

However, Sir Ralph was rather more wily than he appeared. Finding his attentions to Amanda Crowbridge compromised by the competing attractions of the large number of more personable young men who formed the combined Twinning-Crowbridge court, he retired from the lists and devoted his energies to cultivating Mr. and Mrs. Crowbridge. In this, he achieved such notable success that he was invited to attend Lady Richardson's ball with the Crowbridges. Despite the tearful protestations of both Amanda and Alice at his inclusion in their party, when they crossed the threshold of Lady Richardson's ballroom, Amanda, looking distinctly seedy, had her hand on Sir Ralph's arm.

At her parents' stern instruction, she was forced to endure two waltzes with Sir Ralph. As Arabella acidly observed, if it had been at all permissible, doubtless Amanda would have been forced to remain at his side for the entire ball. As it was, she dared not join her friends for supper but, drooping with dejection, joined Sir Ralph and her parents.

To the three Twinnings, the success of Sir Ralph was like waving a red rag to a bull. Without exception, they took it as interference in their, up until then, successful development of their protégées. Even Lizzie was, metaphorically speaking, hopping mad. But the amenities offered by a ball were hardy conducive to a council of war, so, with admirable restraint, the three younger Twinnings devoted themselves assiduously to their own pursuits and left the problem of Sir Ralph until they had leisure to deal with it appropriately.

Sarah was now well down the road to being acknowledged as having suffered an unrequited love. She bore up nobly under the strain but it was somehow common knowledge that she held little hope of recovery. Her brave face, it was understood, was on account of her sisters, as she did not wish to ruin their Season by retiring into seclusion, despite this being her most ardent wish. Her large brown eyes, always fathomless, and her naturally pale and serious face were welcome aids in the projection of her new persona. She danced and chatted, yet the vitality that had burned with her earlier in the Season had been dampened. That, at least, was no more than the truth.

Arabella, all were agreed, was settling down to the sensible prospect of choosing a suitable connection. As Hugo Denbigh had contrived to be considerably more careful in his attentions to Arabella than Darcy Hamilton had been with Sarah, the gossips had never connected the two. Consequently, the fact that Lord Denbigh's name was clearly absent from Arabella's list did not in itself cause comment. But, as the Twinning sisters had been such a hit, the question of who precisely Arabella would choose was a popular topic for discussion. Speculation was rife and, as was often the case in such matters, a number of wagers had already been entered into the betting books held by the gentlemen's clubs. According to rumour, both Mr. Stone and Sir Humphrey Bullard featured as possible candidates. Yet not the most avid watcher could discern which of these gentlemen Miss Arabella favoured.

Amid all this drama, Lizzie Twinning continued as she always had, accepting the respectful attentions of the sober young men who sought her out while reserving her most brilliant smiles for Martin Rotherbridge. As she was so young and as Martin wisely refrained from any overtly amorous or possessive act in public, most observers assumed he was merely helping his brother with what must, all were agreed, constitute a definite handful. Martin, finding her increasingly difficult to lead astray, was forced to live with his growing frustrations and their steadily diminishing prospects for release.

The change in Amanda Crowbridge's fortunes brought a frown to Caroline's face. She would not have liked the connection for any of her sisters. Still, Amanda Crowbridge was not her concern. As her sisters appeared to have taken the event philosophically enough, she felt justified in giving it no further thought, reserving her energies, mental and otherwise, for her increasingly frequent interludes with her guardian.

Despite her efforts to minimize his opportunities, she found herself sharing his carriage on their return journey to Mount Street. Miriam Alford sat beside her and Max, suavely elegant and exuding a subtle aura of powerful sensuality, had taken the seat opposite her. Lady Benborough and her three sisters were following in the Twyford coach. As Caroline had suspected, their chaperon fell into a sound sleep before the carriage had cleared the Richardson House drive.

Gazing calmly at the moonlit fields, she calculated they had at least a forty-minute drive ahead of them. She waited patiently for the move she was sure would come and tried to marshal her resolve to deflect it. As the minutes ticked by, the damning knowledge slowly seeped into her consciousness that, if her guardian was to suddenly become afflicted with propriety and the journey was accomplished without incident, far from being relieved, she would feel let down, cheated of an eagerly anticipated treat. She frowned, recognizing her already racing pulse and the tense knot in her stomach that restricted her breathing for the symptoms they were. On the thought, she raised her eyes to the dark face before her.

He was watching the countryside slip by, the silvery light etching the planes of his face. As if feeling her gaze, he turned and his eyes met hers. For a moment, he read her thoughts and Caroline was visited by the dreadful certainty that he knew the truth she was struggling to hide. Then, a slow, infinitely wicked smile spread across his face. Caroline stopped breathing. He leaned forward. She expected him to take her hand and draw her to sit beside him. Instead, his strong hands slipped about her waist and, to her utter astonishment, he lifted her across and deposited her in a swirl of silks on his lap.

"Max!" she gasped.

"Sssh. You don't want to wake Mrs. Alford. She'd have palpitations."

Horrified, Caroline tried to get her feet to the ground, wriggling against the firm clasp about her waist. Almost immediately, Max's voice sounded in her ear, in a tone quite different from any she had previously heard. "Sweetheart, unless you cease wriggling your delightful *derriére* in such an enticing fashion, this lesson is likely to go rather further than I had intended."

Caroline froze. She held her breath, not daring to so much as twitch. Then Max's voice, the raw tones of an instant before no longer in evidence, washed over her in warm approval. "Much better."

She turned to face him, carefully keeping her hips still. She placed her hands on his chest in an effort, futile, she knew, to fend him off. "Max, this is madness. You must stop doing this!"

"Why? Don't you like it?" His hands were moving gently on her back, his touch scorching through the thin silk of her gown.

Caroline ignored the sardonic lift of his black brows and the clear evidence in his eyes that he was laughing at her. She found it much harder to ignore the sensations his hands were drawing forth. Forcing her face into strongly disapproving lines, she answered his first question, deeming it prudent to conveniently forget the second. "I'm your *ward*, remember? You know I am. You told me so yourself."

"A fact you should strive to bear in mind, my dear."

Caroline wondered what he meant by that. But Max's mind, and hands, had shifted their focus of attention. As his hands closed over her breasts, Caroline nearly leapt to her feet. *"Max!"*

But, "Sssh," was all her guardian said as his lips settled on hers.

CHAPTER NINE

THE TWYFORD COACH was also the scene of considerable activity, though of a different sort. Augusta, in sympathy with Mrs. Alford, quickly settled into a comfortable doze which the whisperings of the other occupants of the carriage did nothing to disturb. Lizzie, Sarah and Arabella, incensed by Amanda's misfortune, spent some minutes giving vent to their feelings.

"It's not as if Sir Ralph's such a good catch, even," Sarah commented.

"Certainly not," agreed Lizzie with uncharacteristic sharpness. "It's really too bad! Why, Mr. Minchbury is almost at the point of offering for her and he has a much bigger estate, besides being much more attractive. And Amanda *likes* him, what's more."

"Ah," said Arabella, wagging her head sagely, "but he's not been making up to Mrs. Crowbridge, has he? That woman must be all about in her head, to think of giving little Amanda to Keighly."

"Well," said Sarah decisively, "what are we going to do about it?"

Silence reigned for more than a mile as the sisters considered the possibilities. Arabella eventually spoke into the darkness. "I doubt we'd get far discussing matters with the Crowbridges."

"Very true," nodded Sarah. "And working on Amanda's equally pointless. She's too timid."

"Which leaves Sir Ralph," concluded Lizzie. After a pause, she went on: "I know we're not precisely to his taste, but do you think you could do it, Bella?"

Arabella's eyes narrowed as she considered Sir Ralph. Thanks to Hugo, she now had a fairly extensive understanding of the basic attraction between men and women. Sir Ralph was, after all, still a man. She shrugged. "Well, it's worth a try. I really can't see what else we can do."

For the remainder of the journey, the sisters' heads were together, hatching a plan.

ARABELLA STARTED her campaign to steal Sir Ralph from Amanda the next evening, much to the delight of Amanda. When she was informed in a whispered aside of the Twinnings' plan for her relief, Amanda's eyes had grown round. Swearing to abide most faithfully by any instructions they might give her, she had managed to survive her obligatory two waltzes with Sir Ralph in high spirits, which Sarah later informed her was not at all helpful. Chastised, she begged pardon and remained by Sarah's side as Arabella took to the floor with her intended.

As Sir Ralph had no real affection for Amanda, it took very little of Arabella's practised flattery to make him increasingly turn his eyes her way. But, to the Twinnings' consternation, their plan almost immediately developed a hitch.

Their guardian was not at all pleased to see Sir Ralph squiring Arabella. A message from him, relayed by both Caroline and Lady Benborough, to the effect that Arabella should watch her step, pulled Arabella up

short. A hasty conference, convened in the withdrawing-room, agreed there was no possibility of gaining His
Grace's approval for their plan. Likewise, none of the
three sisters had breathed a word of their scheme to
Caroline, knowing that, despite her affection for them,
there were limits to her forbearance.

"But we can't just give up!" declared Lizzie in tren-
chant tones.

Arabella was nibbling the end of one finger. "No. We
won't give up. But we'll have to reorganize. You two,"
she said, looking at Sarah and Lizzie, quite ignoring
Amanda and Alice who were also present, "are going
to have to cover for me. That way, I won't be obviously
spending so much time with Sir Ralph, but he'll still be
thinking about me. You must tell Sir Ralph that our
guardian disapproves but that, as I'm head over heels in
love with him, I'm willing to go against the Duke's
wishes and continue to see him." She frowned, pondering her scenario. "We'll have to be careful not to paint
our dear guardian in too strict colours. The story is that
we're sure he'll eventually come around, when he sees
how attached I am to Sir Ralph. Max knows I'm a
flighty, flirtatious creature and so doubts of the strength
of my affections. That should be believable enough."

"All right," Sarah nodded. "We'll do the groundwork
and you administer the *coup de grâce*."

And so the plan progressed.

For Arabella, the distraction of Sir Ralph came at an
opportune time in her juggling of Sir Humphrey and Mr.
Stone. It formed no part of her plans for either of these
gentlemen to become too particular. And while her
sober and earnest consideration of their suits had, she

knew, stunned and puzzled Lord Denbigh, who watched with a still sceptical eye, her flirtation with Sir Ralph had brought a strange glint to his hazel orbs.

In truth, Hugo had been expecting Arabella to flirt outrageously with her court in an attempt to make him jealous and force a declaration. He had been fully prepared to sit idly by, watching her antics from the sidelines with his usual sleepily amused air, waiting for the right moment to further her seduction. But her apparent intention to settle for a loveless marriage had thrown him. It was not a reaction he had expected. Knowing what he did of Arabella, he could not stop himself from thinking what a waste it would be. True, as the wife of a much older man, she was likely to be even more receptive to his own suggestions of a discreet if illicit relationship. But the idea of her well-endowed charms being brutishly enjoyed by either of her ageing suitors set his teeth on edge. Her sudden pursuit of Sir Ralph Keighly, in what he was perceptive enough to know was not her normal style, seriously troubled him, suggesting as it did some deeper intent. He wondered whether she knew what she was about. The fact that she continued to encourage Keighly despite Twyford's clear disapproval further increased his unease.

Arabella, sensing his perturbation, continued to tread the difficult path she had charted, one eye on him, the other on her guardian, encouraging Sir Ralph with one hand while using the other to hold back Sir Humphrey and Mr. Stone. As she confessed to her sisters one morning, it was exhausting work.

Little by little, she gained ground with Sir Ralph, their association camouflaged by her sisters' ploys. On

the way back to the knot of their friends, having satis-
factorily twirled around Lady Summerhill's ballroom,
Arabella and Sir Ralph were approached by a little lady,
all in brown.

Sir Ralph stiffened.

The unknown lady blushed. "How do you do?" she
said, taking in both Arabella and Sir Ralph in her glance.
"I'm Harriet Jenkins," she explained helpfully to
Arabella, then, turning to Sir Ralph, said, "Hello, Ralph,"
in quite the most wistful tone Arabella had ever heard.

Under Arabella's interested gaze, Sir Ralph became
tongue-tied. He perforce bowed over the small hand
held out to him and managed to say, "Mr. Jenkins's
estates border mine."

Arabella's eyes switched to Harriet Jenkins. "My
father," she supplied.

Sir Ralph suddenly discovered someone he had to
exchange a few words with and precipitately left them.
Arabella looked down into Miss Jenkins's large eyes,
brown, of course, and wondered. "Have you lately come
to town, Miss Jenkins?"

Harriet Jenkins drew her eyes from Sir Ralph's departing figure and dispassionately viewed the beauty
before her. What she saw in the frank hazel eyes
prompted her to reply, "Yes. I was…bored at home. So
my father suggested I come to London for a few weeks.
I'm staying with my aunt, Lady Cottesloe."

Arabella was only partly satisfied with this explanation. Candid to a fault, she put the question in her mind.
"Pardon me, Miss Jenkins, but are you and Sir Ralph…?"

Miss Jenkins's wistfulness returned. "No. Oh, you're
right in thinking I want him. But Ralph has other ideas.

I've known him from the cradle, you see. And I suppose familiarity breeds contempt." Suddenly realizing to whom she was speaking, she blushed and continued, "Not that I could hope to hold a candle to the London beauties, of course."

Her suspicions confirmed, Arabella merely laughed and slipped an arm through Miss Jenkins's. "Oh, I shouldn't let that bother you, my dear." As she said the words, it occurred to her that, if anything, Sir Ralph was uncomfortable and awkward when faced with beautiful women, as evidenced by his behaviour with either herself or Amanda. It was perfectly possible that some of his apparent conceit would drop away when he felt less threatened; for instance, in the presence of Miss Jenkins.

Miss Jenkins had stiffened at Arabella's touch and her words. Then, realizing the kindly intent behind them, she relaxed. "Well, there's no sense in deceiving myself. I suppose I shouldn't say so, but Ralph and I were in a fair way to being settled before he took this latest notion of looking about before he made up his mind irrevocably. I sometimes think it was simply fear of tying the knot that did it."

"Very likely," Arabella laughingly agreed as she steered Miss Jenkins in the direction of her sisters.

"My papa was furious and said I should give him up. But I convinced him to let me come to London, to see how things stood. Now, I suppose, I may as well go home."

"Oh, on no account should you go home yet awhile, Miss Jenkins!" said Arabella, a decided twinkle in her eye. "May I call you Harriet? Harriet, I'd like you to meet my sisters."

THE ADVENT OF Harriet Jenkins caused a certain amount
of reworking of the Twinnings' plan for Sir Ralph. After
due consideration, she was taken into their confidence
and willingly joined the small circle of conspirators. In
truth, her appearance relieved Arabella's mind of a
nagging worry over how she was to let Sir Ralph down
after Amanda accepted Mr. Minchbury, who, under the
specific guidance of Lizzie, was close to popping the
question. Now, all she had to do was to play the hardened
flirt and turn Sir Ralph's bruised ego into Harriet's
tender care. All in all, things were shaping up nicely.

However, to their dismay, the Twinnings found that
Mrs. Crowbridge was not yet vanquished. The news of
her latest ploy was communicated to them two days
later, at Beckenham, where they had gone to watch a
balloon ascent. The intrepid aviators had yet to arrive
at the field, so the three Twinnings had descended from
their carriage and, together with the Misses Crowbridge
and Miss Jenkins, were strolling elegantly about the
field, enjoying the afternoon sunshine and a not inconsiderable amount of male attention. It transpired that
Mrs. Crowbridge had invited Sir Ralph to pay a morning
call and then, on the slightest of pretexts, had left him
alone with Amanda for quite twenty minutes. Such
brazen tactics left them speechless. Sir Ralph, to do
him justice, had not taken undue advantage.

"He probably didn't have time to work out the odds
against getting Arabella versus the benefits of Amanda,"
said Sarah with a grin. "Poor man! I can almost pity
him, what with Mrs. Crowbridge after him as well."

All the girls grinned but their thoughts quickly
returned to their primary preoccupation. "Yes, but," said

Lizzie, voicing a fear already in both Sarah's and Arabella's minds, "if Mrs. Crowbridge keeps behaving like this, she might force Sir Ralph to offer for Amanda by tricking him into compromising her."

"I'm afraid that's only too possible," agreed Harriet. "Ralph's very gullible." She shook her head in such a deploring way that Arabella and Sarah were hard put to it to smother their giggles.

"Yes, but it won't do," said Amanda, suddenly. "I know my mother. She'll keep on and on until she succeeds. You've got to think of some way of…of removing Sir Ralph quickly."

"For his sake as well as your own," agreed Harriet. "The only question is, how?"

Silence descended while this conundrum revolved in their minds. Further conversation on the topic was necessarily suspended when they were joined by a number of gentlemen disinclined to let the opportunity of paying court to such a gaggle of very lovely young ladies pass by. As His Grace of Twyford's curricle was conspicuously placed among the carriages drawn up to the edge of the field, the behaviour of said gentlemen remained every bit as deferential as within the confines of Almack's, despite the sylvan setting.

Mr. Mallard was the first to reach Lizzie's side, closely followed by Mr. Swanston and Lord Brookfell. Three other fashionable exquisites joined the band around Lizzie, Amanda, Alice and Harriet, and within minutes an unexceptionable though thoroughly merry party had formed. Hearing one young gentleman allude to the delicate and complementary tints of the dresses of the four younger girls as "pretty as a posy," Sarah could not resist a grimace, purely for Arabella's benefit. Arabella bit hard on her lip to stifle her answering giggle. Both fell back a step or two from the younger crowd, only to fall victim to their own admirers.

Sir Humphrey Bullard, a large man of distinctly florid countenance, attempted to capture Arabella's undivided attention but was frustrated by the simultaneous arrival of Mr. Stone, sleekly saturnine, on her other side. Both offered their arms, leaving Arabella, with a sunshade to juggle, in a quandary. She laughed and shook her head at them both. "Indeed, gentlemen, you put me to the blush. What can a lady do under such circumstances?"

"Why, make your choice, m'dear," drawled Mr. Stone, a strangely determined glint in his eye.

Arabella's eyes widened at this hint that Mr. Stone, at least, was not entirely happy with being played on a string. She was rescued by Mr. Humphrey, irritatingly aware that he did not cut such a fine figure as Mr. Stone. "I see the balloonists have arrived. Perhaps you'd care to stroll to the enclosure and watch the inflation, Miss Arabella?"

"We'll need to get closer if we're to see anything at all," said Sarah, coming up on the arm of Lord Tulloch.

By the time they reached the area cordoned off in the centre of the large field, a crowd had gathered. The balloon was already filling slowly. As they watched, it lifted from the ground and slowly rose to hover above the cradle slung beneath, anchored to the ground by thick ropes.

"It looks like such a flimsy contraption," said Arabella, eyeing the gaily striped silk balloon. "I wonder that anyone could trust themselves to it."

"They don't always come off unscathed, I'm sorry

to say," answered Mr. Stone, his schoolmasterish tones evincing strong disapproval of such reckless behaviour.

"Humph!" said Sir Humphrey Bullard.

Arabella's eyes met Sarah's in mute supplication. Sarah grinned.

It was not until the balloon had taken off, successfully, to Arabella's relief, and the crowd had started to disperse that the Twinnings once more had leisure to contemplate the problem of Sir Ralph Keighly. Predictably, it was Sarah and Arabella who conceived the plot. In a few whispered sentences, they developed its outline sufficiently to see that it would require great attention to detail to make it work. As they would have no further chance that day to talk with the others in private, they made plans to meet the next morning at Twyford House. Caroline had mentioned her intention of visiting her old nurse, who had left the Twinnings' employ after her mother had died and hence was unknown to the younger Twinnings. Thus, ensconced in the back parlour of Twyford House, they would be able to give free rein to their thoughts. Clearly, the removal of Sir Ralph was becoming a matter of urgency.

Returning to their carriage, drawn up beside the elegant equipage bearing the Delmere crest, the three youngest Twinnings smiled serenely at their guardian, who watched them from the box seat of his curricle, a far from complaisant look in his eyes.

Max was, in fact, convinced that something was in the wind but had no idea what. His highly developed social antennae had picked up the undercurrents of his wards' plotting and their innocent smiles merely confirmed his suspicions. He was well aware that Caroline, seated beside him in a fetching gown of figured muslin, was not privy to their schemes. As he headed his team from the field, he smiled. His eldest ward had had far too much on her mind recently to have had any time free for scheming.

Beside him, Caroline remained in blissful ignorance of her sisters' aims. She had spent a thoroughly enjoyable day in the company of her guardian and was in charity with the world. They had had an excellent view of the ascent itself from the height of the box seat of the curricle. And when she had evinced the desire to stroll among the crowds, Max had readily escorted her, staying attentively by her side, his acerbic comments forever entertaining and, for once, totally unexceptionable. She looked forward to the drive back to Mount Street with unimpaired calm, knowing that in the curricle, she ran no risk of being subjected to another of His Grace's "lessons." In fact, she was beginning to wonder how many more lessons there could possibly be before the graduation ceremony. The thought brought a sleepy smile to her face. She turned to study her guardian.

His attention was wholly on his horses, the bays, as sweet a pair as she had ever seen. Her eyes fell to his hands as they tooled the reins, strong and sure. Remembering the sensations those hands had drawn forth as they had knowledgeably explored her body, she caught her breath and rapidly looked away. Keeping her eyes fixed on the passing landscape, she forced her thoughts into safer fields.

The trouble with Max Rotherbridge was that he invaded her thoughts, too, and, as in other respects, was well-nigh impossible to deny. She was fast coming to the conclusion that she should simply forget all else and give herself up to the exquisite excitements she found in his arms. All the social and moral strictures ever intoned, all her inhibitions seemed to be consumed to ashes in the fire of her desire. She was beginning to feel it was purely a matter of time before she succumbed. The fact that the idea did not fill her with trepidation but rather with a pleasant sense of anticipation was in itself, she felt, telling.

As the wheels hit the cobbles and the noise that was London closed in around them, her thoughts flew ahead to Lady Benborough, who had stayed at home recruiting her energies for the ball that night. It was only this morning, when, with Max, she had bid her ladyship goodbye, that the oddity in Augusta's behaviour had struck her. While the old lady had been assiduous in steering the girls through the shoals of the acceptable gentlemen of the *ton,* she had said nothing about her eldest charge's association with her nephew. No matter how Caroline viewed it, invoke what reason she might, there was something definitely odd about that. As she herself had heard the rumours about His Grace of Twyford's very strange relationship with his eldest ward, it was inconceivable that Lady Benborough had not been edified with their tales. However, far from urging her to behave with greater discretion towards Max, impossible task though that might be, Augusta continued to behave as if there was nothing at all surprising in Max Rotherbridge escorting his wards to a balloon ascent. Caroline wondered what it was that Augusta knew that she did not.

THE TWINNING SISTERS attended the opera later that
week. It was the first time they had been inside the
ornate structure that was the Opera House; their progress
to the box organized for them by their guardian was
perforce slow as they gazed about them with interest.
Once inside the box itself, in a perfect position in the
first tier, their attention was quickly claimed by their
fellow opera-goers. The pit below was a teeming sea of
heads; the stylish crops of the fashionable young men
who took perverse delight in rubbing shoulders with the
masses bobbed amid the unkempt locks of the hoi polloi.
But it was upon the occupants of the other boxes that
the Twinnings' principal interest focused. These quickly
filled as the time for the curtain to rise approached. All
four were absorbed in nodding and waving to friends
and acquaintances as the lights went out.

The first act consisted of a short piece by a little-
known Italian composer, as the prelude to the opera
itself, which would fill the second and third acts, before
another short piece ended the performance. Caroline
sat, happily absorbed in the spectacle, beside and
slightly in front of her guardian. She was blissfully
content. She had merely made a comment to Max a
week before that she would like to visit the opera. Two
days later, he had arranged it all. Now she sat, superbly
elegant in a silver satin slip overlaid with bronzed lace,
and revelled in the music, conscious, despite her preoccupation, of the warmth of the Duke of Twyford's blue
gaze on her bare shoulders.

Max watched her delight with satisfaction. He had
long ago ceased to try to analyze his reactions to
Caroline Twinning; he was besotted and knew it. Her

happiness had somehow become his happiness; in his view, nothing else mattered. As he watched, she turned and smiled, a smile of genuine joy. It was, he felt, all the thanks he required for the effort organizing such a large box at short notice had entailed. He returned her smile, his own lazily sensual. For a moment, their eyes locked. Then, blushing, Caroline turned back to the stage.

Max had little real interest in the performance, his past experiences having had more to do with the singer than the song. He allowed his gaze to move past Caroline to dwell on her eldest half-sister. He had not yet fathomed exactly what Sarah's ambition was, yet felt sure it was not as simple as it appeared. The notion that any Twinning would meekly accept unwedded solitude as her lot was hard to swallow. As Sarah sat by Caroline's side, dramatic as ever in a gown of deepest green, the light from the stage lit her face. Her troubles had left no mark on the classical lines of brow and cheek but the peculiar light revealed more clearly than daylight the underlying determination in the set of the delicate mouth and chin. Max's lips curved in a wry grin. He doubted that Darcy had heard the last of Sarah Twinning, whatever the outcome of his self-imposed exile.

Behind Sarah sat Lord Tulloch and Mr. Swanston, invited by Max to act as squires for Sarah and Arabella respectively. Neither was particularly interested in the opera, yet both had accepted the invitations with alacrity. Now, they sat, yawning politely behind their hands, waiting for the moment when the curtain would fall and they could be seen by the other attending members of the *ton,* escorting their exquisite charges through the corridors.

Arabella, too, was fidgety, settling and resettling her

pink silk skirts and dropping her fan. She appeared to be trying to scan the boxes on the tier above. Max smiled. He could have told her that Hugo Denbigh hated opera and had yet to be seen within the portals of Covent Garden.

Lady Benborough, dragon-like in puce velvet, sat determinedly following the aria. Distracted by Arabella's antics, she turned to speak in a sharp whisper, whereat Arabella grudgingly subsided, a dissatisfied frown marring her delightful visage.

At the opposite end of the box sat Martin, with Lizzie by the parapet beside him. She was enthralled by the performance, hanging on every note that escaped the throat of the soprano performing the lead. Martin, most improperly holding her hand, evinced not the slightest interest in the buxom singer but gazed solely at Lizzie, a peculiar smile hovering about his lips. Inwardly, Max sighed. He just hoped his brother knew what he was about.

The aria ended and the curtain came down. As the applause died, the large flambeaux which lit the pit were brought forth and re-installed in their brackets. Noise erupted around them as everyone talked at once.

Max leaned forward to speak by Caroline's ear. "Come. Let's stroll."

She turned to him in surprise and he smiled. "That's what going to the opera is about, my dear. To see and be seen. Despite appearances, the most important performances take place in the corridors of Covent Garden, not on the stage."

"Of course," she returned, standing and shaking out her skirts. "How very provincial of me not to realize." Her eyes twinkled. "How kind of you, dear guardian, to attend so assiduously to our education."

Max took her hand and tucked it into his arm. As they paused to allow the others to precede them, he bent to whisper in her ear, "On the contrary, sweet Caro. While I'm determined to see your education completed, my interest is entirely selfish."

The wicked look which danced in his dark blue eyes made Caroline blush. But she was becoming used to the highly improper conversations she seemed to have with her guardian. "Oh?" she replied, attempting to look innocent and not entirely succeeding. "Won't I derive any benefit from my new-found knowledge?"

They were alone in the box, hidden from view of the other boxes by shadows. For a long moment, they were both still, blue eyes locked with grey-green, the rest of the world far distant. Caroline could not breathe; the intensity of that blue gaze and the depth of the passion which smouldered within it held her mesmerized. Then, his eyes still on hers, Max lifted her hand and dropped a kiss on her fingers. "My dear, once you find the key, beyond that particular door lies paradise. Soon, sweet Caro, very soon, you'll see."

Once in the corridor, Caroline's cheeks cooled. They were quickly surrounded by her usual court and Max, behaving more circumspectly than he ever had before, relinquished her to the throng. Idly, he strolled along the corridors, taking the opportunity to stretch his long legs. He paused here and there to exchange a word with friends but did not stop for long. His preoccupation was not with extending his acquaintance of the *ton*. His ramblings brought him to the corridor serving the opposite arm of the horseshoe of boxes. The bell summoning the audience to their seats for the next act rang shrilly. Max was turning to make his way back to his box when a voice hailed him through the crush.

"Your Grace!"

Max closed his eyes in exasperation, then opened them and turned to face Lady Mortland. He nodded curtly. "Emma."

She was on the arm of a young man whom she introduced and immediately dismissed, before turning to Max. "I think perhaps we should have a serious talk, Your Grace."

The hard note in her voice and the equally rock-like glitter in her eyes were not lost on the Duke of Twyford. Max had played the part of the fashionable rake for fifteen years and knew well the occupational hazards. He lifted his eyes from an uncannily thorough contemplation of Lady Mortland and sighted a small alcove, temporarily deserted. "I think perhaps you're right, my dear. But I suggest we improve our surroundings."

His hand under her elbow steered Emma towards the alcove. The grip of his fingers through her silk sleeve and the steely quality in his voice were a surprise to her ladyship, but she was determined that Max Rotherbridge should pay, one way or another, for her lost dreams.

They reached the relative privacy of the alcove. "Well, Emma, what's this all about?"

Suddenly, Lady Mortland was rather less certain of her strategy. Faced with a pair of very cold blue eyes and an iron will she had never previously glimpsed, she vacillated. "Actually, Your Grace," she cooed, "I had rather hoped you would call on me and we could discuss the matter in…greater privacy."

"Cut line, Emma," drawled His Grace. "You knew perfectly well I have no wish whatever to be private with you."

The bald statement ignited Lady Mortland's temper. "Yes!" she hissed, fingers curling into claws. "Ever since you set eyes on that little harpy you call your ward, you've had no time for me!"

"I wouldn't, if I were you, make scandalous statements about a young lady to her guardian," said Max, unmoved by her spleen.

"Guardian, ha! Love, more like!"

One black brow rose haughtily.

"Do you deny it? No, of course not! Oh, there are whispers aplenty, let me tell you. But they're as nothing to the storm there'll be when I get through with you. I'll tell—Ow!"

Emma broke off and looked down at her wrist, imprisoned in Max's right hand. "L…let me go. Max, you're hurting me."

"Emma, you'll say nothing."

Lady Mortland looked up and was suddenly frightened. Max nodded, a gentle smile, which was quite terrifyingly cold, on his lips. "Listen carefully, Emma, for I'll say this once only. You'll not, verbally or otherwise, malign my ward—any of my wards—in any way whatever. Because, if you do, rest assured I'll hear about it. Should that happen, I'll ensure your stepson learns of the honours you do his father's memory by your retired lifestyle. Your income derives from the family estates, does it not?"

Emma had paled. "You…you wouldn't."

Max released her. "No. You're quite right. I wouldn't," he said. "Not unless you do first. Then, you may be certain that I would." He viewed the woman before him, with understanding if not compassion. "Leave be, Emma. What Caroline has was never yours and you know it. I suggest you look to other fields."

With a nod, Max left Lady Mortland and returned through the empty corridors to his box.

Caroline turned as he resumed his seat. She studied his face for a moment, then leaned back to whisper, "Is anything wrong?"

Max's gaze rested on her sweet face, concern for his peace of mind the only emotion visible. He smiled reassuringly and shook his head. "A minor matter of no moment." In the darkness he reached for her hand and raised it to his lips. With a smile, Caroline returned her attention to the stage. When she made no move to withdraw her hand, Max continued to hold it, mimicking Martin, placating his conscience with the observation that, in the dark, no one could see the Duke of Twyford holding hands with his eldest ward.

CHAPTER TEN

EXECUTION OF THE first phase of the Twinnings' master plot to rescue Amanda and Sir Ralph from the machinations of Mrs. Crowbridge fell to Sarah. An evening concert was selected as the venue most conducive to success. As Sir Ralph was tone deaf, enticing him from the real pleasure of listening to the dramatic voice of *Señorita Muscariña,* the Spanish soprano engaged for the evening, proved easier than Sarah had feared.

Sir Ralph was quite content to escort Miss Sarah for a stroll on the balcony, ostensibly to relieve the stuffiness in Miss Twinning's head. In the company of the rest of the *ton,* he knew Sarah was pining away and thus, he reasoned, he was safe in her company. That she was one of the more outstandingly opulent beauties he had ever set eyes on simply made life more complete. It was rare that he felt at ease with such women and his time in London had made him, more than once, wish he was back in the less demanding backwoods of Gloucestershire. Even now, despite his successful courtship of the beautiful, the effervescent, the gorgeous Arabella Twinning, there were times Harriet Jenkins's face reminded him of how much more comfortable their almost finalized relationship had been. In fact, although he tried his best to ignore them, doubts kept appearing in his mind, of whether he would be able to live up to Arabella's expectations once they were wed. He was beginning to understand that girls like Arabella—well, she was a woman, really—were used to receiving the most specific advances from the more hardened of the male population. Sir Ralph swallowed nervously, woefully aware that he lacked the abilities to compete with such gentlemen. He glanced at the pale face of the beauty beside him. A frown marred her smooth brow. He relaxed. Clearly, Miss Sarah's mind was not bent on illicit dalliance.

In thinking this, Sir Ralph could not have been further from the truth. Sarah's frown was engendered by her futile attempts to repress the surge of longing that had swept through her—a relic of that fateful evening in Lady Overton's shrubbery, she felt sure—when she had seen Darcy Hamilton's tall figure negligently propped by the door. She had felt the weight of his gaze upon her and, turning to seek its source, had met his eyes across the room. Fool that she was! She had had to fight to keep herself in her seat and not run across the room and throw herself into his arms. Then, an arch look from Arabella, unaware of Lord Darcy's return, had reminded her of her duty. She had put her hand to her head and Lizzie had promptly asked if she was feeling the thing. It had been easy enough to claim Sir Ralph's escort and leave the music-room. But the thunderous look in Darcy's eyes as she did so had tied her stomach in knots.

Pushing her own concerns abruptly aside, she transferred her attention to the man beside her. "Sir Ralph, I hope you won't mind if I speak to you on a matter of some delicacy?"

Taken aback, Sir Ralph goggled.

Sarah ignored his startled expression. Harriet had warned her how he would react. It was her job to lead him by the nose. "I'm afraid things have reached a head with Arabella. I know it's not obvious; she's so reticent about such things. But I feel it's my duty to try to explain it to you. She's in such low spirits. Something must be done or she may even go into a decline."

It was on the tip of Sir Ralph's tongue to say that he had thought it was Sarah who was going into the decline. And the suggestion that Arabella, last seen with an enchanting sparkle in her big eyes, was in low spirits confused him utterly. But Sarah's next comment succeeded in riveting his mind. "You're the only one who can save her."

The practical tone in which Sarah brought out her statement lent it far greater weight than a more dramatic declaration. In the event, Sir Ralph's attention was all hers. "You see, although she would flay me alive for telling you, you should know that she was very seriously taken with a gentleman earlier in the Season, before you arrived. He played on her sensibilities and she was so vulnerable. Unfortunately, he was not interested in marriage. I'm sure I can rely on your discretion. Luckily, she learned of his true intentions before he had time to achieve them. But her heart was sorely bruised, of course. Now that she's found such solace in your company, we had hoped, my sisters and I, that you would not let her down."

Sir Ralph was heard to mumble that he had no intention of letting Miss Arabella down.

"Ah, but you see," said Sarah, warming to her task,

"what she needs is to be taken out of herself. Some excitement that would divert her from the present round
of balls and parties and let her forget her past hurts in
her enjoyment of a new love."

Sir Ralph, quite carried away by her eloquence,
muttered that yes, he could quite see the point in that.

"So you see, Sir Ralph, it's imperative that she be swept
off her feet. She's very romantically inclined, you know."

Sir Ralph, obediently responding to his cue, declared
he was only too ready to do whatever was necessary to
ensure Arabella's happiness.

Sarah smiled warmly, "In that case, I can tell you
exactly what you must do."

IT TOOK SARAH nearly half an hour to conclude her instructions to Sir Ralph. Initially, he had been more than
a little reluctant even to discuss such an enterprise. But,
by dwelling on the depth of Arabella's need, appealing
quite brazenly to poor Sir Ralph's chivalrous instincts,
she had finally wrung from him his sworn agreement to
the entire plan.

In a mood of definite self-congratulation, she led the
way back to the music-room and, stepping over the door
sill, all but walked into Darcy Hamilton. His hand at her
elbow steadied her, but, stung by his touch, she abruptly
pulled away. Sir Ralph, who had not previously met
Lord Darcy, stopped in bewilderment, his eyes going
from Sarah's burning face to his lordship's pale one.
Then, Darcy Hamilton became aware of his presence.
"I'll return Miss Twinning to her seat."

Responding to the commanding tone, Sir Ralph
bowed and departed.

Sarah drew a deep breath. "How *dare* you?" she uttered furiously as she made to follow Sir Ralph.

But Darcy's hand on her arm detained her. "What's that…country bumpkin to you?" The insulting drawl in his voice drew a blaze of fire from Sarah's eyes.

But before she could wither him where she stood, several heads turned their way. "Sssh!"

Without a word, Darcy turned her and propelled her back out of the door.

"Disgraceful!" said Lady Malling to Mrs. Benn, nodding by her side.

On the balcony, Sarah stood very still, quivering with rage and a number of other more interesting emotions, directly attributable to the fact that Darcy was standing immediately behind her.

"Perhaps you'd like to explain what you were doing with that gentleman on the balcony for half an hour and more?"

Sarah almost turned, then remembered how close he was. She lifted her chin and kept her temper with an effort. "That's hardly any affair of yours, my lord."

Darcy frowned. "As a friend of your guardian—"

At that Sarah did turn, uncaring of the consequences, her eyes flashing, her voice taut. "As a friend of my guardian, you've been trying to seduce me ever since you first set eyes on me!"

"True," countered Darcy, his face like granite. "But not even Max has blamed me for that. Besides, it's what you Twinning girls expect, isn't it? Tell me, my dear, how many other lovesick puppies have you had at your feet since I left?"

It was on the tip of Sarah's tongue to retort that she

had had no lack of suitors since his lordship had quit the scene. But, just in time, she saw the crevasse yawning at her feet. In desperation, she willed herself to calm, and coolly met his blue eyes, her own perfectly candid. "Actually, I find the entertainments of the *ton* have palled. Since you ask, I've formed the intention of entering a convent. There's a particularly suitable one, the Ursulines, not far from our old home."

For undoubtedly the first time in his adult life, Darcy Hamilton was completely nonplussed. A whole range of totally unutterable responses sprang to his lips. He swallowed them all and said, "You wouldn't be such a fool."

Sarah's brows rose coldly. For a moment she held his gaze, then turned haughtily to move past him.

"Sarah!" The word was wrung from him and then she was in his arms, her lips crushed under his, her head spinning as he gathered her more fully to him.

For Sarah, it was a repeat of their interlude in the shrubbery. As the kiss deepened, then deepened again, she allowed herself a few minutes' grace, to savour the paradise of being once more in his arms.

Then, she gathered her strength and tore herself from his hold. For an instant, they remained frozen, silently staring at each other, their breathing tumultuous, their eyes liquid fire. Abruptly, Sarah turned and walked quickly back into the music-room.

With a long-drawn-out sigh, Darcy Hamilton leaned upon the balustrade, gazing unseeingly at the well-manicured lawns.

HIS GRACE OF TWYFORD carefully scrutinized Sarah Twinning's face as she returned to the music-room and joined her younger sisters in time to applaud the singer's operatic feats. Caroline, seated beside him, had not noticed her sister's departure from the room, nor her short-lived return. As his gaze slid gently over Caroline's face and noted the real pleasure the music had brought her, he decided that he had no intention of informing her of her sister's strange behaviour. That there was something behind the younger Twinnings's interest in Sir Ralph Keighly he did not doubt. But whatever it was, he would much prefer that Caroline was not caught up in it. He was becoming accustomed to having her complete attention and found himself reluctant to share it with anyone.

He kept a watchful eye on the door to the balcony and, some minutes later, when the singer was once more in full flight, saw Darcy Hamilton enter and, unobtrusively, leave the room. His eyes turning once more to the bowed dark head of Sarah Twinning, Max sighed. Darcy Hamilton had been one of the coolest hands in the business. But in the case of Sarah Twinning his touch seemed to have deserted him entirely. His friend's disintegration was painful to watch. He had not yet had time to do more than nod a greeting to Darcy when he had seen him enter the room. Max wondered what conclusions he had derived from his sojourn in Ireland. Whatever they were, he wryly suspected that Darcy would be seeking him out soon enough.

Which, of course, was likely to put a time limit on his own affair. His gaze returned to Caroline and, as if in response, she turned to smile up at him, her eyes unconsciously warm, her lips curving invitingly. Regretfully dismissing the appealing notion of creating a riot by kissing her in the midst of the cream of the *ton,* Max merely returned the smile and watched as she once more directed her attention to the singer. No, he did not need to worry. She would be his long before her sisters' affairs became pressing.

THE MASKED BALL given by Lady Penbright was set to be one of the highlights of an already glittering Season. Her ladyship had spared no expense. Her ballroom was draped in white satin and the terraces and trellised walks with which Penbright House was lavishly endowed were lit by thousands of Greek lanterns. The music of a small orchestra drifted down from the minstrels' gallery, the notes falling like petals on the gloriously covered heads of the *ton.* By decree, all the guests wore long dominos, concealing their evening dress, hoods secured over the ladies' curls to remove even that hint of identity. Fixed masks concealing the upper face were the order, far harder to penetrate than the smaller and often more bizarre hand-held masks, still popular in certain circles for flirtation. By eleven, the Penbright ball had been accorded the ultimate accolade of being declared a sad crush and her ladyship retired from her position by the door to join in the revels with her guests.

Max, wary of the occasion and having yet to divine the younger Twinnings' secret aim, had taken special note of his wards' dresses when he arrived at Twyford House to escort them to the ball. Caroline he would have no difficulty in detecting; even if her domino in a subtle shade of aqua had not been virtually unique, the effect her presence had on him, he had long ago noticed, would be sufficient to enable him to unerringly find her in a crowded room blindfold. Sarah, looking slightly peaked but carrying herself with the grace he expected of a Twinning, had flicked a moss-green domino over her satin dress which was in a paler shade of the same colour. Arabella had been struggling to settle the hood of a delicate rose-pink domino over her bright curls while Lizzie's huge grey eyes had watched from the depths of her lavender hood. Satisfied he had fixed the particular tints in his mind, Max had ushered them forth.

On entering the Penbright ballroom, the three younger Twinnings melted into the crowd but Caroline remained beside Max, anchored by his hand under her elbow. To her confusion, she found that one of the major purposes of a masked ball seemed to be to allow those couples who wished to spend an entire evening together without creating a scandal to do so. Certainly, her guardian appeared to have no intention of quitting her side.

While the musicians were tuning up, she was approached in a purposeful manner by a grey domino, under which she had no difficulty in recognizing the slight frame of Mr. Willoughby. The poor man was not entirely sure of her identity and Caroline gave him no hint. He glared at the tall figure by her side, which resulted in a slow, infuriating grin spreading across that gentleman's face. Then, as Mr. Willoughby cleared his throat preparatory to asking the lady in the aqua domino for the pleasure of the first waltz, Max got in before him.

After her second waltz with her guardian, who was otherwise behaving impeccably, Caroline consented to a stroll about the rooms. The main ballroom was full and salons on either side took up the overflow. A series of interconnecting rooms made Caroline's head spin.

Then, Max embarked on a long and involved anecdote which focused her attention on his masked face and his wickedly dancing eyes.

She should, of course, have been on her guard, but Caroline's defences against her dangerous guardian had long since fallen. Only when she had passed through the door he held open for her, and discovered it led into a bedroom, clearly set aside for the use of any guests overcome by the revels downstairs, did the penny drop. As she turned to him, she heard the click of the lock falling into its setting. And then Max stood before her, his eyes alight with an emotion she dared not define. That slow grin of his, which by itself turned her bones to jelly, showed in the shifting light from the open windows.

She put her hands on his shoulders, intending to hold him off, yet there was no strength behind the gesture and instead, as he drew her against him, her arms of their own accord slipped around his neck. She yielded in that first instant, as his lips touched hers, and Max knew it. But he saw no reason for undue haste. Savouring the feel of her, the taste of her, he spun out their time, giving her the opportunity to learn of each pleasure as it came, gently guiding her to the chaise by the windows, never letting her leave his arms or that state of helpless surrender she was in.

Caroline Twinning was heady stuff, but Max remembered he had a question for her. He drew back to gaze at her as she lay, reclining against the colourful cushions, her eyes unfocused as his long fingers caressed the satin smoothness of her breasts as they had once before in the carriage on the way back from the Richardsons' ball, with Miriam Alford snoring quietly in the corner. "Caro?"

Caroline struggled to make sense of his voice through the haze of sensation clouding her mind. "Mmm?"

"Sweet Caro," he murmured wickedly, watching her efforts. "If you recall, I once asked you if, were I not your guardian, you would permit me to be alone with you. Do you still think, if that was the case, you'd resist?"

To Caroline, the question was so ridiculous that it broke through to her consciousness, submerged beneath layers of pleasurable sensation. A slight frown came to her eyes as she wondered why on earth he kept asking such a hypothetical question. But his hands had stilled so it clearly behoved her to answer it. "I've always resisted you," she declared. "It's just that I've never succeeded in impressing that fact upon you. Even if you weren't my guardian, I'd still try to resist you." Her eyes closed and she gave up the attempt at conversation as his hands resumed where they had left off. But all too soon they stilled again.

"What do you mean, *even* if I weren't your guardian?"

Caroline groaned. "Max!" But his face clearly showed that he wanted her answer, so she explained with what patience she could muster. "This, you and me, together, would be scandalous enough if you weren't my guardian, but you are, so it's ten times worse." She closed her eyes again. "You must know that."

Max did, but it had never occurred to him that she would have readily accepted his advances even had he not had her guardianship to tie her to him. His slow smile appeared. He should have known. Twinnings and rakes, after all. Caroline, her eyes still closed, all senses focused on the movement of his hands upon her breasts, did not see the smile, nor the glint in her guardian's very blue eyes that went with it. But her eyes flew wide open when Max bent his head and took one rosy nipple into his mouth.

"Oh!" She tensed and Max lifted his head to grin wolfishly at her. He cocked one eyebrow at her but she was incapable of speech. Then, deliberately, his eyes holding hers, he lowered his head to her other breast, feeling her tense in his arms against the anticipated shock. Gradually, she relaxed, accepting that sensation too. Slowly, he pushed her further, knowing he would meet no resistance. She responded freely, so much so that he was constantly drawing back, trying to keep a firm hold on his much tried control. Experienced as he was, Caroline Twinning was something quite outside his previous knowledge.

Soon, they had reached that subtle point beyond which there would be no turning back. He knew it, though he doubted she did. And, to his amazement, he paused, then gently disengaged, drawing her around to lean against his chest so that he could place kisses in the warm hollow of her neck and fondle her breasts, ensuring she would stay blissfully unaware while he did some rapid thinking.

The pros were clear enough, but she would obviously come to him whenever he wished, now or at any time in the future. Such as tomorrow. The cons were rather more substantial. Chief among these was that tonight they would have to return to the ball afterwards, usually a blessing if one merely wanted to bed a woman, not spend the entire night with her. But, if given the choice, he would prefer to spend at least twenty-four hours in bed with Caroline, a reasonable compensation for his forbearance to date. Then, too, there was the very real problem of her sisters. Despite the preoccupation of his hands, he knew that a part of his mind was taken up with the question of what they were doing while he and his love were otherwise engaged. He would infinitely prefer to be able to devote his entire attention to the luscious person in his arms. He sighed. His body did not like what his mind was telling it. Before he could change his decision, he pulled Caroline closer and bent to whisper in her ear. "Caro?"

She murmured his name and put her hand up to his face. Max smiled. "Sweetheart, much as I'd like to complete your education here and now, I have a dreadful premonition of what hideous scandals your sisters might be concocting with both of us absent from the ballroom."

He knew it was the right excuse to offer, for her mind immediately reasserted itself. "Oh, dear," she sighed, disappointment ringing clearly in her tone, deepening Max's smile. "I suspect you're right."

"I know I'm right," he said, straightening and sitting her upright. "Come, let's get you respectable again."

AS SOON AS SHE FELT sufficiently camouflaged from her guardian's eye by the gorgeously coloured throng, Lizzie Twinning made her way to the ballroom window further from the door. It was the meeting place Sarah had stipulated where Sir Ralph was to await further instructions. He was there, in a dark green domino and a black mask.

Lizzie gave him her hand. "Good!" The hand holding hers trembled. She peered into the black mask. "You're not going to let Arabella down, are you?"

To her relief, Sir Ralph swallowed and shook his head. "No. Of course not. I've got my carriage waiting, as Miss Sarah suggested. I wouldn't dream of deserting Miss Arabella."

Despite the weakness in his voice, Lizzie was satisfied. "It's all right," she assured him. "Arabella is wearing a rose-pink domino. It's her favourite colour so you should recognise it. We'll bring her to you, as we said we would. Don't worry," she said, giving his hand a squeeze, "it'll all work out for the best, you'll see." She patted his hand and, returning it to him, left him. As she moved down the ballroom, she scanned the crowd and picked out Caroline in her aqua domino waltzing with a black domino who could only be their guardian. She grinned to herself and the next instant, walked smack into a dark blue domino directly in her path.

"Oh!" She fell back and put up a hand to her mask, which had slipped.

"Lizzie," said the blue domino in perfectly recognizable accents, "what were you doing talking to Keighly?"

"Martin! What a start you gave me. My mask nearly fell. Wh…what do you mean?"

"I mean, Miss Innocence," said Martin sternly, taking her arm and compelling her to walk beside him on to the terrace, "that I saw you come into the ballroom and then, as soon as you were out of Max's sight, make a bee-line for Keighly. Now, out with it! What's going on?"

Lizzie was in shock. What was she to do? Not for a moment did she imagine that Martin would agree to turn a blind eye to their scheme. But she was not a very good liar. Still, she would have to try. Luckily, the mask hid most of her face and her shock had kept her immobile, gazing silently up at him in what could be taken for her usual innocent manner. "But I don't know what you mean, Martin. I know I talked to Sir Ralph, but that was because he was the only one I recognized."

The explanation was so reasonable that Martin felt his sudden suspicion was as ridiculous as it had seemed. He felt decidedly foolish. "Oh."

"But now you're here," said Lizzie, putting her hand on his arm. "So I can talk to you."

Martin's usual grin returned. "So you can." He raised his eyes to the secluded walks, still empty as the dancing had only just begun. "Why don't we explore while we chat?"

Lately, Lizzie had been in the habit of refusing such invitations but tonight she was thankful for any suggestion that would distract Martin from their enterprise. So she nodded and they stepped off the terrace on to the gravel. They followed a path into the shrubbery. It wended this way and that until the house was a glimmer of light and noise beyond the screening bushes. They found an ornamental stream and followed it to a lake. There was a small island in the middle with a tiny summer-house, reached by a rustic bridge. They crossed over and found the door of the summer-house open.

"Isn't this lovely?" said Lizzie, quite enchanted by the scene. Moonbeams danced in a tracery of light created by the carved wooden shutters. The soft swish of the water running past the reed-covered banks was the only sound to reach their ears.

"Mmm, yes, quite lovely," murmured Martin, enchanted by something quite different. Even Lizzie in her innocence heard the warning in his tone but she turned only in time to find herself in his arms. Martin tilted her face up and smiled gently down at her. "Lizzie, sweet Lizzie. Do you have any idea how beautiful you are?"

Lizzie's eyes grew round. Martin's arms closed around her, gentle yet quite firm. It seemed unbelievable that their tightness could be restricting her breathing, yet she found herself quite unable to draw breath. And the strange light in Martin's eyes was making her dizzy. She had meant to ask her sisters for guidance on how best to handle such situations but, due to her absorption with their schemes, it had slipped her mind. She suspected this was one of those points where using one's wits came into it. But, as her tongue seemed incapable of forming any words, she could only shake her head and hope that was acceptable.

"Ah," said Martin, his grin broadening. "Well, you're so very beautiful, sweetheart, that I'm afraid I can't resist. I'm going to kiss you again, Lizzie. And it's going to be thoroughly enjoyable for both of us." Without further words, he dipped his head and, very gently, kissed her. When she did not draw back, he continued the caress, prolonging the sensation until he felt her response. Gradually, with the moonlight washing over them, he deepened the kiss, then, as she continued to respond easily, gently drew her further into his arms. She came willingly and Martin was suddenly unsure of the ground rules. He had no wish to frighten her, innocent as she was, yet he longed to take their dalliance further, much further. He gently increased the pressure of his lips on hers until they parted for him. Slowly, continually reminding himself of her youth, he taught her how pleasurable a kiss could be. Her responses drove him to seek more.

Kisses were something Lizzie felt she could handle. Being held securely in Martin's arms was a delight. But when his hand closed gently over her breast she gasped and pulled away. The reality of her feelings hit her. She burst into tears.

"Lizzie?" Martin, cursing himself for a fool, for pushing her too hard, gathered her into his arms, ignoring her half-hearted resistance. "I'm sorry, Lizzie. It was too soon, I know. Lizzie? Sweetheart?"

Lizzie gulped and stifled her sobs. "It's true!" she said, her voice a tear-choked whisper. "They said you were a rake and you'd want to take me to bed and I didn't believe them but it's *true*." She ended this astonishing speech on a hiccup.

Martin, finding much of her accusation difficult to deny, fastened on the one aspect that was not clear. "They—who?"

"Sarah and Bella and Caro. They said you're *all* rakes. You and Max and Lord Darcy and Lord Denbigh. They said there's something about us that means we attract rakes."

Finding nothing in all this that he wished to dispute, Martin kept silent. He continued to hold Lizzie, his face half buried in her hair. "What did they suggest you should do about it?" he eventually asked, unsure if he would get an answer.

The answer he got was unsettling. "Wait."

Wait. Martin did not need to ask what for. He knew.

Very much later in the evening, when Martin had escorted Lizzie back to the ballroom, Max caught sight of them from the other side of the room. He had been forced to reassess his original opinion of the youngest

Twinning's sobriety. Quite how such a youthful innocent had managed to get Martin into her toils he could not comprehend, but one look at his brother's face, even with his mask in place, was enough to tell him she had succeeded to admiration. Well, he had warned him.

ARABELLA'S ROLE in the great plan was to flirt so outrageously that everyone in the entire room would be certain that it was indeed the vivacious Miss Twinning under the rose-pink domino. None of the conspirators had imagined this would prove at all difficult and, true to form, within half an hour Arabella had convinced the better part of the company of her identity. She left one group of revellers, laughing gaily, and was moving around the room, when she found she had walked into the arms of a large, black-domino-clad figure. The shock she received from the contact immediately informed her of the identity of the gentleman.

"Oh, sir! You quite overwhelm me!"

"In such a crowd as this, my dear? Surely you jest?"

"Would you contradict a lady, sir? Then you're no gentlemen, in truth."

"In truth, you're quite right, sweet lady. Gentlemen lead such boring lives."

The distinctly seductive tone brought Arabella up short. He could not know who she was, could he? As if in answer to her unspoken question, he asked, "And who might you be, my lovely?"

Arabella's chin went up and she playfully retorted, "Why, that's not for you to know, sir. My reputation might be at stake, simply for talking to so unconventional a gentleman as you."

To her unease, Hugo responded with a deep and attractive chuckle. Their light banter continued, Arabella making all the customary responses, her quick ear for repartee saving her from floundering when his returns made her cheeks burn. She flirted with Hugo to the top of her bent. And hated every minute of it. He did not know who she was, yet was prepared to push an unknown lady to make an assignation with him for later in the evening. She was tempted to do so and then confront him with her identity. But her heart failed her. Instead, when she could bear it no longer, she made a weak excuse and escaped.

THEY HAD TIMED their plan carefully, to avoid any possible mishap. The unmasking was scheduled for one o'clock. At precisely half-past twelve, Sarah and Sir Ralph left the ballroom and strolled in a convincingly relaxed manner down a secluded walk which led to a little gazebo. The gazebo was placed across the path and, beyond it, the path continued to a gate giving access to the carriage drive.

Within sight of the gazebo, Sarah halted. "Arabella's inside. I'll wait here and ensure no one interrupts."

Sir Ralph swallowed, nodded once and left her. He climbed the few steps and entered the gazebo. In the dimness, he beheld the rose-pink domino, her mask still in place, waiting nervously for him to approach. Reverently, he went forward and then went down on one knee.

Sarah, watching from the shadows outside, grinned in delight. The dim figures exchanged a few words, then Sir Ralph rose and kissed the lady. Sarah held her breath, but all went well. Hand in hand, the pink domino and her escort descended by the opposite door of the gazebo and headed for the gate. To make absolutely sure of their success, Sarah entered the gazebo and stood watching the couple disappear through the gate. She waited, silently, then the click of horses' hooves came distantly on the breeze. With a quick smile, she turned to leave. And froze.

Just inside the door to the gazebo stood a tall, black-domino-clad figure, his shoulders propped negligently against the frame in an attitude so characteristic Sarah would have known him anywhere. "Are you perchance waiting for an assignation, my dear?"

Sarah made a grab for her fast-disappearing wits. She drew herself up but, before she could speak, his voice came again. "Don't run away. A chase through the bushes would be undignified at best and I would catch you all the same."

Sarah's brows rose haughtily. She had removed her mask which had been irritating her and it hung by its strings from her fingers. She swung it back and forth nervously. "Run? Why should I run?" Her voice, she was pleased to find, was calm.

Darcy did not answer. Instead, he pushed away from the door and crossed the floor to stand in front of her. He reached up and undid his mask. Then his eyes caught hers. "Are you still set on fleeing to a convent?"

Sarah held his gaze steadily. "I am."

A wry smile, self-mocking, she thought, twisted his mobile mouth. "That won't do, you know. You're not cut out to be a bride of Christ."

"Better a bride of Christ than the mistress of any man." She watched the muscles in his jaw tighten.

"You think so?"

Despite the fact that she had known it would happen, had steeled herself to withstand it, her defences crumbled at his touch and she was swept headlong into abandonment, freed from restraint, knowing where the road led and no longer caring.

But when Darcy stooped and lifted her, to carry her to the wide cushioned seats at the side of the room, she shook her head violently. "Darcy, no!" Her voice caught on a sob. "Please, Darcy, let me go."

Her tears sobered him as nothing else could have. Slowly, he let her down until her feet touched the floor. She was openly crying, as if her heart would break. "Sarah?" Darcy put out a hand to smooth her brown hair.

Sarah had found her handkerchief and was mopping her streaming eyes, her face averted. "Please go, Darcy."

Darcy stiffened. For the first time in his adult life, he wanted to take a woman into his arms purely to comfort her. All inclinations to make love to her had vanished at the first hint of her distress. But, sensing behind her whispered words a confusion she had yet to resolve, he sighed and, with a curt bow, did as she asked.

Sarah listened to his footsteps die away. She remained in the gazebo until she had cried herself out. Then, thankful for the at least temporary protection of her mask, she returned to the ballroom to tell her sisters and their protégées of their success.

HUGO SCANNED the room again, searching through the sea of people for Arabella. But the pink domino was nowhere in sight. He was as thoroughly disgruntled as only someone of a generally placid nature could become. Arabella had flirted outrageously with an unknown man. Admittedly him, but she had not known that. Here he had been worrying himself into a state over her getting herself stuck in a loveless marriage for no reason and underneath she was just a heartless flirt. A jade. Where the hell was she?

A small hand on his arm made him jump. But, contrary to the conviction of his senses, it was not Arabella but a lady in a brown domino with a brown mask fixed firmly in place. "'Ello, kind sir. You seem strangely lonely."

Hugo blinked. The lady's accent was heavily middle European, her tone seductively low.

"I'm all alone," sighed the lady in brown. "And as you seemed also alone, I thought that maybe we could cheer one another up, no?"

In spite of himself, Hugo's glance flickered over the lady. Her voice suggested a wealth of experience yet her skin, what he could see of it, was as delicate as a young girl's. The heavy mask she wore covered most of her face, even shading her lips, though he could see these were full and ripe. The domino, as dominos did, concealed her figure. Exasperated, Hugo sent another searching glance about the room in vain. Then, he looked down and smiled into the lady's hazel eyes. "What a very interesting idea, my dear. Shall we find somewhere to further develop our mutual acquaintance?"

He slipped an arm around the lady's waist and found that it was indeed very neat. She seemed for one instant to stiffen under his arm but immediately relaxed. Damn Arabella! She had driven him mad. He would forget her existence and let this lovely lady restore his sanity. "What did you say your name was, my dear?"

The lady smiled up at him, a wickedly inviting smile. "Maria Pavlovska," she said as she allowed him to lead her out of the ballroom.

They found a deserted ante-room without difficulty and, without wasting time in further, clearly unnecessary talk, Hugo drew Maria Pavlovska into his arms. She allowed him to kiss her and, to his surprise, raised no demur when he deepened the kiss. His senses were racing and her responses drove him wild. He let his hand wander and she merely chuckled softly, the sound suggesting that he had yet to reach her limit. He found a convenient armchair and pulled her on to his lap and let her drive him demented. She was the most satisfyingly responsive woman he had ever found. Bewildered by his good fortune, he smiled understandingly when she whispered she would leave him for a moment.

He sighed in anticipation and stretched his long legs in front of him as the door clicked shut.

As the minutes ticked by and Maria Pavlovska did not return, sanity slowly settled back into Hugo's fevered brain. Where the hell was she? She'd deserted him. Just like Arabella. The thought hit him with the force of a sledgehammer. *Just like Arabella?* No, he was imagining things. True, Maria Pavlovska had aroused him in a way he had begun to think only Arabella could. *Hell!* She had even *tasted* like Arabella. But Arabella's domino was pink. Maria Pavlovska's domino was brown. And, now he came to think of it, it had been a few inches too short; he had been able to see her pink slippers and the pink hem of her dress. Arabella's favourite colour was pink but pink was, after all, a very popular colour. Damn, where was she? Where were they? With a long-suffering sigh, Hugo rose and, forswearing all women, left to seek the comparative safety of White's for the rest of the night.

CHAPTER ELEVEN

AFTER RETURNING to the ballroom with Caroline, Max found his temper unconducive to remaining at the ball. In short, he had a headache. His wards seemed to be behaving themselves, despite his premonitions, so there was little reason to remain at Penbright House. But the night was young and his interlude with Caroline had made it unlikely that sleep would come easily, so he excused himself to his eldest ward and his aunt, and left to seek entertainment of a different sort.

He had never got around to replacing Carmelita. There hardly seemed much point now. He doubted he would have much use for such women in future. He grinned to himself, then winced. Just at that moment, he regretted not having a replacement available. He would try his clubs—perhaps a little hazard might distract him.

The carriage had almost reached Delmere House when, on the spur of the moment, he redirected his coachman to a discreet house on Bolsover Street. Sending the carriage back to Penbright House, he entered the newest gaming hell in London. Naturally, the door was opened to His Grace of Twyford with an alacrity that brought a sardonic grin to His Grace's face. But the play was entertaining enough and the beverages varied and of a quality he could not fault. The hell claimed to be at the forefront of fashion and consequently there were a number of women present, playing the green baize tables or, in some instances, merely accompanying their lovers. To his amusement, Max found a number of pairs of feminine eyes turned his way, but was too wise to evince an interest he did not, in truth, feel. Among the patrons he found more than a few refugees from the Penbright ball, among them Darcy Hamilton.

Darcy was leaning against the wall, watching the play at the hazard table. He glowered as Max approached. "I noticed both you and your eldest ward were absent from the festivities for an inordinately long time this evening. Examining etchings upstairs, I suppose?"

Max grinned. "We were upstairs, as it happens. But it wasn't etchings I was examining."

Darcy nearly choked on his laughter. "Damn you, Max," he said when he could speak. "So you've won through, have you?"

A shrug answered him. "Virtually. But I decided the ball was not the right venue." The comment stunned Darcy but before he could phrase his next question Max continued. "Her sisters seem to be hatching some plot, though I'm dashed if I can see what it is. But when I left all seemed peaceful enough." Max's blue eyes went to his friend's face. "What are you doing here?"

"Trying to avoid thinking," said Darcy succinctly.

Max grinned. "Oh. In that case, come and play a hand of piquet."

The two were old adversaries who only occasionally found the time to play against each other. Their skills were well-matched and before long their game had resolved into an exciting tussle which drew an increasing crowd of spectators. The owners of the hell, finding their patrons leaving the tables to view the contest, from their point an unprofitable exercise, held an urgent conference. They concluded that the cachet associated with having hosted a contest between two such well-known players was worth the expense. Consequently, the two combatants found their glasses continually refilled with the finest brandy and new decks of cards made readily available.

Both Max and Darcy enjoyed the battle, and as both were able to stand the nonsense, whatever the outcome, they were perfectly willing to continue the play for however long their interest lasted. In truth, both found the exercise a welcome outlet for their frustrations of the past weeks.

The brandy they both consumed made absolutely no impression on their play or their demeanour. Egged on by a throng of spectators, all considerably more drunk than the principals, the game was still underway at the small table in the first parlour when Lord McCubbin, an ageing but rich Scottish peer, entered with Emma Mortland on his arm.

Drawn to investigate the cause of the excitement, Emma's bright eyes fell on the elegant figure of the Duke of Twyford. An unpleasant smile crossed her sharp features. She hung on Lord McCubbin's arm, pressing close to whisper to him.

"Eh? What? Oh, yes," said his lordship, somewhat incoherently. He turned to address the occupants of the table in the middle of the crowd. "Twyford! There you are! Think you've lost rather more than money tonight, what?"

Max, his hand poised to select his discard, let his eyes rise to Lord McCubbin's face. He frowned, an unwelcome premonition filling him as his lordship's words sank in. "What, exactly, do you mean by that, my lord?" The words were even and precise and distinctly deadly.

But Lord McCubbin seemed not to notice. "Why, dear boy, you've lost one of your wards. Saw her, clear as daylight. The flighty one in the damned pink domino. Getting into a carriage with that chap Keighly outside the Penbright place. Well, if you don't know, it's probably too late anyway, don't you know?"

Max's eyes had gone to Emma Mortland's face and seen the malicious triumph there. But he had no time to waste on her. He turned back to Lord McCubbin. "Which way did they go?"

The silence in the room had finally penetrated his lordship's foggy brain. "Er—didn't see. I went back to the ballroom."

MARTIN ROTHERBRIDGE paused, his hand on the handle of his bedroom door. It was past seven in the morning. He had sat up all night since returning from the ball, with his brother's brandy decanter to keep him company, going over his relationship with Lizzie Twinning. And still he could find only one solution. He shook his head and opened the door. The sounds of a commotion in the hall drifted up the stairwell. He heard his brother's voice, uplifted in a series of orders to Hillshaw, and then to Wilson. The tone of voice was one he had rarely heard from Max. It brought him instantly alert. Sleep forgotten, he strode back to the stairs.

In the library, Max was pacing back and forth before

the hearth, a savage look on his face. Darcy Hamilton stood silently by the window, his face showing the effects of the past weeks, overlaid by the stress of the moment. Max paused to glance at the clock on the mantelshelf. "Seven-thirty," he muttered. "If my people haven't traced Keighly's carriage by eight-thirty, I'll have to send around to Twyford House." He stopped as a thought struck him. Why hadn't they sent for him anyway? It could only mean that, somehow or other, Arabella had managed to conceal her disappearance. He resumed his pacing. The idea of his aunt in hysterics, not to mention Miriam Alford, was a sobering thought. His own scandalous career would be nothing when compared to the repercussions from this little episode. He would wring Arabella's neck when he caught her.

The door opened. Max looked up to see Martin enter. "What's up?" asked Martin.

"Arabella!" said his brother, venom in his voice. "The stupid chit's done a bunk with Keighly."

"Eloped?" said Martin, his disbelief patent.

Max stopped pacing. "Well, I presume he means to marry her. Considering how they all insist on the proposal first, I can't believe she'd change her spots quite so dramatically. But if I have anything to say about it, she won't be marrying Keighly. I've a good mind to shove her into a convent until she comes to her senses!"

Darcy started, then smiled wryly. "I'm told there's a particularly good one near their old home."

Max turned to stare at him as if he had gone mad.

"But think of the waste," said Martin, grinning.

"Precisely my thoughts," nodded Darcy, sinking into

an armchair. "Max, unless you plan to ruin your carpet, for God's sake sit down."

With something very like a growl, Max threw himself into the other armchair. Martin drew up a straight-backed chair from the side of the room and sat astride it, his arms folded over its back. "So what now?" he asked. "I've never been party to an elopement before."

His brother's intense blue gaze, filled with silent warning, only made him grin more broadly. "Well, how the hell should I know?" Max eventually exploded.

Both brothers turned to Darcy. He shook his head, his voice unsteady as he replied. "Don't look at me. Not in my line. Come to think of it, none of us has had much experience in trying to get women to marry us."

"Too true," murmured Martin. A short silence fell, filled with uncomfortable thoughts. Martin broke it. "So, what's your next move?"

"Wilson's sent runners out to all the posting houses. I can't do a thing until I know which road they've taken."

At that moment, the door silently opened and shut again, revealing the efficient Wilson, a small and self-effacing man, Max's most trusted servitor. "I thought you'd wish to know, Your Grace. There's been no sightings of such a vehicle on any of the roads leading north, north-east or south. The man covering the Dover road has yet to report back, as has the man investigating the road to the south-west."

Max nodded. "Thank you, Wilson. Keep me informed as the reports come in."

Wilson bowed and left as silently as he had entered.

The frown on Max's face deepened. "Where would

they go? Gretna Green? Dover? I know Keighly's got estates somewhere, but I never asked where." After a moment, he glanced at Martin. "Did Lizzie ever mention it?"

Martin shook his head. Then, he frowned. "Not but what I found her talking to Keighly as soon as ever they got to the ball this evening. I asked her what it was about but she denied there was anything in it." His face had become grim. "She must have known."

"I think Sarah knew too," said Darcy, his voice unemotional. "I saw her go out with Keighly, then found her alone in a gazebo not far from the carriage gate."

"Hell and the devil!" said Max. "They can't all simultaneously have got a screw loose. What I can't understand is what's so attractive about *Keighly*?"

A knock on the door answered this imponderable question. At Max's command, Hillshaw entered. "Lord Denbigh desires a word with you, Your Grace."

For a moment, Max's face was blank. Then, he sighed. "Show him in, Hillshaw. He's going to have to know sooner or later."

As it transpired, Hugo already knew. As he strode into the library, he was scowling furiously. He barely waited to shake Max's hand and exchange nods with the other two men before asking, "Have you discovered which road they've taken?"

Max blinked and waved him to the armchair he had vacated, moving to take the chair behind the desk. "How did you know?"

"It's all over town," said Hugo, easing his large frame into the chair. "I was at White's when I heard it. And if it's reached that far, by later this morning your ward is going to be featuring in the very latest *on-dit* all over London. I'm going to wring her neck!"

This last statement brought a tired smile to Max's face. But, "You'll have to wait in line for that privilege," was all he said.

The brandy decanter, replenished after Martin's inroads, had twice made the rounds before Wilson again slipped noiselessly into the room. He cleared his throat to attract Max's attention. "A coach carrying a gentleman and a young lady wearing a rose-pink domino put in at the Crown at Acton at two this morning, Your Grace."

The air of despondency which had settled over the room abruptly lifted. "Two," said Max, his eyes going to the clock. "And it's well after eight now. So they must be past Uxbridge. Unless they made a long stop?"

Wilson shook his head. "No, Your Grace. They only stopped long enough to change horses." If anything, the little man's impassive face became even more devoid of emotion. "It seems the young lady was most anxious to put as much distance as possible behind them."

"As well she might," said Max, his eyes glittering. "Have my curricle put to. And good work, Wilson."

"Thank you, Your Grace." Wilson bowed and left. Max tossed off the brandy in his glass and rose.

"I'll come with you," said Hugo, putting his own glass down. For a moment, his eyes met Max's, then Max nodded.

"Very well." His gaze turned to his brother and Darcy Hamilton. "Perhaps you two could break the news to the ladies at Twyford House?"

Martin nodded.

Darcy grimaced at Max over the rim of his glass. "I

thought you'd say that." After a moment, he continued, "As I said before, I'm not much of a hand at elopements and I don't know Keighly at all. But it occurs to me, Max, dear boy, that it's perfectly possible he might not see reason all that easily. He might even do something rash. So, aside from Hugo here, don't you think you'd better take those along with you?"

Darcy pointed at a slim wooden case that rested on top of the dresser standing against the wall at the side of the room. Inside, as he knew, reposed a pair of Mr. Joseph Manton's duelling pistols, with which Max was considered a master.

Max hesitated, then shrugged. "I suppose you're right." He lifted the case to his desk-top and, opening it, quickly checked the pistols. They looked quite lethal, the long black barrels gleaming, the silver mountings glinting wickedly. He had just picked up the second, when the knocker on the front door was plied with a ruthlessness which brought a definite wince to all four faces in the library. The night had been a long one. A moment later, they heard Hillshaw's sonorous tones, remonstrating with the caller. Then, an unmistakably feminine voice reached their ears. With an oath, Max strode to the door.

Caroline fixed Hillshaw with a look which brooked no argument. "I wish to see His Grace *immediately,* Hillshaw."

Accepting defeat, Hillshaw turned to usher her to the drawing-room, only to be halted by his master's voice.

"Caro! What are you doing here?"

From the library door, Max strolled forward to take the hand Caroline held out to him. Her eyes widened as she took in the pistol he still held in his other hand. "Thank God I'm in time!" she said, in such heartfelt accents that Max frowned.

"It's all right. We've found out which road they took. Denbigh and I were about to set out after them. Don't worry, we'll bring her back."

Far from reassuring her as he had intended, his matter-of-fact tone seemed to set her more on edge. Caroline clasped both her small hands on his arm. "No! You don't understand."

Max's frown deepened. He decided she was right. He could not fathom why she wished him to let Arabella ruin herself. "Come into the library."

Caroline allowed him to usher her into the apartment where they had first met. As her eyes took in the other occupants, she coloured slightly. "Oh, I didn't realize," she said.

Max waved her hesitation aside. "It's all right. They already know." He settled her in the armchair Hugo had vacated. "Caro, do you know where Keighly's estates are?"

Caroline was struggling with his last revelation. They already knew? How? "Gloucestershire, I think," she replied automatically. Then, her mind registered the fact that Max had laid the wicked-looking pistol he had been carrying on his desk, with its mate, no less, and was putting the box which she thought ought to contain them back, empty, on the dresser. A cold fear clutched at her stomach. Her voice seemed thin and reedy. "Max, what are you going to do with those?"

Max, still standing behind the desk, glanced down at the pistols. But it was Hugo's deep voice which answered her. "Have to make sure Keighly sees reason, ma'am," he explained gently. "Need to impress on him the wisdom of keeping his mouth shut over this."

Her mind spinning, Caroline looked at him blankly. "But why? I mean, what can he say? Well, it's all so ridiculous."

"Ridiculous?" echoed Max, a grim set to his mouth.

"I'm afraid you don't quite understand, Miss Twinning," broke in Darcy. "The story's already all over town. But if Max can get her back and Keighly keeps his mouth shut, then it's just possible it'll all blow over, you see."

"But…but why should Max interfere?" Caroline put a hand to her head, as if to still her whirling thoughts.

This question was greeted by stunned silence. It was Martin who broke it. "But, dash it all! He's her *guardian!*"

For an instant, Caroline looked perfectly blank. "Is he?" she whispered weakly.

This was too much for Max. "You know perfectly well I am." It appeared to him that his Caro had all but lost her wits with shock. He reined in his temper, sorely tried by the events of the entire night, and said, "Hugo and I are about to leave to get Arabella back—"

"No!" The syllable was uttered with considerable force by Caroline as she leapt to her feet. It had the desired effect of stopping her guardian in his tracks. One black brow rose threateningly, but before he could voice his anger she was speaking again. "You *don't* understand! I didn't *think* you did, but you kept telling me you *knew.*"

Caroline's eyes grew round as she watched Max move around the desk and advance upon her. She waved one hand as if to keep him back and enunciated clearly, "Arabella did not go with Sir Ralph."

Max stopped. Then his eyes narrowed. "She was seen getting into a carriage with him in the Penbrights' drive."

Caroline shook her head as she tried to work this out. Then she saw the light. "A rose-pink domino was seen getting into Sir Ralph's carriage?"

At her questioning look, Max thought back to Lord McCubbin's words. Slowly, he nodded his head. "And you're sure it wasn't Arabella?"

"When I left Twyford House, Arabella was at the breakfast table."

"So who…?"

"Sarah?" came the strangled voice of Darcy Hamilton.

Caroline looked puzzled. "No. She's at home, too."

"Lizzie?"

Martin's horrified exclamation startled Caroline. She regarded him in increasing bewilderment. "Of course not. She's at Twyford House."

By now, Max could see the glimmer of reason for what seemed like the first time in hours. "So who went with Sir Ralph?"

"Miss Harriet Jenkins," said Caroline.

"Who?" The sound of four male voices in puzzled unison was very nearly too much for Caroline. She sank back into her chair and waved them back to their seats. "Sit down and I'll explain."

With wary frowns, they did as she bid them.

After a pause to marshal her thoughts, Caroline began. "It's really all Mrs. Crowbridge's fault. She decided she wanted Sir Ralph for a son-in-law. Sir Ralph had come to town because he took fright at the thought of the marriage he had almost contracted with Miss Jenkins in Gloucestershire." She glanced up, but none of her audience seemed to have difficulty understanding events thus far. "Mrs. Crowbridge kept throwing Amanda in Sir Ralph's way. Amanda did not like Sir Ralph and so, to help out, and especially because Mr. Minchbury had almost come to the point with Amanda and she favoured his suit, Arabella started flirting with Sir Ralph, to draw him away from Amanda." She paused, but no questions came. "Well, you, Max, made that a bit difficult when you told Arabella to behave herself with respect to Sir Ralph. But they got around that by sharing the work, as it were. It was still Arabella drawing Sir Ralph off, but the other two helped to cover her absences. Then, Miss Jenkins came to town, following Sir Ralph. She joined in the…the plot. I gather Arabella was to hold Sir Ralph off until Mr. Minchbury proposed and then turn him over to Miss Jenkins."

Max groaned and Caroline watched as he put his head in his hand. "Sir Ralph has my heart-felt sympathy," he said. He gestured to her. "Go on."

"Well, then Mrs. Crowbridge tried to trap Sir Ralph by trying to put him in a compromising situation with Amanda. After that, they all decided something drastic needed to be done, to save both Sir Ralph and Amanda. At the afternoon concert, Sarah wheedled a declaration of sorts from Sir Ralph over Arabella and got him to promise to go along with their plan. He thought Arabella was about to go into a decline and had to be swept off her feet by an elopement."

"My sympathy for Sir Ralph has just died," said Max. "What a slow-top if he believed that twaddle!"

"So that's what she was doing on the balcony with him," said Darcy. "She was there for at least half an hour."

Caroline nodded. "She said she had had to work on him. But Harriet Jenkins has known Sir Ralph from the cradle and had told her how best to go about it."

When no further comment came, Caroline resumed her story. "At the Penbrights's ball last night, Lizzie had the job of making sure Sir Ralph had brought his carriage and would be waiting for Sarah when she came to take him to the rendezvous later."

"And that's why she went to talk to Keighly as soon as you got in the ballroom," said Martin, putting his piece of the puzzle into place.

"All Arabella had to do was flirt outrageously as usual, so that everyone, but particularly Sir Ralph, would be convinced it was her in the rose-pink domino. At twelve-twenty, Arabella swapped dominos with Harriet Jenkins and Harriet went down to a gazebo by the carriage gate."

"Oh, God!" groaned Hugo Denbigh. The horror in his voice brought all eyes to him. He had paled. "What was the colour? Of the second domino?"

Caroline stared at him. "Brown."

"Oh, no! I should have guessed. But her *accent.*" Hugo dropped his head into his large hands.

For a moment, his companions looked on in total bewilderment. Then Caroline chuckled, her eyes dancing. "Oh. Did you meet Maria Pavlovska?"

"Yes, I did!" said Hugo, emerging from his depression. "Allow me to inform you, Miss Twinning, that your sister is a minx!"

"I know that," said Caroline. "Though I must say, it's

rather trying of her." In answer to Max's look of patent enquiry, she explained. "Maria Pavlovska was a character Arabella acted in a play on board ship. A Polish countess of—er—" Caroline broke off, blushing.

"Dubious virtue," supplied Hugo, hard pressed.

"Well, she was really very good at it," said Caroline.

Looking at Hugo's flushed countenance, none of the others doubted it.

"Where was I?" asked Caroline, trying to appear unconscious. "Oh, yes. Well, all that was left to do was to get Sir Ralph to the gazebo. Sarah apparently did that."

Darcy nodded. "Yes. I saw her."

Max waited for more. His friend's silence brought a considering look to his eyes.

"So, you see, it's all perfectly all right. It's Harriet Jenkins who has gone with Sir Ralph. I gather he proposed before they left and Miss Jenkins's family approved the match, and as they are headed straight back to Gloucestershire, I don't think there's anything to worry about. Oh, and Mr. Minchbury proposed last night and the Crowbridges accepted him, so all's ended well after all and everyone's happy."

"Except for the four of us, who've all aged years in one evening," retorted Max acerbically.

She had the grace to blush. "I came as soon as I found out."

Hugo interrupted. "But they've forgotten one thing. It's all over town that Arabella eloped with Keighly."

"Oh, no. I don't think that can be right," said Caroline, shaking her head. "Anyone who was at the unmasking at the Penbrights' ball would know Arabella was there until the end." Seeing the questioning looks, she explained. "The unmasking was held at one o'clock. And someone suggested there should be a…a competition to see who was the best disguised. People weren't allowed to unmask until someone correctly guessed who they were. Well, no one guessed who Maria Pavlovska was, so Arabella was the toast of the ball."

Max sat back in his chair and grinned tiredly. "So anyone putting about the tale of my ward's elopement will only have the story rebound on them. I'm almost inclined to forgive your sisters their transgression for that one fact."

Caroline looked hopeful, but he did not elaborate. Max stood and the others followed suit. Hugo, still shaking his head in disbelief, took himself off, and Darcy left immediately after. Martin retired for a much needed rest and Caroline found herself alone with her guardian.

Max crossed to where she sat and drew her to her feet and into his arms. His lips found hers in a reassuring kiss. Then, he held her, her head on his shoulder, and laughed wearily. "Sweetheart, if I thought your sisters would be on my hands for much longer, I'd have Whitney around here this morning to instruct him to break that guardianship clause."

"I'm sorry," mumbled Caroline, her hands engrossed in smoothing the folds of his cravat. "I did come as soon as I found out."

"I know you did," acknowledged Max. "And I'm very thankful you did, what's more! Can you imagine how Hugo and I would have looked if we *had* succeeded in overtaking Keighly's carriage and demanded he return the lady to us? God!" He shuddered. "It doesn't bear thinking about." He hugged her, then released her.

"Now you should go home and rest. And I'm going to get some sleep."

"One moment," she said, staying within his slackened hold, her eyes still on his cravat. "Remember I said I'd tell you whether there were any gentlemen who we'd like to consider seriously, should they apply to you for permission to address us?"

Max nodded. "Yes. I remember." Surely she was not going to mention Willoughby? What had gone on last night, after he had left? He suddenly felt cold.

But she was speaking again. "Well, if Lord Darcy should happen to ask, then you know about that, don't you?"

Max nodded. "Yes. Darcy would make Sarah a fine husband. One who would keep her sufficiently occupied so she wouldn't have time for scheming." He grinned at Caroline's blush. "And you're right. I'm expecting him to ask at any time. So that's Sarah dealt with."

"And I'd rather thought Lord Denbigh for Arabella, though I didn't know then about Maria Pavlovska."

"Oh, I wouldn't deal Hugo short. Maria Pavlovska might be a bit hard to bear but I'm sure he'll come about. And, as I'm sure Aunt Augusta has told you, he's perfectly acceptable as long as he can be brought to pop the question."

"And," said Caroline, keeping her eyes down, "I'm not perfectly sure, but…"

"You think Martin might ask for Lizzie," supplied Max, conscious of his own tiredness. It was sapping his will. All sorts of fantasies were surfacing in his brain and the devil of it was they were all perfectly achievable. But he had already made other plans, better plans.

"I foresee no problems there. Martin's got more money than is good for him. I'm sure Lizzie will keep him on his toes, hauling her out of the scrapes her innocence will doubtless land her in. And I'd much rather it was him than me." He tried to look into Caroline's face but she kept her eyes—were they greyish-green or greenish-grey? He had never decided—firmly fixed on his cravat.

"I'm thrilled that you approve of my cravat, sweetheart, but is there anything more? I'm dead on my feet," he acknowledged with a rueful grin, praying that she did not have anything more to tell him.

Caroline's eyes flew to his, an expression he could not read in their depths. "Oh, of course you are! No. There's nothing more."

Max caught the odd wistfulness in her tone and correctly divined its cause. His grin widened. As he walked her to the door, he said, "Once I'm myself again, and have recovered from your sisters' exploits, I'll call on you—say at three this afternoon? I'll take you for a drive. There are some matters I wish to discuss with you." He guided her through the library door and into the hall. In answer to her questioning look, he added. "About your ball."

"Oh. I'd virtually forgotten about it," Caroline said as Max took her cloak from Hillshaw and placed it about her shoulders. They had organized to hold a ball in the Twinnings' honour at Twyford House the following week.

"We'll discuss it at three this afternoon," said Max as he kissed her hand and led her down the steps to her carriage.

CHAPTER TWELVE

SARAH WRINKLED her nose at the piece of cold toast lying on her plate. Pushing it away, she leaned back in her chair and surveyed her elder sister. With her copper curls framing her expressive face, Caroline sat at the other end of the small table in the breakfast-room, a vision of palest cerulean blue. A clearly distracted vision. A slight frown had settled in the greeny eyes, banishing the lively twinkle normally lurking there. She sighed, apparently unconsciously, as she stared at her piece of toast, as cold and untouched as Sarah's, as if concealed in its surface were the answers to all unfathomable questions. Sarah was aware of a guilty twinge. Had Max cut up stiff and Caroline not told them?

They had all risen early, being robust creatures and never having got into the habit of lying abed, and had gathered in the breakfast parlour to examine their success of the night before. That it had been a complete and unqualified success could not have been divined from their faces; all of them had looked drawn and peaked. While Sarah knew the cause of her own unhappiness, and had subsequently learned of her younger sisters' reasons for despondency, she had been and still was at a loss to explain Caroline's similar mood. She had been in high feather at the ball. Then Max had left early, an unusual occurrence which had made Sarah wonder if they had had a falling-out. But her last sight of them together, when he had taken leave of Caroline in the ballroom, had not supported such a fancy. They had looked...well, intimate. Happily so. Thoroughly immersed in each other. Which, thought the knowledgeable Sarah, was not especially like either of them. She sent a sharp glance to the other end of the table.

Caroline's bloom had gradually faded and she had been as silent as the rest of them during the drive home. This morning, on the stairs, she had shared their quiet mood. And then, unfortunately, they had had to make things much worse. They had always agreed that Caroline would have to be told immediately after the event. That had always been their way, ever since they were small children. No matter the outcome, Caroline could be relied on to predict unerringly the potential ramifications and to protect her sisters from any unexpected repercussions. This morning, as they had recounted to her their plan and its execution, she had paled. When they had come to a faltering halt, she had, uncharacteristically, told them in a quiet voice to wait as they were while she communicated their deeds to their guardian forthwith. She had explained nothing. Rising from the table without so much as a sip of her coffee, she had immediately called for the carriage and departed for Delmere House.

She had returned an hour and a half later. They had not left the room; Caroline's orders, spoken in that particular tone, were not to be dismissed lightly. In truth, each sunk in gloomy contemplation of her state, they had not noticed the passage of time. Caroline had re-entered the room, calmly resumed her seat and accepted the cup of coffee Arabella had hastily poured for her. She had fortified herself from this before explaining to them, in quite unequivocal terms, just how close they had come to creating a hellish tangle. It had never occurred to them that someone might see Harriet departing and, drawing the obvious conclusion, inform Max of the fact, especially in such a public manner. They had been aghast at the realization of how close to the edge of scandal they had come and were only too ready to behave as contritely as Caroline wished. However, all she had said was, "I don't really think there's much we should do. Thankfully, Arabella, your gadding about as Maria Pavlovska ensured that everyone knows you did not elope from the ball. I suppose we could go riding." She had paused, then added, "But I really don't feel like it this morning."

They had not disputed this, merely shaken their heads to convey their agreement. After a moment of silence, Caroline had added, "I think Max would expect us to behave as if nothing had happened, other than there being some ridiculous tale about that Bella had eloped. You'll have to admit, I suppose, that you swapped dominos with Harriet Jenkins, but that could have been done in all innocence. And remember to show due interest in the surprising tale that Harriet left the ball with Sir Ralph." An unwelcome thought reared its head. "Will the Crowbridge girls have the sense to keep their mouths shut?"

They had hastened to assure her on this point. "Why, it was all for Amanda's sake, after all," Lizzie had pointed out.

Caroline had not been entirely convinced but had
been distracted by Arabella. Surmising from Caroline's
use of her shortened name that the worst was over, she
had asked, "Is Max very annoyed with us?"

Caroline had considered the question while they had
all hung, unexpectedly nervous, on her answer. "I think
he's resigned, now that it's all over and no real harm
done, to turn a blind eye to your misdemeanours.
However, if I were you, I would not be going out of my
way to bring myself to his notice just at present."

Their relief had been quite real. Despite his reputation, their acquaintance with the Duke of Twyford had
left his younger wards with the definite impression that
he would not condone any breach of conduct and was
perfectly capable of implementing sufficiently draco-
nian measures in response to any transgression. In years
past, they would have ignored the potential threat and
relied on Caroline to make all right in the event of any
trouble. But, given that the man in question was Max
Rotherbridge, none was sure how successful Caroline
would be in turning him up sweet. Reassured that their
guardian was not intending to descend, in ire, upon
them, Lizzie and Arabella, after hugging Caroline and
avowing their deepest thanks for her endeavours on
their behalf, had left the room. Sarah suspected they
would both be found in some particular nook, puzzling
out the uncomfortable feeling in their hearts.

Strangely enough, she no longer felt the need to
emulate them. In the long watches of a sleepless night,
she had finally faced the fact that she could not live
without Darcy Hamilton. In the gazebo the previous
evening, it had been on the tip of her tongue to beg him

to take her from the ball, to some isolated spot where they could pursue their lovemaking in greater privacy. She had had to fight her own nearly overwhelming desire to keep from speaking the words. If she had uttered them, he would have arranged it all in an instant, she knew; his desire for her was every bit as strong as her desire for him. Only her involvement in their scheme and the consternation her sudden disappearance would have caused had tipped the scales. Her desire for marriage, for a home and family, was still as strong as ever. But, if he refused to consider such an arrange- ment, she was now prepared to listen to whatever alter- native suggestions he had to offer. There was Max's opposition to be overcome, but presumably Darcy was aware of that. She felt sure he would seek her company soon enough and then she would make her acquies- cence plain. That, at least, she thought with a small, in- trospective smile, would be very easy to do.

Caroline finally pushed the unhelpful piece of toast aside. She rose and shook her skirts in an unconsciously flustered gesture. In a flash of unaccustomed insight, Sarah wondered if her elder sister was in a similar state to the rest of them. After all, they were all Twinnings. Although their problems were superficially quite differ- ent, in reality, they were simply variations on the same theme. They were all in love with rakes, all of whom seemed highly resistant to matrimony. In her case, the rake had won. But surely Max wouldn't win, too? For a moment, Sarah's mind boggled at the thought of the two elder Twinnings falling by the wayside. Then, she gave herself a mental shake. No, of course not. He was their guardian, after all. Which, Sarah thought, presumably meant Caroline would even the score. Caroline was undoubtedly the most capable of them all. So why, then, did she look so troubled?

Caroline was indeed racked by the most uncomfortable thoughts. Leaving Sarah to her contemplation of the breakfast table, she drifted without purpose into the drawing-room and thence to the small courtyard beyond. Ambling about, her delicate fingers examining some of the bountiful blooms, she eventually came to the hammock, slung under the cherry trees, protected from the morning sun by their leafy foliage. Climbing into it, she rested her aching head against the cushions with relief and prepared to allow the conflicting emotions inside her to do battle.

Lately, it seemed to her that there were two Caroline Twinnings. One knew the ropes, was thoroughly acquainted with society's expectations and had no hesitation in laughing at the idea of a gentlewoman such as herself sharing a man's bed outside the bounds of marriage. She had been acquainted with this Caroline Twinning for as long as she could remember. The other woman, for some mysterious reason, had only surfaced in recent times, since her exposure to the temptations of Max Rotherbridge. There was no denying the increasing control this second persona exerted over her. In truth, it had come to the point where she was seriously considering which Caroline Twinning she preferred.

She was no green girl and could hardly pretend she had not been perfectly aware of Max's intentions when she had heard the lock fall on that bedroom door. Nor could she comfort herself that the situation had been beyond her control—at least, not then. If she had made any real effort to bring the illicit encounter to a halt, as she most certainly should have done, Max would have instantly acquiesced. She could hardly claim he had forced her to remain. But it had been that other Caroline Twinning who had welcomed him into her arms and had proceeded to enjoy, all too wantonly, the delights to be found in his.

She had never succeeded in introducing marriage as an aspect of their relationship. She had always been aware that what Max intended was an illicit affair. What she had underestimated was her own interest in such a scandalous proceeding. But there was no denying the pleasure she had found in his arms, nor the disappointment she had felt when he had cut short their interlude. She knew she could rely on him to ensure that next time there would be no possible impediment to the completion of her education. And she would go to his arms with neither resistance nor regrets. Which, to the original Caroline Twinning, was a very lowering thought.

Swinging gently in the hammock, the itinerant breeze wafting her curls, she tried to drum up all the old arguments against allowing herself to become involved in such an improper relationship. She had been over them all before; they held no power to sway her. Instead, the unbidden memory of Max's mouth on her breast sent a thrill of warm desire through her veins. "Fool!" she said, without heat, to the cherry tree overhead.

MARTIN ROTHERBRIDGE kicked a stone out of his path. He had been walking for nearly twenty minutes in an effort to rid himself of a lingering nervousness over the act he was about to perform. He would rather have raced a charge of Chasseurs than do what he must that day. But there was nothing else for it—the events of the morning had convinced him of that. That dreadful instant when he had thought, for one incredulous and heart-stopping moment, that Lizzie had gone away with Keighly was never to be repeated. And the only way of ensuring that was to marry the chit.

It had certainly not been his intention, and doubtless Max would laugh himself into hysterics, but there it was. Facts had to be faced. Despite his being at her side for much of the time, Lizzie had managed to embroil herself very thoroughly in a madcap plan which, even now, if it ever became known, would see her ostracized by those who mattered in the *ton*. She was a damned sight too innocent to see the outcome of her actions; either that, or too naïve in her belief in her abilities to come about. She needed a husband to keep a firm hand on her reins, to steer her clear of the perils her beauty and innocence would unquestionably lead her into. And, as he desperately wanted the foolish woman, and had every intention of fulfilling the role anyway, he might as well officially be it.

He squared his shoulders. No sense in putting off the evil moment any longer. He might as well speak to Max.

He turned his steps toward Delmere House. Rounding a corner, some blocks from his destination, he saw the impressive form of Lord Denbigh striding along on the opposite side of the street, headed in the same direction. On impulse, Martin crossed the street.

"Hugo!"

Lord Denbigh halted in his purposeful stride and turned to see who had hailed him. Although a few years separated them, he and Martin Rotherbridge had many interests in common and had been acquainted even before the advent of the Twinnings. His lordship's usual sleepy grin surfaced. "Hello, Martin. On your way home?"

Martin nodded and fell into step beside him. At sight of Hugo, his curiosity over Maria Pavlovska had returned. He experimented in his head with a number of suitable openings before settling for, "Dashed nuisances, the Twinning girls!"

"Very!" The curt tone in Hugo's deep voice was not very encouraging.

Nothing loath, Martin plunged on. "Waltz around, tying us all in knots. What exactly happened when Arabella masqueraded as that Polish countess?"

To his amazement, Hugo coloured. "Never you mind," he said, then, at the hopeful look in Martin's eyes, relented. "If you must know, she behaved in a manner which…well, in short, it was difficult to tell who was seducing whom."

Martin gave a burst of laughter, which he quickly controlled at Hugo's scowl. By way of returning the confidence, he said, "Well, I suppose I may as well tell you, as it's bound to be all over town all too soon. I'm on my way to beg Max's permission to pay my addresses to Lizzie Twinning."

Hugo's mild eyes went to Martin's face in surprise. He murmured all the usual condolences, adding, "Didn't really think you'd be wanting to get leg-shackled just yet."

Martin shrugged. "Nothing else for it. Aside from making all else blessedly easy, it's only as her husband I'd have the authority to make certain she didn't get herself involved in any more hare-brained schemes."

"There is that," agreed Hugo ruminatively. They continued for a space in silence before Martin realized they were nearing Delmere House.

"Where are you headed?" he enquired of the giant by his side.

For the second time, Hugo coloured. Looking distinctly annoyed by this fact, he stopped. Martin, puzzled, stopped by his side, but before he could frame any question, Hugo spoke. "I may as well confess, I suppose. I'm on my way to see Max, too."

Martin howled with laughter and this time made no effort to subdue it. When he could speak again, he clapped Hugo on the back. "Welcome to the family!" As they turned and fell into step once more, Martin's eyes lifted. "And lord, what a family it's going to be! Unless I miss my guess, that's Darcy Hamilton's curricle."

Hugo looked up and saw, ahead of them, Lord Darcy's curricle drawn up outside Delmere House. Hamilton himself, elegantly attired, descended and turned to give instructions to his groom, before strolling towards the steps leading up to the door. He was joined by Martin and Hugo.

Martin grinned. "Do you want to see Max, too?"

Darcy Hamilton's face remained inscrutable. "As it happens, I do," he answered equably. As his glance flickered over the unusually precise picture both Martin and Hugo presented, he added, "Am I to take it there's a queue?"

"Afraid so," confirmed Hugo, grinning in spite of himself. "Maybe we should draw lots?"

"Just a moment," said Martin, studying the carriage waiting by the pavement in front of Darcy's curricle. "That's Max's travelling chaise. Is he going somewhere?"

This question was addressed to Darcy Hamilton, who shook his head. "He's said nothing to me."

"Maybe the Twinnings have proved too much for him and he's going on a repairing lease?" suggested Hugo.

"Entirely understandable, but I don't somehow think that's it," mused Darcy. Uncertain, they stood on the pavement, and gazed at the carriage. Behind them the door of Delmere House opened. Masterton hurried down the steps and climbed into the chaise. As soon as the door had shut, the coachman flicked his whip and the carriage pulled away. Almost immediately, the vacated position was filled with Max's curricle, the bays stamping and tossing their heads.

Martin's brows had risen. "Masterton and baggage," he said. "Now why?"

"Whatever the reason," said Darcy succinctly, "I suspect we'd better catch your brother now or he'll merrily leave us to our frustrations for a week or more."

The looks of horror which passed over the two faces before him brought a gleam of amusement to his eyes.

"Lord, yes!" said Hugo.

Without further discussion, they turned *en masse* and started up the steps. At that moment, the door at the top opened and their prey emerged. They stopped.

Max, eyeing them as he paused to draw on his driving gloves, grinned. The breeze lifted the capes of his great-coat as he descended the steps.

"Max, we need to talk to you."

"Where are you going?"

"You can't leave yet."

With a laugh, Max held up his hand to stem the tide. When silence had fallen, he said, "I'm so glad to see you all." His hand once more quelled the surge of explanation his drawling comment drew forth. "No! I find I have neither the time nor the inclination to discuss the matters. My answers to your questions are yes, yes and yes. All right?"

Darcy Hamilton laughed. "Fine by me."

Hugo nodded bemusedly.

"Are you going away?" asked Martin.

Max nodded. "I need a rest. Somewhere tranquil."

His exhausted tone brought a grin to his brother's face. "With or without company?"

Max's wide grin showed fleetingly. "Never you mind, brother dear. Just channel your energies into keeping Lizzie from engaging in any further crusades to help the needy and I'll be satisfied." His gaze took in the two curricles beside the pavement, the horses fretting impatiently. "In fact, I'll make life easy for you. For all of you. I suggest we repair to Twyford House. I'll engage to remove Miss Twinning. Aunt Augusta and Mrs. Alford rest all afternoon. And the house is a large one. If you can't manage to wrest agreement to your proposals from the Misses Twinning under such circumstances, I wash my hands of you."

They all agreed very readily. Together, they set off immediately, Max and his brother in his curricle, Lord Darcy and Hugo Denbigh following in Darcy's carriage.

THE SOUND OF male voices in the front hall drifted to Caroline's ears as she sat with her sisters in the back parlour. With a sigh, she picked up her bonnet and bade the three despondent figures scattered through the room goodbye. They all looked distracted. She felt much the same. Worn out by her difficult morning and from tossing and turning half the night, tormented by a longing she had tried valiantly to ignore, she had fallen asleep in the hammock under the cherry trees. Her sisters had found her but had left her to recover, only waking her for a late lunch before her scheduled drive with their guardian.

As she walked down the corridor to the front hall, she was aware of the leaping excitement the prospect of seeing Max Rotherbridge always brought her. At the mere thought of being alone with him, albeit on the box seat of a curricle in broad daylight in the middle of fashionable London, she could feel that other Caroline Twinning taking over.

Her sisters had taken her words of the morning to heart and had wisely refrained from joining her in greeting their guardian. Alone, she emerged into the hallway. In astonishment, she beheld, not one elegantly turned out gentleman, but four.

Max, his eyes immediately drawn as if by some magic to her, smiled and came forward to take her hand. His comprehensive glance swept her face, then dropped to her bonnet, dangling loosely by its ribbons from one hand. His smile broadened, bringing a delicate colour to her cheeks. "I'm glad you're ready, my dear. But where are your sisters?"

Caroline blinked. "They're in the back parlour," she answered, turning to greet Darcy Hamilton.

Max turned. "Millwade, escort these gentlemen to the back parlour."

Millwade, not in Hillshaw's class, looked slightly scandalized. But an order from his employer was not to be disobeyed. Caroline, engaged in exchanging courtesies with the gentlemen involved, was staggered. But before she could remonstrate, her cloak appeared about her shoulders and she was firmly propelled out the door. She was constrained to hold her fire until Max had dismissed the urchin holding the bays and climbed up beside her.

"You're supposed to be our guardian! Don't you think it's a little unconventional to leave three gentlemen with your wards unchaperoned?"

Giving his horses the office, Max chuckled. "I don't think any of them need chaperoning at present. They'd hardly welcome company when trying to propose."

"Oh! You mean they've asked?"

Max nodded, then glanced down. "I take it you're still happy with their suits?"

"Oh, yes! It's just that…well, the others didn't seem to hold out much hope." After a pause, she asked, "Weren't you surprised?"

He shook his head. "Darcy I've been expecting for weeks. After this morning, Hugo was a certainty. And Martin's been more sternly silent than I've ever seen him before. So, no, I can't say I was surprised." He turned to grin at her. "Still, I hope your sisters have suffered as much as their swains—it's only fair."

She was unable to repress her answering grin, the dimple by her mouth coming delightfully into being. A subtle comment of Max's had the effect of turning the conversation into general fields. They laughed and discussed, occasionally with mock seriousness, a number of tonnish topics, then settled to determined consideration of the Twyford House ball.

This event had been fixed for the following Tuesday, five days distant. More than four hundred guests were expected. Thankfully, the ballroom was huge and the house would easily cater for this number. Under Lady Benborough's guidance, the Twinning sisters had coped with all the arrangements, a fact known to Max. He had a bewildering array of questions for Caroline. Absorbed with answering these, she paid little attention to her surroundings.

"You don't think," she said, airing a point she and her sisters had spent much time pondering, "that, as it's not really a proper come-out, in that we've been about for the entire Season and none of us is truly a débutante, the whole thing might fall a little flat?"

Max grinned. "I think I can assure you that it will very definitely not be flat. In fact," he continued, as if pondering a new thought, "I should think it'll be one of the highlights of the Season."

Caroline looked her question but he declined to explain.

As usual when with her guardian, time flew and it was only when a chill in the breeze penetrated her thin cloak that Caroline glanced up and found the afternoon gone. The curricle was travelling smoothly down a well surfaced road, lined with low hedges set back a little from the carriageway. Beyond these, neat fields stretched sleepily under the waning sun, a few scattered sheep and cattle attesting to the fact that they were deep in the country. From the direction of the sun, they were travelling south, away from the capital. With a puzzled frown, she turned to the man beside her. "Shouldn't we be heading back?"

Max glanced down at her, his devilish grin in evidence. "We aren't going back."

Caroline's brain flatly refused to accept the implications of that statement. Instead, after a pause, she asked conversationally, "Where are we?"

"A little past Twickenham."

"Oh." If they were that far out of town, then it was difficult to see how they could return that evening even if he was only joking about not going back. But he had to be joking, surely?

The curricle slowed and Max checked his team for the turn into a beech-lined drive. As they whisked through the gateway, Caroline caught a glimpse of a coat of arms worked into the impressive iron gates. The Delmere arms, Max's own. She looked about her with interest, refusing to give credence to the suspicion growing in her mind. The drive led deep into the beech-wood, then opened out to run along a ridge bordered by cleared land, close-clipped grass dropping away on one side to run down to a distant river. On the other side, the beechwood fell back as the curricle continued towards a rise. Cresting this, the road descended in a broad sweep to end in a gravel courtyard before an old stone house. It nestled into an unexpected curve of a small stream, presumably a tributary of the larger river which Caroline rather thought must be the Thames. The roof sported many gables. Almost as many chimneys, intricate pots capping them, soared high above the tiles. In the setting sun, the house glowed mellow and warm. Along one wall, a rambling white rose nodded its blooms and released its perfume to the freshening breeze. Caroline thought she had seen few more appealing houses.

They were expected, that much was clear. A groom

came running at the sound of the wheels on the gravel.
Max lifted her down and led her to the door. It opened
at his touch. He escorted her in and closed the door
behind them.

Caroline found herself in a small hall, neatly panelled
in oak, a small round table standing in the middle of the
tiled floor. Max's hand at her elbow steered her to a
corridor giving off the back of the hall. It terminated in
a beautifully carved oak door. As Max reached around
her to open it, Caroline asked, "Where are the servants?"

"Oh, they're about. But they're too well trained to
show themselves."

Her suspicions developing in leaps and bounds,
Caroline entered a large room, furnished in a fashion she
had never before encountered.

The floor was covered in thick, silky rugs, executed
in the most glorious hues. Low tables were scattered
amid piles of cushions in silks and satins of every con-
ceivable shade. There was a bureau against one wall, but
the room was dominated by a dais covered with silks
and piled with cushions, more silks draping down from
above to swirl about it in semi-concealing mystery.
Large glass doors gave on to a paved courtyard. The
doors stood slightly ajar, admitting the comforting
gurgle of the stream as it passed by on the other side of
the courtyard wall. As she crossed to peer out, she
noticed the ornate brass lamps which hung from the
ceiling. The courtyard was empty and, surprisingly,
entirely enclosed. A wooden gate was set in one side-
wall and another in the wall opposite the house presumably gave on to the stream. As she turned back into the
room, Caroline thought it had a strangely relaxing effect

on the senses—the silks, the glowing but not overbright colours, the soothing murmur of the stream. Then, her eyes lit on the silk-covered dais. And grew round. Seen from this angle, it was clearly a bed, heavily disguised beneath the jumble of cushions and silks, but a bed nevertheless. Her suspicions confirmed, her gaze flew to her guardian's face.

What she saw there tied her stomach in knots. "Max…" she began uncertainly, the conservative Miss Twinning hanging on grimly.

But then he was standing before her, his eyes glinting devilishly and that slow smile wreaking havoc with her good intentions. "Mmm?" he asked.

"What are we doing here?" she managed, her pulse racing, her breath coming more and more shallowly, her nerves stretching in anticipation.

"Finishing your education," the deep voice drawled.

Well, what had she expected? asked that other Miss Twinning, ousting her competitor and taking total possession as Max bent his head to kiss her. Her mouth opened welcomingly under his and he took what she offered, gradually drawing her into his embrace until she was crushed against his chest. Caroline did not mind; breathing seemed unimportant just at that moment.

When Max finally raised his head, his eyes were bright under their hooded lids and, she noticed with smug satisfaction, his breathing was almost as ragged as hers. His eyes searched her face, then his slow smile appeared. "I notice you've ceased reminding me I'm your guardian."

Caroline, finding her arms twined around his neck, ran her fingers through his dark hair. "I've given up," she said in resignation. "You never paid the slightest attention, anyway."

Max chuckled and bent to kiss her again, then pulled back and turned her about. "Even if I were your guardian, I'd still have seduced you, sweetheart."

Caroline obligingly stood still while his long fingers unlaced her gown. She dropped her head forward to move her curls, which he had loosed, out of his way. Then, the oddity of his words struck her. Her head came up abruptly. "*Even?* Max…" She tried to turn around but his hand pushed her back.

"Stand still," he commanded. "I have no intention of making love to you with your clothes on."

Having no wish to argue that particular point, Caroline, seething with impatience, stood still until she felt the last ribbon freed. Then, she turned. "What do you mean, *even* if you were my guardian? You are my guardian. You told me so yourself." Her voice tapered away as one part of her mind tried to concentrate on her questions while the rest was more interested in the fact that Max had slipped her dress from her shoulders and it had slid, in a softly sensuous way, down to her feet. In seconds, her petticoats followed.

"Yes, I know I did," Max agreed helpfully, his fingers busy with the laces of the light stays which restrained her ample charms. "I lied. Most unwisely, as it turned out."

"Wh…what?" Caroline was having a terrible time trying to focus her mind. It kept wandering. She supposed she really ought to feel shy about Max undressing her. The thought that there were not so many pieces of her clothing left for him to remove, spurred her to ask, "What do you mean, you lied? And why unwisely?"

Max dispensed with her stays and turned his attention to the tiny buttons of her chemise. "You were never my ward. You ceased to be a ward of the Duke of Twyford when you turned twenty-five. But I arranged to let you believe I was still your guardian, thinking that if you knew I wasn't you would never let me near you." He grinned wolfishly at her as his hands slipped over her shoulders and her chemise joined the rest of her clothes at her feet. "I didn't then know that the Twinnings are…susceptible to rakes."

His smug grin drove Caroline to shake her head. "We're not…susceptible."

"Oh?" One dark brow rose.

Caroline closed her eyes and her head fell back as his hands closed over her breasts. She heard his deep chuckle and smiled to herself. Then, as his hands drifted, and his lips turned to hers, her mind went obligingly blank, allowing her senses free rein. As her bones turned to jelly and her knees buckled, Max's arm helpfully supported her. Then, her lips were free and she was swung up into his arms. A moment later, she was deposited in the midst of the cushions and silks on the dais.

Feeling excitement tingling along every nerve, Caroline stretched sensuously, smiling at the light that glowed in Max's eyes as they watched her while he dispensed with his clothes. But when he stretched out beside her, and her hands drifted across the hard muscles of his chest, she felt him hold back. In unconscious entreaty, she turned towards him, her body arching against his. His response was immediate and the next instant his lips had returned to hers, his arms gathering her to him. With a satisfied sigh, Caroline gave her full concentration to her last lesson.

CHAPTER THIRTEEN

"SARAH?" Darcy tried to squint down at the face under the dark hair covering his chest.

"Mmm," Sarah replied sleepily, snuggling comfortably against him.

Darcy grinned and gave up trying to rouse her. His eyes drifted to the ceiling as he gently stroked her back. Serve her right if she was exhausted.

Together with Martin and Hugo, he had followed the strongly disapproving Millwade to the back parlour. He had announced them, to the obvious consternation of the three occupants. Darcy's grin broadened as he recalled the scene. Arabella had looked positively stricken with guilt, Lizzie had not known what to think and Sarah had simply stood, her back to the windows, and watched him. At his sign, she had come to his side and they had left the crowded room together.

At his murmured request to see her privately, she had led the way to the morning-room. He had intended to speak to her then, but she had stood so silently in the middle of the room, her face quite unreadable, that before he had known it he was kissing her. Accomplished rake that he was, her response had been staggering. He had always known her for a sensual woman but previously her reactions had been dragged unwillingly from her. Now that they came freely, their potency was enhanced a thousand-fold. After five minutes, he had forcibly disengaged to return to the door and lock it. After that, neither of them had spared a thought for anything save the quenching of their raging desires.

Much later, when they had recovered somewhat, he had managed to find the time, in between other occupations, to ask her to marry him. She had clearly been stunned and it was only then that he realized she had not expected his proposal. He had been oddly touched. Her answer, given without the benefit of speech, had been nevertheless comprehensive and had left him in no doubt of her desire to fill the position he was offering. His wife. The idea made him laugh. Would he survive?

The rumble in his chest disturbed Sarah but she merely burrowed her head into his shoulder and returned to her bliss-filled dreams. Darcy moved slightly, settling her more comfortably.

Her eagerness rang all sorts of warning bells in his mind. Used to taking advantage of the boredom of sensual married women, he made a resolution to ensure that his Sarah never came within arm's reach of any rakes. It would doubtless be wise to establish her as his wife as soon as possible, now he had whetted her appetite for hitherto unknown pleasures. Getting her settled in Hamilton House and introducing her to his country residences, and perhaps giving her a child or two, would no doubt keep her occupied. At least, he amended, sufficiently occupied to have no desire left over for any other than himself.

The light was fading. He glanced at the window to

find the afternoon far advanced. With a sigh, he shook Sarah's white shoulder gently.

"Mmm," she murmured protestingly, sleepily trying to shake off his hand.

Darcy chuckled. "I'm afraid, my love, that you'll have to awaken. The day is spent and doubtless someone will come looking for us. I rather think we should be dressed when they do."

With a long-drawn-out sigh, Sarah struggled to lift her head, propping her elbows on his chest to look into his face. Then, her gaze wandered to take in the scene about them. They were lying on the accommodatingly large sofa before the empty fireplace, their clothes strewn about the room. She dropped her head into her hands. "Oh, God. I suppose you're right."

"Undoubtedly," confirmed Darcy, smiling. "And allow me to add, sweetheart, that, as your future husband, I'll always be right."

"Oh?" Sarah enquired innocently. She sat up slightly, her hair in chaos around her face, straggling down her back to cover his hands where they lay, still gently stroking her satin skin.

Darcy viewed her serene face with misgiving. Thinking to distract her, he asked, "Incidentally, when should we marry? I'm sure Max won't care what we decide."

Sarah's attention was drawn from tracing her finger along the curve of his collarbone. She frowned in concentration. "I rather think," she eventually said, "that it had better be soon."

Having no wish to disagree with this eminently sensible conclusion, Darcy said, "A wise decision. Do you want a big wedding? Or shall we leave that to Max and Caroline?"

Sarah grinned. "A very good idea. I think our guardian should be forced to undergo that pleasure, don't you?"

As this sentiment exactly tallied with his own, Darcy merely grinned in reply. But Sarah's next question made him think a great deal harder.

"How soon is it possible to marry?"

It took a few minutes to check all the possible pros and cons. Then he said, uncertain of her response, "Well, theoretically speaking, it would be possible to get married tomorrow."

"Truly? Well, let's do that," replied his prospective bride, a decidedly wicked expression on her face.

Seeing it, Darcy grinned. And postponed their emergence from the morning-room for a further half-hour.

THE FIRST THOUGHT that sprang to Arabella's mind on seeing Hugo Denbigh enter the back parlour was how annoyed he must have been to learn of her deception. Caroline had told her of the circumstances; they would have improved his temper. Oblivious to all else save the object of her thoughts, she did not see Sarah leave the room, nor Martin take Lizzie through the long windows into the garden. Consequently, she was a little perturbed to suddenly find herself alone with Hugo Denbigh.

"Maria Pavlovska, I presume?" His tone was perfectly equable but Arabella did not place any reliance on that. He came to stand before her, dwarfing her by his height and the breadth of his magnificent chest.

Arabella was conscious of a devastating desire to throw herself on that broad expanse and beg forgiveness for her sins. Then she remembered how he had responded to Maria Pavlovska. Her chin went up enough to look his lordship in the eye. "I'm so glad you found my little…charade entertaining."

Despite having started the conversation, Hugo abruptly found himself at a loss for words. He had not intended to bring up the subject of Maria Pavlovska, at least not until Arabella had agreed to marry him. But seeing her standing there, obviously knowing he knew and how he found out, memory of the desire Arabella-Maria so readily provoked had stirred disquietingly and he had temporarily lost his head. But now was not the time to indulge in a verbal brawl with a woman who, he had learned to his cost, could match his quick tongue in repartee. So, he smiled lazily down at her, totally confusing her instead, and rapidly sought to bring the discussion to a field where he knew she possessed few defences. "Mouthy baggage," he drawled, taking her in his arms and preventing any riposte by the simple expedient of placing his mouth over hers.

Arabella was initially too stunned by this unexpected manoeuvre to protest. And by the time she realized what had happened, she did not want to protest. Instead, she twined her arms about Hugo's neck and kissed him back with all the fervour she possessed. Unbeknownst to her, this was a considerable amount, and Hugo suddenly found himself desperately searching for a control he had somehow misplaced.

Not being as hardened a rake as Max or Darcy, he struggled with himself until he won some small measure of rectitude; enough, at least, to draw back and sit in a large armchair, drawing Arabella onto his lap. She snuggled against his chest, drawing comfort from his warmth and solidity.

"Well, baggage, will you marry me?"

Arabella sat bolt upright, her hands braced against his chest, and stared at him. "Marry you? Me?"

Hugo chuckled, delighted to have reduced her to dithering idiocy.

But Arabella was frowning. "Why do you want to marry me?"

The frown transferred itself to Hugo's countenance. "I should have thought the answer to that was a mite obvious, m'dear."

Arabella brushed that answer aside. "I mean, besides the obvious."

Hugo sighed and, closing his eyes, let his head fall back against the chair. He had asked himself the same question and knew the answer perfectly well. But he had not shaped his arguments into any coherent form, not contemplating being called on to recite them. He opened his eyes and fixed his disobliging love with a grim look. "I'm marrying you because the idea of you flirting with every Tom, Dick and Harry drives me insane. I'll tear anyone you flirt with limb from limb. So, unless you wish to be responsible for murder, you'd better stop flirting." A giggle, quickly suppressed, greeted this threat. "Incidentally," Hugo continued, "you don't go around kissing men like that all the time, do you?"

Arabella had no idea of what he meant by "like that" but as she had never kissed any other man, except in a perfectly chaste manner, she could reply with perfect truthfulness, "No, of course not! That was only you."

"Thank God for that!" said a relieved Lord Denbigh. "Kindly confine all such activities to your betrothed in future. Me," he added, in case this was not yet plain.

Arabella lifted one fine brow but said nothing. She was conscious of his hands gently stroking her hips and wondered if it would be acceptable to simply blurt out "yes". Then, she felt Hugo's hand tighten about her waist.

"And one thing more," he said, his eyes kindling. "No more Maria Pavlovska. Ever."

Arabella grinned. "No?" she asked wistfully, her voice dropping into the huskily seductive Polish accent.

Hugo stopped and considered this plea. "Well," he temporized, inclined to be lenient, "Only with me. I dare say I could handle closer acquaintance with Madame Pavlovska."

Arabella giggled and Hugo took the opportunity to kiss her again. This time, he let the kiss develop as he had on other occasions, keeping one eye on the door, the other on the windows and his mind solely on her responses. Eventually, he drew back and, retrieving his hands from where they had wandered, bringing a blush to his love's cheeks, he gripped her about her waist and gently shook her. "You haven't given me your answer yet."

"Yes, please," said Arabella, her eyes alight. "I couldn't bear not to be able to be Maria Pavlovska every now and again."

Laughing, Hugo drew her back into his arms. "When shall we wed?"

Tracing the strong line of his jaw with one small finger, Arabella thought for a minute, then replied, "Need we wait very long?"

The undisguised longing in her tone brought her a swift response. "Only as long as you wish."

Arabella chuckled. "Well, I doubt we could be married tomorrow."

"Why not?" asked Hugo, his eyes dancing.

His love looked puzzled. "Is it possible? I thought all those sorts of things took forever to arrange."

"Only if you want a big wedding. If you do, I warn you it'll take months. My family's big and distributed all about. Just getting in touch with half of them will be bad enough."

But the idea of waiting for months did not appeal to Arabella. "If it can be done, can we really be married tomorrow? It would be a lovely surprise—stealing a march on the others."

Hugo grinned. "For a baggage, you do have some good ideas sometimes."

"Really?" asked Maria Pavlovska.

FOR MARTIN ROTHERBRIDGE, the look on Lizzie's face as he walked into the back parlour was easy to read. Total confusion. On Lizzie, it was a particularly attractive attitude and one with which he was thoroughly conversant. With a grin, he went to her and took her hand, kissed it and tucked it into his arm. "Let's go into the garden. I want to talk to you."

As talking to Martin in gardens had become something of a habit, Lizzie went with him, curious to know what it was he wished to say and wondering why her heart was leaping about so uncomfortably.

Martin led her down the path that bordered the large main lawn until they reached an archway formed by a rambling rose. This gave access to the rose gardens. Here, they came to a stone bench bathed in softly dappled sunshine. At Martin's nod, Lizzie seated herself with a swish of her muslin skirts. After a moment's consideration, Martin sat beside her. Their view was filled with ancient rosebushes, the spaces beneath crammed with early summer flowers. Bees buzzed sleepily and the occasional dragonfly darted by, on its way from the shrubbery to the pond at the bottom of the main lawn. The sun shone warmly and all was peace and tranquillity.

All through the morning, Lizzie had been fighting the fear that in helping Amanda Crowbridge she had unwittingly earned Martin's disapproval. She had no idea why his approval mattered so much to her, but with the single-mindedness of youth, was only aware that it did. "Wh…what did you wish to tell me?"

Martin schooled his face into stern lines, much as he would when bawling out a young lieutenant for some silly but understandable folly. He took Lizzie's hand in his, his strong fingers moving comfortingly over her slight ones. "Lizzie, this scheme of yours, m'dear. It really was most unwise." Martin kept his eyes on her slim fingers. "I suppose Caroline told you how close-run the thing was. If she hadn't arrived in the nick of time, Max and Hugo would have been off and there would have been no way to catch them. And the devil to pay when they came up with Keighly."

A stifled sob brought his eyes to her, but she had averted her face. "Lizzie?" No lieutenant he had ever had to speak to had sobbed. Martin abruptly dropped his stance of stern mentor and gathered Lizzie into his arms. "Oh, sweetheart. Don't cry. I didn't mean to upset you. Well, yes, I did. Just a bit. You upset me the devil of a lot when I thought you had run off with Keighly."

Lizzie had muffled her face in his coat but she looked up at that. "You thought… But whyever did you think such a silly thing?"

Martin flushed slightly. "Well, yes. I know it was silly. But it was just the way it all came out. At one stage, we weren't sure who had gone in that blasted coach." He paused for a moment, then continued in more serious vein. "But, really, sweetheart, you mustn't start up these schemes to help people. Not when they involve sailing so close to the wind. You'll set all sorts of people's backs up, if ever they knew."

Rather better acquainted with Lizzie than his brother was, Martin had no doubt at all whose impulse had started the whole affair. It might have been Arabella who had carried out most of the actions and Sarah who had worked out the details, but it was his own sweet Lizzie who had set the ball rolling.

Lizzie was hanging her head in contrition, her fingers idly playing with his coat buttons. Martin tightened his arms about her until she looked up. "Lizzie, I want you to promise me that if you ever get any more of these helpful ideas you'll immediately come and tell me about them, before you do anything at all. Promise?"

Lizzie's downcast face cleared and a smile like the sun lit her eyes. "Oh, yes. That will be safer." Then, a thought struck her and her face clouded again. "But you might not be about. You'll…well, now your wound is healed, you'll be getting about more. Meeting lots of l-ladies and…things."

"Things?" said Martin, struggling to keep a straight face. "What things?"

"Well, you know. The sort of things you do. With l-ladies." At Martin's hoot of laughter, she set her lips firmly and doggedly went on. "Besides, you might marry and your wife wouldn't like it if I was hanging on your sleeve." There, she had said it. Her worst fear had been brought into the light.

But, instead of reassuring her that all would, somehow, be well, Martin was in stitches. She glared at him. When that had no effect, she thumped him hard on his chest.

Gasping for breath, Martin caught her small fists and then a slow grin, very like his brother's, broke across his face as he looked into her delightfully enraged countenance. He waited to see the confusion show in her fine eyes before drawing her hands up, pulling her hard against him and kissing her.

Lizzie had thought he had taught her all about kissing, but this was something quite different. She felt his arms lock like a vice about her waist, not that she had any intention of struggling. And the kiss went on and on. When she finally emerged, flushed, her eyes sparkling, all she could do was gasp and stare at him.

Martin uttered a laugh that was halfway to a groan. "Oh, Lizzie! Sweet Lizzie. For God's sake, say you'll marry me and put me out of my misery."

Her eyes grew round. "Marry you?" The words came out as a squeak.

Martin's grin grew broader. "Mmm. I thought it might be a good idea." His eyes dropped from her face to the lace edging that lay over her breasts. "Aside from ensuring I'll always be there for you to discuss your hare-brained schemes with," he continued conversationally, "I could also teach you about all the things I do with l-ladies."

Lizzie's eyes widened as far as they possibly could.

Martin grinned devilishly. "Would you like that, Lizzie?"

Mutely, Lizzie nodded. Then, quite suddenly, she found her voice. "Oh, yes!" She flung her arms about Martin's neck and kissed him ferociously. Emerging from her wild embrace, Martin threw back his head and laughed. Lizzie did not, however, confuse this with rejection. She waited patiently for him to recover.

But, "Lizzie, oh, Lizzie. What a delight you are!" was all Martin Rotherbridge said, before gathering her more firmly into his arms to explore her delights more thoroughly.

A considerable time later, when Martin had called a halt to their mutual exploration on the grounds that there were probably gardeners about, Lizzie sat comfortably in the circle of his arms, blissfully happy, and turned her thought to the future. "When shall we marry?" she asked.

Martin, adrift in another world, came back to earth and gave the matter due consideration. If he had been asked the same question two hours ago, he would have considered a few months sufficiently soon. Now, having spent those two hours with Lizzie in unfortunately restrictive surroundings, he rather thought a few days would be too long to wait. But presumably she would want a big wedding, with all the trimmings.

However, when questioned, Lizzie disclaimed all interest in wedding breakfasts and the like. Hesitantly, not sure how he would take the suggestion, she toyed with the pin in his cravat and said, "Actually, I wonder if it would be possible to be married quite soon. Tomorrow, even?"

Martin stared at her.

"I mean," Lizzie went on, "that there's bound to be quite a few weddings in the family—what with Arabella and Sarah."

"And Caroline," said Martin.

Lizzie looked her question.

"Max has taken Caroline off somewhere. I don't know where, but I'm quite sure why."

"Oh." Their recent occupation in mind, Lizzie could certainly see how he had come to that conclusion. It was on the tip of her tongue to ask for further clarification of the possibilities Caroline might encounter, but her tenacious disposition suggested she settle the question of her own wedding first. "Yes, well, there you are. With all the fuss and bother, I suspect we'll be at the end of the list."

Martin looked much struck by her argument.

"But," Lizzie continued, sitting up as she warmed to her theme, "if we get married tomorrow, without any of the others knowing, then it'll be done and we shan't have to wait." In triumph, she turned to Martin.

Finding her eyes fixed on him enquiringly, Martin grinned. "Sweetheart, you put together a very convincing argument. So let's agree to be married tomorrow. Now that's settled, it seems to me you're in far too composed a state. From what I've learned, it would be safest for everyone if you were kept in a perpetual state of confusion. So come here, my sweet, and let me confuse you a little."

Lizzie giggled and, quite happily, gave herself up to delighted confusion.

THE CLINK OF CROCKERY woke Caroline. She stretched languorously amid the soft cushions, the sensuous drift of the silken covers over her still tingling skin bringing back clear memories of the past hours. She was alone in the bed. Peering through the concealing silk canopy, she spied Max, tastefully clad in a long silk robe, watching a small dapper servant laying out dishes on the low tables on the other side of the room. The light from the brass lamps suffused the scene with a soft glow. She wondered what the time was.

Lying back in the luxurious cushions, she pondered her state. Her final lesson had been in two parts. The first was concluded fairly soon after Max had joined her in the huge bed; the second, a much more lingering affair, had spun out the hours of the evening. In between, Max had, to her lasting shock, asked her to marry him. She had asked him to repeat his request three times, after which he had refused to do it again, saying she had no choice in the matter anyway as she was hopelessly compromised. He had then turned his attention to compromising her even further. As she had no wish to argue the point, she had meekly gone along with his evident desire to examine her responses to him in even greater depth than he had hitherto, a proceeding which had greatly contributed to their mutual content. She was, she feared, fast becoming addicted to Max's particular expertise; there were, she had discovered, certain benefits attached to going to bed with rakes.

She heard the door shut and Max's tread cross the floor. The silk curtains were drawn back and he stood by the bed. His eyes found her pale body, covered only by the diaphanous silks, and travelled slowly from her legs all the way up until, finally, they reached her face, and he saw she was awake and distinctly amused. He grinned and held out a hand. "Come and eat. I'm ravenous."

It was on the tip of Caroline's tongue to ask what his appetite craved, but the look in his eyes suggested that might not be wise if she wished for any dinner. She struggled to sit up and looked wildly around for her clothes. They had disappeared. She looked enquiringly at Max. He merely raised one black brow.

"I draw the line at sitting down to dinner with you clad only in silk gauze," Caroline stated.

With a laugh, Max reached behind him and lifted a pale blue silk wrap from a chair and handed it to her. She struggled into it and accepted his hand to help her from the depths of the cushioned dais.

The meal was well cooked and delicious. Max contrived to turn eating into a sensual experience of a different sort and Caroline eagerly followed his lead. At the end of the repast, she was lying, relaxed and content, against his chest, surrounded by the inevitable cushions and sipping a glass of very fine chilled wine.

Max, equally content, settled one arm around her comfortably, then turned to a subject they had yet to broach. "When shall we be married?"

Caroline raised her brows. "I hadn't really thought that far ahead."

"Well, I suggest you do, for there are certain cavils to be met."

"Oh?"

"Yes," said Max. "Given that I left my brother, Darcy Hamilton and Hugo Denbigh about to pay their addresses to my three wards, I suspect we had better return to London tomorrow afternoon. Then, if you want a big wedding, I should warn you that the Rotherbridge family is huge and, as I am its head, all will expect to be invited."

Caroline was shaking her head. "Oh, I don't think a

big wedding would be at all wise. I mean, it looks as though the Twinning family will have a surfeit of weddings. But," she paused, "maybe your family will expect it?"

"I dare say they will, but they're quite used to me doing outrageous things. I should think they'll be happy enough that I'm marrying at all, let alone to someone as suitable as yourself, my love."

Suddenly, Caroline sat bolt upright. "Max! I just remembered. What's the time? They'll all be in a flurry because I haven't returned…."

But Max drew her back against his chest. "Hush. It's all taken care of. I left a note for Aunt Augusta. She knows you're with me and will not be returning until tomorrow."

"But…won't she be upset?"

"I should think she'll be dancing a jig." He grinned as she turned a puzzled face to him. "Haven't you worked out Aunt Augusta's grand plan yet?" Bemused, Caroline shook her head. "I suspect she had it in mind that I should marry you from the moment she first met you. That was why she was so insistent that I keep my wards. Initially, I rather think she hoped that by her throwing us forever together I would notice you." He chuckled. "Mind you, a man would have to be blind not to notice your charms at first sight, m'dear. By that first night at Almack's, I think she realized she didn't need to do anything further, just give me plenty of opportunity. She knows me rather well, you see, and knew that, despite my reputation, you were in no danger of being offered a *carte blanche* by me."

"I did wonder why she never warned me about you," admitted Caroline.

"But to return to the question of our marriage. If you wish to fight shy of a full society occasion, then it still remains to fix the date."

Caroline bent her mind to the task. Once they returned to London, she would doubtless be caught up in all the plans for her sisters' weddings, and, she supposed, her own would have to come first. But it would all take time. And meanwhile, she would be living in Twyford House, not Delmere House. The idea of returning to sleeping alone in her own bed did not appeal. The end of one slim finger tapping her lower lip, she asked, "How soon could we be married?"

"Tomorrow, if you wish." As she turned to stare at him again, Max continued. "Somewhere about here," he waved his arm to indicate the room, "lies a special licence. And our neighbour happens to be a retired bishop, a long-time friend of my late father's, who will be only too thrilled to officiate at my wedding. If you truly wish it, I'll ride over tomorrow morning and we can be married before luncheon, after which we had better get back to London. Does that programme meet with your approval?"

Caroline leaned forward and placed her glass on the table. Then she turned to Max, letting her hands slide under the edge of his robe. "Oh, yes," she purred. "Most definitely."

Max looked down at her, a glint in his eyes. "You, madam, are proving to be every bit as much a houri as I suspected."

Caroline smiled slowly. "And do you approve, my lord?"

"Most definitely," drawled Max as his lips found hers.

THE DUKE OF TWYFORD returned to London the next afternoon, accompanied by his Duchess. They went directly to Twyford House, to find the entire household at sixes and sevens. They found Lady Benborough in the back parlour, reclining on the chaise, her wig askew, an expression of smug satisfaction on her face. At sight of them, she abruptly sat up, struggling to control the wig. "There you are! And about time, too!" Her shrewd blue eyes scanned their faces, noting the inner glow that lit Caroline's features and the contented satisfaction in her nephew's dark face. "What have you been up to?"

Max grinned wickedly and bent to kiss her cheek. "Securing my Duchess, as you correctly imagined."

"You've tied the knot already?" she asked in disbelief.

Caroline nodded. "It seemed most appropriate. That way, our wedding won't get in the way of the others."

"Humph!" snorted Augusta, disgruntled at missing the sight of her reprehensible nephew getting leg-shackled. She glared at Max.

His smile broadened. "Strange, I had thought you would be pleased to see us wed. Particularly considering your odd behaviour. Why, even Caro had begun to wonder why you never warned her about me, despite the lengths to which I went to distract her mind from such concerns."

Augusta blushed. "Yes, well," she began, slightly flustered, then saw the twinkle in Max's eye. "You know very well I'm *aux anges* to see you married at last, but I would have given my best wig to have seen it!"

Caroline laughed. "I do assure you we are truly married. But where are the others?"

"And that's another thing!" said Augusta, turning to Max. "The next time you set about creating a bordello in a household I'm managing, at least have the goodness to warn me beforehand! I come down after my nap to find Arabella in Hugo Denbigh's lap. That was bad enough, but the door to the morning-room was locked. Sarah and Darcy Hamilton *eventually* emerged, but only much later." She glared at Max but was obviously having difficulty keeping her face straight. "Worst of all," she continued in a voice of long suffering, "Miriam went to look at the roses just before sunset. Martin had apparently chosen the rose garden to further his affair with Lizzie, don't ask me why. It was an hour before Miriam's palpitations had died down enough for her to go to bed. I've packed her off to her sister's to recuperate. Really, Max, you've had enough experience to have foreseen what would happen."

Both Max and Caroline were convulsed with laughter.

"Oh, dear," said Caroline when she could speak, "I wonder what would have happened if she had woken up on the way back from the Richardsons' ball?"

Augusta looked interested but, before she could request further information, the door opened and Sarah entered, followed by Darcy Hamilton. From their faces it was clear that all their troubles were behind them— Sarah looked radiant, Darcy simply looked besotted. The sisters greeted each other affectionately, then Sarah drew back and surveyed the heavy gold ring on Caroline's left hand. "Married already?"

"We thought to do you the favour of getting our marriage out of the way forthwith," drawled Max, releasing Darcy's hand. "So there's no impediment to your own nuptials."

Darcy and Sarah exchanged an odd look, then burst

out laughing. "I'm afraid, dear boy," said Darcy, "that we've jumped the gun, too."

Sarah held out her left hand, on which glowed a slim gold band.

While the Duke and Duchess of Twyford and Lord and Lady Darcy exchanged congratulations all around, Lady Benborough looked on in disgust. "What I want to know," she said, when she could make herself heard once more, "is if I'm to be entirely done out of weddings, even after all my efforts to see you all in parson's mouse-trap?"

"Oh, there are still two Twinnings to go, so I wouldn't give up hope," returned her nephew, smiling down at her with transparent goodwill. "Apropos of which, has anyone seen the other two lately?"

No one had. When applied to, Millwade imparted the information that Lord Denbigh had called for Miss Arabella just before two. They had departed in Lord Denbigh's carriage. Mr. Martin had dropped by for Miss Lizzie at closer to three. They had left in a hack.

"A hack?" queried Max.

Millwade merely nodded. Dismissed, he withdrew.

Max was puzzled. "Where on earth could they have gone?"

As if in answer, voices were heard in the hall. But it was Arabella and Hugo who had returned. Arabella danced in, her curls bouncing, her big eyes alight with happiness. Hugo ambled in her wake, his grin suggesting that he suspected his good fortune was merely a dream and he would doubtless wake soon enough. Meanwhile, he was perfectly content with the way this particular dream was developing. Arabella flew to embrace Caroline and Sarah, then turned to the company at large and announced, "Guess what!"

A pregnant silence greeted her words, the Duke and his Duchess, the Lord and his Lady, all struck dumb by a sneaking suspicion. Almost unwillingly, Max voiced it. "You're married already?"

Arabella's face fell a little. "How did you guess?" she demanded.

"No!" moaned Augusta. "Max, see what happens when you leave town? I won't have it!"

But her words fell on deaf ears. Too blissfully happy themselves to deny their friends the same pleasures, the Duke and his Duchess were fully engaged in wishing the new Lady Denbigh and her Lord all manner of felicitations. And then, of course, there was their own news to hear, and that of the Hamiltons. The next ten minutes were filled with congratulations and good wishes.

Left much to herself, Lady Benborough sat in a corner of the chaise and watched the group with an indulgent eye. Truth to tell, she was not overly concerned with the absence of weddings. At her age, they constituted a definite trial. She smiled at the thought of the stories she would tell of the rapidity with which the three rakes before her had rushed their brides to the altar. Between them, they had nearly forty years of experience in evading parson's mouse-trap, yet, when the right lady had loomed on their horizon, they had found it expedient to wed her with all speed. She wondered whether that fact owed more to their frustrations or their experience.

Having been assured by Arabella that Martin had indeed proposed and been accepted, the Duke and

Duchess allowed themselves to be distracted by the question of the immediate housing arrangements. Eventually, it was decided that, in the circumstances, it was perfectly appropriate that Sarah should move into Hamilton House immediately, and Arabella likewise to Denbigh House. Caroline, of course, would henceforth be found at Delmere House. Relieved to find their ex-guardian so accommodating, Sarah and Arabella were about to leave to attend to their necessary packing, when the door to the drawing-room opened.

Martin and Lizzie entered.

It was Max, his sharp eyes taking in the glow in Lizzie's face and the ridiculously proud look stamped across Martin's features, who correctly guessed their secret.

"Don't tell me!" he said, in a voice of long suffering. "You've got married, too?"

NEEDLESS TO SAY, the Twyford House ball four days later was hardly flat. In fact, with four blushing brides, sternly watched over by their four handsome husbands, it was, as Max had prophesied, one of the highlights of the Season.

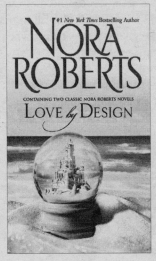

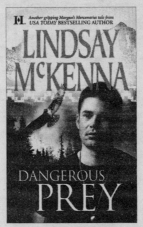

REQUEST YOUR FREE BOOKS!

2 FREE NOVELS
FROM THE ROMANCE/SUSPENSE
COLLECTION PLUS 2 FREE GIFTS!

YES! Please send me 2 FREE novels from the Romance/Suspense Collection and my 2 FREE gifts (gifts are worth about $10). After receiving them, if I don't wish to receive any more books, I can return the shipping statement marked "cancel." If I don't cancel, I will receive 4 brand-new novels every month and be billed just $5.49 per book in the U.S. or $5.99 per book in Canada, plus 25¢ shipping and handling per book plus applicable taxes, if any*. That's a savings of at least 20% off the cover price! I understand that accepting the 2 free books and gifts places me under no obligation to buy anything. I can always return a shipment and cancel at any time. Even if I never buy another book from the Reader Service, the two free books and gifts are mine to keep forever.

185 MDN EF5Y   385 MDN EF6C

Name _____ (PLEASE PRINT)

Address _____ Apt. #

City _____ State/Prov. _____ Zip/Postal Code

Signature (if under 18, a parent or guardian must sign)

Mail to The Reader Service:
IN U.S.A.: P.O. Box 1867, Buffalo, NY 14240-1867
IN CANADA: P.O. Box 609, Fort Erie, Ontario L2A 5X3

Not valid to current subscribers to the Romance Collection,
the Suspense Collection or the Romance/Suspense Collection.

Want to try two free books from another line?
Call 1-800-873-8635 or visit www.morefreebooks.com.

* Terms and prices subject to change without notice. N.Y. residents add applicable sales tax. Canadian residents will be charged applicable provincial taxes and GST. Offer not valid in Quebec. This offer is limited to one order per household. All orders subject to approval. Credit or debit balances in a customer's account(s) may be offset by any other outstanding balance owed by or to the customer. Please allow 4 to 6 weeks for delivery. Offer available while quantities last.

Your Privacy: Harlequin is committed to protecting your privacy. Our Privacy Policy is available online at www.eHarlequin.com or upon request from the Reader Service. From time to time we make our lists of customers available to reputable third parties who may have a product or service of interest to you. If you would prefer we not share your name and address, please check here. ☐

BOB08R

Harlequin® Historical
Historical Romantic Adventure!

THE VISCOUNT CLAIMS HIS BRIDE
Bronwyn Scott

Viscount Valerian Inglemoore
knows exactly what he wants—
Philippa Stratten, the woman he gave
up for the sake of her family years
ago. But Philippa is not the hurt, naive
debutante he once knew, and the
passion between them is too strong
for her to stay angry for long!

*Available January 2009
wherever books are sold.*